THESE WICKED DESIRES

FATES

BOOK THREE

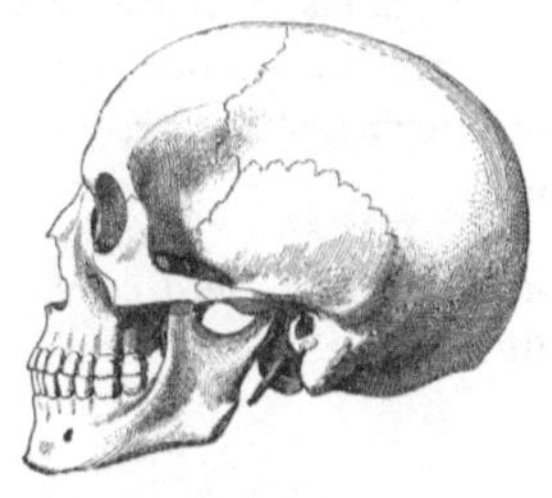

WHITNEY L. SPRADLING

Midnight Tide
PUBLISHING

To my family...

Once again, I beg you, if you are in any way related to me, please put the book down. I really hate awkward encounters, and that is exactly what will happen the next time we see each other if you read this book.

I appreciate the support, but DO NOT READ THIS BOOK!

Thank you.

Content Warning

This book contains adult themes that may not be appropriate for all audiences. These themes include: violence, graphic sexual scenes, language, drug/alcohol use, mention of torture, blood play, and mention of past non-consent encounters and sexual assault.

This is a why choose romance, meaning the main character will end up with at least three guys by the end of the series. If you enjoy tattooed bad guys who'd do anything for their girl, MM relationships, and plenty of heat, then join the fates in These Wicked Desires.

National Domestic Violence Hotline

If you or someone you know needs help, please call the National Domestic Violence Hotline at 800-799-7233.

You are not alone. Help is available.

Ellis

"Spread your legs more," Kai says, leaning against the wall with his arms crossed over his chest. His gray eyes closely watch me and Cade.

"More? Pretty soon I'm going to be doing the splits," I grumble, but comply.

"The wider your legs the more stable your base of support. With those wings, you need a bigger base of support for balance." Kai tilts his head to the side, raising one pierced brow. He knows I already know this.

My hands fall to my sides, fists loosening. "Can we take a break?"

"We just started," Cade says.

My head falls back and I groan. He's right. We've only been outside for five minutes, but learning how to fight, how to move, with these godsforsaken wings is too much. For the past three days these stupid things have been ruining my life. I've knocked paintings off the walls, all the lamps are broken, Cade had to heal Kai's broken nose from where one of my wings smacked him in the face, sleeping has been impossible. And forget about sex.

I just want to have sex again. The one time we tried was when I broke Kai's nose. I haven't had the energy or mind set to try again after that. Every time I do, I catch a flutter of white in my peripheral and instantly go into pissy mode.

I raise my head and grimace as some of my hair gets tangled in feathers. "Son of a bitch!" I yank my hair free and scream, stomping my foot like a child. It feels good. For a second. Then I just feel exhausted. Deep in my bones, the ache of needing a break causes my shoulders to slump, and I hang my head forward, taking deep breaths to try and calm myself.

Sterling steps in front of me. I know it's him by the scent. Pine and winter nights. He gently lifts my chin with his fingers, and I stare into those glacial blue eyes, my mate's eyes. "Hey, let's try something. I think you could use a break from those things."

I snort. "You think? I've tried Sterling. I can't make them go away." I know I'm whining, but seriously, I just want to catch my breath. I want a moment of normalcy. No wings, no threats, no drama. Just me and my guys.

"I've been thinking," Sterling says, ignoring my petulance. "You have Kai's supernatural abilities and Cade's magic. What if the wings are part of my shifting ability?"

I blink. "I hadn't thought of it that way."

"Maybe I can help walk you through shifting to make them go away." His thumb rubs my cheek and I lean into the gesture. I'll never get sick of his affection after going so long without it.

"Okay, let's try it." I nod and take a deep breath as he walks around behind me. I try to not get my hopes up. I know if I do and this fails—which it's likely to—I'll just be even more overwhelmed and ready to give up.

"Close your eyes and try to empty your mind." His voice is gentle and soothing, and I let it flow over me. His presence behind me, safety and comfort, eases the tension in my muscles. The heat from his body soaks into my back, and I have to refrain from leaning against him. "Remember what it's like to not have wings." His finger trails between my shoulder blades, right where the wings sprout from my spine. It's hard to imagine that when little shivers overcome me at his touch. It's so sensitive. "Remember what it's like to lay in bed on your back with nothing in the way. Remember being able to turn around without knocking something over." There is definitely laughter hidden in his voice, and I'm tempted to turn around just to knock him over. "Now feel your wings. Feel their presence behind you." This time his finger brushes through the downy soft feathers near my spine, and I can't control the flutter in my stomach. I need to get laid so badly. "Now, imagine shedding them like a second skin. Picture them falling away."

In my mind, I see my wings shivering, the feathers fluttering wildly. Then, as if a blanket covers them, they disappear. Hands run down my back. My back devoid of wings.

My eyes snap open. "Did it work?" I'm barely breathing, scared it's just my imagination making me think the wings are gone.

In response, Sterling wraps his arms around me from behind and presses a kiss to my mating mark. "It did. Good job, kitten." Pride rings in his voice, and I arch my back against him at the praise.

"Thank you!" I squeal and turn around, wrapping my arms around his neck. "Thank you, thank you, thank you." My words are muffled, buried in his naked chest. Always freaking naked.

Kai grunts, and I turn around to see him push off the wall. "I think I miss them already," he says.

"Well, too bad. I need a break." I shimmy and twist, enjoying the freedom of no wings dragging behind me.

"I think to get them back, you'd just repeat that process. That's what I do with my wolf, at least."

"I'll try that later. Much later." I don't plan on bringing those babies back out for a while. I glance at Cade. He's been quiet through this entire thing, and now he's watching me with a furrowed brow. "What's wrong?" I ask, stepping up to him.

He frames my face in his hands, brushing back loose curls. "I know there is so much we need to do, and so much we have to worry about, but I think we need to take a step back and just do something fun."

I can't help the little spark that lights up inside me. "Really?"

"I'm worried about you. You've been through so much, Ellis, and you haven't had a chance to just ... live. Between Sam, and finding out you're a harpy, and Sterling's capture. It's a lot for one person to deal with." His hands travel down to squeeze my upper arms. "There's so much pressure and stress on you. So much on your mind. We need to remember we can't keep pushing you harder and harder without giving you some time to decompress."

I know Cade isn't an empath, but sometimes I swear he reads me better than Kai does. And even though his words are true and I desperately need some time to unwind, I hesitate. What about my sister? What about Sam and his experiments? What about Cade's and Sterling's families? We can't afford to take a break right now. Can we?

"I think that's a great idea," Kai says, stepping up next to Cade. "What about you Sterling?"

I glance behind me and find Sterling looking at me, indecision in his gaze. Of the three of them, he's the most serious. The one who would say we have to stay focused. Besides me, he's the only one who has experienced Sam first hand. He's the one who saw my sister get tortured.

Sterling searches my face before sighing. "I can't say no to you, Ellis."

Excitement swoops through me at the prospect of doing something normal for a change. "So, what are we going to do?"

"I have an idea," Cade says, slowly. "But it will take a few days to organize. In the meantime, we'll keep working on fighting and magic lessons."

I slump backward against Sterling and grumble. More lessons. More magic. More wings. I could cry.

Cade chuckles and leans forward to kiss me. "Soon, love. It will give you something to look forward to."

THREE DAYS later I'm sitting on the couch in the cabin, enjoying the book about the witch with all of her men—which by the way, she has even more men now—when Cade enters the cabin, arms loaded down with bags. He and Kai had gone off to do something top secret, and they wouldn't tell me what. Sterling kept his mouth shut all evening, only smiling at me when I asked what they were planning.

"What's all of that?" I ask, setting my phone in my lap.

He grins at me. "A surprise for tonight." The bags and boxes thump onto the kitchen table and he digs through them, pulling out a garment bag. He holds it up by the hanger and gives me a wink. "Go take a shower, get ready, and put this on. Meet us down here in two hours."

"Cryptic," I drawl, but snag the bag. It's heavy, and a sneaking suspicion worms through me. His gaze burns into my back as I head upstairs, and I make sure to sway my hips a little extra just for him.

In the bedroom I hang the bag over the bathroom door. My fingers shake slightly as I gather the bottom and slowly lift it up, revealing red satin fabric. My breath catches as I remove the bag completely, unveiling a stunning evening gown.

Biting my lip, I dart into the bathroom and turn on the shower. This seems like the appropriate time to actually wash and fix my hair, so I spend the next hour doing that. The guys have made sure to buy things to make me comfortable here in the cabin. I haven't really had the chance to leave and do any shopping, besides online shopping, because it's not safe. The lavender shampoo isn't something I'd typically use on my curls, but they tried. Same with the make-up. I forgo the concealer Kai bought that is two shades too light, and go with a dramatic eye.

When I'm finished with my hair and makeup, I return to the bedroom and stare at the dress. I wore plenty of evening gowns during my time as Thomas's daughter. All of the stuffy parties and events he'd dragged me to, and then again on Sam's arm as his girlfriend and fiancé. But none of them compare to the dress before me.

I let the towel drop to the floor and take the dress off the hanger. I realize it's not one piece, but rather two. A skirt and bustier. Black lace forms the bustier top, with boning lining the sides and under the breasts. By the time I get the dang thing hooked, my breasts are sufficiently pushed up and on display. The pattern of the lace is thick, but a hint of nipple still peeks through, and I hope wherever we're going it's either really dark or private. It's quite possibly the most revealing thing I've ever worn, and I love it.

The skirt is heavy. The red satin is full and thick, and the fabric glides over my freshly shaved legs making me shiver. It sits high on my waist, over the bustier, and a slit opens almost to my hip. Grinning wickedly, I toss the underwear I had planned to put on. I know where this evening is headed, so why bother with more clothing the guys will have to remove.

I walk to the full-length mirror, the skirts swishing with every step. I feel like a princess as I run my fingers over the smooth fabric. In the mirror I gasp. It's been a long time since I actually looked at myself. I had gotten so used to seeing broken Ellis, this version of myself shocks me.

My amber eyes are practically glowing. There is no overwhelming despair in the depths of my irises. My skin is smooth and unblemished, aside from a few light freckles across my nose. No bruises, no cuts. No dark circles. I've been gaining back the weight I lost, and my cheeks are no longer sunken in. I look happy and healthy. For the first time in years, I look like myself. Powerful. Sexy. Confident.

I blink back the tears that burn the corners of my eyes and take a step back. The dress is stunning, and I look—and feel—incredibly sexy in it. I can't wait for the guys to see me.

"Ellis, love, are you ready?" Cade hollers from downstairs.

I take one last glance in the mirror, fixing a curl that's laying the wrong way, and head for the door. For some reason butterflies erupt in my stomach as I reach for the handle. This is as close to a real date as I've ever had. Growing up with Thomas, he always vetted my boyfriends and I always had a chaperone go on every date with me. Then there was Sam. I guess things started off normal enough, but those memories are tainted now. This will be the first time I'm with my guys, just the four of us, nothing to worry about, nothing to think about. I'm not even sure how to act in this situation.

Taking a deep breath I step through the door and make my way down the stairs, the heavy skirt trailing behind me. Half way down, I stop. All three of my guys are standing at the bottom of the steps, and I don't know who to look at first.

Kai is dressed in black jeans with holes ripped in the knees, black boots, a black shirt, and his black leather jacket. As always, his hair lays in artfully messy waves across his forehead. My beautiful, dark vampire.

Cade is wearing a nice pair of jeans, white sneakers, and a gray long-sleeved Henley. His brown hair is styled to perfection, swept to the side away from his face. My sweet, adorable mage.

And Sterling. My mate. He's wearing a pair of worn jeans, boots, and a black and red flannel shirt, unbuttoned over a white t-shirt. I barely refrain from making a comment at the fact he's not naked for once. His silver hair has been brushed and it gleams as it lays over his shoulders.

My breath catches as I take in each of them. I am, by far, overdressed compared to them, but they look distinctly themselves. And I love it. I swallow as I take the final few steps down, and I notice their expressions. They range from straight up desire from Kai, to awe from Cade, to joy from Sterling. None of them say anything, and I suddenly have this fear I've done something wrong.

"Um, I didn't have any shoes?" I nervously run my hands down my stomach and over the sides of my skirts, looking back and forth between them.

Kai starts and steps forward. He's holding a pair of strappy black heels, and he kneels on the ground in front of me. I lift my skirts and raise my foot, noticing Kai's gaze traveling the length of my leg, up and up to the top of the slit. His eyes are the darkest gray imaginable, and for a second, I get lost in them. Then he runs his hand down the back of my calf, and his touch draws me out of the hold he had on me.

He slips my foot into the first heel, making sure to let his fingers brush my skin at every opportunity. When he's done, he places a soft kiss above my knee and stands. "You are so fucking beautiful," he says, his voice rough.

I expect him to kiss me, but he doesn't. Instead he backs away and heads for the front door, keys jingling in his hand. I blink, thrown off and left wanting. Where is my kiss?

Cade smirks. "Are you ready, love?"

"Where are we going?" I ask, taking his outstretched hand.

He leans in to whisper in my ear, "It's a surprise." His breath tickles my neck and I wait for him to kiss it, but again, he pulls away.

I bite my lip in agitation and look at Sterling. He's grinning from ear to ear like he knows exactly what they're doing and planned it from the beginning. Swallowing my frustration, I let Cade lead me outside into the warm night air. Kai's already in the driver's seat of the hummer, and Sterling hops into the front with him.

"After you, love," Cade says, holding the back door open for me.

I climb in, and get situated. Looking between my three guys, I wait for one of them to say something, but they don't. Cade doesn't even hold my hand as the car descends the mountain. What kind of new torture is this? I think I'd rather be training than sit so close to my guys and not touch them.

"A little hint would be nice. And seriously, why the fuck aren't any of you touching me?"

"Patience, love. Patience," Cade croons.

ELLIS

I'm about to jump out of my skin by the time Kai stops the hummer. They said nothing the entire drive, no matter how many times I tried to get them to tell me where we were going. I didn't recognize the roads Kai took, and when he pulled off the main road and we bounced over uneven terrain, I knew we weren't going anywhere public.

Sterling hops out and opens my door, giving me a hand down. He doesn't let go like I expect him to, since apparently they all agreed to tease me and leave me begging for their touch. He leans in and presses a soft kiss just below my ear. "Almost there, kitten."

My toes curl in my strappy heels as his voice washes over me. "And where is there?" I ask for the hundredth time.

Surprise surprise, no answer.

It's so dark, it's hard to make out where we are. Looking around, I can tell that we're on another mountain. Pine trees surround us and their scent reminds me of Sterling. There is no path that I can see, and besides the four of us and the car, there is nothing around.

"You're not bringing me out here to murder me, are you?"

Kai huffs and shakes his head. "No. That's our plan for next week's date. Come on."

Cade raises his hand and purple light flares in his palm, illuminating the way. I follow them, with Sterling close behind. He has to help me keep my balance because walking through the woods on a mountain in heels and an evening gown is incredibly challenging. Obviously this entire thing, outfit included, was thought out by a guy, because what girl in their right mind would traipse through the woods in high heels?

We walk for a few minutes, when I notice a soft white glow coming from up ahead. The closer we get, the faster my heart beats. Anticipation, excitement, wonder. It all bubbles inside of me, spilling over when I step between two large pine trees into a clearing.

It's the lake we can see from the front porch of the cabin. And hanging from the branches of the pine trees are fairy lights that twinkle softly in the darkness, reflecting off the dark waters of the lake. Off to the side are blankets and pillows spread out in invitation, with trays of food and glasses of wine.

"It's a midnight picnic," Cade says, brushing his fingers down my arm.

"It's beautiful," I whisper. Sterling leads me to the blankets and we sit down, my red skirts puddling around me. "Is it safe? We're so out in the open here." I can't help but glance around. Anyone could be hiding in the darkness beyond the clearing.

Cade sits on the blankets with Kai and shakes his head. "I laid so many wards around here, an ant can't make it through without me knowing." He leans forward to tuck my hair behind my ear, even though it springs right back. "Don't worry tonight, love. Tonight is for you to relax and enjoy yourself. Leave the worrying to us. We'll keep you safe."

I know they will, but it's hard to let go of everything when I've been holding it so close for so long. And just thinking about everything hanging over our heads, and everything we have to do, weighs down my shoulders with heavy guilt.

Kai hands me a glass of wine. "Here. This will help you take your mind off things."

We sit on the blankets, talking, drinking, and eating. Before long, I find myself relaxing. Crickets and cicadas sing their nighttime songs around us, and I let the sound mix with my guys' voices. Since Sterling and I have finally accepted our bond, the tension between the three of them has disappeared. It's almost like watching them interact together for the first time. They joke, harass, and argue with each other like they've been doing it for years. And they have. It's good to see them together again. A unit. A family.

After a time, Kai stands and walks to the edge of the lake. He slowly strips out of his clothing, like he's putting on a show because he knows I can't tear my eyes away from him. I don't have to look at Cade to know his gaze is also glued to the vampire. In the fairy lights, Kai's pale skin almost glows. He reaches above his head and dives straight into the lake, his body perfectly poised and sculpted.

He surfaces and shakes his head, spraying droplets of water in all directions. "Who's going to join me?" A wicked grin spreads across his face displaying his fangs.

I smile but shake my head. "I actually spent time on my hair tonight. I'm not ruining it so soon." It won't last. Especially if we end up having sex. But I'm going to try, at least.

Cade stands and kicks off his shoes. "Why the hell not?"

I watch him strip out of his clothes and dive into the water with Kai. "Are you going to join them?" I ask, turning to Sterling.

He watches them with a smile. "No. I'll let them have some time together."

I scoot closer to him and lay my head on his shoulder, making sure I can still see Kai and Cade in the lake. Watching them swim around, splash, and laugh makes my heart flutter behind my ribs. "Have they always been like this?"

Sterling shakes his head and wraps his arm around my waist. "No. They started having sex to help Kai keep his monster under control. I don't know why they thought that would help, or how they came to that conclusion. But for a while that's all it was. It changed over time. I don't think either of them realized it, or maybe they did and they chose to ignore it. But I noticed the difference."

"How so?"

"I'd catch Kai looking at Cade differently, or Cade watching Kai out of the corner of his eye. There would be the occasional charged moment that was obvious to everyone but them." He huffs a laugh. "It got really annoying actually. There were so many times I wanted to yell at them to open their eyes and see what was happening."

"What changed?"

"You." He squeezes my waist and drops a kiss to the top of my head. "I think it became harder for them to deny their feelings the more time they spent together. And I'm guessing they realized what they felt for you was similar to what they felt for each other. But since you came along, they've been more open about it, and I'm glad."

"I don't think they've admitted it to each other yet," I say, watching them in the lake.

"No, but they will."

We fall silent and continue to watch them. It doesn't take long for the atmosphere between them to go from playful to charged. My stomach tightens as I watch Kai tug Cade closer to him. They whisper something to each other and Cade's eyes flutter shut a moment before Kai kisses him. My breath hitches watching them. It's not rough and dominating. It's deep and sensual. And I'm all here for it.

"You like watching them together, don't you?" Sterling's voice rasps in my ear, making me shiver.

I nod, unable to find words as his fingers trail down my arm raising goosebumps in their wake. When he gets to my fingers, he moves his hand to my leg, the one exposed by the high slit of the skirt. A small moan escapes when he traces my skin, over my knee and up my thigh. My legs spread wider on instinct and Sterling chuckles darkly.

"Are you watching them, kitten?"

I nod again. Cade's hands are tangled in Kai's hair, and their bodies are pressed tight together. They are so beautiful, and watching them move together is mesmerizing and fucking sexy as hell. I bite my lip as Sterling's fingers graze closer and closer to my core where molten heat has been steadily growing. The first brush of his knuckles makes me gasp.

"What's this?" he asks, breath fanning over my ear. "No panties?" He runs a finger through my wetness and I whimper. "That's a bad kitten."

He punctuates his statement by pushing a finger inside. I must make some kind of noise because Cade and Kai both turn in my direction. Kai whispers something to Cade who grins, and they both wade to shore, their bodies glistening as water drips down the hard planes of their chests. Both of them are rock hard and I bite my lip, lifting my hips in a silent plea for more from Sterling.

"Don't stop on our account," Kai mutters as he kneels in front of me and gently pushes me onto my back.

Kai claims my mouth in a hot, wet kiss at the same time Sterling adds a second finger. The wet strands of Kai's hair tangle in my fingers as I try to pull him closer to me, while spreading my legs wider for Sterling. Droplets of water fall from him onto me, and I suddenly want this dress out of the way. I want to feel all three of them around me, on me, in me. I need their skin on mine, our bodies moving together. Just the thought makes me heat from the inside out.

"She was enjoying the show you and Cade were putting on," Sterling says, still pumping his fingers in a frustratingly slow rhythm.

Kai smiles against my mouth before pulling away. "Do you want us to keep putting on a show for you?" His voice is low and guttural and his eyes glitter dangerously.

Unable to form words, I nod my head enthusiastically. I'd like nothing more than to watch them together while Sterling fucks me with his fingers.

Kai nips my lower lip with his fang, not hard enough to draw blood, but enough to make me gasp. "I just want one taste first."

He looks at Sterling and opens his mouth, sticking out his tongue. Sterling slides his fingers out of me and holds them up for Kai. Watching Kai lick my juices off of Sterling's fingers is hotter than I thought it would be because I know Sterling has no desire to take part in Cade and Kai's activities.

Once satisfied, Kai lays on his back and gives Cade a wicked grin. "Do your worst. Make our woman squirm on Sterling's fingers."

Sterling lifts me so I'm sitting in front of him, my back to his chest. With his legs, he spreads mine and draws the skirts of my dress to the side. I'm shaking in anticipation for his touch, but he waits until Cade hovers over Kai, slowly lowering himself for a kiss.

I'm so absorbed in watching the passion between my vampire and mage, I startle when Sterling's fingers unhook my bustier. He tosses it aside and cups my breasts in his palms, squeezing gently.

"I can smell how turned on you are," he whispers, running his nose up the side of my neck. The side where his bite mark claims me as his. I tilt my head to the side, giving him better access, and he gently nips at the mark making liquid heat pool in my core. "Watch them together, kitten. Watch how undone Kai becomes under Cade's touch."

I do. As Cade licks a path down Kai's chest and abs, Kai writhes, and I can feel his heart thumping madly the lower Cade goes. When Cade licks the length of Kai's cock and sucks the tip into his mouth, Kai's head hits the ground and his back arches. He is so fucking beautiful it hurts to look at him.

"How does it feel knowing all you'd have to do is say their names and they'd be over here in an instant? Ready to make you scream as we all fuck you senseless." Sterling pinches my nipples and rolls them into tight peaks. The pleasure inside me is growing, and I can feel my own slickness on my thighs. He keeps working one nipple while the other hand trails down my belly, heading for my center that I desperately need him to touch. "You have all three of us in the palm of your hand, Ellis. Say the word and we'll make it happen. Whatever you want, we will give you."

Fuck. I want that. I want all three of them together. Have dreamt of this moment for so long. There was a time I thought it would never happen. That I'd have to live with just Kai and Cade. And while that would have been wonderful, a piece of me would have been missing. I need all three of them equally. I love all three of them equally. Now, I'm ready to fuck all three of them.

He slips his finger through my folds, pushing inside. I lift my hips, needing more friction, more stretch. More of all of them. It's on the tip of my tongue to call Cade and Kai over. I know Sterling is right. One word and they're mine. But watching Cade's lips spread wide around Kai's cock, watching Kai slowly unravel, it's too fucking hot. I can hold out a second longer.

"Fuck," Kai curses, pulling Cade away by his hair. "You're going to make me come," he says, breathing heavily.

Cade chuckles but his gaze travels to me and he bites his bottom lip. "Was that enough of a show for you? Because watching Sterling finger you is driving me fucking wild."

I whimper when Sterling removes his fingers. He brings them to my lips and I open my mouth, letting him slide them inside so I can clean them off. Kai groans and his cock twitches as he watches me with the fierceness of a predator.

Sterling leans in and whispers in my ear, "I want you to take off that skirt and go ride Kai's cock."

Oh fuck. I quickly realize Sterling is going to be the dominant one in this relationship. He's going to make all the rules and expect us to play by them. We haven't had a chance to explore this dynamic, the four of us together, but I'm all for it. I shimmy out of the skirt and let Sterling toss it aside with the bustier. My gaze locks with Kai's as I crawl to him, cheeks heating slightly at how they're watching me degrade myself by crawling to him on my hands and knees. Kai's fangs bite into his lower lip and it makes me clench my inner walls. I want those in my neck.

I straddle Kai and rub my core along his hard length, making us both groan and shudder. His cock is still wet from Cade's mouth when I take it in my hands and position it at my entrance. Kai's fingers tighten on my hips as I slowly lower down onto him. I hold his gaze and it's not just lust I see in his gray irises. No, there is so much more. Love, fierce and undying. Something so deep my once human brain can't fathom it.

"Oh, baby girl," Kai breathes. "You feel perfect."

I distantly hear Sterling say something to Cade, but I'm too focused on gliding up and down on Kai's cock. His chest is cool and hard under my fingers as I brace myself for more leverage. Looking into his gray eyes is almost enough to make me come. Seeing that devotion almost shatters me completely.

A hand on my back pushes me down so my chest is against Kai's. I'm not prepared for the cool, wet sensation of something sliding between my cheeks. I start, but Kai murmurs something soothing. Looking over my shoulder I see Cade kneeling over Kai's legs, a bottle lube in his hand.

"Relax, love. Look at Kai."

I do as he says and I try to relax. Something probes my back entrance, a finger I think. It's not as big as the plug they used on me, so it slips inside easily. The sensation is strange, but not unwelcome. Kai lifts his hips, encouraging me to keep moving, so I do.

Soon, a second finger gets added, the stretch surprisingly pleasant. Cade moves his fingers around before pulling them out. I frown. I kind of liked that feeling. But my frown doesn't last. I feel the head of his cock push against my back entrance and I stiffen.

"I'm not ready for that," I breathe.

"You are ready for it," Sterling growls. "And you'll take it like you were made for Cade's cock." His words make my inner walls clench around Kai.

"Trust us, baby girl." Kai frames my face in his hands and kisses me. "We'll stop at any point if you want us to."

"Say the word, Ellis," Cade says behind me, his voice rough and strained like he's barely holding himself back.

I glance at Sterling, at his hooded gaze and cock jutting from his body. He leans in and slides his hand between me and Kai, rubbing my clit lightly.

I nod. "Okay."

Sterling and Kai distract me with their kisses and fingers. Hushed words of encouragement and praise float over me and Cade slowly pushes inside, giving me plenty of time to adjust. Once he's seated all the way, everyone stills. It's not so different from the plug, and the longer we wait, the more relaxed I become.

Sterling flicks his finger over my clit and I jolt. The motion causes Cade's cock to move inside me and I groan. I'm so full. With Kai in my pussy and Cade in my ass, I feel like I'll burst. But in a good way.

"Oh my gods," I pant.

"Is this okay?" Kai asks, slowly lifting his hips.

Each movement, each shift of hips causes pleasure to ripple through me. Pleasure like I've never experienced before. I suddenly need them to move. To fuck me and make me see stars.

"No," I choke out, and they all tense. "Move. Fuck me. Don't just sit there." My voice is strained with desperation and untamed desire. I try to thrust my own hips, but being pinned between Cade and Kai makes it difficult.

Cade chuckles and he sets a slow pace. When he pulls out, Kai pulls me down onto his cock. When Kai lifts me off, Cade pushes in. They work together, slowly increasing their rhythm. Sterling rains praise on me, all while his fingers play my clit like a string instrument.

Kai groans. "I can feel Cade. Oh shit, this is ..."

Fingers tangle in my hair and tug my head to the side. Sterling kneels with his cock in his hand, urging me to open my mouth. I don't hesitate, and he slips inside.

I'm lost. Completely filled by my men, my Shields. They move around me and inside me, making me feel things I've never felt before. I'm utterly at their mercy and I let myself fall away. I sink into the moment and the sensations. The sounds of moaning, my wetness, skin slapping. The scent of arousal and nature. My eyes fall shut and I let it all go.

This. This is what I've been desperately waiting for. To take all three of them at one time. To solidify our bonds and what we have. To make sure they know how much I love them, how much I trust them. They don't hold back, and they make sure to show me *everything*.

Fangs scrape along my neck and lightning shoots through me. As soon as Kai bites me, it will be over. I'm already teetering on the edge. I don't want it to end, but I don't think I can hold on much longer.

"Fuck," Cade grunts. His rhythm falters briefly, and his fingers on my waist tighten. "Bite her, Kai."

Two pinpricks pierce my flesh, and the pleasure that tears through me makes me scream. My body moves on its own, my hips searching for that last bit of friction. When Sterling's fingers rub against my clit, my vision fractures. The orgasm crashes through me so hard I black out. Sterling curses as he slams his dick as deep into my throat as possible, and I swallow his release by reflex alone. My inner walls fluttering and clenching set Cade and Kai off. They both stiffen and the chorus of their moans mix together as they come.

When it's all over, I can barely breathe, let alone move. Each guy slowly pulls out and my body jerks, nerve endings sensitive and overworked. I keep my eyes closed as they clean me up and settle around me. I know Sterling is in front of me, his scent is the closest. I rest my head on his shoulder as Kai's cool arm wraps around my middle. Somehow, I know Cade is tucked behind Kai without opening my eyes. It's like now that we've all been together, my bonds with them have sharpened.

I can sense each one of them separately deep in my chest. I've never felt so whole in my life. With that feeling sinking deep into me, I fall asleep, safe in my Shield's arms.

ELLIS

I wish I could repeat that night over and over again. Everything about it was perfect. Being able to finally be with all three of my guys was beyond my wildest dreams. I know we have so much to deal with, but I can't wait for it to all be over so we can repeat everything that happened last night.

Unfortunately, the next day the guys return to battle mode. I've spent the past two days manifesting my wings and making them disappear. Sterling wants me to be able to do it in the blink of an eye. Right now, it takes me about five seconds of closing my eyes and imaging it in my mind. It's mentally exhausting, and by the end of each practice session, my brain is mush.

"Can we take a break?" I ask, shoulders sagging. Sweat coats my skin, and my tank top clings to me uncomfortably. When Sterling nods, I heave a sigh of relief.

"You're doing better," he says, unsticking a curl from my neck. "You just have to keep practicing. And once you have it down, I want you to practice shifting while fighting or under high stress situations."

I stare at him and blink. Just thinking about that makes me want to cry. I've never been so exhausted in my life. Even with the boxing Allie and I used to do, I never experienced this bone deep weariness. It goes further than just muscle. My brain is just as worn out.

He wraps me in his arms, and I let myself collapse against him, not even caring about my sweatiness. "I'm proud of you, by the way," he murmurs.

When was the last time someone said they were proud of me? His words make my throat burn with unshed tears. "Not a lot to be proud of," I mumble.

He scoffs. "Seriously? You know pups take forever to get the shifting thing down. Many of them end up stuck in their wolf form for months at a time until they can shift back. You learned really quickly. Granted, you're not a full shifter, but that's impressive nonetheless."

He kisses the top of my head and I melt a little bit inside. "Sterling?"

"Hmm?"

"Do you think it would be easier to deal with Sam if Noah was out of the picture?"

He stiffens but doesn't pull away. "Why do you ask?"

"If Sam knows we're coming back for Gracie, don't you think he'll be prepared by getting Noah involved? If we have to go against Sam and Noah at the same time ..." I leave the rest unsaid. He'll understand the threat that presents.

Sterling sighs and rubs my back. "It's a possibility. But ..."

"But you don't know if you want to challenge him?" I pull away enough to glance at him. His blue eyes are shadowed and he won't quite meet my gaze. "Sterling."

He drops his arms and I immediately miss his closeness. "I do," he says quietly. "I want to take my place as alpha. I want to save my family. But I can't." His stubble scratches as he rubs a hand down his face.

"Why not? We've accepted the bond, so that's not an issue anymore. I know Cade and Kai would be okay with it. All any of us want is for you to be happy. So why can't you?"

He turns away, and I know I shouldn't push him. Cade's

words come back to me, that Sterling tends to handle his personal stuff alone, but I won't let him do that. Not now that we're mates. If he doesn't take his place as alpha, there will always be a part of him that will regret it. And I don't want that to happen.

I grab his hand and force him to stop. "Sterling, talk to me. Please."

His shoulders sag and when I walk around to face him, his eyes are squeezed shut. "I can't become alpha without my brother. As soon as Cole was born, my wolf knew he was going to be my beta. There is no one else I'd want at my side helping me lead the pack. Without him, I can't do it."

Oh. I bite my lip, hesitating. This is a delicate situation, and I don't want to do or say anything to upset Sterling. "Have you tried to talk to him?" I ask quietly, gently squeezing his hand.

"No." His silver hair glints in the setting sun as he shakes his head. "And he won't talk to me even if I tried."

"You don't know that."

"I appreciate what you're trying to do, Ellis, but it's just not going to happen." The defeated tone of his voice cracks me open. I open my mouth to argue but he cuts me off. "I'm going to go for a run. It's been awhile and my wolf is getting antsy."

I step back, letting my hand drop to my side. "I'm sorry," I whisper. "I didn't mean to upset you."

"You didn't upset me, kitten." He cups my cheek and leans in for a quick kiss. "It's just a lot to think about." He scans my face and must see something he doesn't like, because he pulls me in for a hug. "Hey, I mean it. You did nothing wrong. Now, I'm going to let my wolf out for a bit. Cade and Kai are in town still, but should be back soon. I'll be on the mountain, and the wards will keep you safe. Is that okay?"

"Yeah, okay."

He kisses my forehead before stepping away and stripping out of his sweats. I take a moment to admire him, because who the hell wouldn't? Naked Sterling is impressive. He winks at me before shifting. It's so seamless and smooth. One second he's human, the next he's a wolf.

"I hate how easy you make that look," I mutter. Kneeling down I run my hands through his thick fur. "Hey Fluffy. What's up?"

Fluffy gives me a tail wag and licks the side of my face. I swear I can hear Sterling grumbling about me calling his wolf Fluffy.

"Go run," I say, pressing a kiss to the top of his nose before standing.

I watch the wolf disappear into the trees, worrying my bottom lip. Sterling really needs to make amends with his brother. I know I shouldn't get involved, but something in me tells me if I don't, nothing will ever get better between them. I know what it's like to lose a sibling, and I don't want that for him. Decision made, I grab his sweats from the ground and fish out his phone. Drew's number is saved, and I hit dial without giving myself a chance to change my mind.

"Hey man, what's up?" Drew asks after the third ring.

"Actually, it's Ellis, not Sterling."

"Is everything okay?"

"Yeah. No? Maybe. I need your help with something."

The sound of a door closing and footsteps up a set of stairs echo from the phone. "What do you need?"

"Can you take me to see Sterling's brother?"

A pause on the other end, then, "What the hell for?"

"I need to talk to him. Both of them need to get their heads out of their asses and have a conversation like the adults they are."

"I'm guessing Sterling doesn't know you're calling me about this," Drew drawls.

"You guess correctly."

"Annnd I'm also guessing Cade and Kai don't know?"

"Um, also correct."

"No. Not a chance in hell I'm taking you from that cabin without them knowing. Ellis, they would murder me and there would be nothing left of my body for anyone to find. Not happening."

"Drew, please. This is important. Sterling said he won't challenge Noah unless Cole is his beta." Silence on the other end gives me a slight bit of hope. "I know you agree with me that Sterling needs to take back control of the pack."

"Of course I agree with you on that. I just don't agree with how you're going about making it happen. Why can't Sterling do this on his own? He's a big boy."

"But he's really not," I grouse. "I tried to talk to him and he shut me down. He's stubborn, and he won't do this because he thinks what Cole believes is right. In Sterling's eyes, he'll never be able to make things up to earn Cole's trust and forgiveness."

"But me taking you to see him without any of the guys knowing is not the way to do this."

I'm silent because I don't know what else to say. He's right. I know he is. But I also know that I need to do this. It's something in my gut. Something screaming at me that this needs to happen.

Drew sighs. "If I don't take you you'll go on your own, won't you."

My response is silence, because yes. Yes, I will go on my own if he doesn't take me.

"Fuck me," Drew mutters. "When?"

My heart lurches. "Now?"

Another heavy sigh. "I'll be there in twenty minutes."

———

"I hope you realize by doing this, I have officially signed my own death warrant," Drew says as he drives his small SUV down the mountain.

"I'd like to say quit being so dramatic, but knowing those guys, you're probably right."

Drew snorts. "Gee, you're really making me feel like I made

the right decision here." Sarcasm laces his words heavily, and I roll my eyes.

The ride is bumpy until we turn off onto the road, and then I distract myself with the view out the window. From the moment I hung up with Drew, my stomach has been tumbling. Nervous energy courses through my body and I can't sit still. I have no idea if we will be back before the guys get home, and if we're not, I'm going to be in serious trouble.

"Can I trust Cole?" I ask, forcing my thoughts away from the inevitable consequences of my actions. "Like, can I tell him we're staying at the cabin? He won't run off to Noah will he?"

Drew shakes his head. "You can trust him. He may be angry and hotheaded, but he's a wolf. Family always comes first. No matter what. Besides, if something happened to Sterling, it would destroy their mom and Cole would never do that to her."

"Where is Noah tonight? How much time will I be able to talk with Cole?" I ask, fidgeting with the hem of my tank top.

"Noah's not on pack lands tonight, luckily. And since no one on pack lands will know who you are, we can park in Shari's driveway. Everyone knows I visit them occasionally, so it won't be out of the ordinary to see me there."

"Fate," I mutter. The surety in my gut intensifies knowing Noah will be gone tonight. This is what I'm supposed to do. Maybe this is part of my job as a harpy. Maybe getting Sterling back in the pack as alpha is one of the ways I'm supposed to help balance things. It sure would be nice if this harpy shit came with a manual, but my gut feelings will have to do.

Drew pulls up to the house and my nerves intensify. Golden light spills from the windows onto the porch. As welcoming as it looks, I know my reception will not be that warm. At least not from Cole.

"Do you want me to come in?" Drew asks as he cuts the engine.

"Umm ..." I hesitate. I don't really want him there for the conversation with Cole, but his presence would be comforting.

"How about I hang out on the roof and keep watch," he offers.

"That would be great. Thanks."

I climb out of the car and head for the front porch. I hear the flap of wings before talons scrape along the shingles. Taking a deep breath, I knock on the door. *Here we go.*

The door opens and Shari gasps. "Ellis! What are you doing here? Is Sterling okay?"

"He's fine," I assure her. "I'm actually here to talk to Cole."

She frowns but ushers me inside. "Have a seat. Would you like something to eat or drink?"

"I'm good, thank you." Before I can take a seat she grabs my hand.

"Is he doing okay?" Her eyes shine with unshed tears and my heart aches for her.

"He is. I promise. He misses you, though."

A tear spills over and her lips wobble. "Luna, I miss him too." She shakes herself, quickly wiping away the tear. "Sit, Ellis. I'll get Cole down here."

I perch on the edge of the couch and pull out my phone, checking the time. No new messages or calls. Still good.

Shari returns with a tray of cookies, their delicious scent wafting ahead of her. She sets them on the coffee table and studies me. "He'll be right down. Is this something I need to leave the room for?"

"You don't have to, but it might be hard for you to hear some of the things I need to say." I don't plan on telling Cole the entirety of Sterling's story. But I will tell him my story, and Sterling's role in my story hasn't been sunshine and roses.

She nods and straightens her spine before taking a seat next to me on the couch. Sterling wasn't lying when he said his mom was a strong woman. Footsteps sound on the stairs and I take a page from Shari's book. I straighten my shoulders and raise my chin. I can be just as stubborn as Sterling, and I won't walk away until Cole has at least heard what I have to say.

"You've got to be fucking kidding me," Cole growls as he walks into the living room.

"Cole!" Shari admonishes. "Sit down. Ellis says she wants to talk to you."

"What could she possibly have to say that I'll want to hear?" He crosses his arms over his broad chest. He has the same physical structure as his older brother, but instead of silver hair, his is black, like his mom's. A full beard covers the lower half of his face, and makes his blue eyes even more startling.

"Cole, so help me, if you don't sit your ass down and listen to Ellis ..." Shari gives Cole a look that I store away for use later. It may come in handy with three stubborn guys.

Cole sighs and sits on the chair, crossing his arms again and staring at me with such hate I almost change my mind. He raises one brow impatiently and I quickly gather my thoughts.

"Here's the deal," I begin, clasping my hands in my lap to hide their shaking. "I want to tell you to take the fucking stick out of your ass and talk to your brother, but I know better than to do that." Indeed, he's already stiffening, gaze shuttering as he prepares to stand and walk away. "Instead, since neither you nor Sterling will put on your big girl panties, I'm going to tell you my story in the hopes that maybe, just maybe, it will make you realize your brother is not the enemy."

He snorts, but he relaxes in the chair. I almost wished he would have gotten up and left. Then I wouldn't have had to do this. I wouldn't have had to open myself up and tell these people about my life and the horrors I've endured. I swallow down my fear and push forward.

"When I was sixteen, my entire life came to an end. My mom and sister were murdered in my home. I hid, and somehow survived, only to find out years later it was Sterling who kept me safe that night. He was there with Noah Martin to carry out Noah's orders to kill me, my mom, and sister. But Sterling smelled me as soon as he walked into the house and knew I was his mate."

Shari gasps, but I ignore her. I can't look at her reaction. I can't see her sympathy or sadness. It will crumple me.

"I was raised by Thomas Kennedy and when I turned twenty-three, I started dating Sam Morris, a prominent mage in Thomas's company." My throat tries to close so I swallow and shut my eyes so I don't have to see anyone while I admit this darkest secret of mine. "After two years with Sam, I found out he was only dating me to get into Thomas's good graces. When I tried to leave, he turned into a monster. I spent the next two years being raped and beaten by the man I was supposed to marry."

The room is so quiet I can hear my heart pounding in my chest. The couch dips slightly, like Shari wants to reach out to me, but she doesn't. And I'm glad. I can't handle anyone's touch while I tell this story.

"Thomas creating the contest was the best thing that ever happened to me. Malakai, Cade, and Sterling saved me from a fate I can't even contemplate." I open my eyes and my gaze lands on Cole. His expression is unreadable as he studies me. "There is a lot that has happened since then, but the part I want you to know about is Sterling's role in my story."

I take a deep breath and relax. This is easier. Talking about my mate, even though it started out rough, is as easy as breathing. "Sterling knew if he took me the night my mom and sister were killed, I'd never forgive him. So he left me. He kept an eye on me, making sure I was safe, but he knew if he ever told anyone he had a mate, Noah would have me killed. There was no way he'd let me live after having escaped him once, and the added threat I would create to his rule."

From the corner of my eye I see Shari nod, and I know Cole understands as well.

"He had to decide between his family and his mate, and it tore him apart. If he tried to fight Noah, if he tried to reclaim his title, Noah would have killed you. So Sterling gave all of it up. He lived all of those years without his family and without his mate."

Cole's jaw tenses and he looks down to his lap.

"When he joined Kai during the contest, he didn't tell me I was his mate. He fought the connection we both felt until Thomas blew his cover. Thomas found out Sterling had been there the night my mom and sister were killed, and Sterling finally came clean."

Shari sighs and shakes her head. I swear I hear her mutter something about idiotic boys.

"It hurt a lot to find out he'd lied to me and kept that secret from me. I didn't make it easy on him to get back in my good graces. In fact, when we visited you guys the night I first met you, I hadn't accepted the bond yet. It wasn't until recently, thanks to something you said, Shari, that I realized it didn't matter what happened in the past. All that mattered was that I accept the bond. So I did." I meet Shari's gaze and see unwavering love and acceptance in her eyes. It hits me right in the chest, to know this woman has already decided to welcome me in with open arms.

My phone vibrates on the coffee table and my stomach clenches. I check the screen and see Kai's name. *Shit.*

I swallow thickly and continue. "I wanted you to know that Sterling's choices were not made lightly. He struggled a lot. He had a lot of decisions to make, and he did the best he could. Now, we have more on our plate than you could ever imagine. My ex has been hunting me. He has a warehouse where he's been experimenting on magicals and non-magicals alike. He wants me for ... well, he wants me. And all this time, I thought my sister had been murdered but he has her. She's alive, and she needs us to rescue her." My voice breaks. *Gracie.* I can't imagine what she's been through. "And to top it all off, I found out Thomas isn't my dad. Noah is." I huff a humorless laugh. "Gods. Saying it all out loud sounds insane."

Cole rears back, gaze snapping to mine.

"Yeah. He tried to have me killed. Father of the year right there. Right along with Thomas Kennedy." I snort, but there is no humor to it. "Sterling wants to be alpha. He wants to challenge Noah, but there is so much on our plate and he's scared.

He needs you, Cole. He needs your approval and support. He needs his family behind him."

My phone buzzes again, this time Cade's picture pops up. *Fuck.* I'm going to be in so much trouble.

I clench my phone and prepare to stand. "All I want you to do is talk to him. Hear him out. Listen to his side of the story. Then you can make up your mind as to whether you still blame him for everything." A text comes through, followed quickly by three more. "I really have to go, but we're staying at the cabin if you want to talk to Sterling. And I really hope you do."

I stand from the couch as my phone rings once more. Kai again. Shari jumps up and stops me.

"Ellis." She pulls me in for a hug, and I have to hold back the tears. "I am so sorry for everything. But I'm happy you found your mate." She lowers her voice and whispers in my ear. "I hope your story convinces Cole to talk to Sterling. They need each other."

I nod in agreement. "They really do." Another string of texts come through. "I really have to go. I'm going to be in big trouble for doing this."

She walks me to the door and hugs me one last time. "Tell Sterling I love him."

I nod and walk toward the car. Drew flies down and shifts, quickly slipping into his pants before getting behind the wheel.

"How'd it go?" he asks as he turns the car on.

I hold up my phone, buzzing again. "They're looking for me."

ELLIS

"WHY DON'T YOU ANSWER IT AND LET THEM KNOW you're okay?" Drew asks after my phone buzzes for a solid five minutes.

"Because they'll just yell at me. Then yell at me again when we get back." I shrug. "I might as well wait so I just get yelled at once."

It makes no sense, and I know that, but I've always been the type to put off punishment. Even if it makes it worse later on.

My phone buzzes again, this time a text, and I glance at it. Forty-three messages.

Kai: WHERE ARE YOU

Kai: ellis! are you okay?

Cade: please let us know if you're okay.

Kai: i swear to the gods, if you don't answer me i will lose my fucking my mind!!

Cade: we're really worried, love. Sterling is scouring the mountain in his wolf form, and Kai is about to go berserk.

I grimace and my thumb hovers over the keyboard. Maybe I should just send a quick text and tell them I'm on my way home and I'm safe. But I chicken out and set my phone in my lap, screen face down.

The closer we get to the cabin, the more I feel like I'm going to vomit. This was quite possibly the stupidest thing I've ever done. I should have just waited for Cade and Kai to get home, so they could take me to talk to Cole. Why didn't I do that? Oh yeah, because they would have never agreed to it.

"Fuck me," Drew grumbles. "If I could, I'd make you walk the rest of the way. Kai is going to murder me."

"I'll put a good word in for you," I say, but it doesn't come out as confident as I hoped it would. It's too hard to breathe, even as I take in one deep breath after another in an attempt to calm the roiling in my stomach.

When the cabin comes into view, I swallow thickly, my mouth suddenly dry. Cade and Kai are both on the porch, and I want to crawl under the seat and hide. Purple sparks flicker at Cade's fingertips as he flexes his hands. Kai paces back and forth, his hair a mess from where he's run his hands through it. I slink lower in the seat, guilt and shame riding me hard at their worry and fear.

Both guys jump off the porch before the car comes to a stop and Drew mumbles something under his breath before stepping out. I open my door more slowly, and Cade is upon me in seconds. His magic bursts out of him, purple wisps fluttering around me, caressing my skin as if searching for an injury. Cade's eyes flare in surprise before he reins it back in.

"Are you okay?" He grabs my face in his hands, not as gentle as he usually is, and the fear in his gaze makes me want to sink into the ground and never come back out.

Guilt makes my skin prickle, like it's stretched too tight over my bones. I try to nod, but his grip is too strong. "Yes," I croak. "I'm fine."

"Where the hell did you go? Why didn't you tell us? Ellis, we were worried sick about you!"

"I'm sorry," I mumble, casting my gaze down, unable to look at him as shame heats the back of my neck.

"I'm going to rip out your fucking throat!"

Kai's growl jerks my head up, and I see him pinning Drew to

the side of the car. I pull away from Cade and rush around to grab Kai's arm.

"Wait! Kai, don't hurt him!"

He growls in response, no words, just low, rumbly vibrations I feel in his arms. His eyes are glowing red and his fangs are longer than I've ever seen.

"Kai, let him go! It was my idea to leave. Drew didn't want to take me, but I told him I'd go without him if he didn't." I try to wedge myself between them, but Kai shifts so I can't.

Drew wheezes, Kai's hand around his throat making breathing difficult, but he manages to say, "I made sure she was safe."

"Please, Kai. Let him go." I tug on his arm, but it's like trying to pull down a steel beam. "Don't punish him for my choices."

Kai holds Drew pinned to the car for a second longer before he pushes away. He doesn't go far though. Faster than I can blink, he throws a right hook. I scream as Drew's head snaps to the side and blood sprays.

"Fuck," Drew grunts, holding the side of his face. Blood streams from his broken nose and dribbles down his chin. I try to go to him, but he holds out a hand to stop me. "It's fine. It's the least I deserve."

Kai grunts and turns to me. Under that piercing red stare, I shrink back. Normally, I'd be excited to draw the monster out, but this time I know I really messed up. The monster isn't out to play.

"Kai," I breathe shakily.

"Get inside." His voice is barely recognizable as his own, and his entire body is taut like a bowstring.

Drew hesitates. "Ellis ..."

Kai growls, and his body tenses even more.

"You should leave, Drew," I say, never taking my eyes off Kai. "I'll be fine."

"Inside. Now," Kai says, taking a step forward.

I nod my head and turn around, heading for the porch. Cade watches me with his arms crossed, a look in his eyes that screams with hurt. My heart sinks. I really fucked up. In the living room I perch on the edge of the couch, too nervous to sit all the way back onto the cushions. My gaze bounces between Cade and Kai, and I bite my lip.

"I'm sor—"

Kai holds out a hand, stopping me. I close my eyes and let my head fall forward, hiding my face in the curtain of my hair. The couch dips, and I know who it is without looking. Even without the scent of cedar and lilac, Kai is too wound up to sit down.

Cade puts his hand on my thigh and something settles within me. "Where did you go, Ellis?"

"I went to talk to Cole," I whisper. Sterling isn't back yet, and the guys would have no way to let him know I'm home safe if he's in his wolf form.

"Why?" Cade asks.

"Because they need to talk." I look up to meet his gaze. "I think it would be safer to deal with Sam if Noah was out of the picture. Sterling agrees, but he won't challenge Noah without Cole, and he won't talk to Cole. So, I talked to him."

"Sterling won't like that you got involved," Cade mutters, his gaze guarded like he's holding back his emotions.

"I only told him my story. I'm hoping it will help him put some things in perspective, and he'll be willing to talk to Sterling."

"Why didn't you tell us?" Kai growls, pausing his pacing to stare at me.

I shrug. "I don't know." My voice wobbles and tears blur my vision. "I thought you guys would say no. That you would tell me to not get in the middle of them."

Kai huffs a humorless laugh. "Yeah. You're probably right." He shakes his head. "What you did was so incredibly stupid, Ellis!" His words hit me like a slap, and I flinch. "Did you forget how many people are hunting you right now? What if Sam had found you? What if Noah had come home and found you in his house? You left the fucking wards Cade put down for *your* protection and offered yourself up on a silver fucking platter!"

"It was a mistake. I'm sorry." I stare at Kai, some of my guilt warping into anger. "And see?" I fling my hand toward him, pacing back and forth. "You just said so yourself. You would have said no. What else was I supposed to do?"

"Oh, I don't know. Maybe talk to us?" Kai snaps back at me. "Maybe act like a responsible adult instead of a child!"

I grit my teeth and sit up straighter, glaring daggers at him. "You don't get to talk to me like that just because I messed up."

Kai huffs a laugh but there's no humor in it. "No. I get to talk to you like this because you scared the fucking shit out of us by this stupid stunt you pulled. Put yourself in our shoes, Ellis. How would you have felt?"

That cools some of my anger. A single tear slips down my cheek, and I hastily wipe it away. "I'm sorry," I whisper. I know it's not enough. It doesn't fix anything, but I don't know what else to say.

Kai runs a hand through his hair and sighs. "I need to feed before I say or do something I'll regret."

I suck in a breath and bite my lip, but Kai cuts his blood red gaze to me and shakes his head.

"Not from you. I'm too pissed right now. Cade?"

His words cut through me like a jagged knife. It sucks all of the fight out of me and leaves me reeling. It would have hurt less if he had hit me. I almost wish he would have hit me. That I know I can deal with. But knowing he doesn't want to feed from me, his beloved, it's suffocating.

I gasp for breath and shakily push from the couch. Everything blurs around me as I head for the stairs, feeling like my world has been completely upended. I don't know how I make it to the bedroom, but when I collapse onto the bed, the tears I'd been holding back break free.

I bury my face in the pillow and sob. Soul crushing sobs that shake my entire body. It's my fault. I knew they would be mad, but I wasn't ready to deal with the consequences of my actions. *I'm so fucking stupid.*

I pull a pillow over my head, not wanting to hear anything that happens downstairs. Just thinking about Kai feeding from Cade makes my heart shatter into tiny pieces. *I'm* his beloved. It always made me feel special that I could provide for him in a way no one else could. And here he is, feeding from Cade instead.

With the pillow over my head, I don't hear the bedroom door open. I jerk when it gets pulled away and someone sits on the edge of the bed. Sterling runs his gaze over me, a little wild and scared as he makes sure I'm okay. My lips tremble again and I swallow down a sob.

He sighs heavily and scoots to the head of the bed, leaning against the headboard and holding his arms open for me. The sob I tried to hold back escapes, and I crawl to him, letting him wrap me in his arms. I collapse against his chest and cry. I needed this. I needed one of my guys to hold me and let me know that even though I messed up, everything is still okay.

Sterling holds me tightly, like he needs to be sure I'm safe, like he's trying to hold me together. He doesn't say anything until my tears run their course. When they do, I'm left hiccuping and sniffling, but I feel a tiny bit better.

I pull away and grimace. "I'm sorry," I hiccup, trying to wipe my tears from his chest which is now wet and shiny.

He shakes his head and lifts my chin, wiping my cheeks. "Talk to me, kitten. Where did you go, and why was it so important to have Drew take you without telling us?"

I swallow and duck my head against his chest again, unable to look at him while I admit what I did. "I went to see Cole," I mumble.

He jerks, but he keeps his arms around me. "What? Why?"

"Because I know how much you want to challenge Noah. And I know you won't do it without Cole. But I also know you won't talk to him even though you want to." I pull back and look at him, searching his gaze for anger. It's there, but he's not near as angry as Kai. "I lost my sister. I mean, I thought I lost her. Maybe I still have, who knows what she'll be like when we rescue her. I live with that pain every day. Wanting to talk to her. Wanting to share my life with her. But I can't. And it sucks. It really, really sucks." I have to pause to swallow down more tears. "But Cole is still alive. You haven't lost him. I just thought if I could do something to help you guys repair what's been broken, then you wouldn't have to live with the pain of missing your brother like I miss my sister."

Sterling deflates, his shoulder slumping. He rests his forehead against mine. "How the hell can I be mad at you for thinking like that?" He pulls away and takes my face gently in his hands. "You know you shouldn't have left without us knowing, right? It was dangerous, and if something had happened to you ..." he trails off, unable to finish that thought. "I haven't been that scared before in my life," he whispers, tucking a strand of hair behind my ear. "Not knowing where you were. Not knowing if you were in danger or hurt. It was terrifying."

Tears build on my lashes again, but I blink them away. "I'm sorry. I know it was wrong. I know I shouldn't have done it. I never wanted to scare you guys." I rub my chest. "There was something inside me that told me I had to do it. I can't explain but, it was like a tug in my chest that I had to follow. I almost want to say it was something I *had* to do, like as a harpy. The pull was so strong."

Sterling studies me with a frown. "You're saying you think it's part of your job as a harpy to make sure I become alpha?"

I shrug and wipe my cheeks again. "It makes sense. Noah has to be taken care of for many reasons. Bringing balance back to the wolves seems like a pretty important job."

He nods his head slowly. "What did Cole say?"

"He didn't say anything, but I didn't give him a chance to. I just told him my story in the hopes it would make him realize you did what you had to do."

"You told him everything?" Sterling asks quietly.

"Everything about me. Well, except the harpy part and being bonded to all three of you. There wasn't time to go into that."

He nods. "You still shouldn't have done it without telling us."

"I know. I'm so sorry, Sterling."

"I know you are." He pulls me against him again and I let his warmth wrap around me.

"Cade and Kai ..."

"Give them time. Kai especially. I can't explain the terror we all felt. They'll have to process this in their own way and their own time."

I release a breath and let the knowledge that at least one of my Shields still loves me settle the unease in my gut. He holds me tightly until the bedroom door opens. I look up to see Cade standing in the doorway. His hair is mussed, but I can't tell if that's because he's been running his hands through it or if Kai has. My gaze drops to his neck where two fresh puncture marks mar the surface.

I'm not prepared for the angry jealousy that sweeps through me. I've never felt that way with the two of them. I love how much they love each other, and I've never not wanted them to be together. But this is different. This hurts so much worse because I know it's my fault. Kai chose Cade because of what I did.

I swallow down the tears that burn the back of my throat and bury my face in Sterling's chest, unable to look at Cade and the reminder that Kai fed from him and not me. Cade sighs, and the bed dips as he sits.

"Ellis," he says gently and places his hand on my thigh. When I don't respond, he sighs again and climbs to the top of the bed next to Sterling. "I know you're upset that Kai fed from me, but there was nothing sexual about it this time. He was worried if he fed from you he would end up hurting you. That's all it was."

I still say nothing because it was my fault. And I can't help the guilt that has been weighing me down since I saw them standing on the front porch. I knew they would be angry, but I never really thought about *why* they would be angry. I didn't think about how much me disappearing without a word would scare them. Why did I do it? I wish I could go back and start over. Maybe I'd be able to convince them to take me to talk to Cole. But then again, what if I couldn't have?

I don't lift my head from Sterling's chest, but I raise my gaze to look at Cade. He's leaning against the headboard with his head tipped back and eyes closed. There's a strain around his eyes and mouth, like he still hasn't completely shaken the worry and fear.

"I think making sure Sterling becomes alpha of the pack is part of my duties as harpy," I say. "There was something inside me that wouldn't settle until I talked to Cole. I'm sorry I didn't tell you guys. I'm sorry I scared you. But I was worried you would say no, and I really needed to do this."

Cade opens his eyes and looks at me. He studies me, his violet gaze piercing me straight to my soul. "I could see that being the case. Removing Noah would restore a lot of balance within the wolves." He runs his hand through his hair, messing it up further. "But that doesn't make it okay. You should have told us. You shouldn't have left the wards without one of us. Ellis, what if Sam found you?" His voice cracks, emotion filling him and overflowing as he tries his hardest to keep his fears under control.

While his words make me panic at the just the thought of Sam finding me, I can also see the panic in his eyes as he thinks about it. My lips tremble again, and tears blur my vision ... again.

"I'm sorry," I say between hiccuping sobs. "I don't know what to do to make you guys trust me again. And I ... I know it was wrong. I just ... I needed to ..." Where is my anger? Why do I just feel sad about all of this? I just want my guys to not be angry with me anymore.

"Oh, Ellis. Come here." He holds open his arms, and I can't resist the pull to climb onto his lap. He holds me close and I inhale his scent, letting it calm me. "Love, I know you're sorry. I just need you to understand how dangerous it was. I'm not mad at you. I still trust you. I was just ... terrified." He shudders under me, and his hand traces circles on my back.

With Sterling sitting next to us, and both of their hands on me, the adrenaline coursing through me evaporates. I spent all morning working on shifting with Sterling. Then I shared my entire story with Cole and Sterling's mom. Topping off my day with all the crying and worrying and guilt, I'm utterly exhausted—physically, mentally, and emotionally. My eyes grow heavy, and the steady thumping of Cade's heart under my ear lulls me closer and closer to sleep.

Just as I'm about to drift off, Cade presses a kiss to the top of my hair. "Sleep, love. Everything is going to be okay."

With his reassurance echoing in my mind, I let myself slip away.

KAI

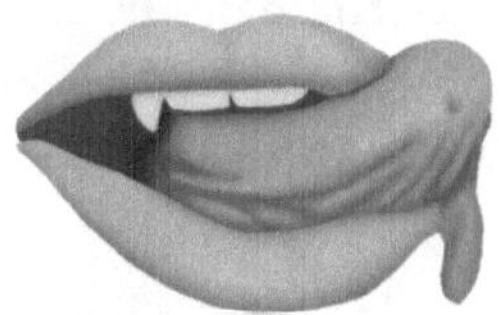

I'm on edge, unable to sit still or calm my heart. The restless feeling could easily be remedied by going upstairs and talking to Ellis, but I'm not ready for that. In all my years of living, I have never lost control of the monster inside me. Tonight, I came really damn close. That alone has left me unsteady and unsure of everything. If it hadn't been for Cade, I for sure would have done something I would have regretted later.

I sit on the porch steps and sigh. The moon reflects off the lake in the distance and just the thought of it makes my chest ache. That night was perfect. Being able to give Ellis what she'd been dreaming of was amazing. And being together, the four of us, finally, was honestly the most special night of my life. But even thinking about that night and the possibility of more like it to come can't help me shake this sensation.

Behind me the door opens and closes, and the sound of bare feet thumping on the wooden porch precedes the scent of pine and winter air. Sterling sits next to me with a heavy exhale. It's been a while since we've been alone, just the two of us. So much got weird between us while he was figuring out his situation with Ellis. It's nice having him back.

"She's asleep," he says. "And so is Cade."

I nod, not surprised by any of it. Ellis had an emotionally draining day. And I took more from Cade than I probably should have. "She told you why she left?" I'm curious to know his reaction to Ellis trying to make peace between the brothers.

"Yeah, and I can't fault her for it. I mean, obviously I wish she wouldn't have gone off without one of us, but her heart was in the right place." He takes the hair tie off his wrist and tugs his hair into a messy bun on the back of his head. "She knows what it's like to lose a sibling, and she didn't want me to go through that."

I nod. Like Sterling, I don't fault her for why she did it. I just don't like the way she went about it. Unfortunately, I think she was probably right. Had she asked Cade and me to take her, we probably would have said no. Neither of us would have wanted to help her get in the middle of something we thought Sterling would want her to stay out of.

It's just one more reason tonight left me so on edge. She didn't trust us to help her so she went behind our back. And she would have been right. What does that say about us? It makes me realize we need to trust *her* more. Not just because she knows us better than we do. But because no one has ever listened to her before. And if she thinks she needs to do something for us, we need to let her.

"I hurt her by feeding from Cade instead of her." The look in her eyes when she realized I chose him over her will haunt me for the rest of my life. But it was the emotions I picked up on that I'll never be able to shake. Betrayed. Heartbroken. Devastated. They were so strong I could barely remain standing. It took all of my self control to remain on my feet. Just thinking about it makes the monster inside me restless.

"Once you talk to her she'll understand," Sterling says. "This is the first time something like this has happened, and I'm sure it won't be the last. We all have a lot to learn. None of us have ever been in a relationship like this and we're bound to make mistakes."

He would know. And based on what I'm picking up from him, he's thinking of exactly that.

"She loves us, and we love her. In the end, that will get us through everything." Sterling grimaces as he stretches out his neck from side to side, the bones popping softly.

He's right, and while that knowledge helps to ease some of my worry, I know I just have to wait to hear it from Ellis to make everything right again.

We sit quietly for a few moments, the only sounds are the crickets chirping in the darkness and the occasional call of an owl or the howl of a wolf. I've always loved the night, and not just because I'm a vampire and hate the sunlight. To me, there is nothing more peaceful than when the world is asleep.

Being the vampire prince and my father's assassin, I never get to spend as much time outside at night just enjoying the stillness as I would like. The blanket of stars overhead in the vast black sky does something to a person. It humbles you. Makes you realize there is so much more out there than you could ever fathom. It's a good reminder for someone like me who has everything they could ever want in the palm of their hands.

I turn to Sterling to find him staring at the stars as well. "We haven't talked in a while," I say. "Ellis seems to think you want to be alpha. Is that the case?"

He nods. "Ultimately, yeah. But it's a decision I would make with all of you. My choice no longer just impacts me. I have all of you to think about now, too."

I nod. That's something that will take some getting used to. Any decisions we make from here on out will have to be as a team. "Well, I'm all for it. Getting the wolves back to what they were when your dad was alpha would benefit everyone."

"What about you?" he asks, turning to me. "You're still the prince, after all."

I sigh. I've never been more conflicted about my future than I have been recently. "I've always wanted to be king after my dad. You know how much I want to change how things are done. I don't know if that's still a possibility. I guess that will also be a group discussion." I run my hands through my hair, looking at the lake in the distance. "But I do know I'm done being my dad's lackey. As soon as all of this is over, I'm making sure he understands Ellis is off limits, and he can find someone else to do his bidding."

He nods. "I have a feeling Ellis will be going after Cade's family next. She won't settle for them being held captive. We need to be prepared for that."

He's right. "Yeah. And this time we'll make sure we do it together."

Silence falls around us once again, until he pushes up from the steps with a soft groan. "I'm going to try and get some sleep. You coming?"

I shake my head. "No. I'm going to hang out here for a bit longer." Even if I wanted to sleep, I'm too hardwired to be awake at night. Besides, until I settle things with Ellis, I won't be able to sleep anyway.

"Sounds good. And Kai?" Sterling stops with his hand on the knob. "Everything will be fine."

———

THE MOON IS low on the horizon when the porch door opens again. This time vanilla and lavender swirl around me, and my heart skips a beat. She doesn't sit next to me, instead she stands behind me until I turn around to look at her. Her arms are wrapped around her middle and her shoulders are curved inward. She looks like she did when we first rescued her from Sam. It hits me so hard in the gut I double over. It's my fault my beloved looks like that.

I climb to my feet and face her. "Ellis," I breathe.

She sucks in a breath, shoulders shaking, and silver lines her eyes as tears gather on her lashes. "I'm sorry," she whispers, her words almost being blown away in the slight early morning breeze. "I messed up, and I'm so, so sorry."

Unable to stop myself, I climb the steps to her and pull her into my arms. She shudders and collapses against me as her tears finally spill over. The tension inside me settles with her in my arms. Even the monster calms down. I carry her to the porch swing and settle her in my lap with her head on my shoulder.

"I'm sorry, too," I say, rubbing her back gently.

"I just—"

"Shh, it's okay. I talked to Sterling already. You don't need to explain yourself again. And it's not entirely your fault." She shifts to look at me with a questioning gaze. "You didn't trust us to let you make a decision you felt you needed to make. And that's on us. We need to do a better job of trusting you." I sigh and tug her head against my shoulder again. "You were right. We would have said no, and we shouldn't have. We need to listen to you and your instincts more, instead of just ours. You're ultimately more powerful than us, and your purpose is greater than ours. We need to remember that."

"I don't want you to think you can boss me around just because I'm your beloved," she says quietly, not quite looking me in the eye. "Sometimes I feel like I'm not heard, so I think that's why I did this without telling you guys."

I release a breath, trying my best to ignore the way my stomach flips at her words. "Fuck, Ellis. I never want you to feel that way. And I'm sorry if I've done that. I mean it. Your happiness and safety are my top priorities. I guess sometimes I focus too much on the safety part."

She says nothing, but she tucks herself tighter against me, and I press a kiss to the top of her head. We sit that way for a few minutes, watching the moon sink below the horizon as the sun begins to make its ascent, painting the sky a brilliant shade of pink and orange. I'll have to go inside soon, but there is one more thing I need to say to her.

"Ellis, I'm sorry I hurt you when I fed from Cade."

She stiffens in my arms, and the thread of contentment I could feel from her disappears, replaced with jealousy and heartache. I don't like that bitter taste of jealousy in my mouth. She's never shown that before when Cade and I have been together.

"I needed to calm the monster. It was out of control, and I was worried I would take too much and hurt you." I push her away so I can look at her, I need her to understand why I did it. "I had no way of knowing what I'd end up doing if I fed from you. For all I know, the monster could have taken over, I could have ended up killing you." The shudder that runs through me is entirely involuntary. Just the thought of ... I shake myself to stop that train of thought.

Her amber eyes search mine and she slowly nods. "I get it," she whispers. "I trust you, though. The monster doesn't scare me, and I honestly don't think it would harm me. But I can respect your decision. Even if I didn't like it."

I take her face in my palms, wiping away the stray tears that still leak from her eyes. "You will always be my first choice, baby girl. Cade's blood helps, but it's not the same. *You* are my beloved, and only your blood can truly satisfy me."

Tears swim in her eyes, and she reaches up to brush her hair from her neck, tilting her head to the side as she does so. I brush my nose along her throat, inhaling her scent and my heart kicks up, both of us reacting to and matching the other. She needs this as much as I do. To wipe away the hurt, to satisfy the need only she can fulfill.

"I love you, Ellis," I mumble against her skin, kissing my mark and making her shudder.

She gasps as I sink my fangs into her neck. That first taste of her blood on my tongue makes me groan. Nothing will ever compare to it. Rich and dark. Like the most decadent chocolate.

I have no intention of making this sexual. This moment is all about repairing trust and moving forward. Ellis has other ideas though. Her hips grind against mine and I can't resist sliding my hands up her thighs and under the t-shirt she's wearing—Sterling's from the scent. I really fucking love when she wears only a t-shirt. Her skin is smooth and warm under my palms and I grip her ass, tugging her down on my hardening cock so she can rub against it.

Before I know what she's doing, her hands are at my waist, yanking my sweats down and wrapping her hand around my length. I groan as my hips lift, seeking more from her. She gives me what I want—what we both want. Slowly, she slides down onto my cock, her wet heat enveloping me. Her hands move to my hair, tangling in the strands as she rolls her hips in a delicious pattern.

I usually would't keep my fangs in her neck while we fucked. There is too much of a risk of tearing through her artery with our movements. But this is slow and sensual. There is nothing rough or hurried about it. I slow my sucking, not wanting to take too much, but not willing to stop either.

"Make me come, Kai," she breathes.

Fuck. With pleasure. It takes a single thought from me to make the feeding sexual—well, more sexual than it already is. She cries out as pleasure rocks her body, her core tightening around me. I slide one hand between us and press down on her clit, and she loses it. I have to remove my fangs as she jerks when her orgasm overcomes her. Her pussy clenching around my cock, her breathy moans, and the way she whispers my name send me over the edge with lightning shooting through my veins.

When we still, she lays her head on my shoulder, and the contentment and peace I felt earlier once again brush against my barriers. The monster is calm, practically purring at having Ellis in our arms again.

"We're okay?" she asks, her words slurred and lazy.

My heart matches hers, steady and slowing down. "We're okay, baby girl. We'll always be okay."

She snuggles closer and I smile. Picking her up, I carry her inside and up the stairs to her two other Shields.

STERLING

It took a few days, but we're all finally back on the same sleep schedule—awake at night and sleeping during the day. Although I sleep less than the others, something about my shifter nature, or maybe my wolf, requires less sleep than most people. We've developed a morning routine, even though our morning is at night, which includes me, Cade, and Kai waking up early to eat breakfast—at least for Cade and me—and have a cup of coffee or tea. We let Ellis sleep in as late as possible before we wake her for more training.

Cade grunts where he sits at the table with his almost empty plate of breakfast. He's staring at his phone, brows pulled down into a V. "They found another body in the river," he says. "The same strange syringe marks and wounds as the others."

"Where was it found?" I ask, taking my plate to the sink to rinse.

"A few miles from the warehouse." Cade scrolls some more, frown deepening. "They identified the body as a missing human, but when the coroner did his exam, they found traces of magic in his bloodstream."

"This makes three bodies now," Kai chimes in. His eyes are

closed and he's resting his head on his arms at the table. "All with syringe marks. All within a three mile radius of the warehouse. And all with the same brutal injuries."

"People are going to start talking," Cade says.

I shrug. "With the syringe marks and area of town, it will get written off as a drug overdose."

"What about the injuries?" Kai asks.

"Drug deal gone wrong? A fight ring? With drugs involved, the possibilities are endless." I return to my seat and take a sip of coffee. It's gone cold already.

Cade shakes his head. "But the magic in his system? A human shouldn't have even the faintest trace of magic."

None of us have an answer for that, and we fall into silence, lost in our own thoughts. Either Sam has a damn good plan up his sleeve, or he's getting careless. Disposing of bodies from his failed experiments in the river where they are sure to wash up is asking for discovery. It leads me to believe he wants people to find them. But I can't figure out why that would be the case.

Finally, Kai sighs. "Whose turn is it to wake up Ellis?" His eyes are still closed, head still on the table.

"Sterling," Cade replies, nursing a cup of tea across from him. He lifts his gaze to mine and the glimmer of mirth is clearly visible.

Kai stifles a yawn. "Good luck, man."

I roll my eyes and quickly make a cup of coffee for my mate before climbing the stairs. Ellis has never been a morning person, but with all the practice we've been doing, she's been extra tired and cranky in the mornings. When I push into the room, I can't help but smile. She's sprawled across the bed on her back taking up as much space as she can now that the three of us aren't in it. Her hair has come out of the bun she sleeps in, and curls riot around her head like a lion's mane. The covers have been kicked aside, and the shirt she's wearing is tugged up around her waist, leaving her lower half completely exposed.

I set the coffee on the nightstand and sit on the edge of the bed. "Ellis, it's time to get up." I gently shake her shoulder and she groans. "Come on kitten, wake up."

She mumbles something that sounds a lot like 'fuck you' and drags a pillow over her head. Grinning to myself, I get up and kneel between her legs. I can think of the perfect alarm clock. But I only get one lick in before she grumbles and thrashes her legs, kneeing me in the face.

Bone crunches and wet, warm liquid trickles out of my nose. "Fuck!" I sit up, pinching the bridge of my nose and tipping my head back.

My shout must have woken her, because Ellis sits up, wild eyed with her hair sticking up in all directions. I'm momentarily distracted by how adorable she looks, and I drop my hand until I feel the blood trickle from my nose.

"Sterling?" she asks groggily. When she sees the blood, she gasps. "What happened?" She crawls toward me and takes my face in her palms.

I raise my brow. "You kneed me."

She gasps. "I did? When? Why?"

"I was trying to wake you up."

"Why were you between my legs?"

I stare at her over my hand until her eyes widen and red creeps into her cheeks.

"Oh no," she whispers.

I nod. "Oh, yes."

"Cade!" She pulls my hand away, immediately more blood dribbles out of my nose. "I'm so sorry, Sterling."

Cade pops into the room with Kai close behind him. "What's wrong?" When his gaze lands on me, blood coating the lower half of my face and Ellis frantically trying to stop it, he laughs. "That went well, huh?"

"Shut up and get over here," Ellis hisses.

He raises his hands in surrender and purple light sparks to life at his fingertips. I close my eyes as his magic squeezes my head like a grape. It only lasts a few seconds, but I absolutely hate that sensation. When I open my eyes again, Kai hands me a wet washcloth to clean my face.

"Well, now that we're all awake," Cade says with his hands on his hips and a grin in my direction. "Let's get moving. We have a lot to do today."

"Like what?" Ellis asks, climbing out of bed and pulling off the t-shirt.

Cade gets momentarily distracted as Ellis walks around the room naked, gathering her clothes and putting them on. I elbow him in the side and he starts.

"Um, yeah," he says, clearing his throat. "We have to keep working on the training thing. I think Sterling wants you to do the wing thing first. Then I want to do some magic work with you. And Kai wants to do some physical training with your wings."

Ellis deflates and she sticks out her lower lip. "All of that? How about we just do one of those things?"

"Sorry, love." Cade places a kiss on her forehead. "The sooner we get you ready, the sooner we can rescue your sister."

She nods, even though her shoulders stay slumped. "Yeah, I know."

"Meet us downstairs. You have ten minutes." Cade kisses her forehead again and tugs Kai out of the room.

Ellis turns her pleading gaze to me and I shake my head. "Sorry, kitten. That look won't work on me."

Her pout turns into a glare and I can't help but chuckle. It's adorable how fierce she thinks she is. Then she blinks and the glare disappears, replaced by a spark in her eyes that I know means trouble. "Ooor," she drawls, taking a step closer so she can run her hands down my chest. "We could finish what you started ..."

"You mean before you broke my nose?" I grab her hands as her fingers loop in the waistband of my sweats.

She steps closer and arches her back, rubbing her hips against mine. Fucking temptress. "Come on, Sterling. I know you want to."

I groan, because I really fucking want to. But Cade and Kai are waiting downstairs and we really do have a lot we need work on. I take her face in my hands and lean in, stopping just shy of our lips meeting. "Get dressed, kitten." I step back and she stumbles forward, her balance thrown off from leaning forward into the almost kiss. An indignant sound escapes her and I grin, backing toward the door. "Cade said ten minutes. You're probably down to seven by now."

Her curses follow me down the stairs.

———

"GOOD, but next time I want you to react quicker." Cade and Ellis have been working on magic lessons for the past forty minutes, and Ellis's reactions have been progressively getting slower as she tires.

"I'm trying, Cade," she says, a hint of whine in her voice.

Kai and I are sitting in the grass, leaning against the cabin. His head has been tipped toward the sky, watching the stars twinkle and the moon slowly drift across the black expanse. I've been watching Ellis.

Sometimes it still hits me unexpectedly that she's my mate. I went so long watching from afar, keeping our bond secret from everyone. Being able to act on it, to act on my feelings for her, has been mindblowing. I'm not sure I'll ever really get over that. And having things restored with me and the guys has been great too. I missed them. My wolf missed them. Even with everything we're dealing with, the little glimpses of what life could be like with Ellis and the three of us, makes my wolf incredibly happy. His pack is whole, and that's all that matters.

Cade fires off two blasts of magic, one right after the other, and Ellis barely manages to duck out of the way of the second. She gives Cade an incredulous look, the wings behind her back shuffling with irritation.

"Do you think she could learn to fly?" I ask Kai quietly.

He shifts his gaze to the pair practicing magic. "I bet she could, but my guess is she'll never learn. The amount of core strength it would require would deter her from ever trying. Once all of this is over, she'll probably put those things away and never get them back out again. And I can't say I blame her." He shrugs as he watches Ellis try to block Cade's magic with her own. "She's never really lived a normal life. Even after we get through this, her life won't be normal. Being fated to three guys?" He snorts and shakes his head.

I nod in agreement. "Yeah, but we can make it as normal as possible for her."

"Oh, for sure. We wi—" Kai cuts off as the sound of a car rumbling up the mountain reaches our ears.

We both stand and walk to the front of the house, Cade and Ellis following behind after a moment for Ellis to tuck those wings away. When the person behind the wheel becomes visible, my stomach flips over. Ellis gasps and comes to stand next to me, wrapping herself around my arm.

"Is that …" she asks, trailing off.

I nod. "Yeah."

The car parks and Cole hops out, his gaze traveling over the four of us standing in front of the cabin. When it lands on me and Ellis, his jaw tightens and he slams the car door shut.

"Let's give them some privacy," Cade says quietly, tugging Kai away.

"You okay?" Ellis asks, peering up at me.

I look down at her and my heart breaks seeing the concern and care in her amber eyes. "Hopefully. I guess it will depend on how this goes."

Before I can turn back to my brother, Ellis stands on her toes and takes my face in her hands. "No matter what happens, I'm here. Just say the word." She lifts a little higher to place a soft kiss on my lips. "I love you, Sterling."

I can't stop myself. My hands tangle in her curls and I hold her to me, deepening the kiss. "I love you too, kitten," I whisper against her mouth.

When she pulls away, she levels a stare at Cole, and my mouth quirks into a smile. No matter how fierce she tries to be, she just looks adorable to me. With a final parting glare, she turns around and follows Cade and Kai.

Cole turns his attention to the cabin. "I didn't know we owned a cabin."

"Yeah. You were only a pup the last time we visited with dad." I still remember that visit. Dad wasn't doing well, but he wanted the family to spend some time together away from pack responsibilities. Cole was three and an absolute menace. He got into everything he wasn't supposed to, and I made sure to help him as much as I could. Mom saw all of it, and let most of it slide.

Cole grunts and runs his hands through his thick, black hair. "Want to take a walk?"

"Sure." I head for the trees to the right of the house, but Cole pauses.

"You're just going to leave your mate here unprotected?"

"She's not unprotected. Cade and Kai are here."

He stares at me and blinks slowly in disbelief. "You trust her safety with someone else?" he asks incredulously.

Wolves are notoriously over protective of their mates. Luckily, mine has two others bonded to her to keep her safe. That gives my wolf the ability to be a bit more chill than others.

I smile. "Yeah. She's perfectly safe with them."

Cole shakes his head in disbelief but follows me. We walk in silence, weaving through the pine trees. The moon lights a dappled path through for us. Dead needles crunch under our feet, and the scent of nature and prey drifts to us on the breeze. My wolf wants to run, to hunt. But he'll have to wait.

"So," I say, clearing my throat.

He sighs. "Ellis came to talk to me."

"Yeah, I know. She did that without my knowledge, by the

way." The paralyzing fear I experienced during that time resurfaces, and I rub my chest to make it go away.

"She told me a little bit about her life." He swallows, the sound loud in the quiet forest. "And damn, she went through a lot."

I nod, anger curling in my gut just thinking about Sam and what he did to her. "Yeah, she's been through hell and back. But it only made her stronger in the end."

Cole pauses and leans against a tree, shoving his hands into his pockets. "Mom's pretty much in love with her."

"I'm glad to hear that," I say, smiling. It makes my heart happy to know I have given my mom something positive to think about.

"So, what's your story, then?" Cole looks at me, cutting straight to chase. His blue eyes, so similar to mine, pierce through me.

I take a deep breath and sit on a fallen log, staring at the ground. If Ellis can share her story, with all the horrible aspects of her past, then I can share mine. "I guess it all started when dad died." That day was horrible. The collective howl of mourning from the pack still echoes in my mind. "I was too young to take dad's place, and it didn't take long for Noah to gain control of the pack."

Cole grunts and I run a hand down my face, refusing to look at him. I don't know what I'll do if I see a negative expression on his face.

"As I'm sure you're aware, he used me and you against mom. She had to do what he said or else he threatened to hurt us. Well, he did that to me too. He made me do what he wanted, and threatened you and mom if I didn't. He told me if I challenged him for alpha, he'd kill you guys. So I spent those years after dad's death doing Noah's bidding."

I risk a glance at Cole. He's looking at the ground, chewing on his bottom lip. None of this should come as a surprise to him. I'm sure our mom has told him what happened.

"One of the things Noah tasked me with, was joining the group of wolves he ordered to kill Ellis, her mom, and her sister." I push up from the log, unable to sit still as I talk about that horrid night. "I knew as soon as I stepped into the house my mate was there. I followed her scent to the kitchen, to the pantry she was hiding in. I contemplated grabbing her and running. But she was only sixteen, and her family had just been murdered. It wouldn't have gone over well for me."

I pace between two trees and face the rush of feelings head on. "I still remember the mix of emotions inside me that night. Joy at finding my mate. Terror at realizing Noah wanted her dead. Heartache at losing her right after I found her.

"I kept her safe that night. I told Noah she wasn't there and I convinced him to let it go. Whatever reasons he wanted her dead, he dropped. I kept an eye on her after that. I made sure she was safe. I made sure Noah never got it into his head again to hurt her. It was pure torture, watching her from afar and not being able to go to her. Not being able to claim her was the hardest thing I've ever done."

"Why did Noah let it go? Why did he want her family dead?" Cole asks quietly.

"I didn't know at the time. But we found out later that Noah was her father. She and her sister were the result of an affair, which is why neither of them had powers. No shifting, no magic. Nothing. Noah didn't want to risk either of them coming back to challenge him, despite the fact they were human." And probably because he found out from Sam that one of them had some kind of special power, not that Cole needs to know that yet.

I sit back down on the log and rest my elbows on my knees. "The night I left the pack, my wolf took over. He tried to challenge Noah. No matter what I did, I couldn't get control of him. Alex fought me. Gave me this scar." I finger the smooth, raised line running from above my right eyebrow to below my eye. "That was the only thing that gave me the ability to take control back from my wolf. I left. I had to. I couldn't risk my wolf taking over again. I couldn't risk challenging Noah and having him hurt you or mom."

I look at him finally. He's watching me, but I can't read the expression on his face. "It wasn't easy, Cole." I have to clear my throat at the thickness that gathers. "Choosing to leave my family behind, knowing they were stuck living under that bastard's rule. It tore me up. But I thought it was for the best. At least you were still alive."

He looks away. "So you just lived your life of luxury knowing mom and I were living with that bastard."

I sigh. "It wasn't exactly luxury. I fell in with Kai. His dad hired me to do his dirty work with Kai and Cade. I went from doing Noah's bidding, to Kai's dad's. Yeah, I had money. Yeah, I had all the perks that came with being friends with the vampire prince. But I was living without my family. Without my mate. I wasn't so much living as surviving. Not too differently from you, I would guess."

"Why wait?" he asks, looking at me again. "You knew your mate was out there. I get you didn't want to risk her at first. But why now? What took you so long to decide to claim her and take back the pack?"

"That's another long, complicated story." I rub a hand down my face and sigh heavily. "It turns out Ellis is a harpy." I hear Cole suck in a sharp breath and shift on his feet, but I don't look at him. "Kai, Cade, and I are her Shields. We're bound to her, to protect her and help her achieve her goal of bringing balance back to the world."

"A harpy?" he breathes shakily.

"She feels that one of her jobs is to restore balance to the wolves by making sure I become alpha." Now I glance at him, to gauge his reaction to that statement.

He studies me for a moment, chewing on his bottom lip. "So, if it weren't for Ellis deciding this, you wouldn't have ever come back? You would have let the pack, and your family, rot under Noah's rule?"

I shake my head. "No. I never would have left you to that fate. I always planned on coming back. With Ellis as my mate I always intended to have a discussion with everyone about taking control of the pack. It would have had to be a team decision, because we're all tied together now." I shrug and look down at the forest floor. "But, Ellis took things into her own hands. And honestly? I'm glad she did." I can't look at him as I continue. If he refuses, I'll never recover from the hurt. "The second you were born, Cole, my wolf knew. He knew you were supposed to be my beta. And without you by my side, I don't want to do this. I don't think I *can* do it."

"Fuck," he mumbles. I risk a glance at him, and find him rubbing his eyes hard enough he's probably seeing stars. "If I'm being honest, I want to say no. I want to hurt you as much as you hurt me."

I recoil like his words are a physical slap across my face. My heart splits into thousands of pieces and crumbles to the forest floor.

"I was only five years old when you left, Sterling. I didn't understand it. You were the person I looked up to the most, and I felt like you abandoned me. Like you didn't care about me as much as I cared about you." Cole's voice cracks and he clears his throat, rubbing the back of his neck.

I shake my head, wanting him to know that is not true. I never stopped loving him. Not a day went by that I didn't think of him and my mom. But he doesn't give me a chance.

"I know now that isn't true, but it doesn't erase the years of hurt I felt." He pushes off the tree and paces the same path I just did moments before.

"I know I'll never be able to make it up to you. I know saying sorry fixes nothing. But I'm truly sorry, Cole. You have no idea how much. I did the only thing I could think of. I don't know if it was the right thing, but in the moment, it was all I had."

He purses his lips, but nods his head. "I'll be your beta."

My head snaps up, breath catching my throat. "Seriously?"

"It needs to be done." He shrugs. "I'd like to help bring the pack back to what it used to be. I can't guarantee ... I don't know if ..." He sighs and rubs the bridge of his nose. "It's going to take me time to open up and let you in."

I nod. "I get that. Take all the time you need." Because even just the hope that I may get my brother back is enough to keep me going.

ELLIS

"WHAT DOES THIS MEAN?" I ask after STERLING FILLS us in on what he and his brother talked about.

"Well, not a whole lot right now." He sits in the grass next to me as I take a break from the grueling training Cade and Kai have been putting me through. "We are going to meet up tomorrow evening to talk about plans and who we can trust to join us. I won't be able to challenge Noah until we have a solid plan in place to make sure the transition goes smoothly for the pack."

"What will happen when you challenge him?" Just the thought is enough to send butterflies tumbling in my belly.

"We'll set a date and time to battle. Our wolves will fight until one of us comes out on top."

I swallow down the lump in my throat. "What does that mean exactly?"

His eyes scan my face and he shakes his head. "Don't worry about it right now, Ellis. There are other things you need to focus on."

I don't particularly like that he won't tell me what's going to happen, because I can imagine it, and it isn't pretty. But I let it go for now. I'll force the conversation later when I have more mental bandwidth to deal with it. If I ever have the mental bandwidth to deal with it. At the rate things are going, I'm just going to turn into a zombie. A walking meatsuit with nothing left to give.

"Hey! Stop that." Kai crouches in front of me, his brow furrowed. "I don't like that emotion." He points his finger in my face and waves it in a circle.

"Sorry," I mumble. "It's just ... hard."

He grabs my chin in his fingers and squeezes gently. "We're going to take things one step at a time. Sterling will challenge Noah and win. With him as alpha and Noah out of the picture, we'll move on to rescuing Grace and removing Sam from the picture. Just focus on one thing at a time. While Sterling prepares, we'll keep training. When it's time to save your sister, you're going to be such a badass." He grins at me, fangs glinting in the moonlight.

He makes it sound easy. And it does ease some of my anxiety. I'm not alone and I need to remember that. But it's still incredibly overwhelming. Kai leans forward and kisses my forehead.

"Now, get up. Break's over. And get those wings back out." He stands and claps his hands twice. The love and gratefulness I just felt toward him melt away in a heartbeat.

I groan, but push to my feet. In my mind, the imaginary blanket slides off my wings, and I know they've reappeared as the breeze slides through my feathers, tickling and teasing. "Okay. Let's do this," I say, mentally prepping myself for another brutal session.

"I want to keep working on magic," Cade says, stepping up to me. "But this time, I want you to dodge my attacks instead of blocking them. I think we can assume Sam won't do anything to harm you too much because he wants you alive."

I swallow as nerves flutter in my belly. "Okay," I say slowly. "You're not really going to throw your magic at me in an attempt to hit me, though, are you?"

Cade grimaces. "I mean, it's the best way to train you to block and dodge attacks."

"Great," I mutter. With a deep breath, I call Cade's magic to me, and let it gather in my palms. Widening my stance, I get a feel for my balance with the wings, and nod my head.

"I'll take it easy on you at first." His magic flares to life, purple light wreathing his arms. It's really beautiful, especially as his violet eyes swirl and sparkle with his magic.

He's true to his word. The first few attacks are aimed wide and are easy to dodge by jumping out of the way. It takes some time to get used to my wings slowing me down, and I eventually learn to tuck them closer to my body to reduce the amount of wind resistance. The quicker I become at dodging, the quicker and closer to me Cade's attacks get.

I'm so focused on Cade and his magic, when a sudden weight appears in my hand, it throws me off balance. I fall to the side, stumbling and just barely catching myself. Confused, I glance at my hand and gasp.

"What the hell?" I shriek.

In my hand is a sword. An actual freaking sword. The handle thing—or whatever it's called—is wrapped in aged black leather. A bright purple stone is perched on the top and shines in the moonlight. There are golden wing-like things sprouting just below the handle. And the blade. Holy shit the blade is gold and silver and sharp as hell. It's heavy, but at the same time, not heavy at all.

I open my fingers to let the sword drop to the ground, but it stays in my hand like it's glued there. My eyes widen and look to Cade for help. "Cade?" My voice has raised a few octaves and my breath comes in quick bursts. "Help!"

All three of the guys approach with varying expressions of confusion, thought, and awe. Kai kneels in front of me and studies the sword, whistling as his fingers trail over the blade. Sterling comes to my side and wraps a supportive arm around my waist below the wings. And Cade turns my hand palm up, supporting the weight of the sword.

"It's … stuck," he says, looking closely at my palm. He tries to grab the handle but it doesn't budge.

"Make it go away," I plead, voice cracking with emotion. "I don't want it!"

"Take a deep breath, Ellis," Cade says. "We'll figure this out."

"Figure it out now, then! I can't walk around with a freaking sword stuck to my hand! I'll stab myself!"

Kai chuckles. "She's right. That thing is dangerous in her hand."

I glare at him, contemplating using it to stab him. "Watch it, Kai."

"Close your eyes," Sterling says calmly. "Just like with the wings, imagine it going away."

I do as he says, forcing my heart to slow and my breathing to even out. I imagine the weight in my hand disappearing, the ancient weapon becoming nothing more than a memory. When I open my eyes, it's gone. I sink to the ground, wrapping my arms around my legs.

"What the hell?" I whisper.

Kai, still kneeling, pulls out his phone and scrolls through the random pictures I've taken of the three of us. When he gets to what he wants, he shows me. "I don't think we should be surprised. The image in the book showed a harpy with wings and a sword. You got the wings. Now you have the sword."

The picture is from the book where we learned what Shields were. The drawing of the harpy indeed is holding a sword that looked just like the one in my hand.

"I don't know how to use a sword," I breathe.

"We can teach you, love," Cade says soothingly. "At least, we can help you learn the basics. We don't have enough time to show you everything. But every little advantage we can give you in this battle could be the difference between winning and losing."

I sigh as the weight on my shoulders only seems to get heavier. A sword is not something I want to learn how to use. It was heavy and weird in my hand, and I didn't like it. But Cade does have a point. "Fine."

Cade nods and releases a breath. "Let's start sword training tomorrow. Right now, let's keep working on dodging."

I shove the thought of the sword away and stand. Practice will take my mind off of what just happened, so I'm all for it. "Yeah. Let's keep going."

Before long, Cade and I are back in rhythm. His magic flies past me, and I dodge. Faster and faster until I'm breathing heavily and my eyes are constantly scanning for his magic. Purple sparks sizzle past my left shoulder as I jump to the side, a few brushing against my wings and making me wince, but I keep going. This time, I jump to the right, his magic coming at me almost continuously now. My legs are getting more shaky the longer we do this, and my reaction time is starting to slow. Cade must not realize that, because the next thing I know, a stream of magic is heading straight for my chest.

My eyes widen and I gasp. I won't be able to dodge that quick enough, but I try. I duck to the right and drop as fast as I can, but I'm not fast enough. The blast hits me in my left shoulder, knocking me backward and sending burning pain ricocheting through my upper body. My heart stutters as electricity pumps through the organ and my vision blackens.

"Fuck!" I hear Kai and Sterling yell through the ringing in my ears.

"Ellis!" Cade's voice is scared, shaky and breathless.

I can't feel anything. I don't know if I'm standing, sitting, or lying down. I think my eyes are open, but I can't see anything. All I can tell is that my heart is racing faster than it ever has. It's pumping so hard and so fast it's tripping over itself, the rhythm erratic. *Thump-thu-thump-thump-thu-thump.*

"Ellis, baby girl, open your eyes. Look at me." Kai's voice is closer now, strained and barely controlled.

I guess my eyes are closed. I try to open them, but I'm not sure if I'm successful. Everything is still black. The longer my heart races, the harder my breathing becomes. Like my lungs are trying to inflate at the same pace as my heart. My head feels fuzzy amid all of the numbness, and each thought in my mind floats past like a cloud on a breeze, just out of reach.

"Ellis. Shit, Ellis are you okay?" Cade's frantic words are muffled as the fuzziness increases. Something warm pulses around me, and from the depths of my slowly unraveling consciousness, I know it's Cade's magic.

I attempt to open my mouth, but I'm not sure if I do. I really have no idea what my body is doing. I'm cold, though. I do know that.

"Heal her, Cade," Kai says. "Her heart rate is all over the place." His words sound pained, like his heart matching mine is causing him discomfort.

Vaguely I notice a purple glow in my vision, or maybe it's behind my closed eyelids. Warmth surrounds me, fighting off the chill that had started to settle in, making me shiver. It floods through my body, flowing through my veins and permeating every bone, muscle, and organ. The rapid, chaotic beat of my heart slows and steadies. My lungs calm, and my breathing becomes easier. The fuzziness lifts, and I'm able to think coherently again.

I open my eyes to find the guys hovering over me. My head is in Kai's lap, and his fingers shakily brush back my curls over and over. Cade's violet gaze is wide in his pale face as he scans me.

"Are you okay, Ellis?" he rasps. His chest is rising and falling as rapidly as mine had been just a moment ago. Purple sparks sizzle at his trembling fingertips and he fists his hands in the grass as if to hide the lack of control.

I nod my head, glad that I'm able to do so. My entire body feels like a wet noodle though, and I'm not sure if that is because of the practice, the blast of magic, or a combo of both. "I think so," I mumble.

Cade exhales heavily and drops his head to my shoulder, arms wrapping around me tightly. "I am so sorry, Ellis. I shouldn't have pushed so hard and put you at risk. This won't happen again. I promise."

I want to tell him it's okay. That I don't blame him. That I need to be pushed, as much as I hate it. But my energy is quickly fading. The effort it would take to open my mouth is too much. I pat his arm, all I'm able to manage, and release a breath, closing my eyes. They're too heavy to keep open anyway.

"Get her upstairs to bed," Sterling says.

The world swoops as I'm lifted in someone's arms. By the cherries and spice scent clinging to the shirt my face is buried in, it's Kai. I pull that smell into my lungs and let it comfort me. The safety of knowing I'm tucked against his chest, and the motion of him walking, causes my eyelids to get heavier and heavier until I can't fight it anymore.

———

THE PULL of sleep is strong when I finally climb from the darkness. My body still feels like wet noodles, and my eyelids still weigh hundreds of pounds. But a comforting presence pulls me into consciousness.

My wings are still out, so Kai must have laid me on my side. Cade is pressed against my front, his arms wrapped around my middle and his head pressed against my chest, like he needs the reminder of my heart beating to know I'm okay. It takes monumental effort to lift my arm and run my fingers through his hair.

He stirs, tucking closer and mumbling in his sleep. I trace his jaw with my finger, his stubble tickling and scratching, and when I reach his lips and brush over them, his eyes flutter open. I could get lost in that violet stare.

"Ellis," he breathes, leaning up on his elbow. He cups my cheek, his thumb brushing back and forth. "I am so, so sorry." Immense sadness and regret darken his eyes.

"It's okay," I whisper. "It was an accident."

He shakes his head, clenching his jaw. "It's not okay. Me hurting you will never be okay. I shouldn't have pushed you so hard."

"I need to be pushed hard, though. Our enemies won't go easy on me, and I need to be prepared. It's the only way to learn," I say. "I don't enjoy the training, but I know it's important. Accidents happen, Cade. I know as long as you're here I'll be fine. If I get hurt during training, you can heal me."

"I don't want to be the one to hurt you, love." His breath leaves him in a rush, fanning over my face and warming my skin. "Shit, my magic recoiled so hard I probably would have lost it forever if I hadn't needed it to heal you. I told you it's more sentient now than it ever has been. I almost get the feeling it's throwing a temper tantrum at me for hurting you."

I smile at the thought of his magic acting out because of his actions. "Kiss me Cade."

He shakes his head, still unhappy with the situation but unable to resist giving me what I want. He leans down and presses his lips against mine. Softly at first, then harder. I open my mouth and let his tongue sweep in, claiming me all over again. My blood starts to heat, and I slip my hand under his shirt, feeling his warmth and smooth skin.

Unbidden, a yawn crawls up my throat mid-kiss. Cade pulls away with a grin. "How about you rest some more before we continue this." He kisses me one last time, and I pout.

"But ..."

"No buts." He presses a kiss to the top of my head. "Sleep, love."

I can't fight it. I'm utterly exhausted. Sleep comes again, and this time it's cedar and lilac that follows me into oblivion.

The next time I wake it's easier to climb from the trenches of sleep. My limbs don't feel like jello, and my head is clear. At least, it's as clear as it can be with someone trailing their fingers through the feathers of my wings. My back arches and a soft moan climbs up my throat as shivers spread through my body, igniting my blood like fire.

"You like that?" Sterling's deep voice whispers in my ear, adding to the heat.

I nod my head, unable to form the words in my suddenly dry mouth. Sterling moves his finger close to the base of my wings where they're even more sensitive. I gasp and squeeze my legs together to try and ease the ache that is rapidly growing.

A dark chuckle rumbles behind me. "Do you want me to stop?" Sterling adds a second finger to the other wing, gently brushing it down the feathers on that side.

"No!" I gasp. I'm pretty sure I could orgasm with just his touch on my wings. But that wouldn't be very fun. I sit up, tucking my wings in at the last minute to avoid whacking Sterling in the face, and tackle him to the bed. He grunts in surprise and grabs my hips as I straddle his waist. "You started this Sterling, now you have to finish it." I roll my hips making his eyes roll back in his head and a soft rumble echoes in his chest.

"Oh, I'll be finishing this, alright," he growls.

Sterling grabs the back of my tank and tears it in two, easing it past my wings and throwing the tattered remains to the floor. As I roll my hips, Sterling's blue eyes darken, taking in the flush that covers my tan skin. When he leans up to scrape his teeth along my nipple, the motion of my hips change. The smooth, teasing motions become sharp and jerky. My breath catches in my throat and I tangle my hands in his hair, holding him to my breast.

The fabric of his sweats is already darkening from my wetness, and I want them gone. I want to feel only him sliding against me. "Your pants," I gasp. "Take them off."

He releases my nipple and places his hands on my hips to force me to still my movements. A dark look crosses his face, and he nips at my lower lip. "You don't get to tell me what to do, kitten." Without any warning he stands up, taking me with him and setting me on the floor. "On your hands and knees," he says nodding to the bed as his hands drop to the waist of his sweats.

I take one quick peek at his cock pushing against the fabric, straining to be let free, and I quickly comply. My wings spread out behind me, and the white feathers flutter in my vision when I look behind me at Sterling. He's already removed his pants and he slowly works his hand up and down his shaft, his eyes traveling over me kneeling on the bed, ass in the air, completely on display for him.

"Fuck," he groans, biting his lower lip. "You drive my wolf fucking wild." The bed dips as he places one knee on the mattress. "Eyes forward, kitten."

My gaze drops to the sheets balled in my fists and I wait with uneven breaths for his touch. He doesn't leave me waiting long. A soft caress down my wings makes my back arch, lifting my ass higher. I'm so wet I can feel the slickness along my inner thighs, and I desperately want him to touch me.

Sterling trails his fingers from my wings, over my ass, to my core. I gasp and press backward, searching for more pressure. I'm so achy I'm desperate.

"Please, Sterling. Quit teasing me." It's almost a whine, and I really don't care. It's been awhile since it's just been me and Sterling, and I want my wolf to give me everything he's got.

Sterling grabs my hips with one hand and trails the head of his cock through my folds. I push back and forward, trying to give myself what I want, but he tightens his grip and stops me.

"Patience, kitten," he growls.

I growl right back. "Damn it, Sterling."

He chuckles, but he positions himself at my entrance and slowly pushes inside. My walls adjust for him, and I moan as he slides all the way in. He sits there for a second, not moving, driving me crazy, then he finally pulls out to push back in. The pace he sets is slow and lazy and not near enough for me.

"If you don't fuck me properly—"

A fist tangled in my hair yanks me up so my wings are flush against his chest. "I already told you. You don't get to tell me what to do." His breath brushes against my ear and I shiver. He tugs my head to the side, the pull on my scalp creating delicious pain that makes me shiver. The flat of his tongue runs over his mark and I cry out.

The sound must snap something in him. The next thing I know, his hips are driving into me, each thrust tugging my hair a little more. His chest brushes against my wings and the added sensation is making my mind fuzzy with sex. When Sterling slips his free hand between my legs, I almost combust. Every nerve ending in my body is on fire with his touch.

"Is this what you wanted?" he growls, rubbing circles around my clit but not touching it.

Sounds fall from my mouth, nothing coherent because my brain can't formulate anything that makes sense. Each time he slams home, stars burst in my vision. I'm so fucking close to losing it. The pressure is building to the point it's almost unbearable. Just when I think I can't take anymore, his teeth close on his mark and he presses down hard on my clit.

I shatter around him, screaming his name as I come. My body shudders, pleasure rolling through me in waves. Sterling wraps his arms around my waist, pressing tight against my wings as he finds his own release. The pressure against my wings sends more tingles through my body, and a second orgasm rocks me unexpectedly.

When I finally settle, I'm laying on my stomach, chest heaving as I suck air into my starved lungs. My wings are sprawled to either side of me, and Sterling climbs under one, the touch making me jerk from overstimulation, and settles next to me.

I peel my eyes open to find him smiling at me, his blue eyes shining incredibly bright. "Whoa," I whisper.

He chuckles. "Whoa is right." His thumb brushes back and forth on my cheek and leans in, pressing a soft kiss to my lips.

"Do you think they heard us?" I mumble, eyes closing again.

"Oh, I'm sure they did. You weren't exactly quiet."

I mumble something, I'm not really sure what, and turn to my side, letting my wings fall behind me. Sterling wraps his arm around my waist and I settle against his chest.

"I'm a huge fan of these, by the way," he says, brushing his knuckles against the feathers peeking over my shoulder.

"Mmm. It definitely made things interesting. And I didn't break your nose."

"Well, it wouldn't be the first time you've done that. Or the second."

Heat creeps up my neck. "Hush and cuddle me."

He chuckles again. "With pleasure, kitten."

CADE

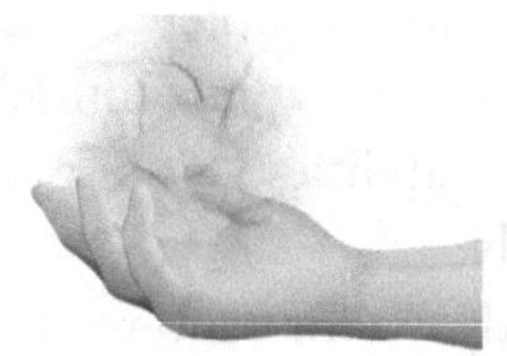

"You're still beating yourself up about hurting Ellis, aren't you?" Kai plops onto the couch next to me causing me to spill my bourbon all over myself.

"Dude! Seriously?" I set my glass down and pull off my shirt, grumbling the entire time about wasting alcohol.

Kai chuckles. "I just wanted you to take off your shirt."

"You could have asked. Asshole." I throw the wet shirt at him and he bats it away. "But to answer your question, yes. I am still beating myself up about it. And you would too if it had been you who hurt her." Looking deep inside of myself, I can barely sense my magic. As soon as it hit Ellis, it recoiled so sharply it hurt my chest, like something was torn from me. If it weren't for the fact I was able to heal her, I'd be afraid I'd lost it for good.

Ever since I met Ellis, my magic has grown more ... intelligent and life-like. Almost as if there is a being living inside of me. Each day is something new, I feel like. It reaches out at random times to caress her or tuck a curl behind her ear without my say so. Now, it's as if it's sulking inside of me, pissed that I used it to hurt her. Like I did it on purpose. I shudder at the thought. I'd never purposefully hurt her. I'd rip my own heart out before I ever did something like that.

Kai shrugs. "Probably. But if it makes you feel any better she's up there fucking Sterling right now. So she's clearly feeling better."

My gaze snaps to the ceiling like I can see through it to the bedroom and my soul-bonded. "She is?"

"Based on the emotions floating down those stairs—and the sounds—yes. They are most definitely going at it."

I glance at Kai to see him adjust himself, like he's picking up things from his empath abilities he can't contain. "Should we go join them?" I ask slowly.

Kai's gray eyes study me for a moment, then he leans over and pushes me onto my back. "No, let's give them some time alone. Sterling has a lot of catching up to do." He brushes his lips over my neck and I instinctually tilt my head to the side. "Besides, it's been awhile since it's just been us."

I shiver as he lightly trails his fangs over the sensitive skin of my throat. I try to think about the last time we did something just the two of us, but it's hard with Kai's weight on top of me. Honestly, I don't think we've been together alone since Ellis came along. And a lot has changed between us in that time.

My heart kicks up at the thought of us messing around just because we want to. Not to help Kai get himself under control. Not because we know Ellis enjoys watching us. But just because we *want* to. What does that mean for us?

"You're thinking awfully hard right now," Kai murmurs, sliding his hands down my chest and abs to the waistband of my joggers.

He's right, and I need to get out of my head before I start down a path I won't be able to return from. I lean up, threading my hands into his hair, and kiss him. I'm not an empath like Kai, but I swear I can sense what he's feeling through this kiss. It hits me deep in my soul and it makes me pull him harder against me.

His hand slips into my pants and he wraps his fingers around my length. I break the kiss and let my head fall back on the cushions as a groan escapes my throat.

Kai leans down and presses his lips to my pulse point. "You are so beautiful, Cade," he whispers.

My breath catches and I squeeze my eyes shut, still not ready to go down that road. Right? Maybe I am ready. Kai pulls me out of my thoughts again when he stands, taking his little bit of body heat with him. I snap my eyes open, worried he picked up that emotion from me and didn't like it. But instead of walking away, he's tugging his clothes off and heading to the bag by the door. The one no one ever unpacked from our night by the lake with Ellis. He fishes out the bottle of lube and returns, raising one brow at me still laying on the couch with my pants on.

I quickly lift my hips to remove them, tossing them to the floor with his clothes. Goosebumps break out over my skin as his heated gaze travels over me. I swear it's like a brand on my skin everywhere he looks.

"That's better," he says, his words a soft growl.

I push up on my elbow and reach for his cock, the piercings on the underside slightly cooler than they would be on a human or shifter. A bead of precum forms on the crown and I lick it away, grinning at the sound that comes from Kai's mouth. Never breaking eye contact, I suck his length into my mouth. Kai threads his fingers through my hair and grips the strands tightly, using it as leverage to set the pace he wants.

He never looks away from my gaze, and my heart stutters. What the fuck is happening? It's been easy to push these feelings aside, to look at them from a different vantage point. Yes, I love Kai. I've loved Kai for a long time. He's my brother. My best friend. He's bonded to Ellis the same as I am.

It's always been fun and exciting with us. Sometimes hot and steamy. But never emotional. And this feels emotional. The eye contact. The deep look of ... adoration. It steals my breath and leaves me feeling like I'm standing on the edge of a precipice.

Kai's hips slow and his chest rises on a rapid inhale. He pulls out, only to settle on top of me, between my legs. I watch him pour the lube into his palm and slick his hand up and down his length. When his gaze catches mine again, neither of us look away. It's like I'm trapped under that piercing gray stare. I lift my knees to my chest, and Kai slowly pushes inside, both of us breathing heavily with limbs trembling. He stills once he's all the way in, fingers digging into my hips hard enough to leave bruises. We stare at each other, lost in the moment and the feelings and the emotions.

"Kai," I whisper.

He leans down and kisses me deeply, moving his hips at the same time. I wrap my legs around him and cling to him, getting lost in the motions and sensations. It doesn't take long for the pressure to build. Even without Kai touching my cock, all I need is him to press those fangs against my neck, and I'm gone. Lightning fires through my veins, and my release tears through me, landing on my stomach but I don't even notice it. I'm too busy watching Kai come with his head thrown back and the tendons of his neck pulled taut.

When he collapses on top of me he groans. "Oh, ew." He pushes back up and looks down at the sticky mess he landed in.

I can't help but laugh at his expression with one fang on display as he curls his lip. I take his face in my hands and bring him back down for another slow kiss. He sighs and flops back down on top of me, heedless of the mess.

We lay together, with Kai's head on my chest, letting our hearts slow and breathing even out. It's the most content I've felt in a while. Unless Ellis is in my arms, my world never seems to be calm. Especially lately, with my worry for my family increasing, and the threats to Ellis growing closer each day. I let myself soak in this moment, and try to keep my feelings from projecting into the ether for Kai to pick up on.

"Do you think they're done?" I ask after a while, tracing random circles on Kai's back with my finger.

He's still for a moment before nodding. "Mm hmm."

"Good. We should get back to training." Even as I say it, my mind rebels at the thought. All I want to do is go upstairs and have a giant, naked cuddle party.

Kai groans. "You are a fucking drill sergeant." But he pushes off of me, grimacing at the dried sticky mess crusted to both of our stomachs. "Oh, gods. I'm gonna puke." He gags dramatically, to the point he actually makes himself gag for real.

"You fucking swallow, Kai. What's the difference?" I ask sitting up.

"The difference is, it's crusty and stuck to me." He shudders. "It reminds me of being a teen again."

I laugh. "You have a history of having crusty come stuck to you? What the hell were you doing back then?"

He levels a flat stare in my direction. "Lots of orgies, Cade. Flying come everywhere."

I snort and push to my feet, grabbing my shirt still wet from the bourbon he made me spill. "Right. Awkward young Malakai attending orgies. You probably came in your pants when a pretty girl looked at you and you had to go the rest of the day at school with it crusting in your tighty whities." I wipe off my stomach before tossing the shirt to him.

He snags it out of the air with glare. "It was more than a look, thank you very much."

I'm still laughing after we've pulled our pants on and stand outside the bedroom door. Kai grabs my arm and spins me around, pinning me to the wall.

"Keep laughing, pretty boy." His chest rumbles against mine with his low growled words. "I'll make you pay for that later."

I press my mouth to his. One last kiss. "Looking forward to it."

———

ELLIS AND STERLING are laying naked in bed together. Her wings are spread out behind her, trailing onto the floor. The gold threaded through them shimmers in the moonlight streaming in through the window. She's fucking beautiful. So beautiful it makes my heart feel like it's cracking into tiny pieces. There's no way someone like her could be mine.

She glances over her shoulder and smiles as her gaze travels from our feet to our heads. "You both look a little disheveled," she says, lifting one brow with a knowing smirk.

I grin. "Says the woman who looks like she's just been thoroughly fucked."

Her smile spreads and she stretches like a cat, displaying all of her gorgeous curves. "I won't deny that," she practically purrs.

And just like that, I'm hard again. This woman drives me absolutely wild. From the corner of my eye I see Kai adjusting himself, and I laugh.

Kai steps forward and crosses his arms over his bare chest, his tattoos flexing with the movement. "So, you keep the wings out for Sterling but break my nose when I try to sleep with you when they're out."

Ellis shrugs one shoulder and gives him a coy smile. "I like him better."

Kai growls, and I swear I see his eyes flash red for a split second. He gives her no warning when he pounces, using his supernatural abilities to jump the distance to the bed. He lands on top of her, pinning her wrists above her head, careful to avoid landing on her wings. She squeals and squirms, trying to get out from under him, but he's too strong.

"What is it with you and Cade testing me today?" He nips at her neck, leaving a red mark but not breaking the skin.

The playfulness in her expression evaporates, replaced with lust, and I know if I don't step in things will get derailed quickly. Not that I don't want that to happen. We just really need to focus on getting ready for all the shit to come.

"Nice package you got there, Sterling," I say, throwing a wink in his direction. Sterling snorts and stretches before standing and walking to the bathroom, careless of the fact he's naked as the day he was born. As he passes me, I smack his ass. "Nice ass, too."

Kai stiffens and looks over his shoulder, glaring at me. "Seriously?"

I shrug and have to bite my cheek as Ellis's face turns red from trying not to laugh. A small gurgling sound comes from her throat and Kai whips his gaze back to her.

"What the hell? Why do you guys do this to me?" He rolls off of Ellis and flops his arm over his eyes dramatically. With a heavy sigh, he sticks his lower lip out in a pout.

"Aw, it's because we love you," Ellis says, leaning over to place a kiss on his cheek.

Kai grunts but drops his arm. He narrows his gaze at me and I smile. It's too much fun teasing him. But, now is not the time.

"Alright. We still have time to get some training in. Let's get moving." I'm met with a chorus of groans from Ellis and Kai, and an evil laugh from Sterling. "Quit complaining. Let's go."

By the time everyone is dressed and ready, we've lost even more time. I'm pretty sure Kai purposely took forever to find a shirt and put it on, and Ellis couldn't find her socks that were laying on the floor right in front of the bathroom door. Just for that, I'm going to make them both work extra hard.

As everyone files past me, I snag Ellis's arm and stop her. "Are you sure you're okay?" I search her amber eyes for any sign of fatigue or pain. They soften as she looks at me, and the only thing I see is love shining through. The tightness in my chest eases as she lifts on her toes and presses a soft kiss to my lips.

"I'm more than okay," she says. "Quit worrying about it, Cade. I love you."

I pull her into my arms and hold her for just a second, letting her vanilla and chamomile scent erase the rest of the unease inside of me. "I love you too, Ellis."

Her smile is blinding and I could stare at her forever, but she says, "Now, I believe you were forcing us to do some more practice?"

This time it's me who groans. "Yeah. Why did I insist on doing this?"

"You could change your mind ..."

I shake my head firmly. "Nice try. But no go."

She sighs, tugging me down the steps and out into the cool night air.

Ellis

I'm getting stronger, and faster. Cade's magic is easier for me to use than it ever has been. Kai and Sterling—when he isn't meeting with his brother—have been teaching me all kinds of defense and attack moves to use in combination with Cade's magic. I can shift into and out of my wings smoothly, however it still takes a second for me to clear my mind to make it happen. As much as I hate the training, I can't deny it's been incredibly helpful.

But the longer we train, the more antsy I become. My sister has been in Sam's clutches for two more weeks now. I can imagine all too well what he's doing to her. After spending years living with his abuse, and seeing what he did to Sterling, the pictures I conjure in my head keep me up at night.

"Shit," I mutter, as I jump out of the way of a blast of purple magic. It just barely misses me.

Cade stops his magical attack and frowns. "What's going on, love? You've been distracted today."

He's not wrong. That's the third time I've almost not moved fast enough. I shrug. "I don't know."

"That's a lie," Kai says, crossing his arms. "You're stuck in your head today." He taps my temple as he speaks. "What's bothering you?"

"I feel like we're not doing anything. Time keeps moving forward and we're just sitting here. And Gracie is still captured. When are we going to rescue her?" My eyes burn as unshed tears build on my lashes.

"You said you thought it would be best to wait until Sterling has dealt with Noah," Cade says, walking closer. "And we all agree. The risk of him showing up to help defend Sam is too great."

"Well, when is that going to happen?" My hands drop to my sides and I have to fight the urge to crumple to the ground. I've kept a positive attitude for so long, but it's starting to fray. My nerves with it.

"It takes time, love." Cade squeezes my shoulder. "He has to make sure he has the right people on his side. And he has to ensure none of Noah's followers cause problems after he becomes alpha. There are a lot of things he has to put into place before he can act."

I sigh, and even I can see myself deflating with the action. "We can't wait much longer," I whisper, looking at the ground and rubbing my sternum. "There's this ... urgency in my chest. We need to act soon. I can feel it."

Kai and Cade glance at each other, the worry in their eyes is palpable. Kai gently grabs my chin and forces me to look at him. "We'll talk to Sterling when he gets back today and see where he's at in this whole process."

Cade tucks a stray curl behind my ear. "We understand now that we need to listen to your gut. So we'll get things moving. I promise."

Just them listening to me and taking me seriously eases some of my anxiety. "Tha—"

Kai's phone rings, interrupting me, and he fishes it out of his pocket. "My dad." He grimaces as he walks away, sliding his thumb across the screen to answer.

"Do you want to try practicing with your magic instead of mine? We haven't done that yet." Cade turns me to face him, but as soon as he sees my expression, he changes his mind. "Okay," he sighs. "Come on."

We head toward the porch steps and Cade tugs me down to sit next to him. I lean my head on his shoulder and watch Kai pace back and forth as he talks on the phone.

"This isn't going to last forever," Cade says, rubbing his hand up and down my arm. "We're going to save Gracie. We're going to deal with Sam and Noah. And we'll figure out our new normal after that. Things won't be like this forever."

"Thanks, Cade." Sometimes I need these reminders when my thoughts get heavy. "I know I can do this," I say quietly. "I've dealt with worse and survived."

"You have. You're incredibly strong. But that doesn't mean this will be easy. You can still be upset, scared, sad. You can still lean on other people and let them help you. That doesn't mean you aren't strong."

I let Cade's voice wash over me, tucking his words close to my heart. "It's hard to remember that sometimes. I lived alone for so long, with no one to rely on. I mean, I had Allie, but there was only so much she could do."

"We'll remind you as often as you need us to." He kisses the top of my head.

We lapse into silence, both of us watching Kai pace back and forth. When he hangs up, he heads over to us with a small frown.

"What's up?" Cade asks.

"My dad seems to be playing nice, and it's making me uneasy."

"What do you mean?" I ask, scooting over to give Kai room to sit next to me.

He sighs as he takes a seat, running his hand through his black hair. "He called to tell me they haven't been able to find any proof Sam was behind the attack on the estate. They did catch three vamps who were clearly working for someone, because they helped get the attackers through the gate, but they wouldn't give any names. And believe me, my dad tried to get it out of them."

I shudder because I can only imagine the kind of torture King Salvatore would inflict on someone he wanted information from.

"He also asked when we would be back because I've been slacking on my duties. Which is much nicer than what he actually said. But I told him we were helping Sterling prepare for challenging Noah, and he relented. He said to give Sterling whatever help he needed, and that I could let him know the vamps stand behind him."

"That makes sense," Cade says quietly. "Especially if Noah is working with Sam and the mages. Having the wolves as allies against the mages would be a huge bonus. Besides, when Sterling's dad was alpha, the vamps and wolves were always pretty tight."

Kai nods. "Yeah, you're right. They were. And my dad knows Sterling. He honestly probably thinks he'll be able to control him."

I snort. "Good luck. That boy is more stubborn than both of you combined."

"Yeah, my dad will be sorely disappointed when he realizes Sterling will not be easily manipulated."

"So this is a good thing?" I ask, looking at Kai.

He nods. "Yeah, I think it is. It will help give Sterling a bit of a confidence boost too. Knowing he has the support of the vampires will be huge. And my dad said to let him know when the challenge takes place and he'll send some guys to provide backup if things go to shit."

I swallow. I don't like to think of things going to shit, because there are so many ways in which they can. And each one gives me so much anxiety it's almost impossible to function.

Instead, I focus on another aspect of Kai's dad's offer. "Can we trust him, though? What if he plans some kind of coup or something?"

Kai shrugs. "We can't. But, I highly doubt he will. Cade's right. An alliance between the wolves and vamps is too much for my dad to pass up. With the attack on the estate, and the almost certainty it was Sam, my dad will never side with the mages."

It doesn't ease my anxiety.

Kai, of course, can sense this. He kisses my forehead before he stands up. "It's going to be fine, baby girl. Have faith in Sterling. He's strong and he wants this. He'll come out on top." He tosses his phone in the air and catches it. "I'm going to call him and let him know what my dad said."

We watch as Kai calls Sterling. He resumes his pacing and I can't help but smile as his free hand waves through the air as he talks. Even at this distance I can see his smile. His laugh reaches us on the wind and Cade takes a deep breath, releasing it loudly.

I glance at him and frown. Cade's brows are drawn down over his violet eyes and he's chewing on his lower lip. "What's wrong?" I ask.

"Hmm?" He doesn't take his eyes off Kai.

I nudge him with my shoulder until he looks at me. "What's wrong?"

"Nothing," he says a little too quickly. I give him a knowing look until he cracks. With a heavy sigh, he turns his gaze back to Kai. "I just ... things between us ... I don't know," he finishes as he deflates.

"You should tell him," I say quietly, not needing to know what he's thinking. It's obvious by the way he looks at Kai. It's been obvious for a while now.

Cade shakes his head. "I can't."

"Why not?"

"It's just better this way." By the tone of his voice I can tell he doesn't mean that.

"What do you mean? Cade, that's the stupidest thing I've ever heard come out of your mouth."

Cade whips his head in my direction, disbelief raising his brows to his hairline.

"Look, I don't like thinking of this because the thought makes me want to scream, and cry, and vomit. But our future is so uncertain." I swallow the lump that makes my voice wobble. The words I say next taste like ash on my tongue. "Anything could happen, and there is no guarantee we'll come out of it alive."

Cade opens his mouth, no doubt to argue with me, but I know it's true. The guys will do everything they can to protect me, even if that means one of them might not survive. There is no promise they can make that would ensure all of our safety.

I shake my head and continue on, not giving him a chance to speak. "You need to tell him how you feel, Cade. If something were to happen," I clear my throat as my voice cracks. "If something were to happen, wouldn't you feel better knowing he knows how you feel?"

"He probably already does. He's an empath."

"It's not the same as hearing it. I can feel how much all of you love me in your actions and your touch. But when I hear you say it, it makes me soar. It soothes every broken part of me. The reminder of someone's love is something we all need."

Cade says nothing for a while, watching Kai continue his conversation. But when he finally says something, it completely throws me off. "Does it bother you?"

"What?" I ask, rearing back so fast I get a crick in my neck. "Does it bother me that you love Kai?"

Cade studies me closely, eyes traveling over my features as he tries to read me. "Well, yeah. I'm your Shield, Ellis. My entire purpose is you. My focus and attention should all be on you. I shouldn't love someone else."

"I take it back," I mutter. "*That* was the stupidest thing I've ever heard you say." I shift so I'm facing him more fully. "Cade, seeing how much you two love each other makes me so happy. I can't even begin to describe what it does to my heart. Besides, I love three guys. Why can't you love more than one person? There is enough room in your heart for both me and Kai."

He shakes his head and glances at his hands in his lap. "What if he doesn't feel the same?"

I've never heard Cade so unsure before, and it makes me sad

to see him this way, but at the same time, I want to laugh. "It doesn't take an empath to know he does. He looks at you the same way he looks at me. And I swear, if neither of you admit your feelings, I'll refuse to sleep with either of you until you do. You're both being incredibly stupid."

"Gee, Ellis. Tell me how you really feel," Cade says wryly.

I grab his face in both of my hands and force him to look at me. "Pull your head out of your ass, Cade."

"What's he doing now?" Kai asks.

I turn to find him swaggering over, a crooked smile leaving one fang on display. I shove down my desire for him, and push to my feet. "I desperately need to go wash my hair for the next couple of hours." I shoot Cade a pointed look and turn for the door. "Have fun," I call over my shoulder, letting the door shut behind me.

Kai

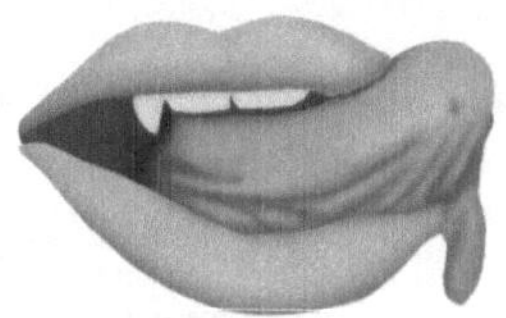

I watch Ellis prance inside, her hips swaying enticingly, until the door closes and blocks my view of her. "What's her deal?" I ask, turning to Cade. His face is turning an alarming shade of red and he refuses to look at me. "Or maybe I should be asking what your deal is?"

"Nothing." It comes out a croak and he clears his throat, rubbing the back of his neck.

"And that was convincing." I sit next to him, debating if I should open my senses to read him, but I've just sat my ass on the step when Cade stands up. "Do I smell or something?" I raise my arm and sniff but all I smell is my deodorant. Cade paces back and forth and I watch him, my eyes like ping pong balls in my head.

I let his emotions filter through my barrier, and I'm almost knocked backward with the amount of nerves and anxiety that hit me in the face. Lately, I've sensed nerves from both of the guys, which is understandable with everything that's going on. But this ... this is extreme. I push to my feet and step in front of him, stopping his pacing with my hands on his chest.

"Cade," I say quietly, lifting his chin with my finger, forcing him to look at me. "What's wrong?"

His violet gaze reluctantly reaches mine. "I ... can we talk?"

I nod. "Of course."

Cade climbs the steps and I follow, my gaze landing on his ass looking perfect in those joggers. If it weren't for the uneasiness in my gut his nerves have created, I'd smack it, or pinch it, or hell, take a bite out of it. I shake myself and sit next to Cade on the porch swing.

"So ..." I say after a minute of silence. Cade inhales and I sense him strengthening his resolve. Determination flaring hotly along my mental barrier. It makes my nerves flutter in my stomach. What the hell could he be so scared to talk about?

"I've been putting this off, but Ellis made me realize how badly I need to say it."

My stomach clenches and I force my hands to relax on my thighs. This could be about anything. There's no point jumping to conclusions.

Cade shifts on the swing, making it sway side to side a little as he turns to face me. "I know we have history, and not just as friends. And I've never denied that I find you attractive and enjoy having sex with you. But ..." he pauses and swallows.

I think I'm going to be sick. This conversation could go two different directions, and I'm worried it's going to go the direction I don't want it to go. It takes all my self control to not shake Cade and yell at him to just say it already. I turn away, unable to look at him in case he says what I'm scared he's going to say. I don't want him to see the hurt that I'm sure I won't be able to hide from him.

"But it's changed for me lately. It's not just ... it's ..." He mumbles something under his breath, something that sounds suspiciously like 'fuck it.' "Kai," he says, and waits for me to look at him.

His violet eyes are shimmering, like his magic is close to the surface. My breath catches at the emotions that slip through my shields even though I have them locked down tightly, not wanting to know what he's feeling.

"I love you, Kai."

My heart stutters, and in my surprise, I lose my grip on the barrier that keeps everyone's emotions from hounding me constantly. Cade's nervous, scared even. But the feeling I'm sensing the most is the same one I pick up from Ellis.

Love.

I stare at Cade as I let his words sink in. The nausea in my gut disappears, replaced by the wings of thousands of butterflies. Three words I never thought I'd hear from him. Three words I've been terrified to say because, what if he didn't feel the same? The longer I stare at him, the more the nervous energy from Cade intensifies, and I realize I probably should say something in return. But my words are stuck in my throat that seems to have closed. So instead, I kiss him.

I crash into him, hard enough to make the swing rock back and forth like a ship on a stormy sea. Cade gasps and I slide my tongue into his mouth, brushing it against his. His hands slide into my hair, pulling on the strands and sending electric pleasure through my veins. When I pull away, I drag my fangs along his lower lip, restraining myself from biting hard enough to draw blood.

Cade's eyes are huge as he looks at me, chest heaving with uneven breaths. "Does that ... I take it as ..."

I don't let him finish that sentence. "I love you too, Cade." The way his eyes light up makes me want to kiss him again. "I think I have for a while now. I've just been too scared to admit it to myself."

Cade frames my face in both of his hands and pulls me against him for another kiss. This one is slow and languid. I let myself feel each of his emotions, amazed that they are coming from him and are directed toward me. It's surreal to even think I have not only Ellis, but Cade as well.

I have no idea how long we sit on the swing, lazily kissing. We only pull apart when Sterling stomps up the steps. "Where's Ellis? I feel like she's missing out."

Cade and I pull away, but we don't turn our attention to

Sterling. Instead, we stare into each other's eyes for a moment longer.

Sterling clears his throat. "Do I need to get naked to get your attention?"

"It wouldn't hurt," Cade says, slightly out of breath.

I snort, breaking the moment and turning to Sterling. "She's inside washing her hair. Apparently it was really dirty."

Sterling raises one silver brow in question but shakes his head. "Well, I have some news. You're all going to want to hear this."

———

WHEN ELLIS DESCENDS THE STAIRS, it's obvious she didn't wash her hair. It's thrown into a messy bun on top of her head, loose curls escaping to fan around her head. If I were to guess, she went upstairs and changed into one of our t-shirts, curled up in bed, and was reading a book.

She glances at Cade and I sitting next to each other, practically glued to each other's side with Cade's arm around my shoulders, and she winks at us. I'm just about to scoot over to make room for her, but she turns toward Sterling and plops into his lap instead. I glare at her and she smiles, shimmying her hips seductively as she scoots closer against him. Lucky bastard.

Sterling wraps his arm around her waist almost absentmindedly, and the t-shirt she's wearing climbs higher up her thighs. I laugh when Sterling's brow furrows and he sniffs Ellis's shoulder, scrunching his nose.

"Do you have to wear Kai's shirt?" he mutters. "You stink."

I cackle, even as the monster inside of me puffs out his chest knowing our beloved smells like me.

"Oh hush," she says, elbowing him in the stomach, earning a soft oomph from the shifter. "I'm sure I smell like all of you. There is no way I'll ever get all of your scents off my skin with how much time I'm stuck with you guys."

Cade's laugh rumbles along the side of my body pressed

against his and I can't stop myself from leaning more against him, getting as close as I possibly can. If I can't cuddle with Ellis, Cade will do just fine.

Sterling clears his throat and we all sober, the atmosphere shifting from playful to serious in the blink of an eye. "I have some news," he says, shifting Ellis on his lap. "Cole and I have been meeting with wolves we can trust to take our side. We've been working on security plans for the day of the challenge as well as after the fact. Noah will have supporters who will not accept the change of leadership easily."

"They shouldn't be too big of a problem, though," Cade chimes in. "I can't imagine they are very powerful. And with Ellis's bond, there won't be anyone strong enough to challenge you."

"You're right, but if they band together, they could cause some issues." He notices Ellis's sharp inhale and he jiggles her softly. "It won't be anything we can't handle, but it will be annoying, and something I'd rather not have to deal with while we have other problems on our plate."

"What can be done to stop that?" she asks quietly looking up at him.

Sterling's blue eyes soften as he stares at her. "Well, thanks to Kai's dad and his offer of assistance, I think we finally have everything in place."

Ellis stiffens, face draining of color. "What does that mean?" Her voice trembles slightly, and her fingers shake in her lap. I can sense her fear. It washes over me in waves.

"It means I'm ready to challenge Noah."

She swallows and presses her hands to her stomach. "So, what's going to happen?"

"Well, I'll officially send Noah a challenge, and he'll pick a date and time. The pack will gather to watch and bear witness to the outcome."

Ellis's shoulders rise on a sharp breath. "And the outcome?"

Sterling hesitates. Even though she already knows what the

options are, hearing them is going to be hard on her. He scans her face, likely debating what to say. But in the end, he tells her the truth. "Our wolves will fight. Only one of us will survive. Whoever that is will be alpha."

My heart pounds erratically in my chest, matching Ellis's, and I realize it's not just everyone else's emotions I'm sensing. It's mine as well. We're all nervous about this challenge. Sterling is my brother. He's been my family for as long as I can remember. The three of us—Cade, Sterling, and I—are a pack. And now Ellis is part of that pack as well. The chance of losing him hasn't really hit until now.

"Okay," she says shakily. Her amber eyes glimmer, most likely fighting back tears. "When are you going to challenge him?"

"I'm going to send the challenge tomorrow."

She closes her eyes and buries her face into his chest. He holds her tightly and looks over at us. I don't need to read him to know he's feeling completely helpless right now.

"Ellis," Cade says quietly. He waits for her to look at him. "I'm assuming you're going to watch the fight?"

She nods, wiping tears from her cheeks.

"Then we need to make sure you're protected. It will be crowded and chaotic, and it will be too good of an opportunity for someone to try and snag you."

"Cole and I have already talked about that," Sterling says. "Along with you two, Cole and Drew will guard her. I've even contemplated calling Connor and asking him."

"I think we should," I say. "I'm not risking anything. Especially because your focus needs to stay on Noah and not Ellis's safety. Having Connor in addition to all of us will help."

"Are there any vamps you would trust her with?" Cade asks, turning to me.

I shake my head. "No. But I think the five of us should be able to handle it."

"My mom will be there too. I know she's not as tough as you guys, but in her wolf form, she'll do anything to protect those she cares about." Sterling tucks Ellis's head against his shoulder. "And she cares a lot about Ellis."

"I still don't like it," Cade mutters. "It's too risky."

Ellis sits up, her eyes wide. "I'm not staying behind," she says vehemently.

"I would never suggest you do, love. I'm just saying I don't like it."

"I don't like any of it," she replies, voice thick with emotion.

Tension and regret flow freely from Sterling, and I know he's hating himself for putting Ellis in this situation. I hop off the couch and kneel in front of her, grasping her hands. They are even colder than mine, which is a first.

"Hey. Don't forget that Sterling is strong. And with your bond he's even stronger. He has so much more to fight for. So much more of a reason to win. Noah is just power hungry. He wants to win for all the wrong reasons." Ellis clings to my words, some of her anxiety easing. "Sterling is fighting for you. For his family. For his pack. In the end, that will go so much further." Her hands in mine have stopped shaking. "Have faith in Sterling, baby girl." I give her a crooked grin, flashing a bit of fang. "Besides. You got to see me in action and now know how much of a badass I am. It's only fair Sterling gets a chance to show off his badassery."

"I don't think that's a word," she mumbles, trying to fight a smile.

I shrug. "Says who?"

She looks at me for a moment before turning to Sterling. "It's not that I don't have faith in your abilities."

"I know, kitten." He kisses her forehead, his icy blue eyes melting for her.

She releases a breath and leans against him. It's then I notice the fatigue lining her features and the way her eyelids seem to be weighed down. "Hey, why don't we all go get some sleep. It's been a long day."

She nods and sits up. Her gaze bounces between me and

Cade. "Did you two talk?" Her tone is accusatory and demanding. I'm guessing if I say no, she'd make us talk before we went to bed.

I smile. "Yes, we talked. Now, upstairs. We all need some sleep."

ELLIS

Cade and Kai have made themselves scarce today. And I know why they did it. Three days ago Sterling officially challenged Noah. Tomorrow they fight. I haven't been able to sleep. Everything I eat comes back up. And I've chewed my nails to the point I almost don't have any. I'm a nervous wreck.

Sterling's hand in mine is big and warm. I would usually find that comforting. His presence has always calmed me, even when we were fighting. I know, without a shadow of a doubt, I'm safe with him. But right now? Right now all I feel is a sense of dread. It's hanging over me like a heavy cloak, pressing me into the ground, making every step I take that much harder.

He leads me through the forest and I take no comfort from the scent of pine that smells so similar to him. The snap of twigs under my feet sounds too much like breaking bones. This walk is having the opposite effect Sterling wanted. Instead of being able to take a deep breath, my lungs have constricted. The forest floor blurs as tears swim in my eyes.

Sterling leads me to a large pine tree. He brushes the limbs aside and pulls me into the shelter they create. Sitting on the ground against the massive trunk, Sterling tugs me into his lap. I can't see anything past the branches. It's just me and Sterling, cocooned in the green needles.

He digs in his pocket, pulling out something shiny. "This is for you," he says, holding up the necklace his mom gave him. The opal dangles from the silver chain, the dim lighting preventing it from showing its facet of colors. "I wanted to wait until we were mated to give it to you, then I decided to ask Cade to put a protection charm on it." He clasps it around my neck, letting the opal settle right above my breasts. "It will get warm anytime there is danger around. And it will provide a bit of protection against someone trying to harm you."

I place my hand over the opal, pressing it against my chest while fighting the anxiety that continues to build inside me.

"I've never not seen my mom wear it." His gaze settles on my hand hiding the gemstone. "My dad gave it to her when I was born."

I want to thank him. I want to tell him how much this means to me, and how much I love it. But I can't form the words. My lips tremble and I press them together, swallowing the lump of emotion obstructing my voice.

"Please don't cry, kitten," he whispers to the top of my head. "I hate when you cry."

"I'm scared, Sterling," I breathe.

He tightens his arms around me and I let his warmth soak through my clothing. "You're going to be fine. Cade and Kai won't let anything happen to you. And with Co—"

"Not for me." My words are strangled, the lump in my throat constricting not just my breath, but my voice. "I'm terrified for you." The first tears slip down my cheeks and soak into his t-shirt.

Sterling says nothing for a moment. He rubs soothing circles on my back that do nothing to calm me. If anything, it only makes me cry harder. What if it's the last time he comforts me? What if this is the last time his arms are wrapped around me? I choke on the sobs that crawl up my throat. My entire body shakes with the force of them, and Sterling holds me tighter, trying to keep me together.

"It's not fair," I gasp. "We just accepted ... accepted the bond. I ... I can't lose you."

"Shh. Ellis, don't say that. You're not going to lose me." He rocks me gently back and forth until my tears slow.

I wipe my face on the sleeve of my shirt. Tears and snot streaking the dark fabric. "You can't promise that."

"I can promise it." He shifts me so I'm straddling his waist, and he grabs my face in his hands. The usual brightness of his eyes is dimmed. "Even if I don't win tomorrow, you will still have me."

He places his hand over my heart. My heart that stops beating entirely at his words. I shake my head, unable to hear or accept what he said, but he doesn't give me a chance to say anything.

"I will always be with you, Ellis. Even if that's just in spirit. Nothing will ever take me away from you. You will always have my love. *Always.*"

My lips tremble and my eyes burn again. *No. No!* That's not what he's supposed to say. My heart is breaking. A crack has formed and is slowly spreading, jagged and uneven. Pieces of it are falling and crumbling to dust.

"No matter what happens tomorrow, you'll be okay," he says gently. I shake my head, because I will never be okay, but he smiles sadly. "Cade and Kai will take care of you, Ellis. At the end of the day, you'll be loved and protected. And that's all I could ever ask for."

I can't speak. My lungs, my mouth, my blood won't allow it. It's like my body is rejecting the very thought of Sterling not walking off that field tomorrow. I won't survive that. I know, deep inside, I would never recover from losing him. From losing any of my Shields.

"Ellis," he breathes, wiping my tears with his thumbs. "I love you."

I sob. The tears flow freely down my cheeks and there is nothing I can do to stop them. My chest aches, and not just from the force of my crying. I'm already hurting where Sterling's bond sits warm and content inside of me, like I can already feel it missing.

Sterling kisses me deeply and slowly. I cry through the entire thing, unable to stop. I cling to him, never wanting to let go, because if I do, he'll disappear and I'll never see him again. His hands slide under my shirt, his skin warm against my chilled body.

"Ellis, make love to me. Be with me right now." The words he doesn't say echo between us. *Let me give you one last memory, just in case.*

I nod and let him tug off my leggings, then my shirt. He lifts his hips and pulls his sweats down while I remove his shirt, because for once he's actually wearing one. With our skin touching, something in me calms enough to stop crying. Something that tells me to be in the moment and not let my fear and anxiety pull me away.

I rock my hips against his cock, working myself until I can feel my wetness slicking him. When I raise onto my knees, he stops me with his hands on my hips.

"Look at me, Ellis," he says, his voice rough and deep. "Let me watch you."

I fall into his blue eyes, tumbling into their depths and getting lost. If only I could stay there forever and not have to face tomorrow. Slowly, I lower myself onto his cock, really letting myself *feel* every inch of him as he fills me.

When I start to move, Sterling grasps my face again and he kisses me. Every movement of our bodies, every brush of our tongues, is slow and purposeful. I fight back the intrusive thoughts that try to worm their way into my mind, stealing this moment from me. *This could be the last time I sleep with my mate.* Tears burn my eyelids and I squeeze my eyes shut tighter. I break the kiss and bury my face in his neck, pulling his scent into my lungs where I hope it never goes away.

Sterling's arms wrap around me tighter, a cage holding me against him, making us one. He runs his nose up my neck, inhaling my scent and his movements turn a bit more sharp. "I love you, Ellis," he breathes against my skin, a moment before he closes his teeth around my mark.

His name leaves me in a soft cry as my orgasm rolls through me in waves. It's not earth shattering. It's not spine tingling. But it's more powerful for the way he holds me closer, like he's never going to let me go. Even as his body gently shakes under me, he holds me. Even as our breathing calms, and our hearts settle, he holds me. And I hope he never, never lets me go.

———

THE DRIVE to the field where the challenge will take place is quiet. I'm plastered to Sterling's side in the back of the Hummer, trying to take deep breaths to quell the nerves that make my stomach unsettled. It's not working. Allie and Connor are following behind us, and knowing my bestie will be there with me makes this a little more bearable.

Cade pulls the Hummer off the road and we bounce over the terrain until he comes to a stop. None of us move. None of us say anything. We all stare out of the windshield at the open field in front of us. The open field where so much could go wrong. Sterling is the first to move. He kisses the top of my head then opens the car door, letting in a chill morning breeze. I want to grab him. Cling to him. Keep him in the car with me. Anything to prevent him from leaving. But I don't. I let him go and I slide out of the car after him.

Cade and Kai immediately surround me, and we make our way to the field. Already, people mill about the open space, some in their human forms, others as wolves. Sterling's mom and brother stand together and we make our way toward them.

Shari pulls Sterling into a hug and I notice the tears glimmering in her eyes. "I'm so proud of you, Sterling," she says when she pulls away.

"Thanks, mom."

He turns to his brother, and I hold my breath as Cole hesitates. Then he grasps the back of Sterling's neck and brings their foreheads together.

"You got this, bro. I know you do."

Sterling swallows and nods, closing his eyes to hide the emotion his brother's support gives him.

A commotion draws all of our attention to the opposite side of the field. It doesn't take a rocket scientist to know it's Noah. A group of men follow behind him looking menacing and threatening. I shrink back against Cade as Noah gets closer, and Sterling steps in front of me. The pearl necklace resting just above my breasts warms slightly as Noah approaches. If I hadn't already known he was a threat, the necklace would have warned me.

"I'll give you one last chance to change your mind, boy." Noah's thick, wavy hair is the same color as mine. His light brown eyes are the same color as Gracie's. While we definitely look like our mom, I can see some similarities that make it obvious he is our father. He's tall and broad shouldered, and he screams wolf energy. Not alpha energy like Sterling does, but it's clear he's a powerful wolf.

Sterling doesn't straighten his shoulders. He doesn't try to stand taller or posture. Yet he still radiates strength, a clear indication of the power resting inside of him, waiting to be unleashed. "I'm not changing my mind. It's time for the wolves to return to their former glory. It's time for the wolves to once again be respected among the magicals like we were when my dad was alpha. Your time running us into the ground and dirtying our name is over. It's time we become the powerhouse we once were."

Noah growls, his upper lip curling to reveal lengthening canines. "Insolent fool. You are going to be destroyed."

Sterling just shakes his head and turns his back to Noah, an insult that screams Sterling is unafraid of the shifter he's about to fight. But this also brings me into Noah's line of sight. His nostrils flare as he scents me, clearly picking up on the fact that I'm his daughter, and his eyes widen. His entire body stiffens and a low growl rumbles from his chest.

Sterling whips back around, stepping in front of me, while Kai and Cade tighten ranks on either side. I notice Cole working his way around toward my back where Connor and Allie are standing.

"Well, this is certainly interesting," Noah drawls, craning his head to the side to see me. "The daughter that got away."

"Walk away, Noah," Sterling growls. "This doesn't involve her."

"It doesn't? Are you sure about that?" He sneers and crosses his arms over his chest. His nostrils flare again and his gaze bounces between me and Sterling, likely scenting our mating bond. "You wouldn't be challenging me if she wasn't here. Is this why you insisted on letting her live all those years ago?"

Sterling says nothing, but his body is tense, practically vibrating with restrained rage.

"You know the rules of a challenge, Noah," Cole says behind me. His hand on my shoulder squeezes slightly, and I relax a bit. "This is between you and Sterling. If anything happens to Ellis, you forfeit the challenge."

Noah narrows his gaze on me and mutters something I choose not to hear before he stalks away. Sterling doesn't relax until Noah is across the field with his cronies. Before he can turn around to look at me, an ancient-looking woman hobbles to the middle of the field.

"That's Agatha," Cade whispers in my ear. "She's the one who gave us the mixture to break your fever so you could mate with Sterling."

Her white hair blows around her shoulders, the red ribbon tying it back not doing anything to keep it contained. Even at this distance I can see her wrinkles. As she comes to a stop, everyone gathered for the challenge falls quiet. It's obvious she's respected in the wolf community, revered even.

"We are gathered today to witness Sterling Harrison challenge

Noah Martin for the position of Alpha of the Iron Shadows pack. You all know the rules," she says in a low, gravelly voice. Somehow it carries across the clearing, almost like she's using magic. "No one may interfere with the fight. No weapons may be used during the challenge. Once it begins, only the death of one of the challengers will end it. The surviving wolf will claim the title of Alpha."

My breath catches at her words. She doesn't mince them, and they cut right through me. Sterling turns to me, taking my face in his palms. I stare into those icy blue eyes, hating the way everything blurs as tears build on my lashes. I furiously blink them away so I can see my mate clearly.

"Remember what I said last night," he says quietly so only I can hear. "No matter what happens, I want you to remain strong. You keep going. Keep fighting. No matter what."

I shake my head and press my wobbling lips together. "Sterling," I whisper brokenly.

"I love you, kitten."

He leans forward to kiss me and I throw my arms around his neck. This will *not* be the last time I kiss him. I refuse to even let that thought take root. Sterling slides his hands down my back and over my ass, gripping it tightly to lift me off the ground. I wrap my legs around him and kiss him even harder. This feels too similar to the time he left and got captured by Sam.

"Sterling and Noah." Agatha's crackling voice echoes through the clearing. "Shift now, and approach."

"Come back to me," I pull away and whisper, just like the last time.

Sterling reluctantly sets me on my feet and kisses my forehead. He steps away, tugging his shirt over his head and tossing it to Kai, never breaking eye contact with me. My heart thunders in my chest, almost painfully. He doesn't look away until he tosses his pants to Kai, and then turns his gaze to my beloved. Kai nods. Sterling glances at Cade. Cade nods. A silent promise that they'll protect me. They'll care for me. If he doesn't make it through this, I'll be okay. At least physically.

In the blink of an eye, a giant silver wolf stands before me, it's head almost reaching my chest. I drop to my knees and wrap my arms around its neck, burying my face in the soft fur. The wolf drops his head to my shoulder, a hug in the only way a wolf can.

"I love you both," I say, pressing a kiss to the top of the wolf's nose. A soft whine from the wolf, a lick of it's tongue on my cheek, and it's gone, running across the field to Agatha.

A dark brown wolf watches him approach. No. It's not watching Sterling. Its beady black gaze is trained on me. Noah is smaller than Sterling, just barely. His dark brown coat doesn't look as soft, either.

I shakily push to my feet and take a deep breath. Cade and Kai both grab my hands, and I practically break their bones as I squeeze them.

Agatha looks at both of the wolves, gaze sharp and full of authority. "Make this a fair fight," she says, looking at Noah in particular. "May the strongest wolf win." With that, she backs away.

They wait until she is clear of the field, and then they begin circling.

ELLIS

THIS IS AWFUL. WATCHING MY MATE CIRCLE NOAH. Waiting for the first move. The anticipation makes my gut roil. I'm seconds from throwing up, even though there is nothing in my stomach to bring back up. Each breath I expel is ten times harder to draw back in. I'm on the verge of a full blown panic attack, and I can't let that happen. Any distraction to Sterling could cost him.

Kai steps behind me and wraps his arms around my waist. "Breathe with me, Ellis." His chest brushes against my back as he inhales, and I match it. Stray curls that have escaped my bun ruffle with each breath Kai exhales. I breathe with him, slow and steady, and eventually it becomes easier. I still feel like I'm going to puke, though.

"Noah is strong, but Sterling is stronger." Cole steps up to fill the space on my right where Kai had been standing. "I've been training with Sterling these past few days, and I know he can beat Noah. As long as Noah doesn't pull anything illegal."

That's what I'm worried about. We all know the kind of person Noah is. He will do anything to come out on top.

Noah makes the first move. He lunges for Sterling, snapping his jaw, and I cry out, covering my mouth with my hands. I've never seen a wolf fight before, so I have no idea what to expect. Sterling doges Noah's jaws and uses his body weight to slam into the other wolf. He knocks Noah down and closes his jaw around a leg, but Noah gets to his feet quickly, seemingly unhindered by the bite.

I close my eyes, too overwhelmed to watch, but the sounds are almost worse. As the fight intensifies, growling, yips, and the occasional whine float across the clearing, and I want to cover my ears. It sounds so awful.

A small hand clutches mine and I open my eyes, expecting to see Allie. But it's Sterling's mom. Her eyes track the fight, mouth pulled into a frown. She's just as worried as I am. I squeeze her hand, and we stand together, watching Sterling fight for his life.

Red blooms in Sterling's white coat, the contrast of colors so jarring. Noah's fur is too dark to see any blood, but I know he has to be bleeding as well. Neither of them appear to be flagging or hurting too badly. The fight continues, getting more and more vicious with each minute that passes. The taste of copper in my mouth tells me I've chewed my cheek so much I made it bleed. I don't care though.

I notice a girl slowly making her way around the field, but I pay her no mind. My attention is glued to my mate. From the corner of my eye, I see Cole tracking her and I know he'll do something if she's trying to hurt me. A few minutes later, she screams behind me. A blood curdling scream that causes Sterling to snap his head in my direction. The distraction costs him. Just as Noah no doubt planned.

Noah lunges and buries his teeth into Sterling's shoulder, clamping down tightly. The whine that escapes Fluffy cracks my heart into jagged little pieces. My breath leaves me in a rush when Noah throws Sterling to the ground, blood rapidly staining his coat.

"Sterling!" His name tears from my throat so loud it hurts. Something inside me writhes, and fire blooms in my stomach. It grows hotter and hotter as I watch Noah bite down harder while

Sterling tries to fend him off with his paws. My mate is in trouble and the need to protect him rises to the surface.

"Shit," Kai says as he grabs my shoulders. "Ellis, calm down!"

His words float through the hazy smoke in my mind. My only thought, though, is to save Sterling.

"Ellis, your flames are sparking to life. You need to keep that under control." Kai's voice is low and urgent in my ear. "Don't let Noah see them."

That registers. He's right. If Noah sees my golden fire, he'll do anything to make sure he gets me to Sam.

"Breathe, Ellis," Kai murmurs, rubbing his hands up and down my arms. "Close your eyes."

I do as he says, blocking Sterling from my vision. It's harder than it should be. Every instinct in my body is screaming at me to not take my eyes off him. To make sure he's okay. But I squeeze them shut and breathe deeply, imagining cool water flowing over my fingers, dousing the flames.

"Good job, baby girl," Kai whispers in my ear.

I keep my eyes closed for a second longer, but a gasp from the crowd draws them open again. The sight drops me to my knees. Sterling is on his back, with Noah's jaws closed around his throat.

Time seems to slow down. My fingers dig into the dirt, and each breath I take hurts my chest. *Fight, Sterling.* The bond inside me goes taut and I cling to it. *Fight!* With each beat of my heart, I push every ounce of love I have for my mate into the bond. I pray he can feel it, that it gives him the strength he needs to overpower Noah. *I need you, Sterling. Don't leave me.*

His head turns to me, blue eyes pained, but he bares his teeth and growls. With a visible effort, Sterling pushes Noah off of him. Blood sprays from the wound at his neck, fur clinging to Noah's mouth. Bile climbs up my throat but I swallow it down.

Sterling is on his feet faster than I can track, and he tackles Noah to the ground. Jaws snap and clumps of grass fly in the air as they tussle. My fingers ache from how hard I'm digging them into the ground.

Come on, Sterling. End this.

Sterling closes his jaw around Noah's leg and bites down hard. Noah yips and backs away, limping, but Sterling doesn't give him the opportunity to regroup. He charges Noah and buries his teeth into Noah's neck. My breath lodges in my throat and every muscle in my body tenses. Sterling swings his head to the side, tearing a chunk out of Noah's throat. Noah falls to the ground, and Sterling is on top of him in seconds. Another viscous bite into his neck, and the brown wolf stills.

Sterling steps away, body heaving with each breath he takes. A second later light flares through the clearing and Noah's wolf form disappears, changing into a naked man. He's unmoving, chest not rising. A gaping hole where his throat should be gushes blood and soaks the grass in red. Sterling stares at him for a second before stumbling backward and collapsing.

I'm up and running before I even realize what I'm doing. My gaze is glued to Sterling, watching his wolf's chest rise and fall rapidly. When I reach him, I drop to my knees, hands hovering over his fur, matted and stained with blood.

"Sterling," I whisper shakily.

His form shimmers, and slower than usual, he shifts back into his human form, bones snapping and popping. Blood streaks his skin, bite marks mar his body. The one on his neck is deep and blood still runs from it steadily.

"Cade!" I yell, but he's already kneeling next to Sterling, purple light flaring around his hands.

People start to gather around us as Cade's magic settles in Sterling, healing all of his injuries. Cole does his best to shoo them away, giving us privacy. Shari stands behind Cade, clutching her stomach, tear tracks trailing down her cheeks.

When Cade steps away I grab Sterling's hand, relieved to find it warm. His eyes open and a slow smile spreads across his face.

"We did it," he whispers.

"You did it." Tears spill over and blur my vision.

Sterling sits up with a grunt and pulls me onto his lap. He

kisses me deeply, and I temporarily forget there are people around watching us and that he's covered in blood—his and Noah's. He hardens under me and I rock my hips, making him moan.

Kai clears his throat, bringing me back to earth. "You might want to wait for that," he says wryly.

Heat burns my neck and I bury my face in Sterling's shoulder. "Oh gods."

He chuckles, but squeezes me tighter, and I sit in his lap, listening to his heart beat. "You know what this means?" he asks.

"What?" I pull away and look into his eyes.

He dries the tears clinging to my cheeks and smiles. "You're my alpha mate."

"And that means what, exactly?"

"You're my equal." He kisses me lightly.

I raise one brow. "I thought I already was."

He chuckles. "No. You are far superior to me, kitten. But in terms of the pack, they have to obey you as well, now."

That sits heavy on my shoulders. More responsibility I don't know what to do with. As if being a harpy wasn't enough.

"Sterling Harrison."

We both look up to find Agatha standing over us. Despite her hunched form, she seems to stand taller than the others around her. She gives Sterling a small smile and a nod.

"You are the new alpha of the Iron Shadows pack."

Cheers and howls rise from the people and wolves surrounding us. I don't fail to notice a group of wolves skulking away, no doubt supporters of Noah. Cole sees them too, and his eyes narrow.

Fatigue suddenly floods me as all of my adrenaline leaves in a rush, and I lay my head on Sterling's shoulder. "Can we go home now?"

He kisses my temple. "Yes, kitten. We can."

———

"CAN I GET YOU ANYTHING ELSE?" I ask Sterling, handing him a bottle of water.

"Lay with me?" His eyes are heavy, and I can see him fighting to stay awake. Cade's healing always takes a lot out of a person.

"Will you eat the sandwich first?" I point to the untouched turkey sandwich on the nightstand.

"Will you lay with me while I eat it?" he counters.

I can't help but smile. "Yes, but if you don't eat I'm getting out of bed."

He holds his arms open for me, and I climb in next to him and lean against the headboard. He immediately curls around me, laying his head on my belly. I nudge his shoulder and stick the plate in front of him. Grumbling, he sits up enough to eat. He somehow manages to eat the entire sandwich in two bites, and downs the bottle of water without coming up for air.

"Happy?" he asks, blinking blearily at me.

"Yes," I whisper and pat my stomach.

He snuggles against me again, sighing in contentment. The way my stomach flutters because this big, alpha wolf is curled next to me like he can't sleep without me makes me smile. His hair is like silk as I run my fingers through it, gently untangling the knots. It takes only seconds before his body relaxes and his breathing evens out.

A soft knock on the door draws my attention and Cade slips inside with a second sandwich. "He's asleep?"

"Yeah. It didn't take him long. I don't think he was sleeping the past few days." I know I hadn't been. But I wasn't just in a fight for my life and healed magically, so I'm able to fight sleep a little better than he was.

Cade nods and climbs onto the bed, sitting at the bottom. "You should eat, too."

I take the plate and my stomach grumbles loud enough I'm surprised it doesn't wake Sterling with his ear against it. I can't remember the last time I ate and it actually stayed down. It's been a few days. I finish the sandwich almost as quickly as Sterling ate his. And I only got a few crumbs in his hair. Cade laughs softly as I try to brush them out with a sheepish grin.

"Everything okay in here?" Kai asks, popping his head inside. Seeing us all settled on the bed, he joins us. After a quick kiss for me, and one for Cade, he lays down with his head in Cade's lap, his feet propped on the pillow next to me.

"So what's next?" I ask, watching Cade brush his fingers through Kai's hair, the same way I am with Sterling.

"Well, we need to start planning how we're going to save your sister," Cade says. "I don't think the same plan we used for Sterling will work. For one, we've done it once already. Two, Sam knew he could let you go because he knew you'd be back for Grace."

I glance at Sterling sleeping on me. "What about getting the other magical races involved? The wolves and vampires?"

"My dad won't be game for that," Kai mumbles. He sounds like he's half asleep, Cade's fingers drawing him closer to the edge. "Even with all the evidence we have against Sam, the mages are too powerful. It would be too much of a risk of them retaliating against us. My dad has no desire to be involved in a war."

"And Sterling would one hundred percent have the wolves help," Cade says, glancing at the sleeping alpha. "But, Cole would step in and stop him. And rightfully so. Even if the vamps and wolves banded together to go after Sam, it would be an act of war. And the last thing Sterling needs to deal with so new in his role as alpha, is an inter-race war. He needs to build up the pack's trust. Not to mention, they are incredibly weak after Noah. They need to rebuild their strength."

"So we go in alone again?" I try to hide the way that makes anxiety writhe in my gut. More people would mean more chance of success and less risk of one of my Shields getting hurt.

"I wouldn't say alone," Cade says. "We have Connor and Drew. And I wouldn't be surprised if Cole stepped in to help."

"So, just mostly alone," I mutter.

Kai huffs a small laugh and cracks open one eye. "Do you not have faith in us?"

I tilt my head to the side, studying him. "It's not you I don't have faith in. It's the fact I know Sam will play dirty."

"And we'll be prepared for that," Cade says. "We just need a solid plan before we go in."

"Tomorrow we'll call Connor and Drew," Kai says, closing his eye again. "Even Cole if he wants to help. We'll get a plan in place and set a time. We are going to get her out of there."

"Thank you," I whisper.

Kai shakes his head, as if to say 'don't thank me.'

"Okay, enough talk." Cade lifts Kai from his lap, ignoring Kai's grumbling, and slides under the covers next to me. "Let's get some sleep. Tomorrow is a new day."

ELLIS

Waking up the next morning is difficult. I'm so warm and cozy with my legs and arms tangled with my guys. Sterling puts off the most heat, and with his chest pressed against my back, his hand resting on my belly, I'm extra warm. I peek an eye open and smile. How Cade is sleeping is beyond me. He's on his back with both me and Kai resting our heads on his chest. My eyes slide closed again, contentment a warm glowing ball inside of me. This is how I want to wake up everyday for the rest of my life.

I'm just about to slip back to sleep when someone's phone rings. Kai twitches and grumbles. Sterling groans and tucks himself closer to me. Cade sighs, his chest deflating under my head.

"Who didn't turn their fucking phone on silent?" Kai mumbles sleepily.

"Just ignore it," I say, snuggling into the bed even more.

The phone stops ringing, and we all relax in our pile of limbs and happiness. Until the phone rings again.

"Seriously?" Kai snaps. "Whose phone is that? I'm going to throw it against the wall."

Cade sighs. "It's mine." He manages to disentangle himself from me and Kai, and climbs out of bed.

Kai immediately scoots over to me. His cooler skin makes me shiver at the loss of Cade's heat. "Mmm," Kai hums. "This is better anyway." He buries his face in my neck, inhaling deeply.

Cade sucks in a breath, and all three of us look up. His throat works on a swallow before he slides his thumb across the screen and puts the phone to his ear. "Hello?"

I watch his eyes widen and his face drain of color. As the rising and falling of his chest becomes more rapid, I sit up. Something is wrong. I crawl to the end of the bed, never taking my eyes off of him.

"Wait!" Cade yells into the phone, but closes his eyes and lets his arm drop. Whoever was on the other end has already hung up. He sets the phone on the dresser with a shaky hand.

"Cade?" I hop to my feet and press my hands to his chest. Under my palms, his heart pounds hard enough I can feel it. "What's wrong?"

He looks at me, his violet eyes devastated. "That was Kennedy," he rasps.

My stomach drops to my feet and I have to sit on the edge of the bed as the room tilts. I already know what he's going to say and I shake my head as if I can ward off the bad news.

"He's threatening my family because I haven't been working." He runs his hands through his hair, yanking roughly on the strands.

Oh, gods. It's my fault. It's hard to breathe through the guilt bombarding me, but I take a deep breath that hurts my chest. "You have to go. Go back home."

He's shaking his head before I even finish speaking. "I'm not leaving. Especially not right now when we're planning to rescue your sister."

"Cade!" I jump from the bed and take his face in my hands. "It's your mom and sister. You know what will happen if you don't."

His heartbreak is evident in his eyes. I can see how much this is killing him. But he places his hands over mine on his cheeks, and he stares at me. "I'm not leaving, Ellis. This is not up for discussion."

"Cade—"

"I'm serious. Drop it." His tone leaves no room for argument. He pulls from my grasp and snags a t-shirt from the floor, tugging it over his head as he heads for the door. "Call Connor and Drew. Tell them to meet us here in an hour."

The door doesn't quite slam behind him, but I still flinch. My eyes burn for more than one reason. I hate that he's letting this happen to his family because of me. One day he'll regret that, and I don't want him to resent me for it when he does. And he's never taken that tone with me. It stings, even knowing he doesn't mean it.

I press my hands to my middle in the hopes it can ease the ball of nerves that formed at his words. The room is quiet, and I spin around to face Kai and Sterling, throwing my shoulders back and preparing for a fight. "We're not ignoring this." I didn't let Sterling's family continue to suffer under Noah, and I won't let Cade's family suffer under Kennedy.

Kai sighs and runs a hand down his face. "No, of course we're not. I just don't know what the fuck to do."

That takes the wind out of my sails and I plop onto the bed, defeated. "There has to be something," I whisper.

"Sneaking in is out of the question," Sterling says. "That building will be under way too much surveillance and there is no way only one or two mages can manage the security and wards Kennedy has surrounding it."

"Not to mention we have no idea where exactly they're being held," Kai chimes in.

An idea starts to take root in my mind, one that only increases the anxiety in my gut, but to save Cade's family, I'll do anything. I swallow thickly and turn to Kai. "You said when you abducted me from my room at the Kennedy mansion, there was video surveillance in my room?"

Kai nods, a frown forming a crease between his gray eyes. "Yeah. Cade was able to hack into it."

"Any chance the footage from that camera gets saved and stored somewhere?" I ignore the way my voice shakes and the way my tongue sticks to the roof of my mouth.

"Most likely. But that would be a Cade question. Why?" Kai narrows his eyes at me, like he suspects what I'm about to say.

I clutch my stomach and bend over. Saying these words brings back the trauma I experienced under that roof. It makes me want to crawl into a hole and never climb back out again. It makes my skin crawl and leaves a sensation of filth covering my body. But if it helps Cade and his family, it's all worth it. "What if I threaten to expose him for everything I went through when he was acting as my dad?" My words are strangled, and I have to force them from my throat.

I don't need to look at Kai and Sterling to know they've gone preternaturally still. "What do you mean?" Sterling asks quietly. Too quietly.

"I mean, if he doesn't release Cade's mom and sister, I'll make sure the world knows what he let happen to me."

"Fuck that!" Kai jumps from the bed and paces back and forth in front of me. "First of all, no one will ever see what happened to you. I'll get my hands on those recordings and destroy them myself to ensure that. Second, you're not going to put yourself in a position that takes you back to that time. Not even to help Cade."

"That's my decision to make, not yours." I stand and step in front of him, stopping his pacing.

"And it's my job to protect you," Kai growls. "That includes more than just physical protection." He sighs and shakes his head, his shoulders drooping. "I want to be supportive, Ellis. I want to support you, but this ..." He shakes his head again. "This is asking too much."

I place my hands on my hips and stand up tall, even though I still only come to his chest. "You know you can't stop me. If you don't help, I'll do it on my own. I've done it once, and I won't hesitate to do it again."

Kai narrows his gaze on me. I know my whirlwind of emotions is feeding into Kai and making it hard for him to control his own. I can see how his eyes churn with everything I'm feeling. "I'll compel you to not do it."

My brows raise to my hairline. I clench my fists hard enough that my nails pinch my palms and let the leash on my magic loosen. Golden sparks flicker at my fingertips and I can see the golden swirling light in my eyes reflected in Kai's. "I fucking dare you, Malakai Thorne," I say, words quiet and shaking with anger. Unbelievable. After that talk we just had about him having to trust me and the first time I need him to, he pulls this shit again.

We stare at each other, Kai's jaw clenching and unclenching, my anger fueling his. If I don't cool my attitude, Kai's will keep rising until he explodes. But I'm not backing down this time.

"Okay, that's enough." Sterling steps between us, gently pushing Kai away. "Take a breath, Kai. Raise your shields before you do something stupid."

Kai growls, baring his fangs at Sterling, but the wolf doesn't back down. He raises one brow, the alpha ordering his pack to obey his command. Kai curses and turns around, heading for the bathroom, and the door slams shut behind him.

Sterling turns to me, and I square my shoulders, prepared to keep fighting. He shakes his head and lifts my chin with his finger. "You too, kitten. Take a deep breath."

I don't want to. I want to show him he doesn't control me like that. He said so himself. I'm his equal, his alphamate. But I have a better chance at convincing them if we all keep level heads. I close my eyes and take a breath, inhaling his pine and winter scent, and releasing it.

I open my mouth to argue with him—calmly—but he beats me to it. "I'm not saying no. *Yet*. But this is a discussion to have with Cade. This will be a group decision, Ellis. No matter what decision we come to, you can't go off and do this by yourself. We're a team, remember?"

I sigh and nod. "Yeah, I know. I didn't really mean that, but when Kai didn't even entertain the idea ..."

"The claws came out?" He smirks, and the sight causes the rest of my anger to melt away. "Come on." He kisses my forehead and threads his fingers through mine. "Let's go downstairs and wait for Kai." Before we can move, the bathroom door opens and Kai steps out. We stare at each other for a moment, and Sterling lets my hand go. "If I leave, will you two play nice?"

I don't answer, because that depends entirely on the vampire. Kai grunts, but there is nothing aggressive in his posture. Sterling must take that for confirmation because he leaves us alone in tense silence. I cross my arms over my chest, unwilling to be the one to break. I never said I wasn't stubborn.

Eventually, Kai sighs and crosses the room. "I'm sorry, Ellis. I should never have threatened to compel you." He frames my face in his palms, using his thumbs to lift my head. "I'm still struggling to keep your emotions out. They feed into mine and it just becomes a perfect storm of anger that I can't control. That's not an excuse, but it's all I have right now. Not to mention you standing up for yourself like that is fucking sexy as hell."

I press my lips together, fighting the twitch that wants to break out into a laugh. He would like to make me mad just because it turns him on. "I just wish you would consider my ideas sometimes. I know they aren't always the best, and I know you only want to keep me safe and happy. But I don't like to be shut down without you even considering what I have to say. And you told me you'd do better, Kai. You told me you needed to trust *my* instincts more."

"I'm so sorry, baby girl," he breathes. "I don't mean to do that. My instincts are hard to fight sometimes. I need to do better. I *will* do better. I don't want you to think I don't value your opinions, because I do." He sighs and presses his forehead to mine. "Sometimes its really fucking scary. You are my world, Ellis. *Nothing* else matters in my life, except you. The thought of you hurt, in any way, makes me crazy. I let that fear win sometimes, and I don't think before I speak or act."

"I get it," I whisper, clutching his t-shirt. "I really do." That fear can be debilitating. Just thinking of losing one of them ...

"I'm sorry," he says again. "I love you so much, Ellis."

I wrap my arms around his middle and bury my face in his chest, inhaling spice and cherries. "I love you too, Kai."

He rests his cheek on top of my head, and we stand together for a second. Under my ear, his heart thumps in time with mine. For once, slow and steady. Calm. It won't last though. Especially because this conversation isn't over.

I pull away and look into his gray eyes. "I still want to talk about this, though. I'm not letting anything happen to Cade's family."

Kai sighs, his breath fanning the curls around my face. "I know."

"Okay." I take his hand and we head downstairs.

Sterling is sitting in the chair where he usually sits. Cade, however, is standing by the window looking outside into the night-darkened yard. I drop Kai's hand and approach Cade, moving slowly so as to not freak him out. His back is tight under my palm, all of his muscles tense. I peek around him and glance at his face, and my heart breaks. His eyes are red, like he's been crying or trying not to cry.

I step between him and the window and hug him tight, lending him what comfort I have. He hugs me back, and I take that as his way of telling me he's not angry with me, even though he raised his voice earlier.

"Ellis has something she would like us to consider," Sterling says, then throws in offhandedly, "Calmly."

Cade pulls away and looks at me, his violet eyes full of sadness. I tug him to the couch and gently push him down next to

Kai. I'm too nervous to sit, so I pace back and forth in front of the couch, Sterling's support bolstering me.

"I refuse to let your family suffer, Cade," I say quietly, but firmly. "I know you say you won't resent me later, but you can't promise that. I'm the reason you're here and not working. It would be my fault if they get hurt."

"Ellis, tha—"

I hold up my hand and stop Cade. "I'm not arguing about this. I don't care how we get them out of there, but we're going to do it." I can see him hesitating. He wants to argue with me, but at the same time he wants to save his family. I know Cade well enough to know that he doesn't want to accept our help. He doesn't want to risk any of us, or make me wait any longer to save my sister. But I've made up my mind. "Cade," I say quietly and sit on his lap. "Please. You've done so much for me. More than you will ever realize. Please let me help you get them back."

He closes his eyes and releases a breath, his shoulders slumping at the same time. "Did you have any ideas?"

Kai snorts and I shoot a glare at him. "Well, yeah," I say timidly. He won't like this, and I know he'll fight me on it. They all will. But I have to make them understand I want to do this. Even if it rips the scab off all of my healing wounds. "Just please consider it before you shoot it down. Like actually consider it. All of you."

His eyes narrow, already not liking the direction this is going. Unable to handle anyone touching me while I talk about this, I push to my feet. Sterling watches me like … well like a wolf watching its prey. But instead of wanting to devour me, he's watching for any signs he needs to step in to protect me from myself. Kai's arms are crossed over his chest and the scowl on his face is top notch.

I take a deep breath, letting it fill my lungs and expand my chest to the point of pain. When I release it, I shake my arms like I can shake off the sensation of spiders crawling over my skin.

"Okay. Since we can't sneak in to rescue them, and asking Thomas to release them will never work, I think our best bet is to blackmail him."

"Blackmail him with what?" Cade's voice is threaded with suspicion, like he already knows the direction this is going to go.

"If we can get the footage from my room, we can threaten to reveal what he let happen to me under his roof." My attempt to sound confident fails miserably. Especially as Cade's eyes darken with anger.

He swallows and leans forward, resting his elbows on his knees and piercing me with his violet stare. "You mean you want me to download the footage of Sam raping you so you can threaten to reveal it for the entire world to see?"

Well, when he puts it that way ... "Yes," I whisper, clutching my hands to my stomach.

"No." That one word, spoken quietly but firmly, snaps my patience.

"Why won't you guys even consider it? Stop being so godsdamn protective for once, and fucking consider one thing I say!"

"I did consider it," Cade says, leaning back and crossing his arms over his chest, the perfect mirror to Kai. "I considered it for .5 seconds and quickly dismissed the idea."

A frustrated, wordless scream climbs up my throat and I stomp my foot. Childish? Yes. But if they are going to treat me like a child then I'll act like one. Kai smirks and my hand tingles with the need to slap him. His eyes flash red, daring me to act on my impulsive reactions. Instead, I take a deep breath and close my eyes, counting to ten before I speak again.

"It's my choice to make. I'm the one who is impacted by the video being released. Not you guys." I cross my arms and shoot Cade a glare when he opens his mouth. "You can't take this choice away from me."

Sterling leans forward, snagging my attention. "You realize

why we're hesitant, right? Ellis, when we first met you, you were a shell of a person. We had to watch you flinch at our touch and break down in tears. You've come so far and the last thing we want is to see that lost look in your eyes again."

Leave it to Sterling to make me second guess myself. But I'm not the same person I was before. In just a short amount of time these guys have helped me become the person I'm meant to be. Now I feel like they're taking it away.

"I understand," I say quietly. "I really do. And you know I appreciate you guys looking out for me. But I'm stronger now. I have your support and love and that has made all the difference." I look at each of them, trying to convey that I'm strong enough to handle this. "I don't want you guys to reject this idea just because you're worried what it will do to my mental health. If I couldn't handle it, I wouldn't have suggested it. You have to trust me."

Sterling looks at me, and I swear I see pride gleaming in his icy blue eyes. I know I'll be able to convince him, it's Cade and Kai I'm worried about.

Cade sits up again, leveling a stern look in my direction. "Let's say we forget about what this will do to you mentally. You're expecting us to accept the fact that *everyone* will be able to watch our mate, our beloved, our soul-bonded, get raped? *No one* gets to see you naked, let alone in a position like that."

Kai growls, the monster making its opinion known on that matter. I look to Sterling, pleading with him to help me convince them, but he says it all with his raised brows and lips pressed together in a small line. I'm on my own in this.

I have to take another deep breath, my frustration is rapidly growing and the last thing I need is for my own anger to filter over to Kai. "I love you guys. You are the breath in my lungs and the beating of my heart. But I'm this close to fucking snapping." I hold my thumb and pointer finger centimeters from each other. "I'm your mate, your beloved, your soul-bonded. But I am still myself. I have my own thoughts and opinions. I control what I do. It's my body, not yours. If you *ever* think you can pull that alphahole possessive bullshit on me, you will be very quickly corrected."

Some of the fire leaves Kai's gray eyes, but it's replaced by a different fire, and he slowly pulls a pillow onto his lap. Cade rubs his face, his stubble scratching softly in the quiet. I watch him closely, because even though Kai will be hard to convince, I'm positive I can do it. Cade, however, will fight me because he doesn't want to be the reason I do this.

Cade pushes from the couch and steps in front of me, taking my face in his palms. "Ellis, love, you know I can't let you do this for me. I'll never forgive myself for it."

"You've done so much for me, though. You've sacrificed so much. *I'll* never forgive *myself* if something happens to them." Tears blur my view of him and my lips tremble. "Please Cade," I whisper. "Please let me do this for you."

He rests his forehead against mine and I cling to his shirt, silently begging him to agree. "Ellis ..." He shakes his head, and my stomach drops.

I pull away, a few tears sliding down my cheeks. "I'm so tired of feeling useless. I'm just an object to protect and keep safe. Someplace for you guys to stick your dick inside with no thoughts or desires of my own. I guess I'll just keep sitting back, looking pretty, and letting everyone make my decisions for me."

My words hit their mark. Cade's eyes widen and I see the devastation in them. I briefly want to take back what I said, but it's the truth. At least how I see it. Swallowing, I open the front door and escape into the cool night air, letting the breeze dry the tears on my cheeks, only for new ones to appear.

The lake glistens in the distance and I turn away from it, not wanting the reminder of that night and how special I felt. How cherished. I know they love me. There is no denying it. But at some point, that love can become too possessive, and I'm scared that's what is going to happen with them. I see their point of view, I hear it, I understand it. But at the end of the day, this should be my decision to make.

The grass tickles my bare feet when I step off the porch. Dew clings to the blades, making my soles damp and cold, but I curl my toes, digging into the hard earth. In just a t-shirt, my skin pebbles, but I'm not ready to go back inside yet. So I stand in the chilly night and look at the stars, wishing the sky would devour me.

CADE

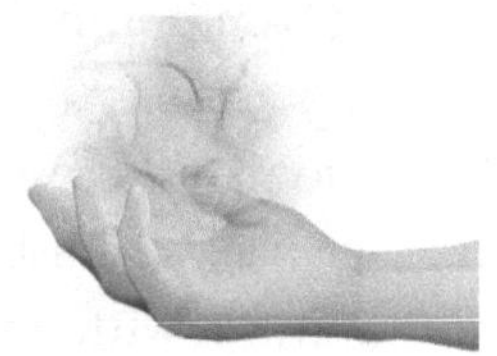

WELL FUCK. NOW WHAT DO I DO? I STARE AT THE DOOR and let Ellis's words cut through me over and over again, burning and slicing like a knife heated over a flame.

"I think we should seriously consider this," Sterling says quietly.

"Are you fucking serious?" Kai snaps. "You want to let your mate release footage of her being raped by her ex?"

Sterling sighs. "Of course I don't want her to do it. It makes me want to rage and destroy things. But she's right. Ellis is her own person. She can make decisions for herself and we need to be able to respect that."

"Sterling's right," I mumble, still staring at the door. "Ellis will always need her freedom. We can't clip her wings and keep her caged no matter how much we may want to. She'll grow to hate us if we do."

Kai laughs but it's lacking in humor. "You agree? Don't you guys realize what this will do to her?"

"Maybe," Sterling says. "But maybe not. We shouldn't discredit her without giving her a chance. She's proven how strong she is. And for Cade? For any of us? That girl would walk through fire and come out on the other side smiling."

She would. And knowing her, it will only make her even stronger. I have to let her do this. No matter how much I hate it. No matter how much I'll end up blaming myself for any pain she has to go through. If I don't let her, something will break within her—between us—that we'll never be able to repair.

I release a breath, shoulders slumping in defeat, and step out into the night. She's standing barefoot in the grass, arms wrapped around her middle, staring up at the stars. Even from here I can see her shivering. Stubborn woman. I cross the yard and wrap my arms around her, pulling her back against my chest. Her skin is chilled, and I do my best to warm it with my own body.

My magic surfaces on its own, weaving through her hair and caressing her bare arms in faint warmth. She holds herself stiff at first, then relaxes, letting her head rest against my shoulder. I can't help but smile, knowing I'll always have this. No matter what's happening between us, I'll always have her.

I place a kiss on her temple, lingering for a few seconds just to inhale her scent. "I'm sorry, love. I hope you know I never intentionally made you feel that way." She says nothing, but nods her head. "I didn't realize that's what I was doing, but I see it now. And I'm so sorry. I never want you to feel like you're just an object. Nothing could be further from the truth."

She turns in my arms, buries her face in my t-shirt, and I hold her a little tighter, hoping I can convey just how sorry I am. "I know you guys don't mean to do it." Her words are muffled, swallowed up by the fabric of my shirt. "I just wish you would take a few seconds to collect yourselves before you act. You didn't even give my idea any thought before shooting it down. All because of how *you* felt about it."

"Yeah. You're right." I pull back far enough to look in her eyes. It breaks my heart to see them so sad. "I need to do better. This is still so new for all of us, and we're all still learning. That's no excuse, I know, but ..." I trail off and shrug.

"Thank you for realizing it," she whispers before snuggling against me again.

I wish I could let her stay like that, but I need to be looking at her for what I have to say next. Pushing her away gently, I tilt her head up with my thumbs under her chin. "I don't like this idea of yours. I don't agree with it. But we can do it. As long as we talk it through and have a solid plan."

Her amber eyes light up, and how she can be so excited for this to happen is beyond me. "Thank you."

"Let's go inside and warm up. We have a lot to talk about."

She nods and threads our fingers together before heading back inside. Kai looks grumpy, arms crossed over his chest and brows drawn down over his gray eyes. Eyes that have the barest ring of red around the iris. This isn't going to be easy on him. Instead of taking a seat, I grab a bottle of blood bourbon and a bottle of regular bourbon from the kitchen and bring them back to the living room. Kai snags the bottle from me and twists the top off with quick bursts of aggressive movement. I open mine much more calmly and offer it to Sterling first.

"I think there are a couple holes in this plan we need to solve before any of us agree to it." Even though we've all caved and know this is going to happen, whether we like it or not. "The biggest issue I see with this is that it doesn't impact Thomas at all."

"Cade's right," Sterling says, handing me the bottle of bourbon. "There is no proof he was aware of what was happening."

Ellis slumps on the couch, and grabs the bourbon from me. "So this idea was pointless afterall," she mumbles. My lips twitch as she takes a big swallow and grimaces, spluttering the entire time the liquid slides down her throat.

"Not pointless," I say, snagging the bottle back. "We just have to find a different angle."

"We need to make it look like Kennedy released the video," Kai grumbles. "Fuck, why am I offering advice when I don't want this to happen."

Sterling sits up. "What do you mean?"

Kai sighs and rubs his eyes, taking a large swallow of his bourbon. The red around his irises looks a little more pronounced, like he's fighting to keep the monster in check. "We tell Kennedy he has to free Cade's mom and sister. If he doesn't, we'll release the video and make it look like *he* released it. Besides Ellis, the only other person impacted would be Sam. I can't imagine he'd be thrilled with the public seeing that side of him."

"He'd go after Kenndy so fast," Sterling agrees. "That would work. Can you make that happen?" he asks, looking at me.

I nod. "Yeah, I can hack into his email and send it from his account. But all this depends on if I can even get access to the footage."

"Ellis," Sterling says firmly, waiting for her to look at him. "I need to make sure you understand. If Kennedy doesn't agree to our demand, we *have* to release the video. If we don't, it will discredit us in the future if we need something else from him."

Ellis takes a deep breath and nods. "Yeah, I understand. I'm prepared for the video to be released." Even though her shoulders are pulled back and her back is straight, she grabs the bourbon from me and takes another large gulp.

Sterling studies her for a moment before nodding. "And if we release the footage and Sam finds out it was us, he won't hesitate to take revenge on you. Including killing your sister."

Her face pales, and her grip on the bourbon bottle tightens until her knuckles are white. "I understand," she breathes.

"Do you really?" His icy blue gaze pierces her. "Because the consequences of going through with this are pretty big. And they all impact you. Are you absolutely sure you want to do this?"

"Yes. I want to do this," she says confidently.

I release a breath and push up from the couch. "Okay. Let's see if I can access the footage."

THREE HOURS and two bottles of bourbon later, I have the footage downloaded to a thumb drive. Ellis is sitting on the swing on the porch, talking to Allie on the phone. And thank goodness. I did my best to keep the footage from playing too much, and I tried my hardest to not watch it. But fuck. I saw enough, and I've never been so keyed up before.

By Kai's stillness, I know he saw some of it, too. I close the laptop and risk a glance in his direction. Ruby red eyes stare at the back of Ellis's head, and while pissed doesn't begin to describe his expression, he also looks heartbroken at the same time. A volatile mixture of emotions I feel as well.

I push up from the couch and run my hands through my hair. Anxious energy courses through me, leaving me jittery and unable to sit still. I can't keep my gaze from traveling to my soul-bonded. Even through the closed window, the occasional laugh filters through. How she survived so long with that fucking piece of shit bastard, I'll never know. And to think that after everything she survived she even wants our touch is a wonder in itself.

Her curly brown hair is in its usual messy bun on top of her head. Stray curls have escaped, wild and untamed. A lioness. That's what she is. Courageous even in the face of her fears. Fiercely protective of those she loves. Possessing a strength I will never be able to comprehend. And she's mine.

I rub my chest, trying to ease the mixture of emotions. I don't understand how one person can make me feel so many things. Love. Pain. Fear. Awe. This woman has completely taken over my life, and I wouldn't want it to be any other way.

"I'll never be able to thank her for this," I whisper to no one in particular.

Sterling shifts in the chair, setting his phone in his lap. "I don't think she wants you to thank her. This is what being a family means. We do whatever we have to for each other and expect nothing in return."

Family. Kai and Sterling have been my family since I lost mine. I know it has been the same for Sterling as well. But with the addition of Ellis, the idea of family has shifted. It's not just me and my brothers anymore. It's no longer late nights, drugs, alcohol, and sex. Well, it's still sex. Now it's sex with Ellis. And Kai. It's nights spent cuddled in bed, memories being made, and … living. And when all of this bullshit we have to deal with is over? I smile. Then we can really live. The four of us. One big happy family. I can't fucking wait.

"So when we rescue your mom and sister …" Kai stops to clear his throat. He's on edge, leg bouncing hard enough to rattle the empty bottle of bourbon on the coffee table. The monster is itching to escape. "Where are they going to go?"

I appreciate that he says *when,* not *if.* "There isn't enough room here," I say, glancing at the ceiling and the one bedroom above it. This place is barely big enough for the four of us. "And I sold the house after my dad died. All I have left is my apartment in the city."

"They can stay at my mom's," Sterling offers. "She has a few empty rooms, and I know she wouldn't mind. Besides, we have no idea what condition they'll be in. My mom will be able to care for them if they need it."

That thought makes me nauseous. Since Kennedy called and threatened their lives, I haven't allowed myself to think about what could have happened to them, or what could be happening currently. If I give it too much thought, I'll lose it.

"Thanks. I appreciate that."

Sterling brushes off my thanks. "I assume you want to leave first thing in the morning?"

I nod. "I don't want to wait too long."

"If you're okay with it, I don't think I'm going to go. I'm not sure it would be appropriate for the alpha of the Iron Shadows pack to get involved in a personal matter, no matter how much I want to. I can head to my moms and help her get things ready, though."

"That's fine," I say, nodding. "I get it. Kai and I can handle this."

"But if something happens, call me. She is still my mate, and I'll do whatever I have to to protect her."

I nod again and glance at Kai. He's staring at Ellis through the window again, eyes practically glowing. "Kai, are you okay?"

He doesn't answer, but a soft growl rumbles in his chest. The tips of his fangs are visible, even with his mouth closed. The monster is riding him hard.

"Sterling, why don't we go ... somewhere else," I say, tipping my head in Kai's direction.

Sterling smirks and pushes to his feet. "Yeah, sure."

ELLIS

The porch door swings open and Cade and
Sterling step out into the night.

"Hey, Allie? I'll call you tomorrow, okay?" I hang up before
she even responds. The nerves that disappeared while I was
talking to her come back in full force. "Is everything alright?" I
press my hands to my stomach in an attempt to quell the
tumbling.

Cade sits next to me on the swing while Sterling leans against
the railing, arms crossed over his chest.

"I was able to get the footage," Cade says quietly. "I
downloaded it to a thumb drive, and deleted the original footage
from the server it was stored on. We now have the only copy of it."

For now. If Thomas doesn't agree to release Cade's family,
then who knows how many copies of that footage will be created
and saved to various devices. The thought makes me double over,
and I swallow back the bile that burns up my throat.

"Ellis, it's not too late to change your mind." Cade rubs my
back, and as much as I want to shy away from his touch, I force
myself to sit still. "Just say the word and I'll destroy that thumb
drive so no one will ever see it."

It's so fucking tempting. But Cade's mom and sister's lives are at stake, and I don't know any other way to get them back. I will shred myself into millions of pieces to keep Cade happy. To keep all of my guys happy. They have done nothing but ensure my safety and happiness. It's the least I can do.

I take a deep breath and sit up, squaring my shoulders. "I'm not changing my mind."

Cade's eyes dart back and forth as he takes in my expression. Finally, he sighs. "I didn't think you would."

"Cade and I are going to talk to my mom about letting his family stay with her. We'll be back shortly." Sterling pushes away from the railing and leans down, grabbing my chin and kissing me. "I love you, kitten."

"Can I come?" I ask. I'd love to get another chance to talk to Shari.

Cade shakes his head. "You need to stay here. Kai is ... on edge." He glances behind me through the window, and it takes all my self control to not look over my shoulder. Cade leans in to whisper in my ear, his breath making me shiver. "Help our boy calm down." After a quick kiss on the cheek, he leaves with Sterling, taking Kai's Hummer.

I watch until the taillights disappear down the mountain, but before I can stand up to head inside, the front door opens, swinging so hard on its hinges it bangs into the wall and rebounds. I jump and slap my hand over my chest, my heart thumping madly under my palm.

"Geez, Kai. You scared me!" I narrow my gaze at him, and a thrill runs through me, tempering the shock.

His eyes glitter like rubies as he stares at me. He's so still, his supernatural otherness blatantly obvious. And being the sole focus of that intense gaze makes me squirm.

"Get inside," he growls.

I know I shouldn't. I know he's on edge and the monster is rearing its head, but I can't help myself. Besides, giving the monster something to focus on, other than what we're going to do tomorrow, will be good. "Why?" My lips quirk in a small, teasing smile.

I didn't think it was possible, but he stiffens further, every muscle tensing to the point of vibration. A rumbling growl echoes in his chest and he curls his top lip, revealing those dangerously sexy fangs. My core tightens in response and I swallow, causing Kai's gaze to drop to my neck.

"Inside. Now." His words are guttural as he grounds them out, and his eyes flash dangerously.

I cock my head to the side and cross my arms. "I don't want to." The sass is strong tonight, and no wonder. After deciding to use that footage, I need to reclaim a sense of ownership over my life.

Kai growls and takes a step toward me. His steps are measured and steadied, each one thumping on the wooden porch. My heart beats in time with them, increasing until he stops in front of me.

"That wasn't a suggestion, little bird," he says, voice low and shivering over my skin. "You can play the brat all you want, I have all the time in the world. It will only increase your punishment."

I tilt my head up to meet his burning red gaze and raise one eyebrow. Daring. Challenging. Pissing off the monster even more.

Kai bares his fangs, running his tongue along one. "Get. Inside. Now."

I smile sweetly. "Make me."

I barely have time to blink before Kai sweeps me off my feet and throws me over his shoulder. I squeal as the world spins, and Kai turns to head for the door.

"You'll regret that, little bird."

A giggle climbs up my throat and Kai's back tenses. "I hope so."

He drops me just inside the cabin, making sure I slide down his body, rubbing against every inch of him. I bite my lip to keep a sigh from escaping.

On instinct, as soon as he lets me go, I turn and run. I have no direction in mind, and I know I won't get far, but the thrill of the chase is what it's all about.

A hand wraps around my ankle, and I scream as I fall face first toward the floor. Of course, with his vampire speed and strength, Kai manages to wrap his arms around me to prevent me from hitting the floor too hard.

Still, the breath is knocked from my lungs in shock. Kai digs his hand into my hair and tugs me to my knees, my scalp prickling with his motions. Keeping his hold on my hair, he walks around to face me and angles my head so I can look at him.

"On your knees," he mutters. "Exactly where I like you."

My gaze travels from his face, down his chest hidden by his shirt, to the prominent bulge in his pants. I lick my lips in anticipation.

"By the time I'm done with you, little bird, you'll know exactly who owns you."

Ah, so that's what this is about. Under normal circumstances, I wouldn't tolerate someone saying they own me. But, in all reality, these guys do own me. They own my heart and my soul. Every breath I breathe is theirs. And I know, in return, they are mine.

And right now, Kai needs that reminder. He may not agree with me threatening to release the footage, but he'll do it because I want to. However, it causes the predator in him to come out. He needs to make sure I know no one will ever be able to claim me again.

I reach up and tuck my fingers under the waistband of his sweats, but he swats me away. With one hand on my chin, fingers digging in to force my mouth open, he pulls his pants down. His cock springs free and he wraps his free hand around it, tracing my lips with the head. The piercing at the tip is cool against my lips.

"Open up, little bird. Swallow me down like a good girl." His fingers tighten, almost to the point of pain.

Something dark inside of me enjoys it. Maybe all that time I spent in darkness, all the hurt and betrayal, have changed me. Maybe the claws of darkness have sunk deep and haven't let go. Or maybe it's just because I trust my guys without question. Whatever it is, I don't mind the pain and dark words. In fact, I find I'm enjoying it.

I open my mouth and let Kai slide his cock inside. He groans softly when I close my mouth around him and suck. The noises he makes send heat straight to my core, and I try to close my legs to ease the growing ache.

Kai tugs my hair, sending more pain coursing through my veins. "Eyes on me, little bird."

I look at Kai through my lowered lids and find his glowing red gaze burning straight into me. I can't take it anymore. I want to feel him touching me. I want him to kiss me, to lick me, to make me scream with pleasure.

"Kai, please," I say, pulling back as much as I can with his fist tangled in my hair.

That evil, crooked grin displays fangs I want buried in my neck. "I don't think so, little bird. Did you forget you're being punished?"

Damn. As much as I enjoy being a brat, I hate the punishment when he refuses to do what I want. But, I know exactly how to get around that.

"You say you own me." My hands slide up his thighs and over his hips, fingers trailing in the grooves of his abs. "Show me."

His eyes flash, and I know I have him. Kai steps out of his pants and grabs me by my waist. The world spins as he throws me over his shoulder and my breath whooshes out of me from it digging into my stomach.

He carries me upstairs and drops me onto the bed. "Take off your clothes, little bird. Let me see you."

He idly strokes himself as I shimmy out of the shirt and undies I threw on when I woke up. That dark look, eager and ready to devour me, makes my heart pound, and anticipation swirls in my gut. I lay back against the pillows and let my legs fall to the sides.

Kai pounces before I stop moving. His fingers bite into my thighs and spread my legs more. The first swipe of his tongue makes me gasp. The sheets bunch in my tightened fists and I lift my hips, silently begging for more.

He gives me more. He gives me everything I could ever ask for. This man knows how to use his tongue. I'm standing on the precipice, ready to fall over the edge when Kai drags one of his fangs over my clit.

My back arches and I scream his name as I come. Waves of pleasure wash through me like a fire consuming a forest. Kai brings me through every last wave, and when he finally lifts his head, his lips glisten with my release.

"That's right, little bird. Only I can make you come that hard."

It's on the tip of my tongue to tell him that's not entirely true, but before I can even think about saying it, he lifts himself over me. Surrounded by Kai, a sense of safety settles within me. He could do anything he wanted to me, and I'd let him. I know he'd never hurt me.

I slide my fingers into his dark hair and tug him down until our lips meet. I can taste myself on his tongue. "Own me, Kai," I say against his mouth. "Make me yours again."

"With pleasure, little bird."

Kai slams home in one thrust. My body accepts him like I was made for him. He sets a punishing rhythm, and I find myself lifting my hips to meet his. If he owns me, I also own him. I may not be able to bite him to mark him, but I have nails, and they work just as well. I claw down his back, loving the way he jerks and moans when I do it.

"Fuck, little bird. You drive me wild."

As much as I love when the monster comes out to play, I want Kai back. So I tip my head to the side, exposing my mark and giving him the nudge he needs.

Kai's fangs lengthen and he sinks them into my skin. The bite of pain quickly disappears, replaced by euphoric pleasure. Every nerve ending lights up. Each place our bodies touch becomes hypersensitive. One brush of his cock on that secret spot inside me is all it takes.

My orgasm overcomes me. I cry out and dig my nails into his back again as my body shakes and comes undone. Kai pulls away from my neck, licking the excess blood away and then kisses me. Copper blooms in my mouth as I taste my blood on his tongue, and I moan.

Kai thrusts one more time and his body shudders over mine, a soft groan climbing up his throat as he orgasms.

I could curl up and close my eyes, my body is worn out and used up. But Kai pulls away, gray eyes meeting mine.

"I'm sorry, baby girl," he whispers, rubbing his thumb along my lower lip.

I give him a sleepy smile and tug him down on top of me. "Don't apologize for great sex."

He chuckles, but rolls over so he can look at me. "I got worked up about the video thing. I couldn't help myself from trying to show you that I own you. And I don't think that I own you."

"It's okay, Kai." I kiss him gently and lay my head on his shoulder. "I think you kind of do own me. And I own you in return."

"Yeah?"

I can hear the hesitation and concern in his voice, and it breaks my heart. I never want him to think he's hurting me in any way. "Yeah," I say. "You're my Shield. I'm your beloved. It's not so much ownership as in owning an object. You're not an object to me. It's more like, I own a piece of you and you own a piece of me. A piece I have willingly given you."

He hums, the sound vibrating his chest under my ear. "I like that."

"I like you," I say with a smile.

He chuckles. "I like you more."

A groan from the doorway draws our attention. "Sorry to interrupt gag me hour," Sterling drawls. "But Allie and Connor are downstairs."

CADE

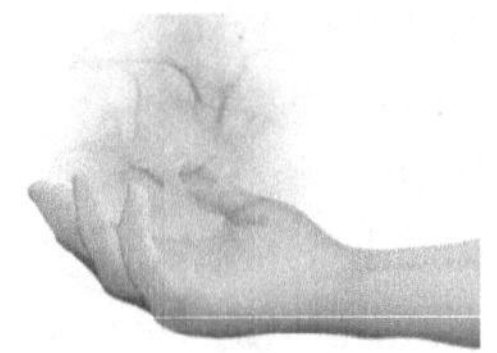

I climb into the back seat of the Hummer, deciding to let Kai drive his car for once. Really, I'm too nervous to drive. My focus is turned inward, on what I'm about to do with Ellis and thoughts of my family.

How are they? Are they healthy? How will this affect them mentally? What if we can't even rescue them?

All those questions, and then some, cloud my mind and take the forefront of my attention. I'll probably crash the Hummer if I drive. Through the open door, I watch Sterling approach Ellis.

"Are you sure you're okay with me not going?" He asks, cupping her cheek. "I'll risk it. For you, I'd risk anything."

"I'll be fine. I promise. Go help your mom. Allie texted me and told me her and Connor are there already. She has everything she'll need, medicine wise. And Connor is laying down some wards. He figured both you and Cade would appreciate the extra protection for your families."

Sterling hesitates a second, but Ellis stands on her tiptoes and kisses him. Without giving him a chance to say anything else, she climbs into the backseat with me, scooting over until she can clasp my hand tightly in hers. It's not a lot, but to me, it's everything.

Just knowing she's here, willing to sacrifice so much for me and my family, it makes me all warm and wiggly feeling inside.

Kai climbs into the driver's seat and glares in the rearview mirror. "I feel like a fucking chauffeur with you both back there."

We drive through the city and I notice Ellis staring in wonder. It's been awhile since we've been here. She's been cooped up on that mountain for a long time. When this is all over, we'll have to plan a date night downtown.

The buildings look the same to me. Gray. Tall. Imposing. Suffocating. I never realized how much I hate the city until now. After spending so much time on the mountain, I'm not sure I could return to city life. It's too hectic. Too fast. It's too easy to lose sight of the important things in the hustle and bustle.

"Wow," Kai says, tugging his hat lower over his eyes. "I don't miss this." A car pulls in front of the Hummer, causing Kai to slam on the brakes and lay on the horn. "Motherfucker! I'm driving a fucking tank! I'll destroy you in your fancy sports car."

"Road rage much?" Ellis mutters.

"I think I hate the city," Kai says, ignoring Ellis's barb.

I snort. "I was just thinking that."

"I don't mind it," Ellis says, looking out the window. "At least for short periods of time."

I clear my throat and turn to face Ellis. "I was thinking, when all of this is over, we could have the cabin renovated. Update it, add on some rooms. As long as it's okay with Sterling. It's on pack lands so he'd be set. Kai can commute to work, it's not that bad of a drive. We could all live there ... if you wanted."

Ellis's eyes light up and she sucks in a hopeful breath. "Really?"

I nod and smile. "Yeah. Obviously we'd have to clear all of that with Sterling, since it's technically his family's."

"I would love that," she breathes, her fingers tightening around mine.

By the time we pull up to the Kennedy building, silence has once again settled heavily atop us. Oppressive, almost, in the way it makes it difficult to breathe. The severity of what we're doing, the impact this could have on Ellis, hangs thick in the air.

Kai pulls the Hummer to the side of the road and cuts the engine. "Okay, I'll wait in the car. You know what to do if you need help."

Before Ellis can climb out, Kai reaches back and grabs her wrist, tugging her between the front seats. "Be careful, Ellis. Try to keep your powers hidden, but if you or Cade end up in trouble, don't hesitate to use them to save yourselves."

"I won't." she promises. With a quick kiss for Kai, she hops out of the Hummer, and I follow her.

"Nervous?" I ask, taking her hand and climbing the steps.

"Actually, I'm not. I'm looking forward to bossing him around for once."

I chuckle. "That's my girl."

We push into the lobby of the Kennedy building and turn toward the elevators. My fingers shake as I press the button for the top floor, and Ellis squeezes my hand tighter. The ride to the top seems like it takes forever and no time at all. My foot taps restlessly on the marble floor until the door opens and the elevator dings.

"Here we go," she mutters, dragging me out and into the hallway.

The elevator opens into a small lobby with a secretary and a few chairs in a waiting room. The secretary sits behind a large desk and smiles. Before she can say anything, Ellis storms past and heads straight for Kennedy's office, ignoring the woman's protests.

I'm amazed at Ellis's determination. I see no fear, no worry, no trepidation on her face. Her shoulders are pulled back and her chin is lifted. I wouldn't be surprised to find her eyes shining with her golden fire.

Her courage and strength when it comes to her Shields is heartwarming.

She knocks three times on the office door, then shoves it open. Inside, Thomas Kennedy sits at his desk, reigning over the room like a corrupt king. His eyes widen and he jerks back as Ellis and I enter.

"Hello *father*," Ellis says, voice thick with sarcasm. "I hope you're doing well."

"What are you doing here? Why did my secretary let you in?" He pushes up from the desk, but Ellis stops him.

"Sit down." Her tone is firm and unyielding, and a pulse of something—magic maybe—makes her words even more powerful.

I blink at the ferocity of her tone. A fucking lioness indeed.

Kennedy gapes for a moment, then smiles. It's twisted and dark, but he sits with his arms crossed over his chest, leaning back in his chair. With a raised brow, he asks, "What can I do for you today?"

"You can release Cade's mom and sister," Ellis says. She widens her feet like she's preparing for a fight and I have to bite back a smile.

Kennedy snorts. "Sure. What are you going to give me in return?"

This time, Ellis scoffs. "Like I'd ever give you anything again. Sick bastard."

"Then we are at an impasse," Kennedy shrugs. "I'm sorry you've wasted your time."

Ellis says nothing. She motions to me, and I take the flash drive out of my pocket, holding it between my pointer and middle fingers.

"I think we have something that might change your mind," I say quietly, forcing the nausea down. This is it. The moment that could break Ellis.

"Camera footage, pulled from the security system at your house. Footage from my bedroom, containing every horrific thing Sam did to me." Her voice trembles slightly, but her shoulders remain straight. Pride courses through me. I never once doubted her strength, but she always surprises me. Just when I think she couldn't handle any more, she does.

Kennedy's eyes narrow. "And I suppose you will threaten to release that footage if I don't release Cade's family?" Neither of us respond, but our silence is answer enough. Kennedy barks a laugh. "I don't see how that will affect me at all. You have no proof I had anything to do with that. Go ahead and release it."

I give Kennedy a small smile, one I know doesn't reach my eyes. "The footage might not affect you. But I'm sure Sam Morris won't be too happy to hear *you've* leaked it. Ruining his pristine reputation." I tsk and shake my head.

Kennedy's gaze shoots to me, suspicion and a tiny bit of fear shining through.

"Go ahead, check your email drafts." I nod toward his computer with a smug grin.

Kennedy pulls up his email and frowns. In his drafts is an email to all the news stations, tabloids, and gossip mills. An email with the footage ready to be shared with the public.

Before he can move the mouse an inch to delete it, I freeze his hand with my magic, giving it a little extra zap in the process.

"This isn't the only copy we have of this," Ellis says. "Even if you deleted that email, we'd get it out there. And I just know how pissed Sam will be when everyone finds out how much of a jackass he really is. And to think, it was all your fault the world found out ..."

Kennedy grinds his teeth together, muscles flexing in his frozen hand. "6428 Mercer Street. Room 3. 928834 is the code to the door."

Ellis smiles sweetly and nods her head. "I knew you'd see it our way."

I toss the flash drive on the desk and turn to follow Ellis, saying over my shoulder. "It's blank, by the way. There is nothing on that drive."

Kennedy's growl makes me chuckle, and I follow Ellis into the hallway, pulling out my phone to delete the unsent message in Kennedy's email before I release my magic.

"Did you get the address?" she asks, peering up at me.

I nod numbly. "Yeah."

She wraps her arms around my waist and lends me her strength as we return to the main floor.

"Hey, can you do me a favor?" I ask as we walk through the lobby to the main doors. A curl has fallen forward and is hiding her eyes from me. A strand of my magic creeps out and tucks it behind her ear before I can stop it. "Can you please let Sterling take you back to his mom's?"

She slows, pulling me to a stop with her. "You don't want me to help you rescue them?" The hurt is evident in her voice, and it breaks me.

"It's not that I don't want your help." I take her face in my hands and rub my thumb along her cheeks. "There is just going to be a lot going on. I'll have not only your safety to worry about, but my mom and sister's as well. Not to mention, I'm sure they are going to be overwhelmed. It might be easier for them if it's just me and Kai."

She bites her bottom lip, scanning my face like she thinks I'm lying. "Okay," she says quietly. "I'll help Allie and Shari."

She tries to turn away but I stop her. "Hey. I can't wait for you to meet them. I just don't know how things are going to go or what state we'll find them in."

"I understand. Just please be careful."

I nod and send a quick text to Sterling, asking him to come pick up Ellis. And then we wait.

———

I stand outside the house—well, more like an apartment complex—and take deep breaths. Looking at the building, you'd never guess there was anything nefarious going on inside. It matches the rest of the buildings on the street. Lower income, could use some work, but normal. If I were to guess, there is a ton of spell work on the building to keep people away.

"Ready?" Kai asks, squeezing my hand.

I appreciate having him with me. I know he'll support me, protect my family, and make sure everything goes smoothly while I try my hardest to focus.

I exhale and nod. "Yeah. Let's do this."

As we approach the front door, it opens, revealing a guard dressed in gray and black fatigues. He scowls at us, but lets us through. Kennedy must have notified him.

I throw a protective shield around me and Kai so we don't have to spend so much energy watching our backs. It will drain me quickly, though, so we have to move fast.

"What's the number?" Kai asks, looking around with a frown.

"Three."

We stop in front of a solid wooden door with an electronic keypad next to it. My finger trembles as I punch the code in.

Kai pushes through first, head swiveling back and forth, blocking my view with his body. He doesn't move until he determines there is nothing for me to see that will hurt me.

My heart beats a mile a minute as I step inside. It's a small apartment, the kitchen and living space one area. A door to the left probably leads to a bed and bathroom. It's sparsely furnished, dust on every surface, and cobwebs hanging from the ceiling.

A rattling cough sounds from the bedroom, and I take a step in that direction. Time seems to slow down, like I'm walking through waist deep mud but also speeding along on a moving walkway. It takes forever and no time at all to reach the entrance. The door has been removed, and I distantly realize the rest have as well.

Huddled on the bed, wrapped in a comforter is my sister. She hovers over my mother, who is bundled in so many blankets I can barely see her. Another rattling cough, and the figure under the blankets jerks with each one.

"Mom? Chloe?" Their names are mere whispers, but they sound loud in silence.

Chloe's head whips in my direction. Blue eyes widening in

shock. "Cade?" Her voice is hoarse, like she's unused to talking. Or has done a lot of screaming.

Tears blur my vision of her, and it doesn't take long for them to fall down my cheeks. I shakily step into the room, each breath I take harsh and uneven. I've imagined this moment for so long, but I never actually thought it would happen. I'm in the same room as my mom and sister. I'm going to get them out of here.

"Are you guys okay?" I rasp.

She shakes her head. "Mom is really sick. They won't give us any medicine."

My heart sinks, but I fortify my resolve. I can fall apart later. Right now, I need to get them to Allie. "I'm getting you out of here," I say and walk to the bed. "Come on."

Chloe is skin and bones under my arm. I help her stand, trying to ignore the way her body trembles from cold and weakness.

"What about mom?" she asks, voice shaking.

"Kai, can you carry her?" I ask.

Kai is already scooping my mom into his arms, careful to keep her wrapped in the blankets. A breathy whimper, followed by more coughing, makes me grit my teeth.

"Got her," Kai says. "Let's go."

We hurry through to the front door as fast as Chloe can manage. I'm supporting her more than she's holding herself up, and we make slow progress.

The guard continues to scowl at us, and we brush past him and head for the Hummer. My chest is tight with my held breath, and I don't release it until Kai takes off down the street.

"Am I dreaming?" Chloe whispers.

I look behind me and my eyes fill with tears again. She looks so haggard. Her brown hair dull and matted. She looks around, her mouth trembling and hands clutched in front her. When was the last time she saw the outside world? 83 years ago? So much has changed since then, I can't imagine how overwhelming this must be for her.

"Chloe," I say. "You're safe now. I'm taking you to a friend's house. There is a nurse waiting, and she'll take care of you and mom."

"I'm not dreaming?" she repeats.

I shake my head, swallowing thickly. "You're not dreaming."

She covers her face and sobs. I resist climbing in the back seat to comfort her. It's been 83 years since we saw each other. So instead, I give her a small smile and turn back around.

We did it. We saved my family, and Ellis didn't have to release that footage. I exhale and Kai reaches over the center console to squeeze my thigh.

"Thank you, Kai."

"Anytime."

ELLIS

"Quit looking at your phone," Allie chides. "They'll get back when they get back."

I sigh and set my phone on the counter. "Sorry. I'm just not used to not being there when they're in danger."

She gives me a sympathetic smile, her blue eyes filled with compassion. "Keep busy. It will take your mind off things."

I grumble under my breath, but fill another bucket with hot water. Before I can lift it and trudge up the stairs with it, a large hand reaches over my shoulder and grabs the handle.

"I can carry it," Cole says, lifting the bucket effortlessly.

I watch him carry it upstairs and turn back to Allie. "Now what? He took my job."

She opens her mouth, but a buzz sounds through the house. With a smile she gestures to the laundry room. "You can fold blankets."

We've been hustling all morning to make sure we have everything we could possibly need for Cade's family's arrival. Not knowing what condition they will be in, we are preparing for everything.

My stomach knots thinking of the worst possible scenarios

and how they will affect Cade. I know Kai is with him and can comfort him if needed, but it still seems like I should be there too.

Snapping in front of my face draws me out of my head. "Earth to Ellis," Allie coos.

"Sorry." I shake my head and turn to the laundry room.

The blankets are warm and smell like a fresh breeze with a hint of pine. I bury my nose in them, inhaling the scent that somehow still clings to Sterling despite him having not lived here in ages. It soothes the nervous part of me, and my shoulders relax.

Allie and I sit on the couch and fold the blankets and sheets. She keeps one eye on me like she's making sure I don't fall apart or run out of the house and head straight for the city.

"I'm fine, Allie. You don't have to keep staring at me."

"I can't help it," she cracks a smile. "You're just so sexy."

"Watch it," Sterling growls, descending the stairs. "She's taken."

"And so are you, Allie" Connor chimes in behind him.

Despite their stern faces, their eyes are alight with humor. Sterling approaches me and leans down, brushing a kiss against my lips.

"Cade texted me just now," he says. "They're on their way back with his mom and sister."

I gasp. "Really? Did he say anything else?"

"No. But they should be here in about forty minutes."

I release a breath and sink back into the couch. "I hope they're okay. At least as okay as they can be." I move a pile of folded blankets to the laundry basket, and Sterling sits on the arm of the couch. "Have you ever met them?" I ask.

He shakes his head. "By the time we met Cade, they had already been held captive for a few years. He didn't start working for Kennedy until his dad died."

Given everything that's about to happen and not knowing their wellbeing, I can't help but feel a tinge of nerves. Meeting Cade's mom and sister is a big deal, and we'll be meeting under extreme circumstances.

Sterling catches on to my change in mood, and I don't know if it's the bond, his wolf, or just him being able to read me, but he seems to know exactly where my thoughts traveled.

"They'll love you, Ellis. My mom fell in love with you the second she met you. And you managed to worm your way into Cole's heart pretty damn quickly. I have no doubt Cade's family will be the same."

Sterling tucks a curl behind my ear and kisses me again. He lingers a second longer, despite Allie and Connor talking softly with each other at the opposite end of the couch.

The front door opening draws us apart, and Sterling hops up to help Shari carry grocery bags in.

"They're on their way back," he tells his mom. "Connor and I moved the beds around upstairs so they will both be in the same room. It'll be easier for Allie to take care of them if they're together."

"Good," Shari says. Ever since we came to her with the idea of bringing Cade's family here, she's been in go mode, making sure her house is ready and welcoming. "Cole, help me get some soup started."

The wait for them to arrive almost kills me. Even Sterling attempting to distract me doesn't keep me from pacing the living room. The scent of vegetables, spices, and herbs float through the house, making it even more welcoming. My stomach grumbles, the aroma enticing me, but the thought of eating makes my stomach clench uncomfortably.

Car doors opening and closing have me rushing to the front door. I throw it open and dart onto the porch. Cade helps a woman out of the backseat, and despite her haggard appearance and matted brown hair, the resemblance is clear. His sister.

My heart stops, though, when Kai lifts a blanket wrapped bundle from the back seat. A rattling cough sounds from the fabric, and Cade's pinched expression deepens.

"Sterling will show you to your room," I say, clutching my

stomach. I search his gaze for ... anything. His violet eyes are dim and clouded with worry. "Allie is up there too."

He nods and leads his sister inside, followed by Kai carrying his mom. I stand on the porch, unsure what to do now. I'm no use to them upstairs. I'll only get in the way. But standing on the porch, I feel so useless.

"Have you eaten yet today?" Cole asks, popping his head around the door frame.

His blue eyes study me, taking in everything from the worry pinching my eyes to the way I chew on my cheek. His eyes are so similar to Sterling's. I realize I'm staring and not answering his question, so I shake my head, cheeks heating.

He ushers me inside and to the kitchen table. "The least I can do is make sure you don't starve to death. Sterling will kill me if you do."

A steaming bowl of vegetable soup appears in front of me, the scent forcing itself up my nose. I swallow, my mouth suddenly watering.

"Here." Cole hands me a spoon and sits across from me. "It's strange. After all that hustle and bustle, and here we are. Sitting quietly in the kitchen with nothing to do."

"I feel so useless," I whisper.

He shakes his head. "Nah. Your skills will be needed later."

"And what skills are those?"

"Comforting Cade. When his adrenaline disappears, and he's exhausted from using his magic, it will be your job to care for him. To make sure he does what he needs to stay healthy."

"I guess," I mumble, between blowing on my soup to cool it. "I just feel like there should be ... more ... for me to do."

"Don't underestimate the power of your presence. Just being here is helping Cade more than you could know."

I nod, even though I'm still skeptical, and eat a spoonful of the soup. Damn. Shari can cook. This is the best vegetable soup I've ever had. It doesn't take long for me to get half the soup eaten, despite it burning my tongue. Once it hit my stomach, I realized how hungry I really was.

Cole clears his throat and rubs the back of his neck. "Hey, Ellis? While we're here, I wanted to thank you."

I choke on the mouthful I'd just taken, a piece of carrot getting stuck in my throat for a moment. "For what?" I finally rasp.

"For being honest with me. For forcing me to see the truth and giving me the encouragement to talk to Sterling." He shrugs, digging at the table with his nail and refusing to look at me. "I don't remember a lot from before he left, I was so young. But I remember the feeling of being lost for a long time. I idolized him when I was a pup. And when he left, I didn't understand why. I just knew that it hurt. And I let that hurt cloud my judgment when I was finally old enough to understand."

"Well, you're welcome. I just know what it's like to lose a sibling. And if I could do something to help you guys, I had to do it."

He nods, and we go back to eating our soup in silence. When I'm finished, I rinse my bowl and place it in the sink, turning around to find Kai descending the stairs. I rush toward him.

"How are ... things?" I ask.

Kai appears to deflate as he releases a breath, and he wraps me in his arms, burying his nose in my hair. "Mmm, you smell good," he mumbles.

"Kai." I poke him the ribs, attempting to get him back on track.

"Chloe is fine. She's just malnourished and exhausted. His mom ... well, I think it's like what happened to Sterling." He links our fingers together and leads me to the couch, sighing again as he sits down. None of us got a lot of sleep last night, and being awake during the day is disorienting. "Their magic was blocked by something that was fed to them. His mom is struggling to fight off an infection caused by a cold. Allie thinks she has pneumonia, and may possibly be septic. Cade and Connor have both tried healing her, but whatever is in her system, it's blocking their magic too. Allie gave her an IV for fluids and antibiotics, as well as a fever reducer. The hope is when her magic comes back, it will help her heal."

I bite my bottom lip, dread curling through me. "Oh gosh. What can I do? Can I do anything?"

"Cade is upstairs," Allie says, overhearing my questions as she comes down the stairs with Shari and Connor. All three of them sit in the living room with heavy sighs. Connor looks drawn and pale, like he used a lot of his magic helping Cade. "He could use you, I think."

I hop to my feet and dash up the steps before the last word leaves her lips. I find Cade sitting on the floor in the hallway. His knees are drawn to his chest, and his head rests on his folded arms across his knees. I kneel next to him, gently running my hand through his brown hair. He slowly turns his head to look at me. His violet eyes are the saddest I've ever seen them. A weight sits on him, heavy and suffocating, and it breaks my heart.

"Cade," I whisper. I sit on the floor next to him and wrap my arms around him. He buries his face in my chest and lets me hold him. I keep running my fingers through his hair, gently scraping my nails against his scalp.

It takes me a moment for me to realize he's crying. His body shakes with small, silent sobs. I hold him tighter, gently rocking back and forth, hoping I can be enough to calm him. He clings to me, wrapping his arms around my waist and crying into my middle. A song comes to me, one my mom used to sing when Gracie and I were upset or sick. The lyrics are just mist in my mind, but the melody is clear.

Softly, I hum the song while I hold my soul-bonded in my arms, giving him the only thing I can. Support. Love. A safe place to just let it all go. When his tears stop, I pull him to his feet and head toward Cole's bedroom. I saw him put clean sheets on his bed, and I've decided to commandeer it.

Cole's room is starkly bare. The white walls and cream carpet are clear of anything. His queen sized bed is covered in a simple navy blanket. It's more than enough for Cade to rest and recharge.

"Let's get you tucked into bed." I let go of his hand and he stumbles, until I grab his waist to steady him. "How much magic did you use?" I ask quietly, peering at his drawn face.

"Too much," he rasps. "But it wasn't enough." Red rimmed violet eyes look straight through me. Dark circles bloom under them, and his mouth is pulled into a deep frown.

"Oh, Cade." I clasp his cheeks, wiping away the tears still clinging to his skin. Lifting onto my toes, I press a soft kiss to his forehead. "Arms up." I drag his shirt over his head before pushing him onto the bed when he stumbles again. Kneeling on the floor, I tug off his shoes and help him swing his legs onto the mattress. "Come here," I say, patting the spot next to me after I climb on the bed.

Cade scootches over until his head rests on my lap and he wraps his arms around my thighs, using me like a body pillow. I lean against the headboard and run my fingers through his hair again.

"Get some sleep, Cade. I'll be here." My heart flutters as he sighs and his body relaxes, sleep already claiming him. Being able to offer him this safe spot means more to him than I ever realized.

I don't stop running my fingers through his hair. The memory of my mom doing the same for me, and the comfort it provided, drives me to keep going. I want to give him that comfort. The door opens and Kai and Sterling step into the room, quietly closing it behind them.

"Is he asleep?" Kai asks, almost whispering.

I nod, watching Kai take off his shirt and shoes before climbing into bed next to Cade, pressing a kiss to his temple. He gets as close as he can to me, pressing Cade tight between us, and I use my other hand to run my fingers through Kai's silken hair. He sighs and closes his eyes, a content smile on his lips.

"Allie just left," Sterling says. "She said she'll be back first thing tomorrow morning." He sits on my other side, still wearing his shirt and shoes. His hand grasps the back of my neck and pulls me toward him for a quick kiss. "Have you eaten?" he asks when he pulls away.

"Yes. Cole made sure I did."

A soft, rumbling chuckle echoes in his chest. "Good. I guess he can be trained after all."

My head falls to the side and I stare at my mate. "Why are you still wearing your shoes?"

"I'm going to meet some of the pack about a few wolves who've been causing some trouble."

I pout, hoping I can convince him to stay with us. I never really feel complete unless all of us are together. It's like some part of me is missing, and it leaves me just slightly off balance.

The smile he gives me tells me he sees my attempt, but has chosen to ignore it. "Get some sleep, kitten. This is technically our nighttime." He kisses me again, lingering a moment longer. Before I can try to deepen it, he pulls away. "I love you, Ellis."

"I love you too, Sterling," I whisper.

He disappears and I sigh, scooting down in the bed to lay my head on the pillow, doing my best to keep from jostling Cade. Still, he mumbles something and re-adjusts, snuggling against me even more. So much has happened today. I faced Thomas again. I threatened to release the footage of me with Sam. Cade rescued his family. My thoughts are so jumbled and overwhelming. There is still so much we have to do. I'm surprised to find my eyelids growing heavy, so I let them close and fall asleep with two of my three guys.

Ellis

The scent of bacon, coffee, and eggs greets me as I descend the steps the next morning. Somehow, Cade, Kai, and I slept all through the rest of the day, and the following night. Sterling joined us at some point, and I didn't even hear him climb into bed. When I left the room, Cade had already turned to Kai and they were snuggled with each other under the covers.

"Good morning," Shari says with a smile, whisk in hand. "Hungry?"

"Actually, I could really use some coffee."

"Not a big breakfast eater?" She digs through the cupboard and hands me a mug with the words "Ew, people" printed in large black letters.

I shake my head. "No. I rely solely on coffee first thing in the morning."

She smiles and hands me the mug. "Cream is in the fridge, sugar on the counter. I have to run a few errands, but the bacon and eggs are done, and there are fresh muffins in the oven. They'll be ready in a few minutes. Do you need anything while I'm out?"

"No, I'm good. Thanks though."

She leaves and I stand in the kitchen, inhaling the steam from my mug and letting it warm me from the inside out. When the oven beeps, I find an oven mitt and place the muffin pan on top of the stove to cool. They smell amazing, nice and golden brown on top with blueberries bursting inside. Shari sure can cook.

"Oh," a soft voice says behind me.

I whirl around to find Cade's sister standing in the kitchen with a blanket wrapped around her. Her brown hair is matted and tangled, hanging in a clump well past her shoulders. Her blue eyes are wide in her sunken eye sockets.

"Hi," I say, standing up straight and tucking a curl behind my ear. "Chloe, right? Would you like something to eat? There's muffins, bacon, eggs. And coffee."

Her throat works on a swallow and she eyes the mug in my hands. "I haven't had coffee in ... a very long time."

"Coffee it is, then." I smile and find a second mug for her. "Do you want anything to eat? These muffins look really good." I hand her the mug, noticing how skeletal her hands look as she cradles it between them.

Instead of answering, she does the same thing with her coffee that I did with mine. She lifts it to her face and inhales. When she opens her eyes, I swear I see tears shimmering along her lashes.

As she opens her eyes, Cade steps into the kitchen and stops. His eyes widen as they land on his sister. "Chloe," he rasps, stopping to clear his throat. "Are you okay?" He grimaces and shakes his head. "I mean, that was a stupid question. Of course you're—" he cuts off with a muttered curse, heat creeping up his neck.

I watch their encounter with my heart in my throat. I know how important this is to Cade, to finally have his family back. But, will they ever truly be 'back?' I have the same thoughts when I think about my sister, and I have to squash the despair that tries to overwhelm me.

Chloe gives Cade a small smile. "I'm ... okay."

He nods and glances around the room, like he's searching for something to do or say. His gaze lands on me and his shoulders drop, his feet bringing him toward me, probably on their own accord.

I give him an encouraging smile. "I'm sure Shari has some tea somewhere in this kitchen. Would you like some?"

He nods, but before I can turn around he pulls me against him. "Thank you," he whispers in my ear.

"Don't thank me. I'm happy to do whatever you need." I pull back and kiss him, just a quick peck since his sister is watching. "Is Kai still sleeping?" Turning for the cabinets, I search through them for tea.

"Sleeping like the dead," Cade replies, a slight smile to his voice.

I roll my eyes, even though he can't see with my back to him. "You are hilarious," I say drily.

"Oooh, my mom made muffins?" Cole asks as he joins us in the kitchen.

"She did. Do you guys have any ..." I trail off as I turn around, my question about tea forgotten when I take in the room.

Cole is frozen in the entryway to the kitchen. His body is tense, still like only a predator can be. Even though he's in his human form, I swear I can see his hackles raised along his neck. His icy blue gaze is locked on Chloe. Each breath he takes sounds loud and harsh in the sudden silence. He takes one step back. Then another. His pulse thrums under his skin hard enough even I can see it in his neck.

I glance at Chloe and frown. She's staring at her hands clasped tightly on the table in front of her, her eyes wide and filled with shock. Blue sparks, the same color as Cole's eyes, fizzle and hiss at her fingertips. They are weak and almost sickly looking, like she hasn't recovered her magic fully from whatever has been blocking it. Cade is tense, glancing between the two.

"Cole?" I ask, stepping around Cade to approach Cole. Cade stops me with a firm grip on my bicep. "Are you okay?"

He shakes his head, squeezing his eyes shut. When he opens

them again, he swallows. "She's my mate." His words rasp through the kitchen, and we all snap our attention to Chloe.

She lifts her head, blue eyes impossibly wide. A startled gasp escapes her open mouth.

Cole takes off, shoving past Cade and me, knocking a chair over, and finally pushing through the back door. He's already shifted into his black wolf before he hits the grass behind the house.

Chloe stands, her chair scraping across the linoleum, the sound loud in the silence. She rushes out of the kitchen and up the stairs without a word. Cade tries to follow, but I stop him.

"Give her some space," I say numbly and tug him to the living room. "Give her time to ... process that."

"Mate?" he repeats. "What the hell?"

"I just passed Chloe upstairs," Kai says, descending the steps. "Is everything okay?"

Cade shakes his head and rubs his eyes. Something between a groan and laugh climbs up his throat. "Fucking mate?"

Kai glances at me, sitting on my other side. "Is he okay? Does he need more rest?"

"Apparently Chloe is Cole's mate," I say, leaning against Kai's shoulder.

"Whoa. Really?" Kai looks around me toward Cade. "And you're not freaking out about this?"

Cade shrugs and huffs a breath. "I mean, she's been captured for so long, I don't feel like I have any room to say anything."

"She's still your sister, Cade. Now more than ever you should be protecting her," Kai counters. "She's been locked away for over 80 years. You think she's ready to take on a mate?"

I frown, brows pulling low over my eyes. "Wait a minute." I hold up my hand toward Kai and stand up so I can look at them both. "You're not going to do anything," I say to Cade. "It's her life. It's her decision to make. Neither of you will say anything to her to try and sway her decision." I cross my arms over my chest and narrow my gaze at them.

Kai smirks before tugging me back down onto the couch. "Of course it's her choice. But it's also Cade's place as head of their family to make sure Chloe is safe. That doesn't mean he wouldn't let her be with Cole."

I sit back and bite my bottom lip. Ever since Cole announced Chloe was his mate, questions have been swirling inside me.

Kai bumps my shoulder. "Don't hurt yourself thinking so hard."

"Don't be an ass." I elbow him hard enough he grunts. "Is it … is it possible for other races to procreate with each other? I mean I know mages can't with non-mages."

Kai stiffens and Cade whips his head in my direction. They both stare at me with wide eyes and open mouths, and I'm pretty sure neither of them are breathing.

"Um, should I not have asked that?" I glance back and forth between them, nerves suddenly fluttering to life in my belly.

Before either of them can answer, Sterling enters the house, surprisingly wearing a shirt. He notices us in the living room, and snags a piece of bacon before sitting across from us in the chair.

"How are you feeling Cade?" Sterling asks, eyeing the mage.

"Better. But, apparently my sister is your brother's mate."

Sterling nods. "Yeah. Cole called me. I just got back from talking with him."

"Is he okay?" I ask, leaning forward. "He seemed really upset when he left."

Sterling huffs. "He will be. Cole has a girlfriend. They've been dating for a few years apparently. But the moment he laid eyes on Chloe it was all over for him." His icy blue eyes land on me, shining with an inner light. "I know that feeling well," he says quietly.

On either side of me, Kai and Cade nod their agreement. My heart flutters like it always does when I realize the depth of their love for me.

"Before you got here, Sterling, Ellis had an interesting

question for us," Kai says, his gray eyes piercing me like a sharp knife.

"Oh?" Sterling raises one silver brow and settles into the chair.

Cade looks at me while he says, "She wants to know if it's possible for other races to procreate."

I learned first hand how the child of a mage and a shifter is essentially human. But what about vampires and shifters? Or any other combination?

Sterling whips his head in my direction, his expression matching Cade and Kai's when I asked the first time. "Why are you asking, Ellis?"

Heat warms my cheeks and I duck my head, using my hair as a shield. "I was just wondering," I mutter, picking at my nails and refusing to look at any of them.

"Just wondering, huh?" Kai says, grabbing my chin in his fingers and forcing me to meet his gaze. "You're wondering about our future, aren't you?"

I swallow, my throat tight and mouth dry. Shrugging, I pull my head free of his grasp and look back at my hands in my lap. Honestly, I hadn't been. Until now. I was just curious about Cole and Chloe. But Kai's question makes me wonder what will happen to us after we deal with Sam. I hadn't ever really thought about children. The brief window of peace I had with Sam didn't last long enough for me to dream. But now? With my Shields?

Sterling gets up and kneels in front of me, a small smile spreading across his face. "We've all thought about that, kitten. A lot." He waits for me to look at him, ducking his head slightly to meet my gaze. "And we all want it."

Kai squeezes my thigh and Cade rubs circles on my back. Some of the tightness in my chest eases as I realize I'm not the only one who's thinking about a family.

"But is it even possible?" I ask. "Cade is a mage, he can't have kids with a non-mage."

Kai sighs and sits back on the couch. "I can't either. Have kids with a non-vamp that is."

My heart sinks. That's two out of three. Two of my guys who I can't have children with. I force a smile to my face. "Well, it was just a thought anyway."

"What about shifters?" Cade asks Sterling.

Sterling watches me carefully. "Wolves have a higher chance of procreating with different races. Well, with humans and other shifters that is. Our pups are strong and stubborn, so it's more likely to be a successful pregnancy." His words don't give me the hope I think he wanted them to. "Don't forget, kitten, you're not normal by any means. I doubt there is any information about harpies and how it works with them. When this is all over, we can talk with Agatha. She might be able to give us some advice."

I nod and bite my lip, forcing my emotions deep inside. Not only will Kai pick up on them, but now is not the time to even be thinking of this. We still have so much to deal with. Starting a family should be the least of my concerns.

A knock on the front door and Allie popping her head inside luckily draws everyone's attention away from me. I hop off the couch and make a break toward her, desperately glad to see her at this particular moment.

"Allie!" I give her a hug, almost knocking her backward. "Thank gods you're here," I whisper so only she can hear.

"Is everything okay?" she asks, untangling herself from me.

I nod, heat creeping into my cheeks once again. "Yes. Just glad to have a distraction right now."

She raises one brow and gives me a look that says I need help, but she lets it drop. "How's your mom and sister, Cade?"

"Chloe is awake. She was downstairs not too long ago. I haven't checked on my mom yet."

"Okay. Well, let's go see if your magic did anything to help your mom yet. Ellis, come with us." Allie links her arm through mine.

I stop Cade before he can climb the stairs. "Are you up to it? You haven't eaten anything yet."

"You haven't eaten?" Kai's tone is laced with concern, and his gray eyes narrow on Cade.

"I'm good," Cade reassures us. "I'll eat in a little bit." He pushes past me and Allie and disappears upstairs before Kai can say anything else.

Upstairs, Chloe is sitting on her mom's bed, placing a fresh compress on her forehead. She glances at us, and I notice her relax when she realizes Cole isn't here.

"Hi Chloe. How are you feeling?" Allie asks, getting down to business.

Chloe shrugs. "I'm ... as okay as I can be."

"Can I scan you again?" Cade asks, purple light flaring around his arms.

"Sure." Chloe closes her eyes, and as Cade's magic flows through her, she sighs. "It feels like dad's magic," she whispers.

Cade jerks back like he was burned. He clears his throat and steps away. "Is your magic coming back yet?"

I hate how awkward he feels around her, and I wish there was something I could do to make things like they used to be between them.

Chloe studies her hands with a frown. "A little. It's like there is all this fog inside of me, and getting through it to my magic is almost impossible. But it does seem like it's getting better. Slowly."

Cade nods and heads toward his mom's side of the bed. "I'm assuming it's the same for mom, then." His magic flows through her body, making her groan, which leads to a coughing fit.

Allie bites her lip. "I'm going to up her antibiotics and give her something else to help reduce the fever."

"Chloe, do you need anything?" I ask. "You didn't eat this morning. I can bring you some food."

"Actually, would it be possible to take a shower or something?" She fingers the matted nest of her hair and grimaces.

"Absolutely," I say, bustling to the attached bathroom to make sure everything she'll need is ready. When I come back out, Cade is hovering over her, looking like he wants to help but is afraid. "You," I say, grabbing his arm and tugging him toward the door, "Go away."

"But—"

"No. I don't want to hear a word out of you. Shoo." I wave my hands and nudge him closer to the door.

"Ellis." He narrows his eyes at me, jaw clenching.

Placing my hands on his chest, I stand on my tiptoes and brush a soft kiss to his lips. "We'll be fine, Cade. Go downstairs and eat something before Kai comes hunting for you and drags you away to force feed you." With that, I give him the final shove out the door, and close it in his face. I turn around with my hands on my hips. "Now. Where were we?"

Ellis

Chloe stares at her reflection in the mirror as I gather the supplies for her shower. I try my hardest not to watch her, to give her the privacy to come to terms with where she is. I understand all too well the story a mirror can tell. Oftentimes, it's not an easy story to hear.

"I'll never get this brushed," she says quietly, fingering the tangled mess of her hair.

I step behind her and study the knots. "I think you might be right. We might need to cut it."

I meet her gaze in the mirror and she sighs, resigned. "Just not too short please?"

"How about a bath instead of a shower?" I ask. "I can work on brushing out your hair while you do your best to relax."

She nods and I turn on the water to fill the freestanding tub, adding a generous amount of bubbles. Chloe steps into the steaming water once it's filled, and I search for a pair of scissors.

"Here, lay your head back on this." I place a soft folded towel on the edge of the tub, and hang her hair down the side. "Ready?"

"Yeah."

Gathering her hair in my hands, I cut off about four inches of pure matted snarls. There is no way I'd ever be able to work those knots out. I wet the rest of her hair and slather it in conditioner. Starting at the ends, I section off a small portion and begin gently working the brush through the strands.

I've made it through two small sections when she shifts in the tub. "So," she asks timidly. "You're dating my brother?"

I smile and huff a small laugh. "Yeah, I am." Along with two other guys.

"How long?" The pain in her voice is evident. Thinking about how much she's missed all these years has got to be hard.

"Not long actually. A few months." Has it really only been a few months? It seems like years ago Kai stormed into my room and threw me out the window into Cade's arms.

"Really?" she asks, surprised. "You seem so ... I don't know. Comfortable. Like you've been together for a long time."

I smile again even though Chloe can't see it. "Well, I'm his beloved."

She whirls around in the tub, causing me to yank on the strands in my hand. Water splashes, threatening to flow over the sides. "Beloved? But ... you're ..." Her blue eyes squint as she studies me.

"I'm not a mage, no." I take a deep breath and motion for her to turn back around. "I'm actually a harpy."

This time water does splash over the sides of the tub as Chloe jerks away, covering herself as best she can with her arms. "A harpy?" she whispers.

"Yeah. A harpy." I laugh quietly, trying to ignore the fear in her eyes. "I pretty much had that same reaction when I found out. I thought I was a monster. A creature of death and destruction." I shrug and grimace. "It's not quite that bad. I'm apparently supposed to bring balance to the world? Find a happy medium between good and evil." This time my laugh is harsh. "Like that's just some simple task."

She studies me, her breathing rapid as she attempts to get herself under control. "And Cade?"

"This entire thing is a relatively new development, but it turns out Cade is one of my Shields. He's one of the guys I get my power from. He's my protector. My ... everything." I motion for her to turn back around so I can continue brushing out her hair, and I hold my breath. Is she going to bolt? Run screaming from the bathroom, too scared to be left alone with a harpy?

She studies me a little longer and swallows thickly. "I guess if Cade trusts you," she mutters so quietly I barely hear her. Her movements are jerky as she turns back around, holding herself tense like she's preparing to run if I try to hurt her.

We're both quiet for a few minutes as I continue to work on her hair. Then she sucks in a breath. "You said, 'one of the guys?'" Chloe asks, her voice only trembling slightly. "There are more?"

"Two more. Kai and Sterling are my other Shields."

"So the four of you ..."

I laugh again, smiling from ear to ear. "Yeah. The four of us. It's kind of wild. Sometimes I still find the entire situation crazy."

"So basically, you have three boyfriends." Chloe shakes her head and I can just picture her eyes wide with shock and surprise.

"Yeah. Three guys I was fated to be with."

"And they all get along? They don't mind sharing?"

"They get along great. They were best friends long before they ever met me. I think it was kind of natural for them to share."

"The sex must be intense," Chloe mutters. "Shit. I'm sorry. That is none of my business."

I laugh, sectioning off another chunk of hair. "It's okay. And yeah. The sex is wild."

Silence falls between us, and I can only guess she's trying to imagine what it would be like to date three guys. However, when she speaks next, her voice is hushed and small.

"How do I move on?" Fear and despair lace her tone. The words hit me right in my soul. How many times did I ask myself that? "Will I ever feel normal again?"

My brushing slows as her words dig deeper into me. I release a breath before I start detangling again. "It seems impossible, doesn't it? You think back to your life *before* and it seems so far away. So hard to reach. And you have no idea how to get that life back."

"You speak as if you understand what I'm going through," she says quietly.

"Because I do." The only thing that keeps me talking is the motion of me brushing her hair. The repetitive up and down of my arm. "Before I met Cade and the other two, I was living in my own personal hell with an abusive fiancé. When I met them, I was nothing but a shell of a person. I was empty inside. Hollow." I swallow thickly. Telling this story will never become easier, but if I can help Chloe, I'll do it. "I thought I'd never be able to handle a man's touch again. I was sure I'd been ruined forever. But Cade came along. And he was so amazing. They all were, but Cade especially. It took time, patience, and love. But they showed me that what I lived through didn't define me. That I was more than what I experienced. They showed me what it meant to be loved and cared for. I'm not perfect by any means. I still have to remind myself sometimes that I'm out. I'm safe. I'm not alone. But I got through it because of them."

"What are you saying?" she whispers. "That I should accept this ... this wolf who claims I'm his mate?"

"No, I'm not saying that. I'm saying it's not going to be easy. And it will take time. But you're not alone. Cade will always be there for you. And I will too."

"What do you know about him?" she asks, changing the subject.

I don't need her to clarify who *him* is. "His name is Cole. He's my mate's brother, and his beta. I don't know a lot about him, but he seems like a good guy."

She falls quiet, thinking over my words. I want to tell her to at least talk to him. That the connection formed with a mate is something so amazing and I wouldn't trade it for the world. But, it's not my place. She's not me. I leaned heavily on all three of my guys to get me through my dark times. Chloe might not need or want that.

"I've almost got this all untangled," I say, changing the subject.

"Really? You're a miracle worker."

I laugh and run the brush through her now unmatted hair. "Living with curly hair has taught me a thing or two about defeating stubborn knots." I pick up the scissors and do my best to even out the cut before washing it thoroughly.

Once Chloe climbs out of the bath, she wraps a towel around herself and looks in the mirror. If I had to guess, her hair was probably down to her mid back before I cut it. It's hard to tell with how matted it was. Now, it hangs just above her shoulders. She fingers the wet strands, a small frown on her face.

"I hope I didn't cut it too short," I say, plugging in a hair dryer. "You'll probably have to get this cut professionally, too. I am by no means a hair stylist."

"No, it's fine. It's been a long time since I had hair this short. Then again, it's been a long time since I actually brushed my hair."

The blow dryer cuts off further conversation, and I take my time drying and straightening her hair. Sometimes just having someone take the time to do something so small can be huge to a person. I have a feeling that's the case for Chloe right now. When I'm done, I leave the bathroom to give her privacy to dress, and I find Cade sitting in a chair in the corner of the room.

"Before you yell at me and kick me out, I ate and Kai watched every bite." He lifts his violet eyes to mine, and they look so sad.

I sit in his lap and brush a strand of brown hair from his forehead. "Good. We all need you to stay strong." I glance at his mom's sleeping form, her hair dull and streaked with gray. Wrinkles mar the surface of her skin, even though I don't think she's old enough to have that many. "How long do you think it will take for her magic to return?" I ask quietly.

"I don't know. It took a day or two for Sterling's. Hopefully by tomorrow."

Looking back at him, I turn him to face me. His stubble

scrapes against my fingertips as I graze them over his cheek. We stare into each other's eyes, getting lost in the quiet moment. I love how his eyes sparkle and shine when he's happy. How they swirl with fracturing light when he uses his magic. I love how just his presence can ease my fears and make me feel safe and loved. His gentle touch, his caring heart. There is no one more perfect than the mage before me.

I lean forward and press my lips to his. I intend for it to be a small peck. A comforting gesture. But instead of pulling away, I linger there, breathing him in. He parts my lips with his own and he deepens the kiss, brushing his tongue along mine. My blood heats like it always does when I kiss him. When he pulls away, I pout. It wasn't enough. It's never enough.

Cade stands, keeping me wrapped tight in his arms, and I lock my ankles behind his back as he walks out of the room and into the room I commandeered last night. He gently lays me on the bed and steps back to slowly tug his clothes from his body. I hesitate for a second, studying his face closely.

But as soon as I see the bleakness in his eyes, I know he needs this. He needs the connection. He needs to know he's not alone. He needs to lose himself in someone he loves and just forget about everything for a little bit. I understand that feeling all too well, and I'm happy to give him what he needs.

I sit up and pull my shirt over my head, smiling as his violet eyes darken with desire. After I shimmy out of my leggings, I lean back on the pillows and beckon him to me.

"Come here, Cade. Kiss me."

He doesn't hesitate. Cade leaps for me and his body surrounds mine, warm and heavy as he claims my lips. I completely surrender to him, letting him take what he needs, giving it willingly. He brushes kisses down my neck, nips at my shoulders and breasts. Each little bite makes my skin redden, and he runs his tongue along the small hurts.

I writhe underneath him. My body reacts to all of my Shields the same way. It takes one look from them, one touch, and I'm ready. Cade's fingers grip my thighs tightly as he spreads them, his fingers leaving marks in my flesh that make me burn even hotter. His gaze on my exposed pussy is like a brand, and he licks his lips before lowering down to run his tongue up my center.

I groan, the sound guttural and almost animalistic. Cade doesn't waste time with teasing strokes. He licks and sucks and bites with a purpose. And that purpose is to get me off so he can taste all of me. It doesn't take long before my thighs clench around his head and my hips move against his face, searching for that last bit of pressure to send me over the edge.

Cade meets my gaze, his purple stare so intense and heated it makes my stomach flutter. When he growls softly and gently bites my clit, I slap my hand over my mouth to muffle my scream as I come apart.

He barely waits until the last wave of pleasure ebbs before he surges up onto his elbows and slides his cock inside of me with one hard thrust. I moan as the pleasure that just washed through me begins to build once again. Cade sets a pace I haven't seen from him before. Fast, rough, and almost desperate.

Looking into his eyes, I can tell he's still not fully present. He needs more to bring him back from the despair that is clutching his soul. So I lean up to kiss him, biting his lower lip hard enough to draw blood. My nails rake down his back, breaking skin and making him grunt. But I can see the heat building in his gaze, slowly pushing away the fear and uncertainty.

"Harder, Cade," I moan. "Fuck me harder." I emphasize my words by sliding my hands into his hair and pulling on the strands roughly. Tugging his head back, I spot two puncture marks from the last time Kai fed from him, and I sink my teeth into his skin right over that mark.

I don't bite him hard enough to draw blood, but with how sensitive those two spots are, Cade curses. His hips stutter for a moment before he regains control. Stopping entirely, he pulls out and roughly flips me over, lifting my ass into the air with a strong grip on my hips.

The force of his thrusts drive me up the bed until I have to brace my hands on the headboard to keep from hitting my head on it. Cade punishes me with his hips. The sound of skin slapping and his cock driving in and out of my slick pussy is only interrupted by our harsh breaths and the moans spilling from my lips.

"Fuck," he groans. The heat from his body washes over me. His sweaty chest rubbing against my back.

Each place where we touch sparks with lightning and it goes straight to my core. "Cade," I beg. "Please. Please. Please." I don't even know what I'm begging for anymore. All I know is him. His scent. His sweat. His cock driving into me harder and faster.

He grunts, and slides a hand around my hips to circle my clit. "Fuck, Ellis." His words are strained like it's taking every bit of his self control to not come.

But I want him to. I want to feel him filling me up while my own orgasm takes me to places I've never been before. With a ragged, harsh breath I whisper, "Please."

Cade finally pinches my clit between his thumb and finger, and I detonate. I bite the pillow under my head to muffle my screams as my body comes undone so hard my toes curl and my limbs jerk uncontrollably. Cade bites my shoulder and the pain only draws out my orgasm even more. His hips slam into me and he holds my hips against his as he shudders through his own release.

When the final waves of our pleasure evaporate, Cade collapses to the side, pulling me with him so my back is pressed against his chest. We're both sweating. Both breathing hard as we pull oxygen into our starved lungs. He doesn't pull out though. Instead, keeping us locked together like he can't bear the thought of separating.

When Cade has his breathing under control he brushes my air from my shoulder and presses a soft kiss to the teeth marks he no doubt left there.

"Thank you," he whispers. "For everything." He sounds

wrecked, his voice filled with emotion that I'd need Kai's abilities to parse through.

"That's what I'm here for." I snuggle against him more. "I would do anything for you Cade. Absolutely anything."

His chest rises as he inhales a deep breath. "None of us deserve you," he whispers, his lips pressed against my temple. "You're far too good for us. And I'm sorry for everything we've done to hurt you."

I want to reply. To tell him that isn't true. That they deserve so much more than they think they do. But his hand rubbing gently over my stomach is too relaxing, and I find it harder and harder to keep my eyes open.

I fall asleep with his whispered, "I love you, Ellis," echoing in my head.

Ellis

The next afternoon, I find myself heading for the front porch. Cade's mom is still not responding to any magic he or Connor have attempted to heal her with. The lines around Cade's eyes deepen every time he looks at her. Chloe hasn't left her side, and it's been almost impossible to get Cade to leave either.

"How is everything up there?" Kai asks, tugging me down onto his lap.

Sterling is off again, doing something alpha related no doubt, and Allie has already left. For all I know, Cole is still hiding somewhere in the woods, and Shari is busy around the house. She refused my offer for help though, and told me Kai was sitting outside on the porch.

"Okay enough, I guess." I shrug and settle more firmly against him. "His mom is still not responding to the magic. I'm giving Cade and Chloe some time to talk."

"They both need that, I think." Kai's arms tighten around me and he rests his chin over my shoulder.

We sit quietly for a few minutes, enjoying the sound of birds chirping in the trees. I tilt my head up to welcome the warmth of the sun on my skin and breathe in the air. It smells different on pack lands. It's probably in my head, but it seems crisper, more fresh. Maybe that's just because it's mountain air, but it's revitalizing.

"Aren't you dying out here in the sun?" I ask, glancing at Kai's squinted eyes.

"Slowly, yes." His grin makes my heart flutter.

"You can't even open your eyes all the way."

"It's your beauty. It blinds me."

I elbow him, and he grunts. "Why don't you go inside?"

"Because I feel like I'm in Shari's way. She practically vacuumed my feet up earlier. And she won't let me help, so I wandered out here to slowly die."

"You are so dramatic." I smile as I kiss him.

I only intend for this kiss to be a quick peck. But it's Kai, and I should have known better. It doesn't take long for it to go from PG-13 to R rated. I'm straddling Kai's lap with his hands under my shirt when someone clears their throat. I jump, the motion causing me to bump into Kai and his fang knicks my lower lip.

"Ow," I say, covering the hurt with my hand.

"If I hadn't come along, would you have just fucked on my front porch?" Sterling drawls, crossing his arms and leaning against the post.

"Probably. Why? You wanna join?" Kai's grin is wicked and makes my toes curl in my shoes.

Sterling snorts and pushes away from the post. "Why are you out here Kai?" He pulls my hand from my lip and bends down, taking my lower lip into his mouth. He sucks off the little bit of blood and my core clenches.

"Excuse me," Kai says, pushing against Sterling's chest. "That's mine."

Sterling chuckles, and the low rasp slithers over me. "Says who? She's my mate."

"She's my beloved. That alone means her blood is mine." Kai glares and pulls me harder against his chest.

I lean back and give Sterling a coy smile. There is nothing

serious in their banter, and I don't mind playing along for a bit. It's been so serious lately. A little light-hearted fun would be nice.

"It's too bad the only way you can make her climax is by biting her." Sterling smirks, and I feel Kai stiffen under me. "Every orgasm I've given her has been pure gods-given talent."

"Or practice," Kai mutters.

Sterling narrows his icy blue eyes. "Do we need to fight this out to prove who is the best mate for Ellis?"

Kai jumps up from the chair so fast I practically fall to the ground. "Oh, you're on, pup!" He leaps over the porch railing, landing on his feet and whipping his shirt over his head at the same time.

"Fucking idiot," Sterling mutters, taking off his own shirt. "He does realize the sun is out, right?"

I shake my head. "I don't think he cares."

"It's just another way to prove I'm stronger than you, and thus proving I'm a more suitable mate for Ellis." Kai lifts his arms and gives Sterling a cocky grin.

Sterling rolls his shoulders and lifts his arms over his head, stretching and flexing his muscles. Kai does his own warm up, his muscles not as big, but no less defined.

Damn, I'm one lucky girl.

Sterling and Kai circle each other a few times, then Sterling pounces. His punch knocks Kai's head back, and even I can hear his nose break. I grimace and lean my arms on the banister. I'll have to get Cade down here to heal them when this is over.

When Kai lifts his head, blood trickles down his lips and he licks it away with a feral grin. A thrill zings through me, hot and needy, and I cross my legs, squeezing them together. Talk about foreplay.

Kai is fast, and his first few punches find their target—Sterling's ribs and abs. Sterling's wolf helps him track the vampire, no doubt without it, Kai would have knocked Sterling on his ass already. My shifter mostly dodges and takes the defensive, leaving Kai to make all the first moves.

I frown as I watch them, and then it dawns on me. Sterling is going to let Kai wear himself out. With the sun shining on him, and Kai only wearing pants, it won't take too long for his energy to drain from him, making him weaker.

Kai comes to the same conclusion. He stops and glares at Sterling. "Seriously? You have to wait until the sun gets to me? That's pathetic."

I wince and glance at Sterling. He only grins and launches for Kai.

"Oh!"

I turn around and find Chloe on the porch, Cade behind her.

Cade sighs and comes to stand next to me. "Who said what?"

"Sterling insulted Kai's ability to get me off." I wince again, as Kai lands a good hit on Sterling.

Cade laughs. "That'll do it."

"Do they do this often?" Chloe asks, standing next to Cade with a white knuckled grip on the banister.

"They used to do it more," Cade says. "It's been awhile since they've duked it out."

"Why do they do it?"

I huff. "They're both arrogant, stubborn assholes?"

Cade nods, ignoring Chloe's wide-eyed stare. He glances at me, watches me watch them, and he leans over to whisper in my ear. "This turns you on, doesn't it?"

I bite my lower lip and squeeze my legs together in response.

He chuckles. "Good to know."

The fight is brutal. Both of them are bleeding, bruised, and breathing heavily. I can't tell who has the upper hand. I watch Kai take Sterling to the ground, and I think for sure, that's the end of it.

"Give in, pup?" Kai growls, pressing Sterling into the grass.

Sterling barks a laugh. "Not a chance." He kicks Kai off of him, and Kai goes flying through the air.

With his vampire reflexes, Kai twists and lands on his feet. My mouth drops open, stunned by that display. I glance back at

Sterling, and find a giant silver wolf where Sterling was, shredded pants next to it.

"Great. There goes his clothes." I sigh and lean against Cade.

"Like you care if he walks around naked." He bumps me, and I elbow him in return.

"Well, no. But I'm sure everybody else minds."

"Eh. I certainly don't mind." The smile in his voice is obvious. And it's obvious, even though Kai and Sterling are fighting, they are still listening to our conversation.

Kai whips around to look at Cade with a 'what the fuck' expression, eyes wide and mouth open in disbelief. The distraction costs him. Sterling tackles Kai to the ground and closes his jaws around Kai's throat. Not enough to break skin, but a clear sign that Sterling has won.

"Son of a bitch," Kai growls.

Fluffy releases him and licks his face, making Kai grimace. I blink, and Sterling is bending down to help Kai to his feet.

"Own up, prince. Who's the better mate?" Sterling taunts.

Kai glares at Cade. "Traitor."

"Oh," Chloe says.

I glance at her and find her staring at Sterling, pink staining her cheeks. A smile tugs at my lips and I lean around Cade. "That's Cole's brother." I wink at her, then laugh when Cade chokes.

Chloe squeaks and turns around, rushing for the door and disappearing inside.

"Seriously, Ellis? That's not at all what I want to be thinking about." Cade stares at me, and I pat his cheek.

"Come on. Let's get them healed up.

———

BACK IN COLE'S room that I commandeered, Kai and Sterling sit on the bed. Both shirtless, one pantless. Both bleeding, bruised, and sweaty. They look dangerous. Sexy. Depraved. All except the tightness around Kai's eyes. The strain from so much sun exposure.

Sterling catches me staring, and he smiles, icy blue eyes lighting with an inner fire. With obvious, exaggerated movements, he inhales. "Do you need some help getting those clothes off?" he asks me, a low growl in his voice. Kai and Cade both turn toward me with wicked smiles and raised brows. Sterling slides back to lean against the headboard, raising his arms behind his head. Sprawled naked and relaxed, blood still leaking from his injuries, I want to pounce on him and lick up every inch of his skin. "Kai, strip her naked. I want to see every bit of her exposed flesh."

I'm so absorbed looking at my wolf and letting his words sink deep into me, that I don't notice Cade slipping behind me until his hands glide under my shirt. He slowly lifts it over my head, then unclasps my bra and lets it slide down my arms, the fabric tickling and making shiver.

My skin prickles from the cool air as well as Kai and Sterling's gazes upon me. Kai kneels in front of me, fingers curling in my waistband, and he pulls down my leggings and panties. I wobble as I stand on one leg to let him slide them off completely, and Cade helps me balance while I dig my fingers into Kai's hair. With Kai shoving his shoulders between my legs, I'm forced to stand with my legs spread, everything on display for my vampire kneeling at my feet.

Before Kai moves, he looks over his shoulder to Sterling, waiting for his orders. I almost scream from need. I just want him to touch me already.

"How does she taste?" Sterling's blue eyes are pinned on me but his question for Kai makes me whimper.

Kai inhales my scent and his eyes flash crimson. "I'm going to devour you," he growls.

Cade supports me, and I tangle my fingers in Kai's hair as he licks up my center. If it weren't for Cade's steady arms, I'd have hit the ground at that first touch.

Kai looks up at me, pupils blown, dried blood on his face. "Fucking delicious," he murmurs, but I know Sterling hears him.

I pull my gaze from Kai and look at my shifter. His cock is hard and straining, and his hand slowly works up and down the thick length. Those icy blue eyes are dark as they watch everything Kai does to me.

"Does seeing us bloodied turn you on, kitten?"

My tongue is stuck to the roof of my mouth, and I have to peel it off and swallow before I can answer. "Yes." My voice is breathy and I sound nothing like myself. "It reminds me of how dangerous you are."

A chuckle rumbles through Kai, the vibrations against my sensitive flesh making me cry out. My voice echoes in the small room, and I hesitate.

"No," I gasp. "Kai, stop." I push his head away with my hands.

All three guys pause instantly, bodies tense, eyes alert. Their response makes my eyes burn. With one word they stop, always making sure to respect my wishes. Kai slides his hands to the backs of my thighs, squeezing gently as he looks up at me. His gray eyes are serious for once, studying me to make sure I'm okay.

"What's wrong, love?" Cade wraps his arms around me, holding me tightly.

I take a breath, trying to calm my racing heart and shove my desire down, down, down. "There are too many people in the house. They'll hear us."

Cade chuckles, and Kai and Sterling relax. I untangle my fingers from Kai's hair as he stands.

"Is that all you're worried about, baby girl?" His fingers trail over my cheek to grip my chin gently, and I nod. He smiles and his eyes smolder once again. "Cade?"

Cade flings his hand out like he's batting away an annoying gnat. Purple light sizzles along the walls, crawls over the ceiling, and floods the floor. It crackles for a moment, a shield of swirling violet light, before sinking into the drywall and carpet and disappearing.

"Problem solved," Cade murmurs in my ear.

With that little worry taken care of, I can focus once again on what was happening. I reach for Kai, wrapping my arms around his neck, and draw him to me. I can taste myself on his tongue, and the faint tinge of blood from his split lip and bloody nose. He sandwiches me between him and Cade, and I wiggle around, trying to feel *all* of them. I get my fingers under the waistband of Kai's pants, but Sterling's voice stops me.

"Uh uh uh," he croons. "You can't have what you want until you get those magnificent wings out."

I don't even hesitate. Stepping away from Cade so I have room, I yank the imaginary blanket off my back and let my wings free. Kai stares with untamed desire at the white feathers laced with gold. Sterling groans, his hand tightening around his cock. And Cade. Cade runs a finger over the sensitive spot near my spine.

My back arches and I gasp, liquid heat pooling between my legs. A whimper climbs up my throat. A sound of desperation. I need them to touch me. To ease the ache. "Please," I whisper, closing my eyes and taking deep breaths.

"Come here, kitten," Sterling growls as he sits up and scoots to the edge of the bed.

I drop to my knees between his legs and keep my gaze locked on Sterling's as I take his length into my mouth. Seeing this bloodied alpha wolf come undone under my touch only turns me on even more. His clenched jaw and sharp breaths, his fingers tangled in my hair tugging painfully. It's a wild storm of desire that fuels my own.

Cade kneels behind me, running his fingers from the nape of my neck, down my back, through the feathers of my wings, and around my hips. He licks my neck, right over Kai's mark, and I moan with Sterling's cock in my mouth. The vibrations make Sterling curse, and he tightens his grip in my hair.

Cade slips his fingers between my thighs at the same time Sterling pulls me closer, forcing me to take him even deeper. My fingers grip his thighs tightly, fire burning through me so hot it leaves me breathless. I swallow reflexively as his cock hits the back of my throat and Sterling curses roughly.

He lifts my head before I can take even more of him and I pout a little, making him smile. He traces my bottom lip with his thumb. "Get up there and ride Kai, kitten. Show him what it's like to fuck with those wings out."

I shiver at his rough voice and dirty words, but I climb onto the bed and straddle Kai's waist, my fingers biting into his chest for balance. Kai's hands land on my hips and his gaze falls behind me, to my wings. Awe laced with pure desire glazes his gray eyes.

My hips grind against him, rubbing my aching clit against his cock. "Is this what you want?" I ask breathlessly.

Kai's fingers tighten, leaving little indents on my thighs. His head thrusts back onto the pillow and he bites his bottom lip with his fangs. "Always, baby girl. But right now? I want more." He lifts me effortlessly and slides me onto his cock. We both groan, and I can't help but lift myself up with my thighs, sliding almost completely off, only to sit back down. "Oh fuck, that's it, baby girl."

With my eyes closed, I have no idea what Cade and Sterling are doing, but I hear the drawer on the nightstand open and someone rifles through it. When I open my eyes, I see Sterling pulling out a bottle of lube. He settles behind me, running his fingers over the swell of my ass. Butterflies swoop in my belly in anticipation. I've taken Cade back there, but Sterling is thicker.

He wraps his hand around my throat and runs his nose over his mark on the opposite side of Kai's. At the same time he slips one finger inside my back hole. I groan, my rhythm faltering, but Kai keeps it going by lifting his own hips.

Sterling preps me, slowly stretching and adding more fingers. The nervous uncertainty has completely fled at his touch, and in its place a molten hot need has taken up residence.

He leans against my back, and whispers in my ear, "Ready, kitten?"

"Yes," I breathe, lowering myself over Kai.

Sterling takes his time, making sure I'm okay every step of the way. Kai rubs my clit, keeping me on edge and ready for more. Each slow inch Sterling pushes in, fills and stretches me almost to the point I can't bear it. Every nerve ending is lit up, each touch is pure bliss. And watching Kai's face, teeth gritted and eyes squeezed shut, as Sterling's cock rubs along his with just the thin wall between them, makes this even hotter.

By the time Sterling is all the way in, all three of us are panting and sweating. I'm aching in places I was never aware of before. A little whimper escapes me, and Kai slowly lifts his hips making me see stars.

"Oh," I gasp, nails digging into his chest. "Don't stop."

"Wasn't planning on it," he grits out.

Cade kneels on the bed by Kai's head and roughly grabs Kai's chin in his fingers, turning his head and forcing his jaws open. Kai eagerly takes Cade's cock into his mouth, and I watch, biting my lip to keep myself from coming already. Cade watches me with a wicked smile, knowing exactly what watching does to me.

It's too much. All the sounds, scents, and sensations are burning deep inside my core, each slight movement sending me closer to the edge. Sterling and Kai take turns thrusting in and out. When Kai removes one of his hands from my thighs and slides it around Cade's backside, I can imagine what he's doing. Especially when Cade grunts and spills his release into Kai's mouth.

I whimper again, my core clenching causing Kai and Sterling to both curse. "I'm ... oh, gods ... I'm ..."

"Not yet, kitten," Sterling growls, wrapping a hand around my throat and squeezing gently.

A strangled noise escapes me—half moan, half cry. I can't hold on any longer. My pleasure sizzles along every nerve ending. It builds inside of me, rising higher and higher until I know I'll combust if he doesn't let me come. Senseless words of pleading fall from my lips and I shake my head side to side.

Sterling brushes his fingers against my wings, right at the base where they meet my back. "Come for us, kitten."

I scream as my orgasm crashes through me, my back arching and toes curling. Wave after wave of pure bliss flows through me, and my guys bring me through all of it. The fluttering of my inner walls set Kai and Sterling off. They grunt and stiffen, their release spilling into me and filling me completely.

When we are all finally still, the only sound in the room is the chorus of our heavy breathing. Sterling slowly pulls out, making me whimper, and Kai opens his eyes. They shine with so much emotion as he looks at me.

"There are no words for how magnificent you are, baby girl," he breathes, touching my face tenderly.

I collapse on top of him and close my eyes, my body spent and ready for a break. I let them take care of me, because I know they always will. Sterling cleans me up gently, whispering soothing words and noises into my ear as I whimper at the oversensitivity of my skin.

With my eyes closed, I listen to Cade healing Kai and Sterling, admonishing them for being idiots. They bicker back and forth, insulting each other good naturedly. A family. A unit. Brothers who don't need blood to bind them together.

I could never have imagined I'd have this. But I do. I have three amazing men who would burn the world for me. A smile tugs at the corner of my lips as my guys settle around me. This is more than I could have ever hoped for. My own family. My own unit. One I hope I can grow one day in the future.

Kai

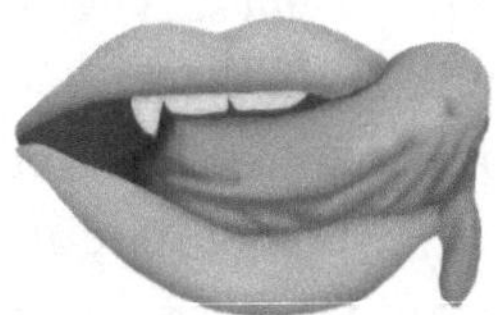

We wait until we're back at the cabin and back in our routine of sleeping during the day and training at night, then we decide it's time to make our move. Grace has been held captive long enough. And two more bodies have washed up from the river not far from the warehouse, both humans with traces of magic. We're running out of time, and I don't know how much more training we can give Ellis that will make a huge difference. I'd prefer another year or two, but that obviously can't happen.

I call Connor, Cole, and Drew and have them meet us one evening at the cabin. We sit in the living room and talk quietly while we wait for Ellis to wake up.

"So, we're really doing this?" Drew asks, taking a drink from his beer.

"We are." I glance at Cade and he gives me an encouraging nod. "And before Ellis wakes up, I want to make sure everyone knows the only thing that matters is her making it out of this alive. Cade, Sterling, and I will give our lives for her. No questions asked."

Cole nods in understanding. "If anything happens to you three, I'll make sure she's okay. She can move in with mom."

"Thanks, Cole," Sterling says quietly. His usually vibrant blue eyes are dull.

I close my eyes and rub my chest. Just the thought of leaving her alone makes me panic. And I don't need to use my abilities to know Cade feels the same way. His eyes are wild, hands fisted tightly at his sides. But the chances of all three of us dying are slim, right? At least one of us will survive to keep her safe and care for her. Fuck. I can't think of that.

"I also want everyone to know Ellis gets the right to kill Sam, if she wants it." I open my eyes and stare at our three companions, making sure they understand the severity of that statement.

They all nod and I sit back in the chair, looking at Sterling. He's been writing down various plans for getting into the warehouse and getting Grace out. He runs his fingers through his silver hair, grimacing as they get caught in knots. "I think our biggest decision is whether or not we do this all in one go, or split it up."

"You mean rescue Grace first, then go back to deal with Sam? Or do it all at once?" Cade asks, sitting on the arm of my chair.

"Exactly. I'm worried splitting it up is pushing our luck. Right now, Sam is quiet only because he knows we'll be coming for Grace." Sterling frowns, flipping through the pages of his notebook. "If we rescue Grace, there will be nothing to keep him from coming after us. Or worse, setting his creatures on Altair."

Cole leans over to glance at the notebook. "What if we break off into groups? One deals with Sam and his creatures, the other rescues Grace."

Sterling bobs his head from side to side. "That's an option. But we'd have to run it by Ellis first."

"Run what by me?" Ellis's sleepy voice cuts through the room as she descends the stairs.

I smile. Her hair is wild and untamed like she didn't even bother to attempt to wrangle it into a bun. A pair of shorts peeks out from under one of our shirts, and her bare feet drag across the floor as she walks to Sterling. He tosses the notebook onto the coffee table and sits back so Ellis can plop onto his lap. She snuggles against him, knees curled to her chest and eyes closed.

"We're making plans for rescuing Grace," Sterling says quietly, brushing her curls away from his face.

She makes a non-committal sound and attempts to bury herself further against him. Cade laughs softly and heads for the kitchen. When he returns, he's holding a steaming cup of coffee which he waves in front of her face. As the steam hits her nose, her eyes pop open.

"Coffee," she breathes, reaching for the mug. She inhales and a beautiful smile spreads across her face.

Cade returns to my chair and sits on the armrest again, draping his arm over my shoulders. I'm hit with a surreal sense of rightness. Take Cole, Connor, and Drew out of the picture, leaving just the four of us. Me and Cade on the chair, Ellis and Sterling on the couch. An early morning with coffee and tea, maybe a fire in the fireplace. No threats. No danger hanging over our heads. Just laughter, peace, comfort. Love.

Laughter and the patter of little feet on the floor.

A visceral need to protect this spreads through me like wildfire. My family, my pack, my entire world is these three people. Without them, there is nothing worth living for. I glance at Cade and he gives me a small, content smile. I glance at Ellis, sleepily drinking her coffee cuddled in Sterling's lap. And Sterling. The brooding, tough alpha, with his features softened as he holds his mate. Fuck. I will do whatever is necessary to make sure my family comes through this alive. I will burn the world to the ground and bathe the ashes in blood to ensure my beloved has an eternity of happiness with the three of us.

After Ellis sets her mug on the coffee table, she looks at all of us. "Okay, now that I'm caffeinated, what decision am I making?"

Sterling shifts her slightly in his lap so he can look at her better. "We were talking about rescuing Grace and taking care of Sam at the same time. I think splitting up into two teams is the best option, but I don't know if you want to be with the team who rescues Grace or the team who takes on Sam."

She bites her lip as she thinks, and indecision draws her brows down. "Will you go with the group to rescue Gracie?" she asks Sterling. "Since she saw you and knows you're my mate. It might help her feel more comfortable."

Sterling's mouth flattens into a thin line. He doesn't like that idea. None of us are going to want to be separated from Ellis, but he nods. "Yeah. I can do that."

"Okay, then I'll go with the group to deal with Sam." Golden light briefly flares in her amber eyes, determination straightening her spine.

Just as we all assumed. Ellis wants the last thing Sam sees to be her ending his life. If I wasn't so worried, I'd find that incredibly sexy.

"So Cade, Kai, and Cole, you guys will go with Ellis. Connor and Drew will be with me." Sterling falls into alpha mode, delivering instructions in a brisk, no-nonsense manner, fully expecting us to obey him. And we do.

When Sterling puts on his alpha panties, he could command anyone to do anything. His presence is that forceful. The plan he has developed is solid, and under normal circumstances, I'd feel confident—probably even cocky—about this entire thing. But nothing about this is normal. My beloved's life is on the line. Her sister's life is on the line. The future of this little unit, my family, my pack, could be forever changed. Too much is at risk for me to feel completely at ease.

Once the plan is in place and everyone is in agreement, Sterling stands. "Okay. Tomorrow evening, we'll meet at the abandoned office building. Connor, make sure Allie is here and ready with all of her supplies." He walks our guests to the door, and when he returns, he finds Cade, Ellis, and me sitting in silence.

We all stare at each other. Ellis's heart is racing. A nervous, uneasy energy has settled in the room, and I have to strengthen my mental shields to keep everyone's emotions from battering me. This is it. This could be the last night we all spend together.

"Can we ..." Ellis pauses, her voice seeming too loud in the silence yet too small at the same time. "Can we spend the day just being together? No training. No talk of tomorrow. Just the four of us. Please?"

Sterling smiles. "Of course. What do you want to do?"

———

THE CORD to the TV drags behind me, lightly thumping on each step as I carry the stupid thing to the bedroom. Ellis wants to cuddle in bed with movies and popcorn, so that is what she's getting.

Sterling is in the kitchen making all kinds of snacks, and Cade ... I almost drop the TV when I get to the room and see what he's doing.

"What the hell?" I ask, setting the TV down on the dresser and glance at the spot the dresser used to be in.

"What?" He looks at me, eyebrows raised, daring me to say anything.

"Did Martha Stewart abduct you and sew herself into your skin?" I look around the room with a wide grin and bat at the sheer curtains Cade hung around the bed to fall in billowing waves to the ground. The dresser has been moved to the foot of the bed, so the curtains will completely surround it and the bed, encasing us in the white material. A veritable love nest.

"Ew, Kai. That's gross." He shudders dramatically then continues hanging the twinkling lights along the ceiling. "I want Ellis to be able to forget about tomorrow, and give her something to remember ... just in case."

My stomach sinks at his words. It's like a roller coaster. One second I'm fine, distracted by something and not thinking of tomorrow. Then the next, I'm plunging down the hill, stomach in my throat, about to vomit. All it takes is one word. One reminder of what's to come.

It's not just Ellis I'm worried about. It's not just the little family I have in these three. It's Cade too. My ... lover? That sounds weird to me, but he is. He's more than my best friend. He's the other half of my heart, the half he somehow managed to pry away from Ellis. This could be the last time we have a moment together.

I snag his waist and spin him around. He gasps in surprise and I take the opening to claim his mouth. The twinkling lights hit the floor and Cade threads his fingers into my hair, pressing his body tight to mine. There was a time we never would have done this. When everything physical between us was to help me get out of my own head. But now it's a conscious choice. To kiss the man I love, to let him know exactly how I feel.

It started hard and fast, dominance and claiming. But it doesn't stay like that. Quickly, the kiss slows. Deepens. Becomes more. My heart feels heavy in my chest, and I try not to think about how this could be the last time I hold Cade in my arms. His cedar and lilac scent surrounds me. His warmth against my chilled skin. The way he seems to fit perfectly against me. I commit it all to memory.

When we finally break apart, I stare into his violet eyes, so full of tenderness and fear. That stupid lock of brown hair that I love has fallen forward across his brow, and I reach up to brush it back, letting my fingers trail through his hair.

"I love you, Kai," he says, a touch breathless.

My heart squeezes painfully, and I swallow down the despair that suddenly drowns me. I give him one last lingering kiss, tasting his lips, breathing in his breath. "I love you too, Cade."

We cling to each other for another few minutes, then Cade pulls away. "Help me get the room ready?"

When Ellis enters a few minutes later, helping Sterling carry trays of various snacks and drinks, she gasps. Her amber eyes glitter in the soft white lights Cade hung from the ceiling and along the walls. I hung blankets over the windows to ensure no sunlight could peek through and dim their brilliance. She smiles when her gaze lands on the bed, the gauzy fabric hanging around it and the piles of blankets and pillows atop it.

"You guys," she breathes, her eyes shining brighter as tears glisten on her lashes.

I pat the spot on the bed next to me and smile. "Hop in."

Cade grabs the tray from her and she climbs into the bed next to me, snuggling against my side and pulling a blanket over her legs. "I can't believe you guys did this for me."

"It's what you wanted," Sterling says, setting his tray at the foot of the bed before laying on Ellis's other side. "And we wanted to make it as special as possible."

"Besides," Cade adds, his tray joining Sterling's. "It's not like we don't benefit from these cuddle sessions. We enjoy them as much as you do." He tries to sit on my other side, but I tug him between my legs, so his back is against my chest. This way he'll be next to Ellis as well.

Sterling turns on the movie, some new comedy that none of us pay attention to. Instead, we talk, laugh, dream. We make plans for our future and discuss the changes we want to make to the cabin. Ellis quietly mentions adding a nursery, and the surge of emotions from Sterling and Cade slips through my shields. Hope. Happiness. Fear.

It's too much right now, and as pressure builds in my chest, I blurt out the first thing I can to diffuse the tension. "Malakai Junior."

"What?" Ellis asks, turning her head to look at me.

I smirk and rub my thumb along her bottom lip. "Our first kid. He'll be named Malakai Junior."

Cade snorts and Ellis raises one brow. But it's Sterling who brings me back down to earth, as always. "What if it's a girl?"

"Uh ... Malakina?" I say slowly as the name forms in my mind.

"Yeah, that's not happening," Ellis says, shaking her head.

"Besides, Sterling Junior sounds better." Sterling crosses his arms without looking away from the movie.

All of us gape at him, and Ellis is the first to burst out in laughter. He's always so serious, so hearing the joke from him while he keeps his gaze glued to the TV and his mouth pressed in a firm line, causes all of us to laugh. Ellis laughs so hard she snorts, and the sound causes Sterling's lips to quirk in a smile.

"There will be no Juniors," Ellis says breathily after we all get ourselves back under control. "That wouldn't be fair."

"Not to mention confusing," Cade mutters. "Two of each of us?"

Ellis shudders dramatically. "I can't handle that. I can barely handle you three alone."

"I doubt you have to worry about that," I say, brushing a curl behind her ear. "I'm sure all of our kids will take after you. Beautiful, sweet, and caring."

"Stubborn, headstrong, and opinionated." Sterling's words are quiet but we all hear them.

"Excuse me?" Ellis gasps in mock outrage. "I am not stubborn."

Sterling snorts. "Yes, you are."

"I am not."

He raises one silver brow. "Fine. You're not."

"Thank you," she says primly, and turns back to the TV.

I grin over her head at the shifter, and wrap my arm around Cade a little tighter, his silent laughter rumbling in his chest. Yeah. I could get used to this.

Ellis is the first to fall asleep, curled between us where she is safe and loved. The three of us watch her, tracing her features with our gazes. By the time the sun begins to set, I don't think any of us have slept, besides Ellis. We stayed awake, trapped in our own minds. Dreaming of a future that might be stolen away all too soon.

Ellis

I'm going to puke. And at the same time, I can't fucking breathe. The abandoned office building spins in my vision, and I drop to the ground. The hard tile floor bites into my knees, but the pain doesn't even register. I'm too focused on trying to get oxygen into my lungs while keeping my stomach from emptying itself. Even though there's nothing in it to empty.

It's not just the fear of losing one of my Shields. It's not just worry over my sister. I'm going to come face to face with Sam today. My tormenter. My abuser. My deepest nightmare. All of the wounds that have been healing because of my guys, are slowly being reopened. The scabs are peeling away, exposing the raw, bloody nerves that hurt just to think about. I will never be able to face Sam and not fall back into the darkness that I lived in for so long.

Kai kneels in front of me and takes my face in his hands. His gray eyes search mine, but I can't even focus on them. I squeeze my eyes shut to block out the way everything is tipping from side to side.

"Look at me, baby girl." His thumb rubs gently back and forth on my cheek. I pry my eyes open, hating how they burn with tears. "I'm going to compel you, okay? Just to help you stay calm."

Relief and shame wash through me at the same time. I hate that I need him to do this, but if he doesn't, I'll never get through what's to come. I nod and stare into his gray eyes as they start to glow with an eerie inner light.

"Breathe, Ellis." His voice sounds hollow and echoey, but at the same time holds a commanding expectation that I'm drawn to. "You're going to remain calm while you face Sam. You won't panic when you see him. Everything is going to be okay."

His words claw through my brain and latch on. Immediately, the panic recedes, and I'm able to take a deep breath. My body droops, already exhausted from how much energy I've expended from worry alone. Kai catches me and hauls me to his chest. I let him hold me for just a moment, letting his strength further bolster my confidence.

"Thank you," I whisper against his black henley.

He kisses the top of my head and helps me to my feet. Everyone is standing around, dressed in various forms of combat gear—leather armor, fatigues, and lots of weapons. I tug my black shirt down and straighten my spine.

"Okay," Sterling says, his voice quiet but still echoing in the empty office building. "My group will wait here for a few minutes to allow you guys time to get inside and distract Sam. Connor will go with you far enough to help Cade break through the wards. Everyone understand?"

We all nod and my group heads for the door. Sterling stops me, grabbing my arm and spinning me to face him. He takes my head in his hands and tilts it up so I'm looking at him. "Be careful, Ellis. Stay with Cade and Kai. No matter what happens, don't leave them." His icy blue eyes search mine, and I nod. He leans forward and presses a kiss to my lips. "I love you," he says against my mouth. "Please come back to me."

The same words I said to him before he ran off and got captured. The same words I said when he challenged Noah. My throat tightens and I have a hard time drawing in a breath, so I wrap my arms around his neck and kiss him. "I love you too, Sterling." My voice breaks on his name and I have to pull away. If I don't, I'm liable to fall apart again, despite Kai's thrall.

Pushing past him, I grab Cade's hand and we walk out the door, leaving Sterling behind. Kai's thrall is helping to keep me semi steady. I'm able to breathe, and my heart isn't racing to the point where I'm afraid I'll pass out. But the nausea hasn't subsided. I press my hands to my stomach and swallow. It doesn't help.

Connor and Cade step up to the ward and they both frown. Cade steps forward, and walks right through. His magic sweeps ahead of him, a faint purple light that races toward the building.

"No ward. At all." He looks at Kai and Cole, worry pinching his brow.

Kai shrugs, taking my hand. "It doesn't surprise me. He wants us to come. Why try to keep us out?"

We walk to the front door, Connor turning around to head back to the other group. Our plan is to distract Sam long enough for them to get in and get Gracie. Then I can end this once and for all. My fingers shake in Kai's grasp and he gives my hand an encouraging squeeze.

Each step brings me closer and closer to the monster of my nightmares. Each step is one step closer to maybe losing someone I love. Unable to stomach that thought any longer, I tear my hand out of Kai's grasp and dash to the edge of the walkway. Bending over, I heave spit and bile onto the grass. There was nothing in my stomach to bring back up, but that doesn't stop my body from trying.

Kai and Cade close in on either side of me. One tucking an escaped curl behind my ear, the other rubbing circles on my back. I take comfort in their presence, reminding myself that they are with me and I don't have to see Sam alone. Their light and love will help banish the memories that try to drag me under. I wipe my mouth on my sleeve and stand, grimacing at the foul taste clinging to my tongue.

"You okay?" Cade asks, peering into my eyes.

I nod, too afraid if I open my mouth to speak I'll either puke again or break down in tears. He kisses my forehead before taking my hand and leading me up the cracked front steps of the building.

The 'warehouse' as Sam calls it, is an old elementary school he purchased from the city. It was never the nicest building to begin with, but under his ownership, it's fallen into more disrepair. Vines cling to the tan brick, digging fingers between the stones in an attempt to claw them from the facade. Many of the windows have been boarded up, but a few remain with intact glass. One of those is how we got in the first time when we rescued Sterling.

The main doors are solid metal with small windows peering inside. It's impossible to see what color they are in the dim light, but they look rusted and derelict. Cole yanks one open and holds it as we file inside.

The air is stale and metallic. Like all the blood from the torture occuring in the basement has permeated the entire structure. There are no wards keeping us out here either, but just inside the main vestibule, a pair of guards stand alert.

Kai steps up to them, flexing his hands like he wants to wrap them around their necks. "We'd like to talk to Sam."

The guard on the left smiles. It's creepy and malevolent, and displays his missing front teeth. The other guard sends chills down my spine. His blank gaze stares at us. No. Not us. Me. He looks at me, but it's more like he's looking through me. I shiver, and Cade steps between us, blocking the guard's view.

"He's been waiting for you," Toothless says, his voice raspy and harsh. "Follow me."

Kai takes the lead behind Toothless, and Cole falls into place behind me and Cade. Sweat slicks my hands, and I know Cade can feel it, but he only holds on tighter. The guard leads us down the hallway, and the closer we get to Sam, the more Sterling's pearl necklace warms under my shirt. A warning I didn't need. An enemy is close by.

The alternating tan and brown linoleum tiles are chipped and peeling. Ceiling tiles stained with water damage line the ceiling; a few of them are missing, leaving the impression of empty eye sockets or gaping teeth. Wooden classroom doors with narrow windows line the hallway, most of them closed. Sterling and his group will be coming in through the windows of one of these rooms.

There are no other guards like the last time. I have a sinking suspicion most of them have been placed in the basement, where the cells and torture chamber are housed. The only other guards I see are the two standing in front of a room that I assume Sam has turned into his office.

"Tell the boss she's here," Toothless says as we come to stop before them.

Similar to the guards at the entrance, one appears more human than the other. The less human one has a blank stare that sees through everything. Like there is nothing alive inside the body. The human guard turns around and opens the wooden door, sticking his head inside to let Sam know I'm here. When he steps back out and holds the door open for us, I take a deep breath and remind myself that I am not alone as I step inside to face my nightmare.

Sam sits behind a rusting metal desk. It's nothing like his office in Thomas Kennedy's building. That office is posh, comfortable, and dripping with wealth. This one ... not so much. The office chair is rickety, the wheels look like they won't even roll, and I think one of the arms may be missing.

The man, though, is as polished and imposing as ever. In his black suit with a light green button-up, he looks like any rich guy you'd meet on the streets of Altair. His brown hair is slicked back, showcasing his strong jaw and brown eyes. If I didn't know any better, I'd say he was attractive. I *do* know better though. Under that facade of a handsome, normal mage, beats the heart of a monster with the blackest possible soul.

He smiles, his gaze landing on me. "Ellis, doll. It's a pleasure to see you again. I've missed you so much."

So genuine. He is so convincing in his earnestness. It's no wonder I fell for his lies. I say nothing. But I straighten my back and lift my chin, a sudden sense of calm settling over me. I won't fall for his lies again. He can't trick me again. I've trained and prepared for this. My guys have made sure I can handle anything thrown at me, and I'm stronger than I was when I was dating Sam.

"We're here for Grace Kennedy," Kai says, stepping in front of me.

Sam chuckles, a dark sound that makes me recoil. "You can have her. If I can have Ellis."

"Not happening." Kai cocks his head, and I can picture his grin, fangs glinting in the dim light.

"Then I keep Grace." Sam crosses his arms and leans back in the chair. I expect it to tip backward, but I'm disappointed when it only creaks. "Although I imagine I'll have both of them in just a few moments."

Kai stiffens and his hands curl. I bet he's wishing he had claws right about now, but his fangs are probably insanely long. "What do you want with Ellis?" Yep. Based on his distorted words, his fangs are huge.

Sam's smile makes me take a step back. "Besides that tight little cunt?" The way he looks at me, his eyes traveling up and down my body, I know he's imagining me naked.

Paralyzing fear spears through me. Naked, bound in burning bands of his green magic, forced to endure his endless assault on my body. Even Kai's thrall can't keep the panic at bay. My fingers tingle, but it's not a sign of my magic. Numbness spreads up my arms, my body going into shock.

Always the observant one, the one that knows what to do, Cade steps closer to me. His hand brushes my lower back, and a pulsing warmth radiates outward from the spot. I've always felt as if Cade's magic was a part of me. Every time it touches me, it's like a bit of myself returning home. As the warmth spreads up my back and down my shoulders, I'm able to take a deep breath.

"I think you know exactly why I want her," Sam continues. "I want her powers. I want her magic. Just think of everything I could achieve with it." An evil grin spreads across his face, his brown eyes sparkling with his green magic. "The use of her body is just a bonus."

I know there is no point in trying to tell him my powers are tied to my Shields. Without them, I'm nothing. Sam is too far gone in his fanatic thoughts to listen to reason, though.

Kai snarls, taking one step forward. "You'll never have her."

Sam's laugh freezes the blood in my veins. "Oh, but you're wrong." He snaps his fingers and faster than I can track, people rush into the room.

No. Not people. Creatures. More of those beings with lifeless eyes. They move faster than any magical creature I know of. Cade, Kai, and Cole don't even get a chance to take up fighting stances. Before I know what's happening, they are held captive by Sam's creations, struggling and cursing, trying to get free. I watch as needles disappear into Cade and Cole's necks, and I know exactly what that means. They will no longer have access to their magic.

I stand frozen in place, heart beating erratically. This time, I think it's Kai's heart that mine is echoing. His gray eyes are wild as he struggles to free himself. But it's useless. Those creatures have them all bound too tightly. Whatever Sam has done to alter them has made them too powerful. We can't fight them.

Sam stands from the chair and walks around his desk. I want to take a step back, to cower, but I keep myself still, imagining Cade's magic still warming me. Green sparks at Sam's fingertips, his magic growing brighter until it wreathes his arms. With a wave of his hand, his magic shoots out and wraps around Kai, Cade, and Cole's throats.

The three of them jerk and gasp, until the bands tighten. Kai's fight intensifies, until Sam steps in front of him and cocks his head. I can see the band tighten further, the indentation digging deep into the pale skin of his neck.

"Stop!" I step forward, reaching a hand out to Sam. "Stop hurting them!" Do I use my magic? Do I reveal it now or wait? Sam already knows I have power, so what would the harm be in trying to stop him?

Golden flames burn to life at my fingertips as I take another step forward. But before I can raise my hands to try to stop Sam, he pulls another syringe from his pocket and waves it in front of me.

"If you get any closer, you'll find yourself just as useless as the others." His eyes shoot to Kai in front of him. "And you'll get to watch as I slowly squeeze the life out of the vampire." The bands around Kai's neck tighten with his words, and his tendons pop as he struggles to free himself and take a breath.

Cole's face is turning red. And Cade's eyes are unfocused and beginning to dim. All of their movements are becoming more jerky. Their fight is slowing. Even if they had been able to break free before, now they never will be able to.

Sam is going to choke the life right out of them.

Sharp, hot panic flares inside of me, making my heart stutter and my breath catch. "Stop! I'll go with you! Just stop hurting them!"

ELLIS

My words are like a gunshot in the room. Kai and Cade both jerk toward me, but they are unable to do anything. Sam looks at me, his smile victorious.

"I knew I could win you over, doll."

"Let them go," I say, clutching my chest where my connection to them is pulling taut as they slowly suffocate.

The bands of magic disappear, but the creatures holding them remain. "I can't let them go yet," Sam croons. "But I promise I'll let them go once we're far enough away they won't cause any trouble."

I don't believe him, but at least they are no longer being choked to death. This gives them a chance to escape. And I know they will. They won't stop fighting.

"Ellis, no!" Cade's words are raspy but forceful.

Kai growls, doubling his efforts to get free. "Don't fucking think about it, Ellis!" He blinks, and from one second to the next, his gray eyes turn crimson. The monster has arrived. But it's still not enough to break away from his captor.

I look at both of them and my magic sizzles against my skin. Sam tsks and moves before I can blink. The syringe is pressed against my neck, the needle not quite penetrating. I freeze.

"I'd rather not have to lock down your magic, but I will if you don't behave," Sam snarls in my ear. "Can you behave, doll?"

I nod, but I glare at him, letting him see all my hatred. I need to keep him distracted. Sterling and the others need more time. But I can't let him hurt Cade and Kai. If I can keep Sam's focus on me, Cade and Kai can free themselves. Then, after Sterling has had time to save Gracie, I can find the right moment to take Sam by surprise. And I *will* take him down.

So instead of fighting, I push my love for Kai to him, hoping he picks it up with his empath abilities. For Cade, I smile. It's small and shaky, but it says everything I need to say. Thank you. I love you.

Their fear and panic hurt more than anything. It cuts straight through me; burns with the heat of the sun, makes me want to tear my insides out just so I can't feel it anymore.

I turn away from their wide eyes, unable to look any longer. Sam grabs my arm and tugs me out the door. When I pass Cole, I nod at him, thanking him for everything.

He shakes his head. "Don't do this," he whispers.

I ignore his words, and the sensation of Cade and Kai's gazes on my back, and let Sam drag me down the hall. Their shouts and curses follow me like ghosts that will haunt me for the rest of my life. However long that is. Sam says nothing, but his fingers bite into my skin hard enough to leave bruises.

He leads me past the set of the stairs we used to get to the basement last time we were here. I force down a flash of panic as I wonder where he's taking me. What if he takes me somewhere out of this building? At least if we're here, the guys will know where I am.

At another set of stairs, Sam drags me down, nearly pulling my arm out of the socket. The doors at the bottom open to a separate room, and my heart stops.

It looks like a medical chamber of some sort. A metal operating table sits in the middle of the space over a drain stained a suspicious shade of copper. Counters and shelves line the walls, various instruments I don't look at too closely sitting on the white surface.

"On the table," Sam says, nudging me in that direction. I don't move, frozen to the spot, and Sam grabs the back of my neck and pushes me. "On. The. Table."

Gone is the handsome businessman. The monster has taken his place.

My arms and legs shake as I climb onto the metal surface and lie down. Immediately, Sam's magic binds me. I hiss through the pain, fighting back the memory of the last time his magic wrapped around my skin.

I debate the best time to let my magic free, but it doesn't feel right yet. There is nothing in my chest tugging me toward the golden flame I harbor inside of me. As hard as it is, I need to trust my instincts. And right now is not the right time.

Sam takes a scalpel from a rolling tray and his gaze roves over my body. The white fog. I need the fog I used to sink into to survive my encounters with him. I search and search for it, but I can't find it.

My guys have made the fog unnecessary.

Sam places the thin blade above my breast bone and carefully slices through my shirt and bra. The fabric falls away, exposing my rapidly rising and falling chest. Sam's eyes heat and he licks his lower lip.

Where is the fog? I need that fucking fog. I need something to mask the shame and hurt and terror. Something to disappear into so I can't feel my own body or hear my own thoughts.

As Sam slices through my leggings and panties, I squeeze my eyes shut. He doesn't touch me, but his gaze on my exposed flesh is more than enough.

"Where is that magic, doll?"

I take a shaky breath and open my eyes. Instead of answering him, I stare. I let him see that I'm not the same person I was a few months ago. He can threaten me, he can torture me, but I won't cry or beg. I won't flinch or shy away from him.

As his gaze travels over my body again, lingering on the apex of my thighs, I realize I don't need the fog anymore.

My guys are the fog I can sink into. My Shields from the pain. Cade's gentle touch and the way he always makes sure I'm okay, every step of the way. Sterling's passion and the way he consumes every part of me. And Kai. I smile despite the situation. My Kai. Despite his possessive tendencies and the monster that lives under his skin, there is no one I feel safer with.

I feel it then. My magic simmering inside me, just under the surface. I know my eyes have turned golden by the shock on Sam's face. This man can't hurt me anymore. He can try all he likes, but he'll never see me cry again. I smile, letting him see all of that in my golden gaze.

The lack of reaction from me and the smile, lights the fuse. Sam darts forward and grabs my throat, squeezing painfully. "Where is the fucking magic?" Spittle flies from his lips in his anger. As quickly as he grabbed me, he lets go. Taking deep breaths, he tries to calm himself, straightening his black suit jacket with rough tugs. He pulls a radio from the counter and speaks into it. "Bring me Grace."

No. Not Gracie. Please, Sterling. Please have gotten her out of here already. I'm not sure if I can hold out if Sam brings Gracie in.

While we wait, Sam talks. I tune him out. Focusing instead on my guys and the strength they give me. There is still no tug in my chest, so I continue to wait to bring out my magic, but I'm getting antsy. Maybe I'm overestimating my abilities. Maybe that instinct I thought I would feel won't come. Should I just act now? I want to act now. I want to wipe this miserable excuse for a mage from the face of the earth.

Sam looks at the clock and mutters under his breath. "What the hell is taking so long," he barks into the radio. "Bring me Grace. Now!"

A few minutes later, the radio crackles. "Sorry sir," a breathless voice comes through the speaker. "We're having a bit of a problem." Muffled noises come from the radio before it cuts off.

"What kind of problem?" Sam asks, his voice dark and promising pain.

There's no response, and I watch as Sam gets angrier and angrier. This is when he becomes dangerous. When his anger takes control, he is liable to do anything.

The next time he looks at me, his brown eyes shimmer with green, the muddy color a sight that haunts me still. I know what happens next will not be good. But there is still no tug in my chest.

Am I waiting for something that isn't going to happen? Are my instincts wrong?

But as soon as Sam takes one step toward me, the door bursts open. Cade rushes in, and the way his face contorts in anger at seeing me bound and naked, makes a thrill rush through me.

"Well, this wasn't planned, but I can certainly use it to my advantage." Sam claps his hands once and smiles.

I've come to realize when he smiles like that, we are always unprepared for what happens next. The thrill inside me turns to fear.

Cade pulls a gun from the waistband of his pants and levels it at Sam.

"I promised Ellis she'd get the chance to kill you." He cocks the gun, the sound loud in the sterile room. "But I'll beg for her forgiveness later."

I jerk as the gun goes off. My ears ring and the breath in my lungs halts. Time seems to slow, and I swear I can see the bullet whizzing through the air toward Sam.

Sam raises his hand and flicks his fingers, like he's shaking water off his skin. The bullet stops mid air, and my stomach drops. Before I can scream, it changes directions and shoots straight for Cade.

He doesn't have time to react. The bullet tears through his chest, a direct hit to his heart.

Stunned, Cade stares at the blood seeping through the

wound, a gory red flower blooming on his chest. His violet eyes meet mine and his knees hit the floor.

A scream tears through my throat as he collapses. A scream that comes from the depth of my very soul. It sears my throat and steals my breath. It drags with it a burst of magic. The bands shackling me to the table sizzle and disappear.

I'm on the ground kneeling next to Cade in seconds. His lifeless violet eyes stare at nothing. The blood from the wound has already stopped flowing.

"Cade," I whisper, shaking his body. "Cade, wake up." He's just sleeping. He'll take a breath and his eyes will sparkle again as he smiles at me. Sleeping. He's just ...

A rift opens inside of me. A gaping wound that bleeds ichor into my bloodstream. My Cade. My sweet mage. He's ... gone.

My heart shatters. Millions of pieces of glass slicing through me, drawing blood and shredding me to ribbons. What do I do now? How do I breathe without him?

A fire sparks inside of me. A golden flicker of a candle. I turn my palms up and draw the magic forth. Golden flames hiss to life in my palms, growing bigger until it climbs my arms.

"There it is," Sam breathes in awe.

I raise my gaze from my soul-bonded and slowly stand. Sam's eyes widen when I take a step over Cade's still form and the white and golden wings flare from my back.

"It's too late," I say, my voice foreign to me. It's dull and numb, unfeeling and uncaring. "You'll never escape me now."

He huffs a laugh. "So dramatic. If you think you can best me with your untrained magic, you are sorely mistaken. I will have your blood. I will have your body to use as I please. You will be my slave, whether willingly or not."

"Go ahead and try." Cold. So cold. My voice and my body. As if Cade took all the warmth with him when he left. *Left.* As if he's just stepped out of the room for a moment and will be back. I crack even more. Splitting wide open and bleeding freely. My flames spread further, covering all of me now, turning me into a walking golden inferno.

Green magic shoots for me. It's not an attack to harm me, but to restrain me. It wraps around my ankles and wrists, snakes around my throat. As soon as it touches my skin, it turns to smoke.

Sam steps backward, eyes widening. "How did you do that?" Another blast of his magic shoots for me. This one less refined, more something that would knock me out if it landed. He's getting desperate. It doesn't land. Fire sweeps before me, golden flames hissing and licking. It burns Sam's attack to ash.

"If you thought you'd get away with killing one of my Shields, torturing my sister, *raping* me, you're dumber than I thought you were." My voice remains cold and detached. Even as they get stuck in my throat thinking about Cade. But my fury is burning hotter than anything else. And I need to see Sam dead at my feet.

The first flicker of fear passes through his eyes as he must recognize the seriousness of my words. He takes another step backward and I follow with slow, matching steps. I take too much enjoyment in the way he glances around, looking for something to help him. I never had help those two years he abused me. He won't find any now.

Another blast of green magic spears for me, and I can taste the terror in it as another puff of smoke erupts in the air when it meets my golden fire.

"Please," he begs, the whites of his eyes visible in his fear. "We can figure something out."

My smile is sharp and pointed, all teeth and the promise of death. "It's over, Sam." There is no point in even refuting him. I'm not going to let him live. Not after everything he's done.

His back hits the wall, a cornered rabbit. His magic is wild around him as he tries anything and everything to get through my golden flames.

The hair that escaped my braid lifts in a phantom breeze. The feathers at my back flutter. My palm tingles and I make a fist. When I open it, the golden sword is clutched in my hand. I spare one glance for the purple gem on the pommel. The same color as Cade's eyes.

Unholy fury spears through me. This man stole too much from me. He took my innocence. He ruined so many years of my life. He gave me trauma I'll never get over.

But Cade's death tops it all. He took my soul-bonded from me. He stole my future, my happiness. He took one of the few good things in my life and destroyed it.

I take a breath and lift the sword. My arm doesn't shake even though the sword is heavy in my hand. It's as if it knows what its purpose is for today. It knows it's taking revenge on someone who has hurt me. Golden fire licks down the blade. Its reflection shines in Sam's wide eyes and I smile.

"Goodbye, Sam."

His magic buffets my fire, but it's not enough. The blade slides effortless through his chest. Through skin and muscle. Past bone. Right into the organ that turned black long ago.

I twist the sword as I pull it free and I watch with impassive eyes as Sam falls to the floor. He blinks at me, green magic fading from his brown eyes.

"Doll," he chokes as blood spews from his mouth and coats his lips and chin.

I sneer. "I was never your doll, you sick bastard." Grasping the hilt like a baseball bat, I swing it down again and again, blood spraying with each hit, splattering my face and arms, until Sam's head rolls from his body.

I stand over him, breathing heavily, making sure he doesn't rise again. I wouldn't put it past him. But he doesn't. I open my hand to drop the sword, and it disappears.

I rush back to Cade and fall to my knees. "Cade," I whisper. My hands are still wreathed in fire when I take his face in my palms. "Cade." My voice breaks, and it cracks me open even more. "I love you." With trembling lips I kiss him one last time.

The dam bursts open. I bury my face in his still chest. My

body shakes with the force of my sobbing. Each tear that falls sizzles on my skin.

Empty. I'm so empty inside. Cade is missing. His presence is gone. I don't know how to breathe anymore without him. He was the one who brought me back from the edge. Who will do it now?

I clutch his body, holding it against mine. The despair, the pain; it grows. It turns to heat inside me, and before I know it, great billowing flames roar from my body.

I feed everything into the fire. I want it to consume me. To destroy me. To make the pain go away. Greater and greater it grows.

I close my eyes and hold Cade close. And I burn.

STERLING

ALL HELL HAS BROKEN LOOSE. I KNEW AS SOON AS WE crawled through the window and found no guards in the hall outside, they would all be waiting in the basement for us. And I was right.

As soon as we stepped out of the stairwell, chaos ensued.

Half of our enemies are magicals—mages and shifters—the other half are the creatures Sam has been creating. Some combination of magical or human laced with the blood of another magical. However it works, it results in almost zombie-like creatures with extreme strength and speed and no sense of pain that I can tell.

Connor's red magic flashes non-stop in the dim lighting. His hits kill the magicals, but the ones who have been altered, the creatures, they get back up—sometimes missing a limb or with smoke rising from an empty eye socket. It's absolutely nauseating to watch.

Drew has given up his crow form. Against these creatures, he's useless. They are too fast, and he almost got his head pulled from his body when one of them caught him mid-air. Instead, he's using fists. It's not doing much, but it is providing a distraction.

I make my way down the hall, dodging what I can, and taking

out what I can't. It would be easier in my wolf form, but I don't want to scare Grace by barging into her cell as a wolf. I'm almost to the room where they're keeping her, when someone calls my name. I turn around and freeze.

"Where is she?" I shout.

Kai, Cade, and Cole have joined the fray in the basement. But there is no sign of Ellis. Or Sam.

"I was hoping you'd seen her!" Kai yells back.

What the fuck does he mean? They were supposed to be with her. I dart back the way I'd come, stopping to slide my knife into a creature's back, right between its ribs and into its kidney. That doesn't kill them, but it stops them long enough for me to wrap my hands around their head and twist. That kills them.

I grab Kai's shoulder and shove him into a room, kicking the door shut behind me. "Where the fuck is she?" I growl.

"Sam had us by the throat," Kai says, panting slightly. His eyes are wild, ruby red and utterly terrified. "Literally. She went with him to save us. Cade and Cole have been injected with whatever you were injected with that one time. They have no access to their magic."

"Fuck. Fuck!" I pace back and forth a few times, tugging at my hair in agitation. Fear and anger swirl inside of me, mixing to create a volatile combination. "He'll have taken her to the torture room, most likely. But I didn't see them come down this way. There must be another way into the room."

"It's at the end of the hall?" Kai asks, already turning back toward the door, ready to go save his beloved.

"Yes."

"I'll get her. You get Grace out of here. Take out as many of these bastards as you can."

He opens the door and rushes into the hall, his image blurring as he taps into his supernatural speed, but he doesn't get far. A creature stops him, and he has to engage it to get past. I use the distraction once again to slip by. I manage to get to Grace's room without having to fight anyone. Behind me, the battle continues.

Flashes of Connor's magic, gun shots, grunts and cries of pain. One look shows me Connor, Drew, Kai, and Cole fighting for their lives. I don't see Cade, but I don't have the time to look for him. Ignoring my anxiety and fear, I push into Grace's room.

She's curled in the corner, looking like a pile of skin and bones with a threadbare blanket wrapped around her frail body.

"Grace?" I say quietly, taking another step inside and closing the door. "Grace?"

She stirs, her body jerking slightly before she lifts her head. It takes all of her strength to do so, and she can only hold it up for a moment before she lays it back down, panting slightly. But her light brown eyes blearily focus on me.

"Grace, it's me. Sterling. Ellis's mate." I kneel in front of her, projecting all of my movements to avoid scaring her. "I'm going to get you out of here."

Her eyes widen and she sucks in a breath. "Ellis?" she rasps, her voice barely audible.

I nod. "Can I pick you up? We need to move fast."

She pales, her skin somehow losing even more color, but she swallows thickly. "Okay."

As gently as I can, I scoop her into my arms. I know she has no visible injuries. Sam makes sure to heal her after every torture session. But her bones protrude from her skin and I can't imagine that doesn't hurt. She weighs nothing in my arms, and before I slip back into the hall I warn her.

"There is fighting in the hallway. I'm going to get you out of there as fast as I can."

She closes her eyes and buries her face in my chest, and I shove through the door into the chaos. It's moved closer to this end of the hallway, no doubt due to Kai trying to get to Ellis. He sees me with Grace and nods, working on opening a path for me to get through.

Between him and Cole I make it to the stairwell, but before I step inside, an explosion rattles the building. I look down the hall to find golden flames billowing from the torture room. They grow quickly, spreading faster and faster toward us. My heart stops.

Ellis.

"Go!" Kai yells, motioning to all of us. "Get out of here. I'll keep going."

Kai would be the only one able to withstand that fire. I hesitate though. My mate is down there. Clearly in trouble. And I need to go for her. But Cole grabs my arm and yanks me through the door. Already, the heat of the golden flames warms the stairwell.

"Get Grace out of here!" Cole yells, darting up the stairs.

Drew gives me a push and we hurry up to the first floor. Golden flames lick up the walls on the first floor, seeping through the floor where they burn the hottest down below. I don't give myself time to think. I follow Cole and Drew into a classroom and hand Grace to Drew before climbing out, running to the edge of the property.

When I turn around, I fall to my knees. The building is consumed in golden fire. It writhes and undulates, dancing and burning as it eats away at the wood and metal.

"Where's Connor?" Cole asks, glancing at Grace. "I think she needs some healing."

I don't take my eyes from the building, barely hearing my brother speak.

"He's not here," Drew says. "Did he get caught inside?"

I don't fucking care about Connor. Where is my mate? Where is Ellis? I jump to my feet, moving faster than I ever have before. As if sensing what I'm about to do, Cole grabs me around the waist and holds me still, keeping me from running into the golden inferno. My heart pounds fast enough to make my chest ache. Or maybe that's the bond that hurts. I thrash against Cole, trying to get free, but he's too strong. My beta is almost equal to me in strength.

"Let me go, Cole!" I growl.

"I can't let you go in there." His voice is irritatingly calm, and I want nothing more than to ram my fist into his nose.

"My mate ..." The words are choked when they come out, and the pain in my chest intensifies. I double over, as much as I can in Cole's grasp. "Ellis," I rasp. My wolf is at the surface. I'm seconds from shifting, when Cole stiffens behind me.

"Wait." He points, and I squint past the brightness of the flames.

I can make out two figures walking toward us. Two figures, each carrying ...

My knees give out, and Cole gently lowers me to the grass. Kai is singed, his clothing hanging in burning tatters to his frame. Dried bloody tears track down his cheeks. And in his arms is my mate. Hanging lifeless and naked. Her white wings trail limply behind them.

And Connor. In Connor's arms is Cade.

The world tips precariously around me. My heart stutters. Stops. Stutters again. Every dream I've had, every hope and fantasy of a life with my brothers and Ellis goes up like smoke. Ash from the warehouse falls around me as Ellis's golden fire continues to consume the building and everything inside of it.

And I wish it would consume me too.

KAI

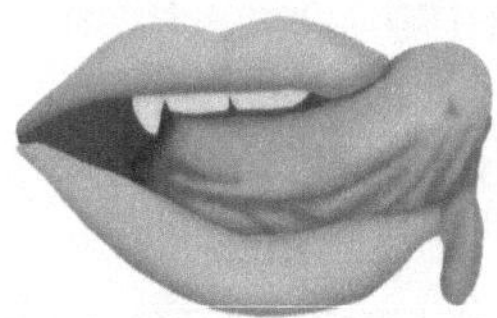

THE HEAT FROM ELLIS'S FLAMES BURNS HOTTER THAN A normal fire. Even knowing I can't be killed by them, I hesitate just slightly. Harpy fire isn't something I've ever trained for. For all I know, it could kill me. But my beloved is in that room and I'd die to get to her. I'd walk through the burning pits of hell to save her.

I hold my hands in front of my face in an attempt to shield against the heat that batters me in a searing wind. My eyes are dried out, my skin too tight over my bones as the fire tries to crispen me. The clothes I was wearing are singed and tattered, a few small fires burning in the fabric. But I pay them no mind as I reach the door to the torture room.

The metal is too hot to touch, so I use my shoulder to shove it open. The blast of hot air almost knocks me backward, and only my supernatural strength and determination of finding Ellis keep me from shrinking away. I scan the room, squinting at the dry wind and brightness of the flames. I can't see anything except a faint impression of a body. And that body is in the center of the swirling vortex of the fire.

I know without a doubt it's Ellis, and the flames are emanating from her in a furious storm that no doubt comes from her emotions. I don't want to know what emotions would make her react in this way.

"Ellis!" I scream, lurching toward her, but my shout is lost in the roar of her flames. Inching closer, holding my hands up to shield my face, I kneel next to her. What I see makes me falter.

She's thrown herself over Cade, and he's laying motionless under her. Everything pulls away from me—my thoughts, my feelings, my very soul—it all pulls away like a tide receding before a tsunami. The breath I suck in burns, and not just from the inferno heating the air around me.

"Ellis?" I rasp, gently reaching out my hand. It passes through the hottest of her flames, the flames surrounding her and Cade. I hiss at the blistering heat, but it doesn't burn my skin away.

As soon as my hand touches her shoulder, the flames nearest us suck back inside of her. The roaring crackle and hiss disappears instantly, leaving my ears ringing in the sudden silence. The building groans ominously, and I know I have to get them out of here now.

Ellis turns her tear streaked face toward me. I have never seen such despair in her eyes. She shudders and sucks in a breath before her eyes roll back and she collapses. I catch her on instinct alone and haul her to my chest. She's naked but I see no major injuries on her. Her heart is still beating, it echoes in my chest slow and steady. She's just overused her magic. Rest and food will help her recover.

My gaze travels to Cade and my own heart stutters. His clothing is singed like mine, like her fire didn't want to hurt us, but the ferocity of it still beat through all the barriers that surrounded us to keep us safe. It's not the singed clothing that steals my breath though. It's the bloodied hole in his shirt, right over his heart.

Is Cade dead? Is that why Ellis had lost it? Why her fire had burned so fiercely?

My fingers shake as I reach out and tug Cade's tattered shirt aside. Fully expecting to see a gaping wound, I'm startled to see pale, smooth flesh. With Ellis still in my arms, I scoot closer and see his chest rise and fall with steady breaths. My body sags under the realization. Something bad happened here, and Ellis must have done something to save Cade.

The ceiling cracks above me, and I glance up to see spiderwebs fissure across the charred and blackened ceiling tiles. This entire structure is going to come down around us. Gritting my teeth, I throw Ellis over one shoulder and snag Cade around the waist, hefting him onto my other shoulder. My legs shake as I walk out of the room, a combination of fear, relief, and exhaustion making me weak.

While Ellis put out the fire in the torture room, the rest of building is still aflame. If I had time, I'd stop to admire the way the golden tongues lick and dance along the walls. There's no smoke, but they put off an incredible amount of heat as they eat away at the building.

More groaning and cracking sounds in the hallway, and I hurry my steps as fast as I can. I'm honestly not positive I'll be able to climb the stairs with both of them. Before I have to try, a figure shimmers in the heat behind the flames. For a second I freeze. Is that Sam? Did he not get caught in her inferno? Before I have to make the decision to put Cade and Ellis down to fight, the figure clarifies. Connor.

His clothing is smoldering, but he is uninjured by the fire. Whatever Ellis did to create this inferno, it doesn't appear to be harming our family and friends. Connor's gaze is somber as he takes in the two bodies thrown over my shoulders.

"Are they …"

"They're alive," I rasp. "I don't know what happened. They're both unconscious, but breathing."

He nods and takes Cade from me, lightening my load. My muscles almost scream in relief. Normally, carrying both of them wouldn't be an issue. But the heat from the fire has sapped my energy, not to mention the tidal waves of fear that washed through me before I found them both alive.

I sling Ellis down into both of my arms. Her wings drag behind us, trailing on the ground, but there is nothing I can do about that.

"The entire building is about to collapse," Connor gasps. "We have to get out of here."

I nod and follow him up the stairs, easier now that I only have one person to carry. The flames continue to crackle and burn. The building creaks and groans. Connor rushes to a classroom, and turning so his back is facing the wall, he shields Cade as he tears through the weakened structure.

I hunch over Ellis as debris falls around us. But Connor has made a man sized hole in the wall, and we both slip through into the cool fresh air. In the distance, I see Sterling, Cole, and Drew waiting, and we make our way toward them.

Sterling collapses to the ground when he sees me with Ellis limp in my arms, and Cade unmoving in Connor's. When I reach him, I kneel on the ground in front of him, staring into his bleak blue eyes.

"Ellis," he croaks, his hand reaching out and hesitating.

"She's alive," I say. "I think she just used too much magic."

It takes all of my will power to hand her off to Sterling. He takes her with shaking hands and presses her tight to his chest, his entire body seeming to deflate when he sees her chest moving. But then he looks up, and his eyes land on Cade.

I take Cade from Connor, cradling him in my lap like a child. He was breathing in the warehouse, I made sure of it, but I need to double check. Placing my hand on his chest, I feel a steady thump under my palm as his heart beats. The last bit of tension inside of me eases.

"What happened?" Sterling asks, looking at the bloody shirt clinging to Cade in tatters.

I pull it aside and graze my fingers over his heart where the bloodiest part of his shirt had been. I couldn't see it in the torture chamber, surrounded by Ellis's flames, but I can feel it. A slightly raised patch of skin, no bigger than a bullet. My throat dries and I press my fingers to his neck, needing confirmation again.

"I think ..." I swallow, the dryness in my throat causing my words to scrape all the way up. "I think he got shot."

Just saying the words causes my heart to pound. Under my fingers, his pulse thrums. There is no denying he's alive. But that is definitely a scar on his chest. A bullet wound he hadn't had before we entered that building.

I squeeze my eyes shut. "Somehow, Ellis healed him. She was laying over him. Her flames were burning so fiercely." The image of Cade looking dead on the floor flashes in my mind, and I snap my eyes open.

Behind me, the building crumbles. Wood splinters and metal groans. And Ellis's fire continues to burn.

I sit in the chair I pulled up to the edge of the bed and watch over the two people I love the most in this world. If I take my eyes off of them, panic creeps in, stealing my breath and making my heart race. What if they stop breathing when I look away? What if their hearts stop beating? It's irrational, but the part of my brain that controls rationality has fled, leaving only the primal, possessive part of me.

"Cole picked up Agatha, they're on their way." Sterling drops into a chair on the opposite side of the bed, heaving a sigh as he rubs his hand down his face.

Neither of us has changed or cleaned up. We're both still wearing torn and bloodied clothing, mine singed and turning crispy along the burnt edges. Downstairs, Allie fusses over Connor and Drew, making sure they aren't hurt. After a quick assessment that Ellis and Cade were alive, I kicked her out of the room. The monster inside of me is too close to the surface, and I'm liable to lash out and hurt anyone who gets too close to my two loves. I think she recognized that and instead of arguing, has decided to distract herself with caring for someone else.

I'm exhausted. Every bone in my body aches. Every muscle overused. Moving requires too much effort when my body feels as if it weighs thousands of pounds. My eyes burn and it's difficult to keep them open. I just want to curl up in bed with my loves and sleep for years. But even if I didn't have that irrational fear of looking away from them, I wouldn't be able to close my eyes.

The image of Ellis laying atop Cade, protecting him, mourning him, is too fresh in my mind. Her eyes when she'd looked at me were haunted, devastated, and completely full of despair. In the moment, with adrenaline coursing through my veins and my instincts roaring to protect them and keep myself safe, the fear had been dulled. But now that I'm no longer moving and my brain has free reign to think about everything, that terror fills me.

I'd thought they were both dead at first. Until Ellis lifted her head, I thought I had lost my entire heart. Then, I'd seen the blood on Cade's chest and the pain in my beloved's eyes, and I knew the worst had happened. It had been too hard to breathe past the band constricting my chest. All I could think about was how I'd care for Ellis, how I'd help her through her mourning, when I couldn't even handle it myself?

When I'd seen the healed smooth skin of his chest, I knew she'd done something to heal him. The relief had been swift, and it had almost knocked me off my feet. I hadn't lost them. They were both still here with me. But the fear was still there, just under the surface waiting for me to close my eyes and let my guard down. I won't forget this moment. Ever.

"We came so close," Sterling whispers, his gaze glued to our family on the bed. "Too close."

I can't respond because my throat has closed up, so I just nod in agreement. There is nothing else to say, really, and we lapse into silence, sinking into our own terror-filled thoughts.

After what felt like hours—hours of fighting the need to close my eyes and sleep—Cole knocks on the bedroom door and pops his head inside. "Agatha is ready. Can I let her in?"

Sterling nods and pushes from the chair with a groan. He looks just as worn down as I am. When Agatha steps into the room, Sterling bows his head to her. "Thank you for coming."

Agatha nods back. "Alpha," she says respectfully. Her gaze drops to the bed, eyes narrowing on Ellis and Cade's unmoving forms. "Tell me what happened." She sits in the chair Sterling had been using, her bones crackling as she does so.

"We don't really know," Sterling answers, taking a seat on the edge of the bed next to Cade. His tone is weary, matching his expression and slumped shoulders. "We were ... taking care of a problem," he says carefully, not wanting to divulge what exactly we were doing.

"I found them in a burning room," I continue. Agatha is smart enough she'll be able to connect the dots once the news of the warehouse hits the media. But I'm not too worried about her knowing. She already knows Ellis is a harpy. "The fire was Ellis's doing, and she was laying atop Cade, cocooned in her flames. Cade had a hole in his shirt, covered with blood, right over his heart. But his skin is smooth and unharmed."

"They have both been unconscious since Kai found them," Sterling finishes for me as I trail off, unable to continue as my throat dries with just the thought of Cade and Ellis dying.

Agatha pushes to her feet, more popping coming from her bones and she leans over Cade. One gnarled finger rubs over the slightly raised scar on his chest. Her brows lower as she thinks, and I can practically see her sifting through all the knowledge she has in that ancient brain of hers. When she finally sits back down, she levels a stare at Sterling.

"It looks like a bullet wound," Agatha says with brutal clarity.

Sterling nods. "Yeah, that's what we think, too."

"There are books and texts that have been long lost to society. The words in these books have been passed down to the wolves from generation to generation. Most of them are considered pure myth and legend, like harpy's themselves. But there are still some facts among the tales." Agatha rests her gnarled hands in her lap, pale gaze alternating between me and Sterling. "There is a story about a harpy that walked the earth long, long ago. On a battlefield, one of her Shields was slain. The harpy's fury was all encompassing. Her flames destroyed their enemy in one blazing hot wall of fire. The story goes that she knelt next to her Shield, her tears freely streaming down her face as her flame surrounded her and her dead lover."

I swallow thickly, imagining how all of this would have played out tonight in that torture room. Cade getting shot. Ellis losing her mind in grief and fury. Sam wouldn't have stood a chance against her.

"What happened next was nothing short of a miracle," Agatha continues, oblivious to my inner turmoil. "With the harpy's tears on her Shield's death wound, and her flames burning hotter and hotter, she somehow brought her lover back to life. She healed him of his mortal injury."

Sterling and I both suck in a breath. We had suspected something like this had happened. It was the only way Cade could have a bullet-shaped scar right over his heart and still be breathing. But just hearing the words said aloud, by someone who has knowledge about supernatural creatures, I'm flooded with fear.

Too close. We were too fucking close to losing them both.

"They should both be fine after some rest," Agatha says. "I imagine they'll sleep for a while, so do not be alarmed. The amount of energy and magic Ellis had to use, and the simple fact that Cade is healing from death, will keep them both down for a while."

Simple fact. I shudder.

Cade died. My ... whatever he is ... died. If it hadn't been for Ellis ...

I can't finish that thought. I can't even try to imagine what life would look like without him. Without both of them. I squeeze my eyes shut and listen to Sterling walk Agatha downstairs for Cole to drive her home. Kneeling on the floor next to the bed where Ellis lays, I bury my face in her neck, inhaling her scent. The rich aroma of her blood pumping through her veins by her heart that beats steadily. It makes my eyes burn.

I hastily wipe them to avoid getting blood everywhere, and reach a hand over her body to grasp Cade's hand. It's warm and I barely bite back a sob. *They are okay. Both pieces of my heart are still here.* I repeat those words over and over, letting Ellis's scent and Cade's skin against mine cement them inside of me.

Sterling returns and the bed dips as he sits next to Ellis. Her hair tickles my face as he tucks a curl behind her ear. "It's going to be okay." His other hand rests on my back, and his words sound like they are more for him than me. Like he's reminding himself they're okay. The same way I am. "We're going to be okay."

CADE

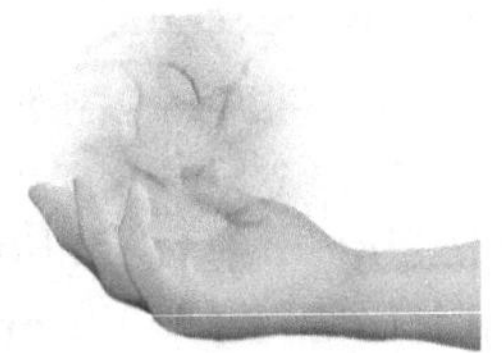

I'm slowly pulled from the depths of unconsciousness, and the first thing I'm aware of is the softness of whatever I'm laying on and the warmth covering me. Am I dead? Is this what heaven feels like? I almost snort because the idea that I'd go to heaven after everything I've done in my life is absurd. I try to open my eyes, but they're still too heavy. So I float for a little bit in the comfort and just enjoy the feeling of peace that has settled over me.

Eventually, quiet sounds filter through to me. Soft breathing. A gentle snore. That snore ... it's familiar. That's Sterling's snore. I snap my eyes open, blinking rapidly at the brightness as my eyes adjust. When I look around, I stifle a gasp.

I'm in the bedroom at the cabin. Ellis is laying next to me in the bed, and Sterling and Kai are asleep on chairs they've pulled up next to us, both of them bent in angles that will no doubt hurt when they wake up.

Slowly, I run my hand over my chest, a slight bump the only sign of what happened to me. I got shot. I remember it so clearly. The burst of fear when I realized the bullet had been stopped and was now heading for me. The look of terror on Ellis's face. The pain that coursed through me only after I'd already hit the ground.

I should be dead. Why am I not dead?

"Kai?" I rasp as quietly as I can.

His head snaps up, gray eyes wide as he looks at me. Then his face crumples. Blood tears fill his eyes and stream down his cheeks as he hangs his head, tugging the strands of his hair. His shoulders shake as he quietly cries, and I crack open seeing him fall apart.

I try to sit up so I can go to him, but before I can move an inch he's by my side. Shaking fingers trail over my cheek, cool on my skin. It takes tremendous effort to lift my arm and wipe away a bloody tear that slides down his face.

"Kai," I whisper.

He swallows hard and buries his face in my neck, climbing onto the bed to lay next to me. "I almost lost you," he breathes. "I almost lost you both."

His words catch in his throat and his body shudders. It takes all of my strength to wrap my arms around him. And when his arms come around me, holding me so tightly I'm positive he'll break my ribs, I turn my head enough to kiss his temple. I let him cry, ignoring the thick, sticky blood that coats my neck. I've only ever seen Kai cry one time, and even then it was only a few tears to honor a friend killed in a car accident.

Never, in all the years I've known him, has he ever been this undone. It does something to me. I want nothing more than to ease his pain, to take away the images I know he's playing on repeat in his head. But I can't do that. So I just lay with him, and do my best to keep my arms around him. But I'm tired, and before long, they start to shake from the effort.

He notices, and immediately lifts his head. "Are you okay?" His face is stained with blood from his crying, and I know my neck and shoulder are as well. The sight jars me, and I'm sure I'll never get used to seeing him cry tears of blood.

"I'm fine. Just tired."

He traces a finger under my eye. No doubt I have dark purple bruises under them. I feel like I could sleep for a year.

"What happened?" I ask tentatively.

Kai wipes at his face, smearing the red onto his hands and he grimaces. "Shit. Sorry." He takes one look at my neck and shoulder and gets up to grab a washcloth from the bathroom. He washes away the blood from my skin while he talks. "I found you and Ellis ..." he has to stop to swallow, his eyes taking on a haunted look. "She was laying on top of you. Her fire was raging around you guys. When I approached, she looked at me with heartbreak in her eyes, and I knew something bad had happened. I saw your shirt. It was soaked in blood, but when I checked for a wound, there was nothing there. Connor and I got you both out of there. You've been sleeping since."

I rub my hand over the raised mark on my chest. "I shot Sam," I say, watching him closely. "But before the bullet could hit him, he used his magic to stop it and turn it back on me. My magic was blocked by whatever that bastard injected me with, so I could do nothing to stop it."

Kai closes his eyes, gripping the cloth tightly in his fist. "I think ... I think you died." His words are choked and harsh. "Agatha said it's believed harpies can heal their Shields with their tears and fire. We think that's how you're ..." His lips tremble and he presses them together.

"Fuck," I whisper. "Lay with me?"

Kai immediately curls against me, tucking his head against my chest and pulling the blanket over us both. He leans up to press a kiss to the scar on my chest. "Don't do that again." His breath fans across my skin as he breathes the words into the silence.

My eyes are drifting shut again, and no amount of effort will keep them open. "Ellis?" I ask, my words slurring slightly.

"She's fine. Resting, like you should be."

"I love you, Kai," I mumble, before I fall asleep once more.

———

THE NEXT TIME I WAKE, it's with the sensation of fingers running through my hair. I roll over, trying to get closer to the body next to me. Kai chuckles softly, tugging me against him. When I open my eyes, he's sitting against the headboard between me and Ellis. While he was playing with my hair, he was holding Ellis's hand, keeping both of us close.

I close my eyes again, content to enjoy the moment. "How long was I asleep?" My voice is thick and hoarse from disuse and thirst.

Kai takes his phone from his pocket and shoots off a text. "Almost two days."

"Two days? Holy shit." I try to sit up, but Kai keeps me glued to his side.

"Stay here. Sterling is bringing up food and water. You need to eat something before you get out of bed."

At the mention of food, my stomach growls. "Yeah, I could definitely go for some food right now."

Kai laughs softly. "I'm sure you can."

"Has Ellis woken up yet?"

"Not yet," he says. "But I don't expect her to wake up for another day at least. I can't imagine the amount of power she used to heal you." His voice is hoarse as he speaks those words, and I hear him swallow. "Not to mention the fire she created to burn the building down."

"What else happened? Did we get Grace out? Is Sam dead?"

Kai sighs. "Grace is at Sterling's mom's house. She's ... she's very withdrawn. I think she needs Ellis. And Sam is dead. I don't know if Ellis did it intentionally, or if her magic had a mind of its own, but even though the entire building was turned to ash, his body and head were spared. But he is most certainly dead."

Body and head. Did she cut his head off? My vicious harpy. I'm so glad she got her revenge. Hopefully this gives her the closure she needs and she can finally move on with her life.

"Is it over?" I whisper.

"It's over. We can start our life together now. Build our family. Live in peace."

Kai's words bring tears to my eyes, and I bury my head in his chest, breathing deeply. When the door opens, Sterling sits on the edge of the bed with a plate of food and a glass of water. I down the water in one gulp, sighing as the cold, wet liquid slides down my throat. The roasted chicken and veggies don't last long either.

With my belly full and almost two days of sleep, I'm feeling more like myself. But one glance at my chest and the dried blood and dirt and ash, and I grimace. "I need to shower."

Kai hops out of the bed and heads straight for the bathroom, and soon the sounds of the shower fill the quiet space. I lean over and press a kiss to Ellis's forehead, studying her sleeping face. She's paler than usual, and a frown pulls her lips down even in sleep. Slight creases surrounded her eyes, and I desperately want to wake her and let her know I'm okay. I can only imagine the pain she's feeling, even in her sleep. But I know she needs that rest.

Instead, I force myself up, not even slightly ashamed I need Sterling to help me. The room spins alarmingly, and I grasp his arm until it stops. He hesitates just outside the bathroom.

"That was the scariest moment of my life," he says quietly, head ducked and gaze averted. "I'm really glad you're okay."

I grin. Sterling has never been big on showing his emotions. His way of showing he cares is by protecting us. By being the alpha of our family and making sure we have everything we need. Words have never been easy for him. I pull him in for a hug, and he thumps me on the back before pulling away. He's not quick enough to hide the shine of his eyes, though.

"I'll sit with Ellis. Take your time." Sterling goes back to the bed and sits next to Ellis, fingers gently tracing over her cheekbone.

When I push through the door, I find Kai standing in the steam with his shirt off. "Get in," he says, voice low and almost growly.

My skin prickles under his intense stare as I tug my sweats down. Kai's gaze is like a brand, burning every inch of my flesh. As turned on as I am, I don't have it in me for this, and I hate to be the one to break it to him.

Kai smiles and shakes his head. "Don't worry. I'm not going to ravish you. I just ... I just want to be here with you."

The vulnerability in his words and the almost timid way he says them cracks me open. So I step into the shower, the hot spray of water cascading over me as I wait for Kai to strip out of his pants and join me.

He stares at me for a moment, fang biting into his lower lip. "Turn around," he says quietly.

I do as he says, and Kai runs his hands over my shoulders, soapy suds slipping down my chest. He slowly and meticulously washes every inch of me. When he gets to my hair, I close my eyes and bite back a moan. His fingers rubbing my scalp, gently massaging, loosens every muscle I've been holding tight since I woke up.

"Rinse off," Kai whispers.

I turn around to rinse off the suds and wash them out of my hair. "Thank you," I say, reaching out my hand and cupping his cheek.

There is a bleakness in his eyes, a haunted look that he doesn't seem to be able to get rid of. It hurts to see it. This strong, cocky vampire is lost. He leans into my touch and I step forward, sliding my hand around to grab the back of his neck. Pulling him against me, I kiss him.

It's like we can't get close enough. Kai clings to me, pressing our bodies together so every inch of our naked skin touches. I thought the kiss would turn desperate, but instead, it stays gentle. The warm water continues to spray down on us, and we lose ourselves in the touches.

If he needs this reminder that I'm okay and alive, I'll give it to him. He doesn't seem to want to take it any further, and I'm okay with that. I don't need to have sex with him to know how much he loves me. I don't need his empath abilities to feel the depth of that love. It's there, in the kiss, in the way he holds me tighter.

When we break apart, the water has cooled. I didn't even realize we'd been in here that long, lost in each other. Kai stares at me with a wild look.

"Never again, Cade. Don't ever die on me again."

ELLIS

Awareness returns slowly. I know I'm in a bed. It's soft, and there's a warm blanket covering me. For a while, that's all I know. And I'm content to float in the warmth and comfort, mindless and numb to everything. I know what awaits me.

Eventually, the sounds of soft conversation filter into my mind. No words. Just the gentle humming of voices. It's familiar. Like the voices are part of me. I let them wash over me, soothing the slowly rising tide of emotions I won't be able to hold at bay much longer.

My fingers and toes are the first parts of my body that I can distinguish in the slowly dissipating fog. My arms and legs are next. Followed by my stomach. I try to keep the feeling at bay. I don't want it to reach my chest where I know it will hurt unbearably.

But the wave crests. No matter how hard I try to stop it, it washes ashore and there is no stopping the complete and utter despair that floods through me. It steals my breath. Burns my throat and lungs. And where my heart should be, it echoes in the empty space, making the missing pieces all that much more recognizable.

Cade is gone.

My soul-bonded. My mage. My world.

He's gone.

Never again will I gaze into those beautiful violet eyes. My skin grows cold knowing I'll never feel his arms around me. I'll never taste his lips or inhale his scent again. His laugh will no longer echo through the cabin.

He. Is. Gone.

I'm cracked open and bleeding. Raw and broken. How do I heal without the one who put me back together into the person I am now? How do I get out of this bed knowing a vital piece of my soul has been removed. Cut out. Destroyed.

The pain is unlike any I've ever felt. Sam's abuse and torture was nothing compared to this. I curl onto my side, squeezing my eyes shut tighter against the tears burning to be let loose. My lungs scream for oxygen but I can't get them to expand. I gasp, a rattling breath that does nothing to ease the ache.

Hands on my cheek, my back, my hair. A combination of voices, soft whispers that I'm unable to process as words. I curl further into myself. Unable to open my eyes and see only two of them in front of me.

"Ellis, baby girl," Kai says, brushing his knuckles down my cheek. "Ellis, listen to me."

I shake my head. Where did the numbness go? Where is the oblivion I so desperately need?

"Ellis, look at me." Kai shakes me slightly, and it infuriates me so much I open my eyes.

"Just leave me alone!" I try to shout, but it comes out more like a croak.

Before I can close my eyes again, his begin to glow. "Listen to me," he says, his voice haunting and demanding.

I have no choice but to listen now. As much as I want to close my ears and bury myself under the covers, I can't. I do glare at him though. Why can't he respect my wishes to be left alone?

"Ellis, Cade is alive."

I blink at him. He forced me to listen but that doesn't mean I comprehend his words. Cade is dead. I watched him hit the ground. I saw him staring lifelessly at the ceiling. I held his unmoving body.

Why would Kai do this to me?

His gray eyes are soft and understanding. He gives me a small smile and turns my head with a finger on my chin. Sitting on the bed next to me, is Cade. I blink, mouth falling open. But ...

"Ellis, love," he whispers, eyes filling with tears. Violet eyes I thought I'd never look into again.

I choke on a sob and clutch my chest. Cade's arms come around me immediately, warm and so very real. All I can do is clutch him and cry. He holds me tight enough to make breathing difficult, but I don't care.

"How?" I gasp between broken sobs. "I saw ..."

Cade rubs his hand up and down my back, the other tangling in my hair to press my face harder to his chest. "Agatha said you healed me."

I pull away, only far enough to look at him. To make sure this is real. To make sure he's real. "What?"

"Something about the combination of your tears and fire." He rubs his chest. The last time I saw him, there was a bloody hole there. "Whatever it was, you saved me."

I stare at him, unable to comprehend the words. "Is this real?" I whisper, lips trembling and tears falling even harder. I'm so afraid to wake up and find this was all a dream.

"It's very real, love." Cade wipes my tears, even though more fall immediately. He gently presses his lips to mine, and I lose all the control I had.

I cry harder than I ever have in my life. Tears and snot flow down my face, and I'm barely able to breathe fast enough to fill my lungs. Cade holds me through all of it. Never once letting go. I cry and cry, until I can't cry anymore.

Cade shifts us so he's leaning against the headboard. I lay my head on his chest, and listen to his heart beating under my ear.

Thump thump. Thump thump. The steady rhythm echoes in my mind as I fight to keep my eyes open. What if he disappears when I close them?

"Sleep, love," Cade whispers, tucking my hair behind my ear. "I'll be right here."

———

WHEN I WAKE AGAIN, I hold my breath. The memory of Cade holding me, telling me he's okay, is too painful. What if it wasn't real? But as I lay here with my eyes closed, his voice washes over me, rumbling in the chest my head is laying on.

"Are you okay, Kai?" he asks.

Someone shifts behind me, and I know it's Kai by the slightly cooler limbs pressed against mine under the covers. I take a moment to breathe. To let the realization sink in that I'm sandwiched between Cade and Kai.

"No," Kai whispers, his breath tickling the nape of my neck.

I feel like I'm intruding on something, but I don't want to move. I don't want to let go of Cade. Besides, knowing Kai, he already knows I'm awake.

"Everytime I close my eyes, I see you both," Kai says. "I see your body, bloody and still. I see Ellis laying on top of you, the brightest golden flames I've ever seen pouring from her. I almost couldn't get to you guys."

The vulnerability in his voice, the trembling echo of fear, makes me ache. I wasn't the only one who thought Cade had died.

"I've never been so scared in my life. I thought I lost you both." His voice cracks, and his chest brushes against my back as he takes a deep breath. "I don't know how I would have ever survived, losing both pieces of my heart."

"Kai," Cade says gently. He leans over, squishing me even more between them, but I don't complain.

I can tell they're kissing by the way my heart speeds up

because of Kai's, and the way Cade's heart beats harder under my ear. I soak it all in. Tears threaten to fall again just thinking about ... No. I won't let myself think that. He didn't die, and I won't let that fear fester and ruin what we have.

A soft knock on the door draws them apart. "Is she still sleeping?" Sterling asks.

"No," Kai says, tugging one of my curls. "She's awake." His smile is evident in his tone.

My eyes pop open and land on Sterling in the doorway. His silver hair is in a bun on the back of his head, and his icy blue eyes pierce me straight to my soul. The first full breath fills my lungs. All three of my guys are okay. All three of my guys are right here, with me.

I haven't seen Sterling since we went our separate ways—me to deal with Sam, him to rescue—

I sit up in bed so fast the room spins. "Gracie!" I look at Sterling, pleading with him with my eyes alone. *Please tell me you got her out of there!*

He walks to the bed and pulls me into his arms. "I got her out," he says, kissing the top of my head. "She's at my mom's."

"Is she ... okay?" I ask, pulling away to look at him.

"She's as okay as can be expected. Allie has looked her over and she has no injuries, besides malnutrition. She'll just need time to heal." He gives me a small smile, cupping my cheek in his big palm. "Her and Chloe have developed a sort of friendship. They don't talk much, but I think they take comfort in knowing they aren't alone anymore."

I close my eyes and lean into his touch. I know all too well what it's like to climb out of the pits of hell. I had my guys, my Shields, to help me through it. Without them, I don't think I'd be where I am today. No. I know I wouldn't be. How will Gracie do it?

Sterling kisses my forehead. "I'm glad to see you awake, kitten. I've missed you."

I scoot to the head of the bed between Kai and Cade, and let

Sterling climb onto the bed in front of me. "How long have I been asleep?"

"Three days," Kai says, taking my hand.

"Three days?" I gasp.

"You used a lot of magic," Cade replies, taking my other hand. "Your body needed to heal and replenish."

"What happened?" I ask, squeezing their hands harder. "I mean, is it ... over?" I know I killed Sam, a fact I don't think has registered in my mind yet. Not that I feel remorse over it. But, taking a life should never be easy.

"The warehouse has been completely destroyed," Sterling says. "I went back with Cole to go through the debris, and there is nothing left of the building. Your flames incinerated it. Along with the building, all of the creatures Sam created were destroyed. Not a single one survived."

"Were there ..." I stop to swallow and lick my lips. "Were there any other prisoners? Did I kill anyone?"

Sterling shakes his head. "Not that we could tell. It seems like he was in between batches of prisoners."

I release a breath, relieved I didn't kill any innocent people. "What about the magicals who supported him?" I ask.

"I can't imagine they will cause many problems with Sam gone," Sterling answers. "Especially after how it all went down. They will slink back into society and pretend like nothing ever happened."

"I think it's safe to say that it's over." Kai gives me a small, encouraging smile. "It's over, Ellis. Your life is yours again. To do with it as you please."

Tears burn my eyes and slide down my cheeks. Over. A word I never thought I'd hear. I'm not being hunted anymore. I can live my life how I've been dreaming of lately. I squeeze my eyes shut and press my lips together.

Over.

My three guys surround me. Their love, support, and

affection fills me. With them holding me, touching me, kissing me, I repeat the word again and again.

Over.

MY LEG WON'T STOP BOUNCING. Anytime Sterling has to stop the Hummer for a stoplight, the entire vehicle shakes. I didn't think I'd be this nervous to see Gracie, but I am. The waves of nerves that keep washing through me make me feel like a livewire.

"Relax, kitten," Sterling murmurs, placing his hand on my knee.

I stop the bouncing ... for a minute. Then it starts back up again. He sighs and returns his gaze to the road. The landscape blurs past, not registering in my mind at all. And before I know it, the Hummer is pulling up the driveway and Sterling throws it in park. How the hell did we get here so fast? I swear we just left the cabin five minutes ago.

Sterling hops out and walks around the car to open the door for me. "Ready, kitten?"

"No." My voice shakes slightly and my fingers tremble as I take Sterling's hand. "Why am I so nervous?"

"Because she's your sister. And you're scared to see how changed she is. And you don't want to do anything that will cause her harm."

I nod and swallow, my throat dry. "What do I say to her?"

"Just let her know you're here. That you love her. And you'll support her however she needs. You don't even need to talk. She might not want it, but your presence alone will make a difference."

"How did you get so wise?" I tease, trying to shake the uncertainty.

Sterling bumps my hip with his and grins. "I've always been

this wise. I just like to let Cade and Kai do all the talking to give them a chance to make asses of themselves."

I laugh and it feels so good to do so. But deep inside, hidden way in the back of my mind, is a tiny seed of fear. My laugh fades, and I bite my bottom lip.

Sterling gently grips my chin and tilts my head up to look at him. "What's wrong, kitten?"

"I'm scared," I whisper, my words barely audible.

He steps closer, brow furrowed. "Of what?"

"This." I wave my hand in front of me, trying to encompass everything that is my life. "The laughter and hope. The peace and dreams. What if it doesn't last? I can't help but think something else will come our way and try to take this happiness from me."

"It's over, Ellis. We won. You can take your happiness and own it. And if anything else comes our way, we'll handle it." He rubs my cheek with his thumb. His bright blue eyes gleam in the evening light. "It doesn't matter how many people try to take this happiness from us. We'll fight for it every fucking day because you deserve it. No matter what comes our way, we'll fight it, and we'll win. We'll get our happily ever after. I promise you that, Ellis." He leans forward and softly kisses me, brushing his lips against mine until I want to melt.

It doesn't last as long as I want it to, and when Sterling pulls away I pout. He laughs, but threads his fingers with mine and pulls me to the front door. Shari greets us with a warm smile and hug and ushers us into the kitchen for dinner. I'm too nervous to eat, despite the delicious scent of roasted chicken and marinated vegetables. I manage a few bites because Sterling pins me with a stare until I squirm in my seat.

When we're done and Sterling is helping Shari clear the table, I make my way upstairs. I pop my head into Chloe's room first and give her a wave before heading to Gracie's room. My fingers tremble as I reach out to knock on the door. There is no answer, so I crack it open and peer inside. She's laying on the bed, covers pulled to her chin, her empty gaze staring at the ceiling.

My breath leaves my lungs in a rush. The last time I saw Gracie alive she was vibrant and full of energy. She was always the one to suggest we do something that would get us in trouble. Like climbing out of the bedroom window and onto the roof, or sneaking out at night to fumble through the woods to the cliffs. She looks so little in that bed, a shell of herself. And it absolutely destroys me.

I somehow manage to swallow my sob, squeezing my eyes shut to hold back the tears. I knock again but she doesn't even blink.

"Gracie? It's me, Ellis."

Nothing.

I push into the room and close the door behind me. Slowly, I approach the bed, making sure to project my movements so I don't startle her. She doesn't acknowledge me as I sit on the edge of the bed, keeping her blank stare pinned on the ceiling.

"I missed you," I whisper, barely managing to keep the brokenness from my voice. "I want you to know you're safe now. He's ... he's dead. I killed him."

Still nothing.

I sit quietly, staring at my hands in my lap. Seeing her sunken cheekbones and pale skin, the dark bruise-like circles under her eyes and limp, matted hair is too much. I dig through my mind for anything to say that won't overwhelm her. Sterling's words come back to me. *You don't even need to talk.* But the longer I sit in silence, the more the heaviness grows in my chest until I can't breathe.

I suck in a ragged breath and gently take her hand. "Do you remember that time we stole d-dad's bottle of vodka?" I stutter over that word, but now is not the time to talk about Thomas Kennedy. "We drank half of it before mom found us puking in the bathtub. Or that time we snuck out at night to go to that boy's house. What was his name? You had the biggest crush on him. Maddox? Yeah, I think it was Maddox. We made it to the end of the driveway and found mom standing there with her arms crossed over her chest. She tried to keep a stern look on her face, but she couldn't. She just laughed at us and drug us back inside."

I smile at the memory. I hadn't thought about these things in a long time. They always hurt too much, knowing I'd lost both of them in one awful night and would never be able to make new memories like that again. My eyes burn, but I don't let the tears fall.

"I have so much to tell you. Like, I'm seeing someone, er, someones?" I huff a laugh. "I think you'd be proud of me. I'm dating *three* guys." I sigh and the smile drops from my face. "I love you so much, and I'm going to keep fighting for you. So don't give up, Gracie. I'm here," I whisper, turning to look at her. "I'm right here, and I'm not going anywhere. Shari is amazing. She's so sweet and she'll take good care of you. If you need anything, just let her know. And I'm always just a phone call away. I'll stop by again later, okay?"

I stand from the bed, and brush a flat curl from her forehead, leaning down to press a soft kiss where the curl had been. I make it to the hallway before the tears fall. Sterling is waiting for me, and he pulls me into a hug, holding me tightly while I cry.

I wish there was something I could do. I wish I could take her pain and fear away. Unfortunately, I know all too well how hard it is to fight trauma like that. I know there is only so much I can do, but the helplessness grates on me.

"Ready?" Sterling asks quietly, wiping my cheeks.

I nod my head and let him lead me to the car.

STERLING

"Here are the plans you wanted," Drew says, handing me a stack of papers.

"Thank fuck," I breathe, riffling through them. "I can't wait to tear this shit down and rebuild it."

Drew looks around Noah's old office with a grimace. "Yeah, It'll be nice to have your own place, one without any hint of that bastard."

The blueprints I had drawn up are exactly what I wanted. A simple building, with two offices—one for me and one for Cole—a front seating area with space for a secretary, a room for file storage, and a meeting room large enough to hold 20 people.

I've been operating out of Noah's old office, and every time I step foot in here I get the creeps. Remembering what I learned after we snuck in here to find proof of Ellis's parentage, the awful realization that Sam was doing horrific things and wanted to use Ellis for her powers, it still haunts me. It will be nice to have my own office. One that nobody associates with Noah. A new office for a new era.

Checking my cell for the time, I finish up what I was doing and power down my laptop. I promised my mom I'd stay for dinner when I picked Ellis up. My mate frequently joins me when

I come to the office, so I can drop her off at my mom's and she can visit with Chloe and Gracie. Knowing I get to see her soon quickens my step as I head for the door.

Before I get to my car, Cole pulls up the driveway and parks. His face has an expression of uncertain nervousness, and my gut clenches. I really hope he doesn't have bad news.

Things have been going fairly smoothly since I took over as alpha of the Iron Shadows pack. There have been a few wolves who we've needed to deal with, ones who supported Noah who no doubt were getting some kind of perk for supporting him. But the majority of wolves were ready for a change and welcomed me back with open arms.

It's still hard to look them in the eyes sometimes and know they did nothing to help me after my dad died. Logically, I know there wasn't a lot they could do, but it still hurts nonetheless.

"What's up?" I ask as Cole steps out of his truck.

"Can we talk for a minute?" He rubs the back of his neck and kicks a rock out of his way.

"Sure."

Cole steps up and sits on the steps rather than head inside into the office, so it must not be anything pack related. Curious, I sit next to him and wait for him to talk.

After a few minutes of silence, he sighs and shakes his head. "I just wanted to thank you for offering me the position as your beta. I'm really glad you're back in my life, and I'm sorry I acted the way I did when you came to see mom that first time."

I hide my surprise at his words. We've been getting along really well, but I never expected to hear these words from him. "You don't need to apologize, Cole. I don't blame you for any of it. The entire situation was fucked up."

He huffs a laugh. "Yeah, but still. I was hurt and I took it out on you and Ellis, and I shouldn't have."

"Well, you're forgiven, so don't worry about it anymore." I shrug and give him a smile. "Besides, it should be me thanking you. You've done a lot by helping us deal with Sam. I appreciate it."

This time it's Cole who shrugs. "It seemed like the best way to make up for being an ass. Besides, I like Ellis. She's spirited."

I laugh. "That's one way to put it."

When we both stand, he hesitates for a second before tugging me in for a hug. I squeeze my eyes shut to hide the way they no doubt glisten with unshed tears. The last time I hugged my brother he was just a pup. I hate that we had so many years apart, so many opportunities for memories stolen from us.

Neither of us say anything as we pull apart and head for our cars, both of us feeling slightly awkward and emotional, and neither wanting to show the other. At least we have time now to figure things out between us, to get comfortable around each other again, and to make new memories. And I have Ellis to thank for that.

———

WHEN WE PULL up to the cabin, it's dark out. My mom cooked us a delicious meal, as always, and we stayed for a bit to talk with her and Chloe. Ellis's relationship with Chloe is growing, and I'm thankful she has another girlfriend to lean on. She deserves it all.

The lights in the cabin spill out onto the porch, warm and welcoming. I've been thinking a lot about how to renovate this place. We definitely need to make it bigger and add bedrooms. At this point, it would probably be easier to just tear the thing down and start over. But that thought makes my heart squeeze. This place was my dad's, and I really don't want to erase every memory I have of him here.

I help Ellis out of the car and link our fingers together, giving her a quick kiss before heading up the steps. We both pause in surprise when we push inside, Ellis's intake of breath telling me exactly how she feels about what we find.

Kai and Cade are both naked. Cade is bent over the arm of the couch with one of Kai's hands pressing down on his neck until his face is buried in the cushions. Kai's hips pound against Cade's ass, the sound of flesh on flesh the only noise besides their grunts and groans.

They both turn toward us with wide eyes. Their faces are flushed and gazes fogged with lust. Ellis's hand tightens around mine and I inhale, taking in her scent. She's already turned on, and that thought makes my cock stir. She loves to watch those two, and if I'm honest with myself, I kind of do too. I'd never join them, it's just not my thing. But watching their powerful bodies come together, and just knowing they are embracing their own wants and desires is heady.

I tug Ellis in front of me, tucking her close against my body, her ass pressing against my growing erection. "Are you mad, kitten?" I whisper against the shell of her ear, loud enough Cade and Kai can hear it. "Are you angry they're fucking without you?"

Neither of them has moved. Cade is pressed into the couch, still impaled by Kai's cock, and they both heave as they watch Ellis's reaction. We all know she isn't mad, and I know her watching them turns them on as much as it does her.

Ellis shakes her head. "No," she breathes.

Kai grins, his fangs on full display, and Ellis squeezes her thighs together, rubbing herself harder against my hips. I bite back a groan at the feel of her ass pressed against my cock.

"Keep going, Kai," I growl. "Show Ellis how hard you fuck Cade."

A small whimper escapes Ellis, and she watches with wide, heated eyes as Kai once again pounds into Cade's ass.

"What do you want, kitten? Do you want them to come? Or do you want them to wait, so they come all over you?" She shivers as my breath washes over the side of her neck, and her lips part. I want to claim those lips for my own.

"I—I want ..."

"Say it kitten," I growl, watching as her cheeks flush and not just from embarrassment at having to speak the dirty words I want to hear from her lips.

She opens her mouth but then clamps it shut in defiance. My hand slides under her shirt and bra, and I pinch her nipple hard, making her gasp.

"If you're going to act like a brat, I'll treat you like one."

She shudders, rubbing herself against my aching cock and I have to restrain myself so I don't throw her over the couch with Cade and take her the same way Kai is taking him.

"Say. It." I pinch her nipple again and her legs shake.

The rosy flush on her cheeks and chest deepens, but she steels herself before saying, "I want them to come on me."

I chuckle darkly and slip her shirt over her head before unclasping her bra and tossing them both to the floor. Cade and Kai are sweating. Cade's face is twisted in pleasure, his hands fisted in the couch cushions. But both of them are watching Ellis and the way she reacts to them.

"Don't make him come, Kai. Our woman wants us to mark her. To make sure everyone knows she's ours."

Kai's eyes flash red, and he pulls out, leaving Cade wanting. Cade looks to Ellis, and through the haze of lust, pride shines in his violet eyes. All three of us want her to smell like us. All the time. For the rest of our lives. No one else will ever have her.

"Cade, tie her wrists behind her back," I order, grasping her hands and crossing them behind her.

Her shoulders tense, her entire body going rigid. Under my thumbs, her pulse hammers and I don't think it's from excitement anymore. I quickly release her as if my skin was burned. It never even crossed my mind what asking her to be tied up would do to her. Fuck.

"Shit, I'm sorry, Ellis," I mutter against her neck, bringing my hands around to rest on her belly. "We don't have to do that."

Kai is standing as still as a predator, his lips pressed into a thin line. Cade steps up to Ellis and cups her cheek.

"Do you want me to tie you up?" he asks quietly. "Just like before, you say the word, love."

His magic caresses her, purple wisps of light gently teasing and stroking her flesh. One thin strand flicks against her nipple and she arches her back, a moan slipping from between her clenched teeth. He lets his magic roam over her body, licking at every inch of exposed skin, letting her know there are no bands of burning green magic to hurt her. Just pleasure. And love.

She nods her head and Cade grips her chin tightly. "Say the words, Ellis. I need to hear you say you want it." Cade's demand isn't an order of dominance, but one of care and making sure she truly agrees to this.

Ellis sucks in a breath. "I want you to tie me up."

I can't see her eyes, but from the way Cade's blaze, I know some of her inner fire is pouring out. My beautiful, strong, determined harpy.

"Kneel on the couch," I demand. "And face Kai."

Her legs are shaky as she walks to the couch and kneels, facing Kai. I give him a look and he pulls a dagger from his discarded pants and slices through her leggings and panties. She gasps, and I don't miss the way she clenches her thighs once Kai has her clothing in ribbons on the floor.

Cade waits until I give him a nod, and he approaches Ellis, running the tips of his fingers over her shoulders and down her arms. Goosebumps break out on her skin at his touch. He gently takes her wrists and tugs her arms behind her back, never breaking eye contact with her. His magic follows the same path his fingers took until it wraps around her wrists, restraining them at the small of her back.

Her breath hitches, but Cade lowers his head to her neck and trails kisses over her throat and down her chest. I step up behind her, gripping her hips and grinding myself against her. Her back arches and her head falls onto my shoulder.

"Why are you still dressed?" she asks me, her voice husky and sexy.

Instead of answering her, I ask, "Do you want to taste Cade, kitten?"

"Yes," she moans, already bending forward to take him in her mouth.

I support her with my hands around her waist as Cade kneels on the couch facing her. Cade's eyes roll back as she swallows him down.

"Fuck, love. That's it." He thrusts his hips slowly, making sure to not push her too hard yet.

Kai, unable to stand around anymore and watch everyone else, leans forward and grabs Cade's throat from behind, before running his fangs along the sensitive skin. Cade shudders and moans, hips thrusting harder into Ellis's mouth.

Running my fingers down Ellis's spine, I slip them over her ass and between her thighs, which are already slick with her arousal. I hiss as I glide my fingers over her clit, just barely touching it. But she groans around Cade's cock, her hips pressing back in search of more pressure.

I hold her firm with my other hand before slowly pushing two fingers inside of her. Her inner walls clamp down on my fingers, and I laugh darkly. "Oh yeah. You like that, don't you." Curling them, I hit the spot I know drives her wild, and she rewards me with a muffled noise.

Cade curses, fisting his hands in her hair. "You're going to end this too quickly if you keep doing that, love."

I make Ellis squirm on my fingers for a few minutes before I pull them out and reach over Cade's shoulder to let Kai lick them clean. He groans and fists his cock, pumping up and down.

I need to be naked. Now. I need to feel her skin against mine. When I step away, she almost falls forward without her hands to support her. Cade's magic immediately wraps around her, holding her up and helping her bob up and down. I remove my clothes quicker than I ever have and step up behind her, pressing myself against her ass. Her warm skin is like a drug and I want to wrap myself around her and never let go.

"Fuck, kitten." I grasp my cock and rub the tip through her wetness, and fuck if it doesn't make me almost come undone. My fingers dig into her hips so hard I know there will be bruises tomorrow, and I revel in that fact. Unable to wait anymore, I slam into her, making her cry out around Cade's length.

The motion rocks her forward and she chokes, causing Cade to curse as his dick hits the back of her throat. She's so fucking warm and addicting. Each thrust makes her clench around me. The noises she makes burrow into my bones and I want to hear them every fucking day.

I realize I've completely forgotten to give orders to the rest of them when Kai says, "Fuck this." He pulls Cade back, popping Ellis off of his cock, then pushes him down and thrust into his ass.

Cade groans low and dark, and Ellis clamps down on me watching them. I slide my fingers through her folds, flicking her clit and making her squirm.

"Look at me, baby girl," Kai growls, a hint of red creeping across his gray eyes.

Cade's magic releases her enough so she can straighten and meet Kai's gaze, but I keep her hips firmly in my grasp as I pump in and out. Each of her breaths is torn from her throat, and her complexion is rosy and flushed. She's fucking beautiful like this. Eyes hazy with lust, hair tangled from our fingers, sweat dampening her brow.

Kai grips her chin and drags her forward, claiming her mouth in a rough kiss. He knicks her lower lip with a fang, running his tongue along the hurt to collect the drop of blood.

She whimpers, fingers squeezing tightly behind her back. "Please," she gasps. "Please, please." Her words are choked out of her, raspy and full of need.

"Please what, kitten?" I grit out from between my teeth. She's squeezing me so tightly, I won't last long like this.

"I ... I need ..." Her words trail off in a moan as I rub her clit. "Please!"

I have to gather every scrap of control and hold it tightly inside of me. "Bite her, Kai."

He strikes fast as a cobra, and Ellis screams as she comes undone. Her body shakes and trembles, her pussy clamping on my dick as each pulse of pleasure rocks through her. I bite down on my lip to keep myself from coming.

When she finally hangs limply in my hands, her breaths heaving out of her, I flip her over. She's like a ragdoll, limbs flopping everywhere as if she can no longer control them. Her face is flushed and a satisfied smile pulls her lips up.

One glance at Kai and Cade and I know they are barely hanging on, the same as me. I fist my cock and with one nod, the two of them do the same and Ellis watches with feral intent as we come on her stomach. It seems like my orgasm lasts forever. Seeing my release hitting her tan skin, mixing with Kai and Cades, and the way she revels in it, it makes me come even harder.

When we're all spent, we stand over her, watching her trail her fingers through the sticky mess on her stomach. Holy. Fucking. Shit. This woman. Even after one of the most intense orgasms of my life, I'm about ready for round two. By the looks on Cade and Kai's faces, they are as well.

I scoop Ellis in my arms, and head for the steps, the other two falling into step behind me. "Time for a shower. And round two."

Kai

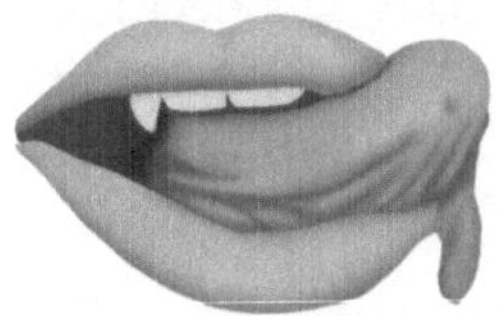

Three weeks after I almost lost Ellis and Cade, I find myself standing outside my father's estate, hand in hand with my beloved. The past two weeks have been phenomenal. We've done nothing but lay around the cabin, eat, drink, talk, and fuck. It was pure bliss. But time doesn't stop, even to let us celebrate, dream, and plan.

My father has been calling me non-stop, and I've put off this meeting for as long as I can. I take a deep breath and step up to the door, but hesitate before opening it.

"Did you forget how to open doors? Do you need me to do it for you?" Ellis squeezes my hand, a wry tilt to her lips.

I squeeze her hand back, perhaps a tad harder than I should, but I can't help it when she gets sassy like that. "No, I did not forget how to open doors." I cut my stare to her and wait until she rolls her eyes. Returning my attention to the massive wooden door in front of us, my humor drops away. "Do I want to do this? Do I want to go inside and tell my dad I still want to be prince?" Ellis says nothing, but she steps closer to me, her arm brushing against mine. "Choose for me," I say, turning to her with renewed energy. "Make this life-changing decision for me."

She shakes her head, a small smile playing about her lips. "I'm not making this decision for you, Kai."

I sigh. "Fine. At least blink once if you think I should. Twice if you think I shouldn't." She doesn't blink at all. "What does that mean?" I ask, pointing at her face. "What does no blink mean?"

She stands on her toes and takes my face in her palms. "It means, only you can make this decision. But whatever decision that is, I will support you and be right here with you. We all talked about this the other night. No matter what choice you make, we're all here for you."

I sigh and turn back to the door. She's right, unfortunately. Only I can make this decision. But it helps knowing she has my back no matter what I decide. I pull open the massive door and tug Ellis in behind me. The opulence of this place is lost on me. After having been raised in the estate, the grand marble floors, gold trim, and expensive decorations no longer phase me. But I notice Ellis looking around with wide eyes. At first I think she's awed taking it all in, but when she tugs me to stop outside the library-turned-man cave, I detect something else from her.

She opens the door and stands in the doorway for a moment before stepping inside. Sadness and longing are the two most prominent emotions I pick up on, but I also detect hope and wonder. She walks around the room, looking at the strange dichotomy of old-fashioned grandeur and modern conveniences.

"This room holds a lot of memories," she whispers, fingers trailing over spines of books tucked on the shelves that have been pushed to one side. "This is where I reclaimed myself. Where I decided I wouldn't let him have a hold over me anymore." She huffs a small laugh and picks up the stuffed wolf with painted blue eyes. Hugging it to her chest, she walks to the pool table and turns to face me. "I learned what love is in this room." Her eyes sparkle with emotion and something I can't quite put my finger on. "I learned that pleasure doesn't equal pain."

Ah. There it is. Desire. I have no doubt she's remembering the time Cade used his magic to bind her to the pool table and I fucked her senseless. The first time magic was used not as a means to hurt her during sex, but to enhance it. I walk toward her, my fingers itching to pin her to the table again, but instead, I lift her and sit her on top, stepping between her thighs.

"Have I told you how proud I am of you?" I ask, taking her face in my hands and tipping it up with my thumbs under her chin.

"No," she whispers, eyes turning glassy with unshed tears.

"Well, shame on me, then." I step closer, brushing my lips lightly against her forehead. "Because I am so incredibly proud of you, Ellis. Your strength and courage leave me in awe everyday. And I am honored to have you by my side."

A single tear escapes and slips down her cheek as she hugs that damn stuffed animal tighter to her chest. She opens her mouth to say something, but her lips tremble and she closes them, pressing them tight together. I don't give her another chance to say something. I claim her mouth and pour all of my feelings into the kiss, making sure she understands every word I said was true.

When I pull away, I brush the tears from her cheeks with my thumbs and help her down from the table. "Thank you," she whispers.

"You never need to thank me, baby girl. Now, let's go see if I can be as brave as you." She snorts and I look at her with mock outrage, placing my hand on my chest. "What? You don't think I'm brave?"

"Oh, it's not that I don't think you're brave. It's that I have no doubt you're going to make a complete fool of yourself somehow."

I can't argue that, so I grunt and we leave the library behind, heading for my dad's office. The estate is quiet, but it usually is. Most of the people who work here are human and keep to a normal schedule of sleeping at night and working during the day. Only a few selected staff members are vampires that keep nighttime hours.

When we reach my dad's office, Ellis looks around, holding

the stuffed wolf and biting her lip. Eventually she sighs and sets the thing in a potted plant. When I raise my brow at her in question, she shrugs. "I can't look like a child holding a stuffie in front of your dad."

My lips twitch but I keep myself from laughing, because the nerves that suddenly batter my mental shield are all hers. I take her hand and give it an encouraging squeeze. "Don't worry. I won't let anything happen to you."

She nods and I knock on the door before opening it. My dad, Salvatore Thorne, king of the vampires, sits behind a massive mahogany desk. The curtains that, during the day, cover the floor to ceiling windows behind him have been pulled open to let the full moon shine in. His long black hair hangs down in a shiny smooth curtain and reflects the moonlight.

His dark eyes land behind me, on Ellis, and I stiffen. "Well," he says, his voice low and full of hunger. "What have we here?"

I tug Ellis to my side and my gaze goes hard as I stare at my dad. "Before we go any further, there are a few things I need to make clear. Ellis is my beloved, and I will not tolerate anything from you." My dad jerks back in his seat, eyes going wide. He studies Ellis and I do my best to not shift in front of her. "You will not lay a hand on her or direct any vile comments toward her. She is off limits."

My dad crosses his arms over his chest and nods. "Very well. Anything else?"

I blink. Okay. That went better than I thought it would. "I am no longer going to do your dirty work. And neither will Cade and Sterling. You can find someone else to be your lackeys, but it won't be us. If you can't accept that, I will walk out of here and never return."

My dad smirks, something glinting in his eyes, and a weird emotion filters past my shields. Is that ... pride? "Well, it's about time."

"What?" I ask, taken aback and thoroughly thrown off my guard.

"Sit down, Malakai." He motions to the chairs in front of his desk, and I pull one out for Ellis before taking my own. My dad steeples his fingers and looks at me with a hard gaze. "I've been waiting for you to grow a backbone. Now that you've shown me you won't let someone walk all over you, I can let you take up more responsibilities within the court."

"Actually, about that," I say, tightening my grip on the arms of the chair. "I would like to focus on the inequality between the races. Between *all* races. Humans included."

One dark brow shoots up and my dad gives me a bewildered look. "Why ever would you want to do that?"

"Because I've seen what my beloved has gone through. I've seen what my friends have gone through. All because of power hungry men that hold prominent places in society. It's time for that to stop."

My dad studies me for a moment before nodding once. "Very well. But I expect you to report here for work. I'll have an office prepared for you."

"Thank you," I say, not quite feeling relief yet. It hasn't settled in that this has been resolved. That Ellis is safe. My friends no longer have to live under my dad's thumb.

I stand and give Ellis my hand, pulling her to her feet. Back in the hallway, Ellis snags the wolf from the potted plant and dusts it off, brushing the dirt from the bottom. She turns to me and smiles.

"Well, prince. What now?"

Something curls in my gut at her use of my title. My eyes flash ruby, and she gasps. "Oh, I can think of something," I growl, throwing her over my shoulder and heading for the library.

I kick the door shut behind me, stopping long enough to turn the lock. It's been so long since we've been here, I have no idea what Cade's wards are doing, if they are even still working. Gently, I lower Ellis onto the pool table, hovering over her to kiss her thoroughly.

"Too bad Cade isn't here to tie you up," I murmur against her neck, my fangs brushing lightly over her pulse.

She whimpers and arches her back, fingers darting to the hem of her pale blue shirt. I stop her and step back, just looking at her. It's been awhile since I've seen her dressed in something other than leggings or just a t-shirt. The white denim shorts she's wearing are frayed on the hems and her belly is on display where her shirt has ridden up. She's a fucking goddess.

I run my fingers over the sliver of exposed skin, watching as it raises in goosebumps. Bending low, I kiss my way from her belly button up her torso, gliding the shirt up as I go, exposing even more of her delicious skin. With the shirt tossed to the side, only a lacy white bra stands in my way. And the shorts.

I yank the shorts off, taking the matching panties with them. My fingers itch to run over all of her smooth skin, so I glide them up her thigh, over her hips, and around to her back where I unclasp the bra. Laying naked on the pool table, she watches me through lowered lids as I slowly strip out of my clothes. It gives me a thrill to see the way she reacts to each inch of skin I display. Flushed, thighs squeezing together, chest rising and falling with each rapid inhale.

I wanted to take this slow, to really enjoy this time alone together, but I'm not sure I'll be able to. I lower myself over her, our skin touching in so many places. Her warmth is so enticing against my cooler skin. I kiss her deeply, and she wraps her legs around my waist, rubbing her wet heat against me and I groan.

"Fuck, Ellis," I breathe, tangling my fingers in her hair. "I want you so fucking badly."

"Then take me, prince. I'm always yours to take."

Her words spear through me, igniting my soul and making the monster inside me practically purr. For some reason though, it slows me down. The reminder I can have her whenever I want gives me the ability to slow down and enjoy the moment.

"Patience, baby girl. Let's make this last." I kiss my way down her body and tug her to the edge of the table. Placing her legs over my shoulders, I dive in for the taste of heaven I love so much.

She pulls my hair and arches her back, seeking more, and I give it all to her. I let her writhe on my face, chasing her pleasure and taking what she wants. When she comes on my tongue, fingers gripping my hair hard enough to sting, I take every last drop. Her hair is splayed around her head like a lion's mane, and her skin is rosy and glimmering with sweat. The sight stops my heart. This beautiful, strong, courageous woman is all mine.

I tug her up to my chest, wrapping my arms around her at the same time I glide my cock inside her. The pool table suddenly doesn't feel like enough. I carry her to the couch, never breaking our kiss, and lower her onto it. If I want to make this last, I need to keep things slow, as hard as that will be. Somehow I manage. I'm not one for slow love making. I'm all for a rough and dirty fuck. But Ellis deserves this, and more. I can make this work this one time.

The noises she makes drive me wild, along with her nails on my back and her fingers pulling my hair. I know she wants it harder, but I'm not giving her that this time. So instead, I kiss her. Deep, languid, sensual. She melts under me, her body going pliant under my touch. Our hearts, beating in time with each other, are rapid flutters in my chest, like a hummingbird's wings.

When I can't take it any longer, I graze my fangs along her neck, mouth watering at the promise of her blood.

"Yes," she moans, tilting her head. "Please bite me, Kai. Make me come."

I can't refuse her that. My fangs sink into her skin, her blood blooming in my mouth like rich decadent wine. She cries out and her pussy flutters around my cock, the sensation combined with her blood sends me over the edge. Lightning shoots through my veins and I pump my hips harder as I come inside of her.

Before I can catch my breath, she tugs my head up and kisses me. "I love you, Kai."

I look at her, her blood now staining her lips from that kiss, and I fall away. I tuck her tight against me and kiss her temple. "I love you too, Ellis."

ELLIS

"Hey! Where are you going?" I jump from the couch, dropping my book on the coffee table and dart after Sterling.

He turns around and opens his arms for me, and I crash into him. "Heading into town real quick. Why?"

"Can you drop me off at your moms? I want to visit Gracie."

"Of course." He bends down to kiss me and pulls me harder against him.

I don't think I'll ever get sick of this. Sterling's kisses are my favorite. I feel guilty for thinking that, but he always kisses me with a deep passion, like he's scared it might be the last one and he wants to make it last. I can't say I blame him. With our history and everything that we just went through, there were many times when we thought we maybe had our last kiss.

When he pulls away I pout, making him chuckle. "Come on, kitten. Quit trying to distract me."

"Have you talked to Cole?" I ask once we're on the road.

He nods. "Yes."

I wait for him to continue but he doesn't. "Seriously, it's like pulling teeth to get you to talk sometimes." I huff, and narrow my eyes at him when he smirks.

"You asked me a question, and I answered it. If you wanted to know something else, you should have asked a different question." He's fighting his smile, and I can't help but stare at him while he does so. He hasn't always been so free with his smiles.

"And you guys say I'm stubborn," I mutter under my breath. "Have you talked to Cole about Chloe?" I ask, clarifying my question.

"Ah, see? That's a completely different question." He smiles and I hit him in the chest. "Yes, I have."

Again, he falls silent. "Oh for fuck's sake, Sterling."

He chuckles and reaches over to squeeze my thigh. "They have been talking. Cole says he's taking things super slow with her, but he suspects he might be her soul-bonded."

"Why does he think that? Although, it would make sense, wouldn't it? If two people from different races are fated to be together, wouldn't that be the case?"

Sterling shrugs. "It's not that common. I mean, it happens, but not enough for me to be aware of the details like that." He glances at me briefly before returning his attention to the road. "But, I think it's going to become more common. I think that's something you may have ushered in. Mixing of the races."

"Is that a bad thing?" I ask. I'm not sure how that will play out with the different ways races procreate. If races mixing becomes commonplace, that would risk magicals being wiped out completely.

"I don't think so. I think nature will find a way to make things work."

I don't reply, because I really don't know what to think about that. So I return my thoughts to Chloe and Cole. "Do you think they'll get together? I think they would be great for each other."

Sterling smiles. "I'd like to see my brother claim his mate. There is nothing quite like it." He squeezes my leg again, his hand sliding slightly higher on my bare thigh.

The memory of him finally claiming me is one I will never forget. The connection that I always sensed magnified and glowing golden in my chest. It still does, and it warms me knowing it's there. Knowing Sterling is there. Not to mention the sex.

I take a deep breath and push those thoughts aside, but Sterling inhales and his fingers tighten on my leg.

"What are you thinking about, Ellis?" he growls softly.

"Nothing," I say sweetly, innocently.

His grip slips higher, and if he goes up any more, he'll find out exactly what I'm thinking about. Although with his shifter senses, I know he already scents my arousal, but it's too late. I am aroused, and only one thing will take care of that problem.

He growls again, this time lower and more forceful. The land rover bounces over the curb as Sterling pulls off the road and into the grass lining the street. He throws the car in park and climbs into the back seat, tugging his sweats down as he does so.

"What are you waiting for?" he asks, taking his hard cock into his hand. "Do you need an invitation?"

No. I don't need an invitation. I climb over the seat and onto his lap, taking his face between my palms and kissing him. I love the way he always tastes like mint, and his scent of winter and pine permeate everything he touches.

"What kind of mate would I be if I left you needy and wanting?" he asks when I pull away. His fingers slide up my thighs and under my dress, hooking in my panties and slipping them down.

I shimmy out of them awkwardly. Even though there is more room in the land rover than most cars, it's still cramped. Especially with Sterling taking up most of the space. "I was thinking about when you claimed me," I breathe as I sit back on his lap, gliding over his cock and coating him in my arousal.

His eyes darken to a stormy blue, but it's not just desire I see glimmering in their depths. His voice is thick with emotion when he speaks. "Something I thought would never happen. That night was a dream come true, Ellis."

"For me, too." I lift up and angle his cock at my entrance

before slowly sitting down. This is similar to the first time we had sex, before I knew he was my mate. We were on the couch in the estate, in this exact position. And I knew at that moment, I would never be able to walk away from him. Even after his betrayal, I still needed him. I will always need him.

Sterling builds me up slowly, controlling my speed with his hands on my hips. He keeps it slow and steady. His gaze searing into me, seeing all the way to my soul. I can't look away from that stare. Just like that time at River's Edge, I'm lost to him.

"Come for me, kitten," he finally says, running his tongue along my mating mark at the same time his thumb finds my clit.

I grip his shoulders and come apart with his name on my lips. He follows me, holding me tightly as he shudders through his own orgasm. When it's over and the last trembling shivers work through my body, I lay my head on his shoulder, content to stay right where we are. Safe. Satisfied. Loved. In his arms I feel it all.

"We really need to go," he says, rubbing my back. "I do have a meeting I have to be at in like ... twenty minutes."

I nod, but I don't move. He doesn't try to make me either. We stay there for another few minutes before he sighs. "Okay. For real this time."

Reluctantly, I slide off his lap and tug my panties back on while he tucks himself into his pants. "That was fun," I say. "We should do it more often." I grin at him, while he climbs back into the driver's seat.

"Just say the word. You know I'll be there."

He pulls into the driveway and gives me a lingering kiss before I step out and walk to the porch. As always, Shari's house smells of some kind of delectable baked good, and judging by the cinnamon scent, it's something I will love. I head to the kitchen, to say hi and to also see if there is anything ready to eat.

"Hi Shari," I say.

She turns around, wiping her flour covered hands on an apron and beams at me. "Ellis! I didn't know you were coming today. How are you?"

"I'm good. I wasn't planning on it, but I caught Sterling leaving and hitched a ride with him."

She looks over my shoulder, eyes hopeful. "Is he here?"

"No. He just dropped me off. But I'll make sure he stops in when he picks me up." I eye the counter, looking for something to snag, and she catches me.

"Would you like a cinnamon cookie? They're Sterling's favorite." She smiles and waves to the counter where a plate of fresh baked goodness waits.

"Thank you." It's still warm, like she just took them out of the oven, and the cinnamon and brown sugar on top flake off into my palm. I take a bite and my eyes close. "Oh my gosh," I mumble around the soft chewy cookie. "This is delicious." I can totally see why these are Sterling's favorite.

Shari chuckles. "Thank you. It was my grandmother's recipe." She hands me a couple more on a napkin. "Take one to Grace. See if you can get her to eat one."

"How has she been?" I ask, my stomach falling.

"About the same. Chloe has been trying to get her to eat, but she only picks at her food. She has been more willing to leave the room, but she needs to be assured there are no men in the house when she does."

My heart clenches. I don't think Sam did anything to her like he did to me. But just the brutal treatment she endured from him is enough to scar her. I understand that feeling all too well. I've put off forcing her to talk to me, but I think maybe I should step in.

"Thank you. For everything. For letting her stay here. Her and Cade's family. We really appreciate it."

Shari waves off my thanks. "Don't mention it. With Cole out of the house helping Sterling, it's nice to have other people around. And it gives me an excuse to cook."

I laugh and snag one more cookie before heading upstairs. Chloe and her mom are still in the same room. Cade's mom has improved, but is still incredibly weak. I haven't ventured in to talk to her yet. My nerves always get the better of me, and I chicken out. I'm not sure why I'm so scared to meet her. Maybe it's because she's sick and so weak, I'm afraid it will just be awkward.

Gracie has a separate room right next door, and I knock before poking my head in. "Gracie? It's me, Ellis."

She's out of bed, wrapped in a blanket and sitting next to the window looking out. She doesn't acknowledge my presence, but I step into the room anyway and sit on the edge of the bed.

"Shari made cinnamon cookies. They are really good. Would you like one?"

No answer. I bite my lip and glance out the window. The view overlooks the woods behind the house. The same woods we crept through all those months ago for Sterling to see his mom and brother. The same woods I realized I wanted to accept him as my mate. The man who was there the night I thought my sister was killed. She may have not truly died that night, but her life did end. The life she knew with her family, the life of comfort and love, was taken from her. She lived so long under Sam. Longer than I did. I'm not sure it will be possible for her to come back from it. But I'm certainly going to try.

"The weather is really nice today," I say. "It's the kind of weather we used to love as kids. When the last few days of summer warmth were joined with a chilly fall breeze." I look at her, hoping to see some kind of reaction, but her face is blank. I don't even know if she's hearing what I'm saying. "Do you want to sit outside with me?" I hold my breath. If she says no, or ignores me, I'm not sure I'll be able to handle it. It's one of the reasons I haven't visited as often as I should.

It hurts to see her like this. Gracie was always so full of life. She was the one who encouraged me to do things I was too scared to try. She was the reason we got into so much trouble with our mom. I never saw her without a smile. This zombie version of her is just too painful.

I'm about to get up and leave when she nods. My heart leaps

into my throat and I swallow back the lump it forms. "Yeah? Okay. Let's go."

She keeps the blanket around her, and I lead her downstairs to the porch. Shari has a rocking bench with cushions and pillows positioned to look out over the beautiful landscape of the pack lands. Her house is off on its own, tucked away in a clearing in the woods. It's peaceful with the wind blowing through the trees and the sounds of insects. The sky is just starting to turn the palest shades of pink and orange as the sun slowly sinks lower to the horizon.

We sit in silence for a few minutes while I gather my courage to say something. Before I get the opportunity, the Hummer pulls up the driveway. Cade and Kai climb out and approach the house, hand in hand. I don't give them the chance to get close to Gracie. When she saw them get out of the car, her entire body stiffened. So I hop down the porch and stop them.

"What are you doing?" I ask.

"You woke up early today," Kai says, leaning down to kiss me. "And you left without saying goodbye."

"Sorry. I was scared to wake you up."

He snorts. "I'm not the difficult one to wake up."

"Yes you are! You are just as bad as I am." I glare at him, daring him to say something.

"Let's ask Cade who he thinks is worse to wake up, shall we?"

Cade rolls his eyes and holds up his hand. "You bit me. Kai has never bitten me." He frowns and his lips twitch. "At least, not like you did."

Kai flashes his fangs. "See? Told you."

"Whatever." I cross my arms over my chest and eyeball them. "Seriously though, what are you doing here?"

"Sterling asked me to come help him with something," Cade replies, snaking out his arm to tug me close. "I didn't want to deal with Kai this early, so I'm dropping him off here for you to deal with."

"Oh, please don't," I say. "I've been having such a good morning."

"I'm right here, you know. I can hear everything you're saying." Kai tugs one of my curls and I swat his hand away.

"I just got Gracie outside, so I don't want to freak her out with you guys being here."

"I'm leaving anyway," Cade says, bending down to kiss me. "I'll be back later. Take care of Kai while I'm gone." He grins and turns to the vampire in question. "Be good."

"What does that mean?" Kai grins and grabs Cade's face in his palms. The kiss is dominant and extremely hot. He pulls away and smirks at me. "We better stop, or Ellis is going to jump us right here."

"Whatever," I mutter and turn back toward the porch. "Shari is inside baking. You should join her. Maybe she can teach you a thing or two."

Gracie doesn't relax again until Cade pulls away and Kai disappears inside. I bite my lip and turn to her, ready to ask my question, but once again, I don't get to.

She turns to me, eyes focusing on me for the first time, and says, "Tell me about them."

I gape at her for a moment before shaking my head. "Cade and Kai?"

She nods. "Isn't there another one, too?"

"Yeah. Sterling. This is his mom's house."

"Tell me about them."

"I think to really get the full picture I need to start back at the beginning. The night I thought you died." I watch her closely as I dive into the story. I'm sure it's not easy for her to hear about how I mourned her loss, dealt with the injustices of being human, and was raped and beaten for two years by the same man who held her captive. It's not easy for me to talk about. Even after the number of times I've shared this story, and the fact that it's all over, it's still hard to put myself back in those moments. But I do it for her.

And I'll do it again, I'm sure, for someone else who needs to hear it. Like Chloe did.

Gracie looks down at her hands, twisting and squeezing them together. "How did you do it?" she whispers.

"Do what?" I ask gently.

"How did you move on? How did you learn to let a man touch you after ... after ..."

"I was lucky. I met my mates. But it took time, and it wasn't easy. It's still not always easy. But knowing I have people who care about me helps a lot. I know I can go to them if I need to. I have to remind myself that I'm not alone anymore, and I frequently need them to remind me as well."

She nods and swallows. "I don't know how to do that."

"I get it, Gracie. I really do. But you're not alone anymore either. And keeping yourself locked in that room where all you do is think about everything that's happened is not going to help. You need to dig deep and find that courage I know you possess. I'm always here to talk to you. Or not talk, if you just want someone to sit with you. Chloe also went through something similar. I know she could use the company sometimes too."

Gracie nods, chewing on her bottom lip. "I'm scared," she whispers.

"I know," I say gently. "I was too. Sometimes I still am. But I promise it does get easier." We fall silent as the sun sinks lower, the first few stars appearing in the darkening sky. "Do you remember when we used to wish on the first star we saw at night?"

She lifts her head to the sky, and a small smile twitches on her lips. She doesn't say anything, but she nods.

"Make a wish, Gracie. I think you'd be surprised at how often they come true."

ELLIS

"Ellis, wake up." Cade's quiet voice filters through my sleepy thoughts, along with an incessant gentle shaking.

I roll over, tugging the blanket higher.

"Ellis, love. Wake up."

The blanket around my shoulders disappears, and I grumble something unintelligible that one hundred percent was supposed to be 'fuck you,' as I search for the missing covers. Cade rubs my cheek, and I turn my head, biting down on the first thing my mouth comes into contact with.

"Ouch, fuck!" he yells, tugging his hand from my mouth.

Movement on either side of me jostles me, and I pry my eyes open to find Sterling standing naked on one side of the bed, hands tipped in claws and icy blue eyes scanning the room for danger. On the other side, Cade and Kai are holding their heads grumbling where Kai sat up so fast he collided with Cade who was leaning over to wake me.

Serves them right.

I snag Kai's pillow and cover my head with it, curling into a ball.

"What the hell?" Sterling growls. "What's going on?"

"She bit me," Cade says indignantly. "Again."

"So … there's no danger?" Kai asks. "Why am I awake then?" Based on the way the bed bounces, Kai flops back down and curses. "Where is my pillow?"

Said pillow gets pulled from my head and I ball my fists and hit the mattress. "Why won't you let me sleep?"

Cade looks at his hand and shakes it like he's trying to ease the pain. "Because I have a surprise for you."

I glance at the clock and groan. "It's three in the afternoon. The sun is out. It can wait until tonight." I try to take Kai's pillow again, but his head is on it, and he opens one eye to glare at me.

"Don't even think about it," he says, tucking it further under his head.

"It can't wait," Cade says, grabbing my hand and trying to pull me out of bed. "Come on."

Instead of making it easy for him, I go limp so he has to drag my dead weight from the bed. As he pulls me over Kai, Kai gets frustrated and tosses me to the floor. I land with a thump, and stare at the vampire in disbelief.

He smirks and closes his eyes. "Just go already, so I can go back to sleep."

"Unbelievable," I mutter, climbing to my feet.

Cade pushes me toward the bathroom. "I already have coffee made for you. It's waiting downstairs."

"Whatever." I shut the bathroom door in his face and sigh. I hate mornings to begin with, and it's not even technically morning for me. I'd only been asleep for about four hours before Cade so rudely woke me up.

I debate a shower, but I don't have the energy to do all that extra stuff, so I settle with fixing my bun and brushing my teeth. I'm working on that second task when the bathroom door opens and Sterling steps in.

He grabs his toothbrush and smiles at me. "I'm awake now, so I'm going for a run."

Crazy wolf. I roll my eyes and say, "oood or oo." With my

mouth full of toothpaste and toothbrush, I'm not sure he caught that.

He raises one silver brow, his blue eyes sparkling. I spit and rinse my mouth, turning to glare at him.

"You have a little bit of toothpaste, just there." He points to my chin, voice shaking with laughter.

"I hate all of you." I wipe my chin on his shoulder as I walk past him and back into the bedroom.

Downstairs, Cade waits for me with the keys to the Hummer and a big cup of coffee. If it weren't for him waking me up at this ungodly hour, I'd kiss him for the coffee. Instead, I grab it out of his hand, glaring the entire time.

He chuckles, and opens the front door. "After you, m'lady."

"Fuck off."

In the Hummer, I take the first sip of the steaming black liquid and exhale. In all honesty, Cade makes the best coffee. Which is weird because he hates the stuff. He remains quiet as we drive to ... wherever we're going, and I appreciate it while I wait for the caffeine to kick in.

It's obvious we're heading into the city and a little flutter of excitement hits me. I haven't been to the city for a while. Not counting the few times we made trips for various purposes while all the shit was going down.

When he pulls the Hummer to a curb and stops, I look at him in question. "This is Allie's place."

"Yes it is," is all he says.

Bewildered, I stare at him. "Am I supposed to get out?"

But before he can answer, Allie pops out of the lobby with a cup of coffee and climbs into the back. "Here ya go, El." She hands me the cup over the console and winks.

"Oh, I love you. Will you marry me?" I inhale the steam, smiling.

She snorts. "I don't think I can take a mage, a vampire, and a wolf. Sorry."

"So, what's going on?" I ask her, now thinking she has something to do with this.

"I have no idea. Cade texted me and told me to be ready and have a coffee for you."

I look at him, and find I can't keep mad any longer. Sure he woke me up, but he made sure I had two coffees. His smile as he pulls away from the curb tells me he knows he won.

"Okay prince charming, what is this surprise?" I ask.

He shakes his head. "If I told you, it wouldn't be a surprise."

I slump in the seat, grumbling under my breath, and drink my coffee. Fine, I'll pout in silence and drink my coffee while I wait.

When he pulls into a small parking lot next to an empty building and gets out, I turn around to look at Allie.

"How much do you trust him?" she asks. "He could be plotting to kill us and hide our bodies."

I nod. "Be on your guard."

We climb out and let Cade lead us around to the front of the building. My eyebrows raise to my hairline when he pulls a key out of his pocket and unlocks the door. He holds it open for us, but sighs when we look at him suspiciously and he enters first.

"Seriously, you two are too much to handle." He stops in the middle of the room, and turns to face us. "Well, what do you think?"

I look around at the empty space. Cheap linoleum floors that desperately need an upgrade. Walls that used to be painted white but have faded to a dingy yellow. Fluorescent lights above hum and flicker, casting weird lighting over the entire space. A door in the back leads to something I'm too scared to investigate.

"Umm, it's ... nice?" I say, ending my statement in more of a question than a certainty.

"I'm sure if you added a plant to the corner it would really liven the space up," Allie offers.

Cade shakes his head. "Imagine new floors. Fresh paint. Updated electricity. Maybe a few blue workout mats, some punching bags, mirrors. Now what do you think?"

I stare at him, mouth hanging open. He can't possibly be thinking what I think he's thinking. "Cade ..." I whisper, taking a step toward him.

"It's officially yours," he says, digging in his pocket and pulling out a second key. He tosses it to Allie who lets its sail past her head, her expression a mirror of my own.

"Cade," I whisper again, looking around the room, imagining all the things he said.

He closes the distance between us and takes my hands. "Make your dream come true, Ellis. Open your gym for women. Provide them with an opportunity to learn how to defend themselves."

"I know nothing about ... any of this. Remodeling, running a business, finances."

"Don't worry about that. I'll help you with all of it. In fact, I also bought the space next door." He looks to Allie with a small smile. "And I could use your help with that."

"Mine?" she screeches. "What for?"

"I'm going to open a clinic for humans. Give them an opportunity to get the same healthcare magicals have."

My eyes burn. They weren't kidding when they said they were going to help me fight for equality. I throw my hands around Cade's neck and hug him, hard. "Thank you," I breathe. "Thank you so much."

"You're welcome, love."

———

"WHAT ARE YOU DOING?" I ask, looking around as Cade pulls the Hummer to the side of the road.

He says nothing, but he gets out of the car and walks to my side, opening the door and pulling me out. When I'm standing outside, bewildered and confused, he hops into the passenger seat and buckles the seatbelt.

"Umm ..." I look around again, thinking I'll spot Kai and Sterling somewhere, but it's just us. "Cade?"

"Get in," he says, nodding at the empty driver's seat. "You're driving us home."

My eyes pop out of my head and I stare at him. "Oh no. No. No. No. I don't know how to drive!"

"That's why it's time you learned. The drive back is relatively simple. We're out of the city, so it's mostly two-lane highway until we get to the mountains. Easy peasy."

"Cade!"

He checks his watch and looks back at me. "Time is ticking, love."

Huffing, I walk around the Hummer and climb into the driver's seat. My palms are sweating, and I wipe them on my thighs before gripping the wheel in a white knuckled grasp. "Okay. Now what?" I ignore how my voice is trembling. I faced my abuser and ended his miserable life. Driving a car has got to be easier. I can do this!

Cade walks me through the steps, and before I'm ready for it, the car inches forward. Panicked, I slam my foot on the brake pedal, making us both jerk forward in our seats.

"Okay, that was a little uncalled for," he says, wincing. "We were only going like two miles per hour."

I make a noise, something between a squeak and growl, and I really have no idea what I'm trying to convey with it. My heart is fluttering rapid fire in my chest, and sweat drips down my back and between my breasts, making me sticky and gross.

"Take a deep breath, and try again," Cade says calmly. "You're a fucking harpy for fuck's sake. You can learn to drive."

"Right," I mutter. "I'm a harpy. I can do this. I'm a harpy. I can do this." I keep up my mantra and ease off the brake, sucking in a breath as the Hummer starts to roll forward.

"Don't stop again," Cade says. "Keep going."

I move to the gas pedal and softly press on it. The car shoots forward, and I scream, removing my foot from the pedal. I don't brake, but I let the car roll slowly before I try again.

By the time we reach the bottom of the mountain, I'm pretty

sure Cade regrets his decision to teach me how to drive. He's grasping the oh shit handle hard enough to break it off if he were Kai or Sterling. And his eyes are probably permanently stuck wide open in fear.

"Okay, stop here. I'm not about to let you drive up the mountain without a road." He waits until I put the car in park before he lets go and unbuckles himself.

I wait until he comes around the driver's side and opens the door. Giving him a look of pure defeat, I slowly slide out.

"Hey, you did good for your first time." He presses me against the side of the Hummer and kisses me.

"But you never want to let me try again, right?"

"Of course I will, Ellis. Everyone has to start somewhere. I think it's probably harder to learn the older you are. You're not as fearless as you are when you're a teenager. You value your life too much to not be afraid of driving."

I duck my head and bury my face in his chest, inhaling his cedar and lilac scent. "What if I never learn?"

He shrugs. "Then we'll drive you around. But I don't think that's going to happen. Come on. I'm pretty sure Kai is still sleeping and Sterling is probably still out for a run. We can play a game when we get back."

I raise one brow and push back to look at him. "A game?"

His smile turns wicked. "Yeah. It's called Don't Wake the Vampire."

I've never climbed into a car so fast in my life. When we get to the cabin, Cade carries me up the stairs, kissing me thoroughly and deeply. He doesn't set me down until we're in the bathroom and the door is closed behind us. He gets the water going while I strip out of my shorts and tank top.

The memory of the last time we had sex in the shower rushes to the surface. I almost broke that day, but Cade held me and promised me I would only ever know pleasure from that day forward. And he kept that promise. It hasn't always been easy getting to this point. We had our share of battles and fights to get here. But we're here now. And that's all that matters.

The bathroom fills with steam, and I step into the shower, letting the hot water rush over my skin. Cade joins me and pushes me against the shower wall. His violet eyes sparkle as he slides one hand down my abdomen and between my thighs.

"I remember another time we did this," he breathes against my neck, pushing his finger inside me. "I remember when you admitted how much you liked watching me and Kai together." He adds a second finger, making me grasp his shoulders to keep from falling to the floor. "I remember how even then I knew I would never walk away from you. You had already burrowed so deep into my soul by that point, there was no going back for me."

"Cade." My eyes burn, and I blink to keep any tears from falling. Only Cade can ever be this sweet.

He picks me up, wrapping my legs around his waist and he uses his strength to slowly slide me onto his cock. "I'll always have you, love. I'll catch you every time you fall."

And I fall. I fall in love with this man all over again. It started that first time we had sex in the shower. And I never stopped falling after that.

His arms flex as he lifts me up and down. Drops of water cling to his lashes, and his violet eyes are so dark they're almost navy. I hold his gaze while he thrusts slowly, each slide of his cock sending me a little bit higher.

Cade drops his face to my neck and he bites and licks along Kai's mark. Sparks of pure pleasure shoot through my veins, lighting me up from the inside. I have to dig my fingers into shoulders for purchase, and I'm sure I'll leave marks from my nails in his skin, but that thought only makes me shiver.

I don't have a mark from Cade like I do for Kai and Sterling. And leaving little scratches and bruises on his flesh, the same way he does to me, has become incredibly important to me. I like wearing my marks for everyone to see. I want people to know who

I belong to. But it's just as important for people to know who belongs to me.

"I ..." I have to stop and swallow to get moisture back in my mouth. "I want to get a tattoo."

Cade huffs a laugh, his warm breath fanning over my neck, but he doesn't stop thrusting. "It's an odd time to talk about that, love."

I grip his chin in my fingers and push him back so he's looking at me. "No. I want a mark from you. Like I have with Kai and Sterling. Something that everyone can see."

Cade's eyes darken further and his pace falters. "Fuck, Ellis. Name the time and I'll fucking be there."

It's as if just the idea of me having something of him permanently etched onto my skin turns him feral. His hips move faster and he pushes me harder against the shower wall. Pleasure curls low in my belly, heating and spreading to my limbs. I'm so close, and I arch my back to change the angle just a smidge.

Cade's magic slithers over my body in purple sparks, and I moan. It slides down my chest, over my breasts where it squeezes and pinches my nipples until I cry out. Cade watches with rapt fascination, and I have a feeling he's not in control of his magic at the moment.

When the violet light slides lower, I gasp and Cade grins. It slips between my folds and pulses warmly around my clit before it flicks the bundle of nerves. I erupt. Cade captures my scream with his mouth, and he pumps his hips faster as he draws me through my orgasm.

When I've finally caught my breath, Cade pauses. "What would you say if I wanted to get a tattoo as well? One to let the world know who owns me?"

My stomach flutters, and I have to close my eyes to keep the sudden tears from falling. "I'd love that."

Leaning forward, I kiss him, tangling my tongue with his and urging him to chase his own orgasm. With a nip on his bottom lip, Cade tenses and his hips falter as he shudders through his release.

I never would have survived my past if it hadn't been for Cade. I realize that now. Despite my bonds with Kai and Sterling, despite how much I love them, it was Cade who was the one to save me. And it couldn't be more perfect to have his mark on me, and mine on him.

"Thank you," I whisper, clinging to him as the steam from the shower billows around us. "Thank you, Cade."

"I love you, Ellis. And I'll always love you."

———

The bedroom is empty when I get out of the bathroom. I hear all three of the guys talking downstairs, so I make my way to them. On the last step, I freeze.

"What is all of this?" I ask, slowly approaching the coffee table.

It's piled with papers that curl at the ends, like it wants to return to its rolled position. Mugs and beer bottles, and even a dagger, weigh the corners down to keep the paper in place.

Sterling looks up and smiles at me. "Come and look." He scoots over so I have room to sit next to him on the floor, across from Cade and Kai.

They all watch me approach, a mix of anticipation and excitement lining their features. I sit next to Sterling and glance at the papers.

"Are those ..." I trail off, eyes bouncing around and taking it all in.

"Blueprints," Kai says with a smile, fangs glinting in the lamplight.

Cade waves his hand over the papers. "Additions and updates to the cabin."

I'm completely speechless as I take it all in. I realize there are words on the page, room labels, but I can't seem to make sense of them. It's just too ... unbelievable.

"We meant it when we said we were going to live here," Sterling says, running his hand down my back in comfort. "With these updates and additions, this will be the perfect place for us. It's on pack lands and close to the city while remaining remote enough for us to have all the privacy we need."

I swallow and rub my eyes, brushing away the tears gathering on my lashes so I can see the blueprints better.

Cade points to the lower floor. "A bigger kitchen and living room with updated appliances and open floor plan. The master bedroom will be down here with an attached bath that has a massive tub, per Kai's request."

I glance at the vampire and find him smirking. He does love his baths.

Cade continues. "There will also be a bathroom for guests down here. And this room," he moves his finger to a smaller space that looks to have a ton of windows. "This will be yours. A library just for you."

I clutch my chest, sure my heart is going to stop. These guys thought of everything.

Kai points to the second level. "Up here will be guest rooms with bathrooms. A couple offices. And ..." he trails off, letting Sterling take up the explanation.

"And this." Sterling points to a room.

"What is that?" I whisper, already suspecting the answer.

"A nursery," Sterling replies. "Because one way or another we will have children in this house. Either our own or adopted."

The tears that I'd been trying to hold back, spill over. Each of their faces is filled with emotion. They all look at the nursery longingly, and I so desperately want to be able to fill this house with the laughter of their babies.

I suck in a shaky breath. "I ... I don't know what to say," I gasp before a sob climbs up my throat. "I ..."

"You don't have to say anything," Cade murmurs. "This is our gift to you."

Sterling wraps his arms around me, and I bury my face in his shirt, softly crying. I hear the coffee table being moved, the legs dragging on the carpeted floor. Then Kai and Cade surround me as well.

"We just want you to be happy," Kai says, kissing my temple.

Sterling kisses the top of my head. "And we'll do whatever we have to to make that happen."

Cade takes my hand and squeezes it. "This is it Ellis. This is the beginning of your happily ever after."

I squeeze my eyes shut, Cade's words echoing and bouncing in my head. With my three guys, my Shields, and their never ending love for me, he's right. This is the beginning of my happily ever after. And I'm going to make the most of it.

KEEP READING for a sneak peek at These Beautiful Moments: Fates Through The Seasons, A Novella

Keep reading for a sneak peek at These Beautiful Moments: Fates Through The Seasons, A Novella

Summer

Ellis

"I HAVE NO FUCKING CLUE WHAT TO GET HER," I grumble to Allie as we walk down the street, bundled in our coats. "What do you get someone who has been held captive by a sociopath for half of their life?"

Allie sighs, her breath fogging in front of her. "Shit, I have no clue. Maybe books? Something she can lose herself in?"

"Maybe. I mean, I lost all interest in reading when I was going through my ordeal. But, I guess it's better than nothing?"

"We can at least check out the bookstore. At the very least we can buy ourselves something!"

I laugh and link my arm with hers. "Always the optimist."

"How is she doing?" Allie asks, sobering.

I shrug. "About as well as can be expected. I don't think she'll ever fully recover from it. She's doing better about being around more people, but men still make her nervous." I shake my head, my heart squeezing for everything my sister has gone through. While Sam didn't treat her the same way he treated me, she was surrounded by guards who leered and made comments. Not to mention all the torture at Sam's hands. "I don't know. I just wish there was something I could do, but I know it's just going to take time and patience."

Allie squeezes my arm where hers is linked with mine. "You're doing everything you can, El. Don't beat yourself up over it. She might not say it, but I know she appreciates everything."

I swallow back the lump that tries to choke me. It's been three months since I killed Sam. Three months since I freed my sister from his cruelty. Three months since I freed *myself* from that monster's clutches. A weight has been lifted. I finally have relief and comfort I hadn't known since before my mother's death. Killing Sam didn't solve every problem. I still have moments of panic and wake from dreams screaming and sweating. But my guys are always there to bring me back down. To remind me I'm safe. Loved.

We're still fighting for humans and weaker magicals. It's a fight we'll probably always be fighting, but it feels good to be doing something. And doing it with my Shields by my side has been everything I've ever needed. Learning how to live again, how to be normal—or at least as normal as I can be when I'm a Harpy with three mates—has been fun. Stressful at times, but truly an amazing experience.

Allie and I push into the bookstore. Warmth surrounds us, thawing our frozen exposed skin. Winter in Altair is brutal with the icy wind blowing off the river and streaming between the buildings. I stomp my feet, trying to regain feeling in my toes despite the fur lined boots Sterling bought for me.

Allie grins. "Meet back up in thirty?"

"Thirty minutes will do some serious damage to our bank accounts." But I grin back and we separate, each going to the section of books we prefer.

Allie is a mystery and thriller lover. I prefer romance. The spicier the better. But before I head to that section, I browse the aisles for something my sister may possibly like. We were so young when everything happened. I have no idea what her taste in books would even be, but I find myself in the inspirational section, and while it might be cheesy, it feels right.

My fingers brush the spines of books, not really reading the titles, but trusting my Harpy instincts. Something inside me tells me to stop, so I pull out the book my fingers rest on. A collection of inspirational quotes. Better than a book about healing and learning to live with your trauma. I tuck it under my arm and turn to head toward the romance section.

Before I get there, I pass a row of poetry books. Gracie used to love to write poetry. I walk down the aisle, stopping when I feel like I should, and tug a book off the shelf at random. The cover is beautiful with flowers and stars, so I add it to the quote book. And then I find the crown jewel. On the endcap of the poetry aisle is a selection of notebooks. A deep purple leather notebook with golden stitching and shiny golden edged paper catches my eye. I grab that as well. Maybe she'll be able to journal her way through her trauma. Or start writing poetry again.

With my sister's gift selected, I head to the romance section to do some serious shopping.

———

THE FIRST THING the guys did after things settled down was have a driveway put in so we didn't have to drive over the rocky terrain to get to the cabin. So, Cade's red Corvette smoothly climbs the mountain. Despite my first attempt at driving being an epic fail, Cade is a great teacher, and it only took me a few weeks to get the hang of it, and now he trusts me enough with his car to let me borrow it. It's nice to have this bit of freedom. Something I've never had before in my life.

The cabin comes into view, the sun just starting to sink below the horizon, and I grin. "What's this?" I ask, climbing out of the car with my bags.

Sterling waves his hand toward the house. "We're decorating for Christmas. Wanna help?"

"I don't know, guys," Cade says, eyeing my bags. "We might need to return all of the decorations just to pay for the books she bought."

I flip him off as I walk past, swaying my hips enticingly. "I'd love to help. You could use some pointers, anyway."

I set the books just inside the door and when I return outside, Kai takes a chair from the porch and puts it in the yard, facing the house. "Your throne, my queen." He bows dramatically with a grin. "You can sit here and direct us peasants where to put the decorations."

I spend the next two hours, wrapped in a blanket with an endless supply of hot chocolate, and watch my guys string lights and hang garland. Sitting back and watching them bicker and tease makes my heart swell. And Kai wearing a Santa hat makes me chuckle every time I look at him.

By the time they're done I can't say they did a good job, but it's festive. The lights are droopy in places, the garland is wrapped asymmetrically around the porch pillars. A sad looking gingerbread man made of lights is about to lose an arm, and poor Frosty's hat won't stay on his head. It's a bit messy. Sloppy even. But I love it.

"I bought a tree and a bunch of ornaments, too," Sterling says tugging me inside. "Do you want to put it up now or later?"

"Now, please." I can't keep the smile off my face.

Kai steals me from Sterling and wraps me in his arms, pulling me to his chest. "It's our first Christmas together," he says, lips brushing against my temple. "I knew that would make you happy, but being able to actually sense the joy this brings you is truly special."

I don't have the words to tell him how this makes me feel. My first Christmas with my guys, totally free and able to live my life. Luckily, I don't have to find the words. Kai can sense it all. He kisses me gently, and I melt under his touch.

"Gross," Cade says, slipping a hand between us and shoving us apart. "Get a room."

I bite my lip and giggle, stepping away. With the three guys, the tree is assembled in record time and we get to work hanging the generic ornaments Sterling bought. When it's done, we all step back to admire our work.

"Not too bad," Kai says.

"It's just missing one thing." Sterling hands me something wrapped in white paper.

I peel the wrapping away to reveal a delicate spun glass golden feather. It catches the light as I hold it up, and my breath sticks in my throat. "It's ... beautiful," I whisper.

Sterling leans over and kisses my cheek. "Seemed appropriate for our first tree."

I squeal as Sterling crouches down and shoves his head between my legs. He stands, making me grab his hair for support as he lifts me onto his shoulders. Once I have my balance, I place the feather on the top of the tree where everyone will be able to see it. I'm pretty sure my smile will remain permanently on my face this entire holiday season.

ACKNOWLEDGMENTS

These are always so hard for me.

Endings are always hard. I love the world of Lustros and as I started wrapping this book up, I knew I wasn't finished with the world or the characters. I wanted to make sure Ellis got all the happiness she deserves, and I wanted you to be able to read it. So the novella came to life. And with the novella, the vision of the future of these characters came to me as well. So while this book may be the end of the trilogy, it's not the end entirely. Stay tuned for more, because I have plans for Ellis, Kai, Cade, and Sterling.

Thank you so much for all of your support and love for these four. Your excitement for these books is what kept me going when writing got hard. I hope I gave them the ending you all wanted.

About the Author

Whitney L. Spradling is a neurospicy, full-time Occupational Therapist and autism mama, who has had a dream to write and publish a novel since she was a little girl. She lives outside of Cincinnati with her husband, son, and two cats.

She is a strange mixture of Disney adult, elder emo, and board game nerd with a love of tattoos, skulls, moths, bees, Gengar, and otters.

When she is not writing, she can be found in her craft room making custom tumblers, or curled up with a good book and a cup of coffee (or glass of wine).